LIBERATION ROAD

Also by David L. Robbins

DAVID L. ROBBINS

LIBERATION ROAD

A NOVEL OF

WORLD WAR II

AND THE

RED BALL EXPRESS

BANTAM BOOKS

LIBERATION ROAD
A Bantam Book / January 2005

Published by
Bantam Dell
A Division of Random House, Inc.
New York, New York

Bantam Books is a registered trademark of Random House, Inc., and the colophon is a trademark of Random House, Inc.

Library of Congress Cataloging-in-Publication Data

Robbins, David L., 1954–
Liberation road : a novel of World War II and
the Red Ball Express / David L. Robbins.
p.   cm.
ISBN 0-553-80175-9
1. World War, 1939–1945—African Americans—Fiction.
2. World War, 1939–1945—Transportation—Fiction.   3. World War,
1939–1945—France—Fiction.   4. Chaplains, Military—Judaism—Fiction.
5. African American men—Fiction.   6. Americans—France—Fiction.
7. Cotenin (France)—Fiction.   8. Truck drivers—Fiction.   9. Jewish men—
Fiction.   10. Traitors—Fiction.   11. Rabbis—Fiction.   I. Title.

PS3568.O22289L53 2005
813'.54—dc22   2004055063

Printed in the United States of America
Published simultaneously in Canada

10 9 8 7 6 5 4 3 2 1
BVG

JAN 0 5 2005

For Dan McMurtrie, a new man.

And as always, this book is dedicated, as I am, to my wife, Lindy.

AUTHOR'S NOTE

Though *Liberation Road* is a work of fiction, it is closely based on authentic events and the actual wartime conduct of individuals and military units, both U.S. and German, during the desperate first three months of the Allied struggle to liberate France. The true designations and histories of divisions, regiments, battalions, and companies have been utilized, while most real names of soldiers and chaplains have been replaced by fictional ones. Places, dates, battles, and the intricacies of the Paris black market have been re-created with as little dramatic license and as much accuracy as my research and abilities have allowed.

At the rear of the book, a glossary is included with explanations of abbreviated military terms used in the novel. A series of annotations will supply the actual names and some additional historical details for several of the events and participants referred to in the narrative.

Many people have contributed to the writing of this novel. Principal among them are:

Kenneth J. Leinwand, Chaplain (Colonel), U.S. Army; Dr. John C. Stevens, Chaplain (Captain, retired), U.S. Army; Dr. John Brinsfield, historian at the Chaplain's Museum, Columbia, SC; former Red Ball driver William Bennett of Pertersburg, VA; Sorlie Bigman for her recollections of Pittsburgh; Jim and Rebecca Redington for their company in Normandy and Paris, and Jim for everything medical in this book; the unknown French dairy farmer whose tractor pulled my car out of a muddy hedgerow in the middle of the night; Alexandra Duckworth for her research and enthusiasm; all my MFA students at VCU for their own mistakes and surprising talents; Tracy Fisher of William Morris for her constant good advice and measured ways; Kate Miciak of Bantam for her incisive editing and fond e-mails; and my old friends Gary Green, Tom Kennedy, and Tucker Connelly who insisted this book should be written.

DLR
Richmond, VA

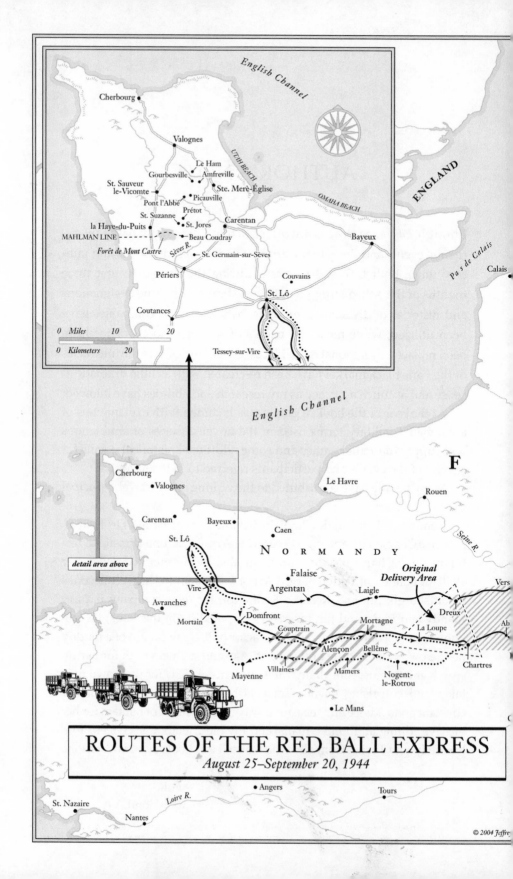

ROUTES OF THE RED BALL EXPRESS

August 25–September 20, 1944

© 2004 Jeffrey

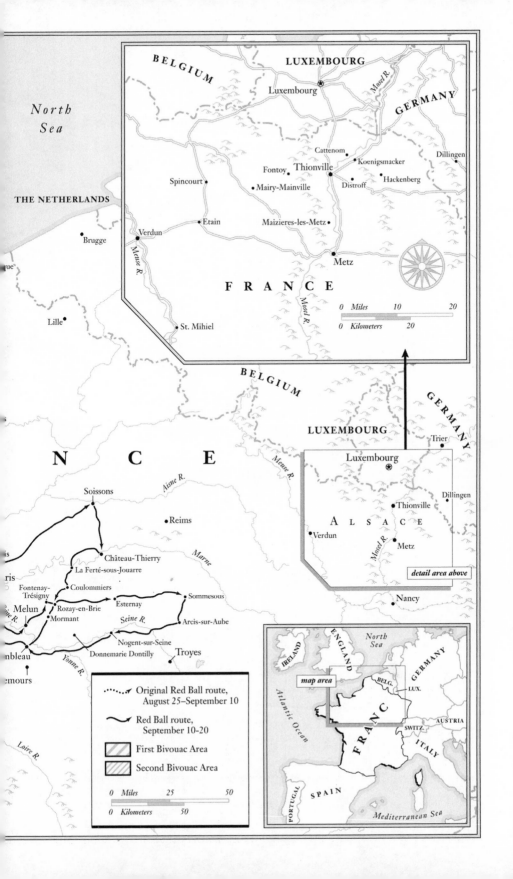

North Sea

BELGIUM

LUXEMBOURG

Luxembourg ✇

GERMANY

Mosel R.

THE NETHERLANDS

Cattenom
Koenigsmacker
Dillingen
Fontoy   Thionville
Spincourt   Hackenberg
Mairy-Mainville   Distroff
Brugge

Meuse R.
Verdun
Etain
Maizieres-les-Metz

Lille

FRANCE

Metz

St. Mihiel

Mosel R.

| 0 | Miles | 10 | 20 |
| 0 | Kilometers | 20 | |

BELGIUM

GERMANY

N   C   E

Aisne R.

Soissons

Reims

Meuse R.

LUXEMBOURG

Luxembourg ✇

Trier

Dillingen

Thionville

ris

Château-Thierry
La Ferté-sous-Jouarre

Marne

ALSACE

Verdun

Metz

Mosel R.

Fontenay-
Trésigny
Coulommiers
Melun   Rozay-en-Brie
Mormant

Esternay

Sommesous

ue R.
Seine R.

Arcis-sur-Aube

detail area above

Nancy

nbleau

Nogent-sur-Seine
Donnemarie Dontilly   Troyes

Yonne R.

emours

IRELAND   ENGLAND   *North Sea*   GERMANY

map area

BELG.
LUX.

Atlantic Ocean

FRANCE

AUSTRIA

Loire R.

SWITZ.

ITALY

.... Original Red Ball route,
August 25–September 10

〜 Red Ball route,
September 10-20

▨ First Bivouac Area

▨ Second Bivouac Area

PORTUGAL   SPAIN

Mediterranean Sea

| 0 | Miles | 25 | 50 |
| 0 | Kilometers | 50 | |

LIBERATION ROAD

D+100

The search for his son stopped here.

Ben Kahn toted up the sum of the young man standing in front of him. Well fed in a starving city. White-skinned and clean where millions lived without soap. Clothes expensive and dark. The long occupation, the fight for Paris, a nation's hunger—none of it had marked him. He'd flourished.

Ben waited while black eyes added him up as well.

The boy shrugged.

"You got me all wrong, Pop."

"Don't call me Pop." Ben winced. A pain in his side threatened to rip open. He put a hand there to hold it in.

"S'matter?" the boy asked. "You got no stomach for business? That's all it ever was—business. Everybody did it. Get serious."

Ben felt unsteady. He reached for a tabletop to catch himself.

His son had been a pilot. That was honorable. A year and a half ago he was shot down over France. The crash didn't kill him. Paris killed him. Paris murdered everything honorable and good about his son, and he in turn killed others. Ben stared at the monster, traitor, in front of him and thought, My son became . . . *this.*

The room was a big space, a garage hung with chains and grimy tools, metal rafters and water pipes. A Citroën waited under a jacket of dust; for four years no one had worked on civilian cars in Paris—little gas to run them. The walls of the building were thick, the street outside was a quiet alley. The thoroughfares beyond were still flush with the Liberation. No one was looking for this young man. He was missing. Presumed dead.

"So, Pop. What are we gonna do? I can't stand here all day chattin' about old times. You don't look like you want to, either."

Ben did not correct him for calling him Pop.

He reached under his olive jacket. He hauled the .45 pistol from his waistband. The gun filled his hand and lifted his arm. Ben felt as though he could let go and the pistol would stay in the air, hammer cocked.

"What are you gonna do, shoot me?"

Untold deaths had passed through Ben's hands.

"Yes."

Ben stared at the white face turned incredulous, cringing. This was a coward, too. Of course he was.

"You can't do that!"

"Yes I can." Ben's voice was cool.

"No, no, no. You're . . . you're a man of God."

Ben answered down the barrel.

"Not anymore."

REVERSE

FIRST

Logistics were the lifeblood of the Allied Armies in France . . . without supplies, we could not move, shoot, eat.

General Omar Bradley
A General's Life

D+5

The first body of the second war in Ben Kahn's life drifted past.

The corpse bobbed on a thieving wave, a little salty crest that snuck onto the beach and floated away the soldier beneath anyone's notice. The water tried to ferret its catch back out to sea, a quiet and greedy bier. A cotton mattress cover had been buttoned around the corpse in its wait for burial somewhere close to this beach. Soaked, the sheath matted to its knees, shoulders, boot tips, even the nose and hollows of the eyes.

He leaned over the rail of the truck bed, where he rode to shore. The truck, a deuce-and-a-half in an armada of vehicles, churned through the long shallows of the Norman coast, making for the beach. Colored boys drove all the trucks. Ben Kahn looked through the rear window at the two black boys in the cab of his truck. Both craned their necks to see the corpse bob off the right fender. Ben scooted across crates of ammunition to the tailgate of the truck. The water here off OMAHA should not want more, he thought. How red has it been already? He jumped into the water, hip deep. The truck stopped at his splash.

The driver shouted, "Hey, you alright?"

"Yeah. Figure I'd fetch this fella back to shore. You two go ahead. Thanks for the lift."

The driver nodded, said something to his assistant, and pulled away. Ben waded to the body, grabbing the mattress cover. The tug of the Channel seemed jealous. Ben pulled against it and plowed forward to the beach.

The walk was long, almost two hundred yards to the low-tide shelf. The body stayed buoyant behind him. Ben imagined how bloated it must be to float like it did. He towed the corpse in its white sack past obstacles the Germans had hammered into the sand. Allied engineers had been hard at work here, clearing paths for the constant invasion. Ben and his dead soldier passed steel tetrahedrons that would gut any boat floating across them at high tide, Belgian gates eight feet high laced with teller mines, barbed-wire lattices, and fat poles jutting in pyramids clotted with barnacles. The hulks of burned, stove-in landing craft, each a fiery story to itself, made the surface of the water jagged. Left and right Ben looked, dragging the body, now in shallower water dragging its own heels as if saddened like Ben to return to France.

A medic jogged into the skim of water to help lug the corpse onto dry sand. Together, the two pulled the soldier back to where the wave had stolen him at a Graves Registration detail. Ben let go of the mattress cover once the soldier lay again in a neat line, one white picket in a long, knocked-down fence.

Ben's boots sloshed, his pantaloons drizzled. The medic left him with a nod. Ben did not know what to do or where to go; he was four days late reaching OMAHA beach. Activity welled everywhere. As a soldier, as the father of a son missing in action, all of it was his concern. This dizzied him, joining the fatigue of dragging the corpse ashore. Ben sat on the sand and gazed at America's arrival.

Landing craft towing barrage balloons ran themselves aground to disgorge machines, men, and matériel. Offshore, Navy ships prowled. Frequently, one of them let go a salvo at some target a mile inland. Each report rattled everything on the beach. An entire division, fifteen thousand men with rifles and machine guns slung over every shoulder, trudged through the shallow water. None of the men paused on the beach, all drudged up the slopes of the high dunes where the Germans had been, away to the front line. Tanks and towed artillery filled the parade, making their separate way to the draw between the bluffs. Working the water behind the landing craft, dozens of tugboats wrestled pieces of the huge artificial harbor called "Mulberry" into place. Fifty-

gallon drums were rolled together by the hundreds to make instant depots. Trucks backed and spit forward, loaded to the gills.

Ben Kahn looked at the one thing he'd done so far since arriving in
France, the body in its wet cocoon he'd retrieved. He unbuttoned the mattress cover to reveal the soldier's face. A boy, a brown-haired boy. Ben fingered for the remaining dog tag under the tunic and read a name, a blood
type, Catholic. Ben could not guess how this soldier died, if he might have
had a last moment to spend with a priest or if he was taken too fast.

He laid a hand on the cold, pallid forehead.

"Hail Mary, full of grace. The Lord is with Thee. Blessed art Thou
among women and blessed is the fruit of Thy womb, Jesus. Holy Mary,
Mother of God, pray for us sinners, now and at the hour of our death."

With his thumb, Ben drew the sign of the cross.

"Amen."

He lifted his gaze. He'd known for more than a year he would do
this as soon as he landed in France. He knew, too, that it would be fruit-
less. Ben Kahn cast his eyes across the beach, at the slogging thousands
of American doughs, wondering if he might spot a lost face, a gait,
something. He would do this the rest of his life—keep looking—until he
was certain.

Rabbi Ben Kahn buttoned the sheath over the dead boy's face and
stood, at war.

"Damn!"

Joe Amos slid across the bench seat until his rear collided with
Boogie John's leg. The big driver shoved him away.

"Get off me, boy!"

"Damn, you see that?" Joe Amos was slow to ease back to his
passenger-side window. Boogie John leaned right to look for himself.

"That's a dead man, sure enough."

Joe Amos nodded. He set his elbows on the window frame. The
corpse floated just below, bagged in a white cotton cover.

"You ain't never seen no dead man before, huh?"

Joe Amos shook his head, longer than just to say no. He watched the
outgoing tide take the body into the Channel and wondered if it would
get all the way to England. That boy wants to go home, Joe Amos
thought.

With a splash, the chaplain riding in the truck bed jumped down. Boogie John hit the brakes. Joe Amos leaned out farther to see behind the truck. The water stood above the Jimmy's tires and running boards and came to the chaplain's belt. One minute the chaplain had been riding high and dry, now he was sopping wet. Good for him, Joe Amos thought. And this wasn't no young man, this chaplain, this was a skinny sharp-nosed type, wiry, some kind of roadrunner. Back on the LCM, when he asked for a ride into shore, Joe Amos saw he was a Jew. The chaplain had a little Ten Commandments badge on his collar with his captain's bars. The chaplain kicked through the water to the floating body.

"Thank you, Jesus," Joe Amos mumbled.

Boogie John leaned out his driver's window.

"Chaplain, you alright?"

The man answered he was going to fetch the body back to the beach. Boogie John waved to the chaplain and said to Joe Amos, "Let's go." Boogie got the Jimmy moving, shoving up to second gear to close the gap in their convoy through the water. Joe Amos brought his gaze forward. The first dead man he'd ever seen was wrapped in white. It was bad but got easier to look at. He knew there'd be dead men, and was grateful to get the first one out of the way like that, better than he'd imagined. Something started when that corpse floated by. Joe Amos looked at Boogie John, the closest living man to him. He reached for Boogie's shoulder and left his hand on it.

"Here we go."

The truck surged forward. The water took a long time to grow shallow, the beach was far off and misty. Boogie closed up on the bumper of the truck ahead of him. Joe Amos twisted in his seat to see everything, gandering at the enemy obstacles strewn like a million jacks as far as he could look to the west, all the way to Pointe du Hoc. Sunken transports, sleek back in England when they were defiant and full of white boys with guns and tanks, were like craters in the water. Boogie told Joe Amos to sit still, but his view was blocked by the truck in front, the ammo crates behind, and Boogie's big face to the left.

When the Jimmy finally pulled onto the sand, the convoy turned left. An MP windmilled one arm to direct them to a gathering station for their battalion. Joe Amos opened his door. He climbed out on the running board to get a better view of the invasion force streaming ashore. An uncountable number of boats plied back and forth in the Channel.

Big Navy ships patrolled the outer limits, rhino ferries and DUKWs hauled supplies and vehicles up to the beach. Trucks, tanks, and bulldozers came out of the water dripping like summer dogs. Activity buzzed for miles down the beach. Joe Amos figured the Brits were doing the same farther east, where their zone was.

I'm in France, Joe Amos thought. Damn a mule, *France.*

"Look at that, Boog!" he shouted over the din of the diesels around him. Three huge roadways spanned from the sand out to a chain of concrete piers sunk a thousand yards offshore. Engineers swarmed over them, securing the last pieces of the bridges to pontoons. "They get that done, won't be no more driving through the water!"

"Nope," Boogie answered.

Joe Amos hung on and gazed over the canvas roof of the rolling Jimmy's cab. Offshore, east of the piers, a string of Liberty ships and tankers had been sunk five hundred yards out from OMAHA to make a breakwater. The blockships lay in a row so tight they almost touched bow to stern. "Well, I'll be," Joe Amos mumbled, impressed. America, all this, so many ships we can sink them on purpose. He swelled with his America.

Boogie drove alongside the cliffs in line with the rest of the truck battalion. Their first assigned stop was a maintenance area where they would strip the hoses from the carburetor and exhaust and unpack the waterproof cosmoline grease from the wires and plugs that allowed the GMC truck to drive through the water. On the slopes of the bluffs, thousands of GIs had dug foxholes, an odd honeycomb, a sort of Yank infestation. None of the soldiers lifted their faces to greet the convoy, they smoked or slept. Over their heads, crowning the bluffs, two pillboxes stood guard no more. The Germans had called this their Atlantic Wall. Shoot, Joe Amos thought. Now those bunkers are just broken concrete, black-eyed and hollow, shut up and done in by these guys curled in their holes in the sand. Joe Amos made a fist and shook it at one soldier whose drawn eye he caught. The man nodded back, a dent in his helmet. The pillboxes were payback for that dent and for the busted landing craft in the water, too, for the white-wrapped, floating body, and for Joe Amos Biggs and all of them being over here in France, and paybacks were hell.

"We're gonna get off this beach!" he cheered. "We're gonna kick their whole ass! What you think?"

Boogie struck out his flat hand for some skin. Joe Amos reached in the window and smoothed his palm across Boogie's.

"Boy!"

Joe Amos looked out the windshield. Boogie slowed the Jimmy to let an MP stride in front of the high grille.

"You! Boy! Get your fanny back in that truck."

Joe Amos straightened on the running board. He fumbled for the door latch.

"Yeah, okay."

The MP banged the butt of his rifle against the passing front fender. "*Now,* boy."

Joe Amos climbed on the bench beside Boogie. The driver's big smile was gone.

"Son of a bitch."

"Leave it, Boog."

Boogie sped the truck past the glaring MP, then pulled one hand from the wheel, the hand that a moment ago was offered to Joe Amos open and pink. Now one finger stabbed close to Joe Amos's eyes.

"You leave it. Don't tell me what I got to do over here."

"Alright, Boog, alright."

"*Boy.*" Boogie drove, ironcast now behind the wheel. "Cracker son of a bitch. I want to know how big they grow the men where he come from."

Joe Amos rode in the silence of the engine, the Jimmy's gears laboring over the sand. He looked again up the slope at the charred pillboxes. A flight of P-47 Thunderbolts streaked in low from over the Channel in tight formation, owning the sky. Out to sea the horizon shuttled with ships, the concrete harbor grew by the minute.

Oh, yeah, Joe Amos thought. America. It's here, alright. It's all here.

D+6
JUNE 12

Ben Kahn kneeled beside another litter. He set his lantern in the sand. Both knees ached from six hours of bending, his kneecaps were chafed from salt and sand, and his trousers were stained with blood where he'd taken soldiers' hands in his lap.

"Son," he said in a firm voice. "I'm Chaplain Kahn. Can I get you anything?"

This soldier smiled under crinkling eyes. He blinked; the smile wavered.

"Got a right foot you can spare, Chaplain?"

Ben opened his hands, empty.

"You know anyone needs a right boot, I left a good one up in Vierville-sur-Mer."

Ben patted the soldier's chest.

"We'll get you out of here pretty quick, son. I've got some water."

Ben poured from his canteen into a steel cup. The soldier worked his way up to his elbows to drink. He grunted. Ben slid a hand under his neck to hold him while he sipped from the cup.

"Minefield," the soldier uttered between swallows. He needed to explain his weakness, the reason why this older man needed to help him drink.

"I know," Ben answered, laying the soldier down, taking back the emptied cup. "There's good boots laying all over this place."

The soldier began to breathe harder through his nose. He fought nausea, tears, something he would not release. Ben looked down the length of the blanket covering the soldier, ending in the one boot. He laid his palm gently on the damaged leg.

"You want to pray with me, son?"

"Yeah."

Ben had no kit with him, that was lost, he'd need to requisition another. In his pack he carried New and Old Testaments, one book of prayers, and another of hymns, issued by the Chaplain Corps. He had a canteen, a cigarette lighter, he'd stolen the lantern. His helmet bore a red cross on a white field to identify him as a non-combatant.

"What's your name, soldier?"

"Lombardy, sir. Kevin. Pfc."

"I'm Ben Kahn. Where you from?"

"Chicago."

"Pittsburgh."

"Go Pirates," the soldier said, in better control of himself.

"Go Cubbies."

Lombardy gestured to the pin on Ben's collar, a double tablet bearing Roman numerals to ten, capped by the Star of David, the insignia for rabbi chaplains.

"I'm Protestant, Chaplain. I never prayed with no Jew before."

Ben grinned. He smoothed the soldier's hair.

"I think you've done tougher things today, Kevin."

The soldier closed his eyes beneath Ben's touch. Ben stayed quiet, watching the young face crease and still in the lantern light. Ben made his prayer in silence. He lowered his face and asked God again in this evacuation station for *tsedoke*, charity. For grace for this poor kid, for courage, luck, something to turn it around for Kevin Lombardy. God could do it. God could do it for any soldier, no matter how hurt, scared, or missing. But God had to choose to do a *mitzvah*. Mercy, please, God. Not for me. For this boy. For my boy and all of them. Hear O Israel . . .

"Chap?"

Ben looked up from his prayer, jarred and not finished. He delved deep for God every time, never just cast his prayers on the surface like bread. Ben Kahn sank them to the bottom, probing.

"Yes."

"I feel better." The soldier dabbed his sleeve across his eyes. "Rabbi, huh? That felt good. That was okay."

"I'm glad."

"You might think about taking a rest, Chap."

"I'm fine."

"You look worse than me."

"I'm a lot older than you. I've had more time to work on my look."

"What division you with?"

Ben slid the Red Cross helmet off his head to scratch his crew cut. This was the first soldier on a stretcher to ask about him. Ben poured himself a cup of water, his first in six hours of wounds and soldiers' hometowns and trying to snag God's attention from a world on fire.

"Don't know yet. I'm a replacement. I was supposed to be here six days ago. Got crossed up. I'll find out where I'm supposed to be when I get to the repple depple."

"When'd you get here?"

"This morning."

"What time is it? You slept any?"

"Alright, Private." Ben screwed the cap on his canteen. "I take my orders from God and Ike. But you take one from me. You go home and you be the same man you always have been. Tell me about your family."

"Mom and Dad. Sister."

"Okay. You take care of them."

Ben made a light fist and tapped it on the soldier's chest, a gentle blow to offset the one that tore this boy off at the ankle. He set his helmet back on his head and pushed off the sand to rise. His knees and hips griped.

Outside the evac tent a clamor erupted. Men shouted, automatic weapons barked.

"What's that?" Ben froze in a half-standing posture.

"Bedcheck Charlie."

"What?"

The gunfire thickened on every side, from the beach and the cliffs. A powerful engine roared past, low and searing over the night sands.

"Jabo," the soldier said, pulling up his blanket, shifting on his stretcher.

Ben ran the few steps to the open tent flap. Outside, orange tongues of small arms and mounted machine guns yelped after the screeching German fighter. The plane left them in its black wake and flew over another ten thousand Americans a mile farther down OMAHA, waking them and their guns. Ben heard the cannons of the fighter, strafing, harassing, then disappearing south over the German lines.

He walked inside the evac tent. Every soldier who could sit up from his stretcher was erect and alert. The medical staff, a dozen doctors and nurses, moved along the lines of tables and litters, through tubes, bags, and poles, pressing the men to lie down. Ben settled again beside Private Lombardy.

"They come in threes," the soldier said.

His knuckles were white on the blanket. Ben sat close and waited.

In another minute when the engines appeared and the cannons and gunfire cranked, Ben lay across the private. The soldier shivered. His arms went around Ben's back and clutched him there.

The orders seemed more than words typed on paper. They weighed that of a commandment, chiseled and sent down. The sheet sank Ben's hand to his side. He thanked the personnel officer and turned away.

The town square of Isigny-sur-Mer brimmed with soldiers, most of them replacements. No civilians milled, moved out long ago by the Germans. Around the cobblestone center, every building was rubble. Desks and filing cabinets had been moved outside, there was not a floor or roof to be trusted in the village. Fresh soldiers waited in clots and lines, swapping cigarettes and glances. Convoys of trucks, always driven by the Negroes, rolled across the Aure River bridge and into the square, heedless of the men who jumped out of the way. The drivers were in a hurry, the replacements were not. Sergeants herded the clean GIs into the truck beds and they were hauled off in fifties and hundreds, chambered into the war an hour after splashing onto OMAHA or UTAH.

Ben read his orders again. He folded the sheet. He did not look into the blue morning sky for God. There was no reason to believe God was up there any more than He was everywhere. Ben had been told at the Chaplain School at Harvard this seemed a very Jewish instinct. He sometimes admired the Gentile way of believing God was in a high heaven, that secure sense that God resided in one place where He could be found. Right now Ben felt God in the orders, like a stone tablet in his pocket.

"The 90th," he said.

He stared at the empty bed of an arriving two-and-a-half-ton truck, one of the olive drab GMC Jimmies that were pouring into France almost as fast as soldiers and guns. The truck swerved around a broken fountain, squealing rubber on the cobbles, then stubbed to a stop. In the cab the Negro driver began tapping on the wheel.

To be heard, a sergeant funneled his hands over his mouth.

"357th Infantry, 90th Division! Let's go! Mount up!"

Soldiers filtered out of the crowd to the idling Jimmy. Ben closed his eyes to listen. The jangles of rifles, bandoliers, buckles, the scuffles of boots, and the mumbles of frightened boys—none of this had been different twenty-six years earlier. The mix of jitters with grease and wool was the same on the French breeze as it had been in the other war, the one they fought to prevent this one.

He opened his eyes. The backs of his hands were not smooth anymore, but spotty, his legs were not as sure. This hurrying truck would carry him back to his old division, the 90th, where he was once young and fierce. How far was he right now from the old trenches? And what of the quarter century wedged in between? What did those years mean, when all they did was return him here? They were just *mishegas*, craziness. All those years were just chisels, carving a circle that led back to the beginning.

Ben climbed into the bed of the truck with a squad. The driver hit the gas the moment the last man clambered up. The sergeant had to run behind to slam the tailgate.

There were no benches in the truck bed. Soldiers clung to the rails and each other for the careering ride out of the town. Ben stood wobbling in the center, pressed against rifle stocks, web belts, packs, and shoulders. A few of the men took hold of him, laying open hands against his chest and spine to buffer the ride.

"Thank you," Ben said to the closest faces. "What's your MOS, soldier?"

The boy answered, "745, Chaplain."

Another piped up over the jostling. "Hell, we're all 745s."

This was military jargon for riflemen. These doughboys were headed straight to the lines.

No one else spoke. A few tried to light cigarettes but gave up under the wind. To the rear, another Jimmy filled with troops closed fast. Behind it, yet another truck left the town. Emptied transports roared past, going back to Isigny. How bad is it, Ben wondered, that replacements are needed in this kind of conveyor belt?

The convoy ran west, away from OMAHA. To the north, the beaches faded behind long marshy flats and scrubby hills dotted with burned-out vehicles and tanks from the fight for Isigny. On both sides of the road, deep craters had been blasted by the mammoth Allied flights of pre-invasion bombers. Ben marveled that so many of the bombs had fallen back here instead of on the Germans' beach defenses. That mistake must have made D-Day even more miserable for the landing forces.

One soldier, a big boy, thick chested and needing a shave, reached across a shorter man to tap Ben on the helmet.

"Chaplain?"

Ben leaned his way to be heard. "Yes?"

"You're a Jew, ain't you?"

"Yes. I'm a rabbi." He had to shout over the truck's passage on the bomb-rutted road. The hands holding him stiffened.

"Well, no offense or nothin'," the soldier drawled out over helmets, "but it's just that I ain't seen many of y'all over here. I mean, I figured with what they say the Krauts have done, you folks'd be crawling all over France to get at 'em. Christ, from what I heard . . ."

The soldier paused.

Ben asked, "And what do they say the Krauts have been doing?"

"You know . . . Taking them out of their homes, shutting down all their shops, stickin' 'em in work camps and such."

Ben put nothing on his face. "And such."

"Yeah, you know."

Ben did not know, and with every living Jew in the world, he lived in fear of learning.

"I'm just sayin', if it was me," the soldier said. "No disrespect."

"None taken, soldier. You go get them for me, alright?"

The doughboy grinned, anointed. Ben recalled the fear that made men speak like this, to hear tough words fly from their own lips. He recalled also that it was not his mission to correct ignorance. It was his job only to see that ignorance served the purposes of the United States Army.

"Alright, Chap! We'll make 'em say Uncle for you."

One soldier angled his head in; his helmet bumped Ben's.

The young GI whispered, "Don't worry, Rabbi. We're here good enough."

Ben smiled and lowered his head, the boy did the same. Ben whispered back words from Joshua:

"It was not because of your own strength nor because you were great in number, for you were the fewest of all people. But it was because the Lord your God loved you, and because He would keep the oath which He had sworn unto your fathers."

The truck jolted through another pit in the road. Ben was held in place, but the young Jewish soldier staggered sideways. The Southern boy, the ignorant one, stuck out an arm to steady him.

"It ain't your job. Sit still."

Boogie John smoked and stared out the windshield to the rising sun. Joe Amos fidgeted on the bench seat.

"Man, I can't just sit like this. I got to *move.*"

The big driver turned to glance in his sideview mirror back at the Quartermaster crew loading the truck bed with jerricans of gasoline.

"What you gon' do, College?" he asked into the reflection. "Get back there and help them load up? It ain't your job. You're the driver."

Joe Amos tugged on the passenger mirror to let him watch the soldiers. The men labored across the sand in a sort of bucket brigade, one slung the jerricans to the next. The last in line hoisted the five-gallon containers up to two big fellows on the bed who stacked the cans.

"Maybe I'll get out and watch. Stretch my legs."

"Yeah." Boogie John coughed a smoky chortle. "Just what I need. Sit here and listen to a bunch of white boys loading my truck while a colored man stands by and watches. Yeah, I'll enjoy that. You go ahead, College. And I'll shoot you."

Boogie John tapped the two stripes on his sleeve, making the point that Joe Amos had only one.

"Now sit still. They load it. We move it. We ain't back in England."

Boogie tempered his command with an offered cigarette. Joe Amos took it and a light from Boogie's Zippo. He inhaled and pushed the passenger mirror back.

"England was nice," he said. "Those were nice girls."

"Yeah," Boogie agreed. "White girls."

Joe Amos never stopped marveling how quickly Boogie could re-place a grimace with a smile.

He said, "And those Red Cross dances. I'm gonna miss them."

Boogie dropped his cigarette to the floorboard and crushed it. They'd all heard stories about a driver in Cornwall who'd tossed a lit cigarette out his window while loading gasoline. Boogie's grin de-parted. "Don't talk to me about the Red Cross."

"It kept us out of trouble, Boog. When you gonna understand that?"

"When am I . . . ?"

Agitated again, the driver shifted on the bench to face Joe Amos. He was wide, dark, and against him Joe Amos felt thin and pale. He never liked the way Boogie did this, lectured him, made him feel the lesser for his light skin, for his three years of college, for his desire to get along.

"Man, you don't know what trouble is. Segregating dances is trouble. Segregating blood by race is trouble. Separate movie halls, sep-arate rooms at pubs. What you gonna call trouble if that ain't it? You need a bomb to fall on your head before you call somethin' trouble?"

With a grunt, Boogie settled back behind the steering wheel.

"Look at these crackers back there. Wouldn't pee on you and me if we was burnin'. And the Red Cross wouldn't give 'em your blood nei-ther if their lives depended on it." Boogie fumbled for another cigarette. "They Jim Crowed us back home and they gonna Jim Crow us over here. You best learn that. Damn."

Joe Amos looked away from the man who'd been his driving partner since training camp, almost two years past. Joe Amos wouldn't change his mind; England hadn't been so bad. The camps were segregated, sure, but that was the way the Army worked, and they all knew it. Maybe it was Jim Crow, but England was still a hell of a lot better than Fort Lee back in Petersburg, where a black man was a nigger half the time and scared the other half. In England, you got to do your job, run-ins with white soldiers only happened in town once in a while. No one in their 688th Truck Battalion had got into any serious dustups, none that got re-ported, anyway. But how had Boogie survived growing up in Cleveland with that kind of anger? He's mad about something new every day in the Army. He's a big man, Joe Amos figured, maybe no one back home ever took him on.

"Boog, you hear the one about that old lady in Tewksbury?"

"No."

"Yeah. She wrote a letter to a Colonel over in Cheltenham. Said she wanted him to send six soldiers from the base over to her house for tea. And she said No Jews."

Boogie shook his head at the British. "Everyone got to have somebody to whup."

Joe Amos finished the tale. He didn't know if it was true or not, but it was funny.

"So Sunday noon the old lady opened her door and standing there were six big colored boys. She says there must be some mistake. And the biggest brother says, 'No, ma'am. Colonel Berkowitz didn't make no mistake.' "

Boogie chuckled, his big stomach rubbed the steering wheel. He laid out his hand. Joe Amos slapped it.

"You take her for a while," Boogie said.

Joe Amos slid over top of the burly driver, and the two exchanged places without getting out. They could do this at sixty miles an hour with no problem.

The Quartermaster crew finished loading the truck. The last man jumped down and shut the gate. He pounded on it.

Joe Amos charged the gears. The instant he pulled from the depot, another Jimmy took his place. An approaching truck honked. Joe Amos tapped the brake to let him go past. The entire beach was choked with traffic and materials. He dodged to get in line with his platoon waiting near the D-1 draw. Everywhere on OMAHA, mounds of ammo crates were built like bunkers in the sand. Dunes of ration cartons swept in and rolled away, to be rebuilt in another hour. A million five-gallon jerricans sucked the loads from tanker trucks dry, then the tankers tiptoed back into the water and up the ramp of one odd-looking ship or another to motor back across the Channel, returning tomorrow with more fuel for the war machines. Toting these crates and cans onto the beach was every shape of vehicle: amphibious DUKWs, giant bladed 'dozers, landing craft great and small laying themselves open to spill in the shallows, rhino ferries, jeeps, Sherman tanks, and hundreds of Jimmies. Joe Amos recollected what a transport officer had told their battalion before the invasion: the plan called for three thousand vehicles a day to land in Normandy. "That's how we're going to beat them," the officer said. "Wheels."

Joe Amos took his place in line with his 1st platoon. He was the tenth truck back from the jeep that waited at the head of their column. With closed eyes, he waited in the warming cab for the rest of his unit to finish loading. Joe Amos Biggs and Boogie John Bailey drove in Dog Company, in the 688th QM Battalion, eleven hundred Negroes led by forty officers, most of them white. The battalion had five hundred trucks, divided into four companies, each broken into four platoons of about thirty vehicles each. When the 688th moved in echelon, the column snaked over eight miles long, and thirteen hundred tons of whatever Eisenhower's U.S. Army ordered went for a ride.

Dog Company had not been off the beach since their arrival yesterday, Sunday. Joe Amos cast his thoughts back to Danville, Virginia. An ocean and two calendars had spread themselves between him and home. His mother and four sisters and four brothers-in-law were all praying for him yesterday, sure enough, uncles, aunts and cousins, too. Every one of them were on their farms or at the textile mill today. Across the Atlantic, Joe Amos idled on an invasion beach in a truck piled high with gasoline cans. He sat in the front seat of a rolling firebomb he was about to drive straight to the front lines. Eyes closed, he said a quick prayer for himself and for his family, because a farm, the mill, Danville, France, these all had dangers.

The truck behind nipped his bumper. Joe Amos opened his eyes. Beside him Boogie shivered awake. The line of Jimmies ahead had moved off. Joe Amos shifted into gear and began his first run of the war.

It took forty minutes to get all the platoon's trucks off the beach and up on the battered road. In single file, the convoy crept through the ravine, labeled D-1, the first of four breaks in the steep green bluffs that allowed vehicles to drive off the five-mile expanse of OMAHA. D-1 was the westernmost and the most prized draw on D-Day because it had been the right-hand, exposed flank of the American invasion sector. According to the maps Joe Amos had seen in England, D-1 was also the narrowest of the paths off the beach, and the best defended by the Germans.

Joe Amos eased the Jimmy between the dunes. Scars hemmed the draw, a dozen blasted pillboxes lay in ruins. Bunkered German machine guns with interlocking fields of fire must have made this five-hundred-yard stretch a slaughterhouse for any soldier fighting his way through. Blackened concrete spoiled the slopes, kicked there by naval artillery and hand-delivered satchel charges. Acres of beach grass were cordoned with barbed wire and posted with skull-and-crossbones signs reading *Achtung! Minen!* Joe Amos gaped at the destruction, slowing so much he drew a honk from the deuce-and-a-half behind and a glare from Boogie John.

Up on the road, the convoy straightened its ranks and picked up speed, headed west. The column hauled POL—petrol, oil, and lubricants. Over the last year, Joe Amos and every driver in the battalion had it drilled in their heads: An American army can fight in dirty uniforms; soldiers can be hungry and low on ammo. But if they don't move fast, if the tanks, transports, tractors, and jeeps stall, then the greatest advantages America brought to the war—manufacturing and mobility—went right to hell. One in ten soldiers actually saw combat. The rest, the service divisions, bore the task of supplying the combat troops. The chain was a long one, stretching from American factories to ports, then onto ships, over the ocean, into English harbors, across the Channel, onto landing craft, then the beaches and into the truck beds. There the drivers took over. They would deliver the matériel when and where it was needed. Without their hands on the steering wheels, the hardware of war—America's real Sunday punch—would stay stacked on the sand. And here in Europe, seven out of ten of those drivers' hands were black.

Joe Amos kept his Jimmy twenty feet behind the truck in front, right where he was supposed to be. The pace of the convoy hovered at twenty-five miles per hour, the speed designated in the transport manual. He didn't know where they were going. That was the job of the jeep out front and the officer with the map. Joe Amos wiped his palms on his thighs. He sweated with excitement and pride. His convoy looked good, long and olive drab, strong and aimed straight at the Jerries. Joe Amos Biggs himself hauled five thousand pounds of fuel in his truck bed.

"I wish they'd let me fight."

"Why you wanna say something stupid like that?" Boogie John asked. "That's the second dumbass thing you said this morning. Take a break."

Joe Amos shrugged. "I don't know. Just figure I could do as good a job as them. That's all."

"Maybe you could, you being a dumbass."

Boogie seemed to laugh at himself, how mean he could be.

The truck tilted and jounced in and out of a deep pothole. Joe Amos struggled to keep his grip on the wrenching steering wheel. The laden truck swayed.

"Get your head on the road!" Boogie barked. "Pay attention to the job, boy! Say you wanna fight? You can't even drive a damn truck."

Joe Amos tightened his lips. Boogie would get under his skin if he didn't, the man could rile an anvil. Joe Amos fixed his gaze on the narrow bit of road sluicing between his hood and the truck ahead.

But the scorched litter of combat drew his gaze. Beyond the shoulder, tanks with broken tracks and burned-out turrets squatted in scorched fields. Deep craters from mortars and artillery scooped the land; two bullet-riddled Jimmies on flat tires had been bulldozed off the road, one of them had caught fire. There were no bodies anywhere, though Joe Amos looked hard to see one on the ground or in the wrecks. He barely kept his hands on the wheel. Every second he wanted to point something out to Boogie, but his big partner only scowled at the carnage. Joe Amos drove and gawked.

His wheels struck another pothole. In the truck bed the jerricans squealed and bumped, the Jimmy shuddered. Joe Amos feared for the axles. Boogie John drew an impatient breath. Joe Amos braced for the rebuke. Boogie's head did not turn his way, but leaned out his passenger window.

A flight of Thunderbolts blared overhead, slicing across the road at four hundred miles an hour. Six Pratt & Whitney engines drowned every noise on the ground. The Jimmy and its load shuddered to the vibrations of the roaring fighters passing low and hot, seeking enemies to the south.

Joe Amos whooped. He balled a fist out his window.

"Damn, Boogie! Look at 'em!"

Boogie lowered his head and watched the six planes snap by. Somewhere over the green terrain to the south—miles off now in the seconds since they were overhead—the Thunderbolts broke formation. They dove, each zeroing in on some target. Joe Amos heard their cannons pound. Smoke plumes rose where they struck. The planes climbed and circled to hit again whatever prey they'd found.

The convoy pressed westward. The power of the Thunderbolts' assault faded, replaced by more war debris beside the road. Trucks and tanks were the largest dead denizens, but the earth was littered with smaller bits. Joe Amos noted everything along the ground: discarded fieldpieces, artillery casings, windblown medical rubbish, lost helmets. He imagined the combat that boiled through here only days ago, the fight for this key road that connected OMAHA and UTAH beaches. He cast back a week earlier, before the invasion, and peopled this road with Germans, black-clad soldiers riding where he rode now, in their convertible staff cars, enjoying the mild Normandy sun. The Germans had been chased south off this highway, but not very far. The attacking P-47s over-head told him how close the Krauts were, and how hard they were going to be to push farther back.

The road stretched long and straight. The convoy rolled through ru-ined villages, and some that had escaped damage. There seemed no for-mula for this other than where the Germans had made a stand and where they'd backed away without a fight. Wherever they'd put up their dukes, like in Longueville, La Cambe, d'Arthenay, and Isigny, the towns were eradicated. What looked like ancient buildings, not made of bricks so much as stones, had been gutted. Joe Amos looked into peo-ple's sliced-open rooms, saw curtains and tidily made-up beds where walls lay in the street. He slowed in front of a church steeple with no church attached, just stones and charred beams. The towns stated their names on signs, sometimes shot-up placards, and again, at the city lim-its, announced you were leaving with a red line through the name. He tried to pronounce the towns in his head, but did not know which of the letters to leave out in the odd French pronunciations; instead, he enlisted Boogie to say the towns out loud and the two chuckled, easing their path through the battle zone.

"Boog?"

"What."

"Can we drive one of those?"

Joe Amos pointed at the Jimmy in front. The truck was one of four in their platoon with a .50 caliber machine gun welded to a ring behind the cab.

"You go ahead," Boogie said. "I'm fine where I am."

Joe Amos rattled his head in reply and drove. Boogie clucked his tongue.

He said, "Where'd you get this notion about fightin'? The man told you we won't gonna fight. We're gonna drive trucks. That's what the black folk came over here to do. And that's what I'm gonna do."

Both men had stowed their M-1 Garand rifles under the seat. In training camp, Joe Amos had made himself a proficient shot. As a ser-vice unit, their battalion was not given regular rifle practice. Joe Amos hadn't fired his weapon once in 1944, but he kept the rifle clean and close at hand. No matter the truth of what Boogie was saying, when Joe Amos carried the M-1 or oiled it, he felt like a soldier.

"College, show me one boy in this whole Army doin' one thing more than he's supposed to, I'll show you a moron. That's FUBAR and you know it. And don't think the Army's gonna do anything extra for you, neither. We ain't wanted here and that's fine with me, I don't wanna be here. They drafted me and I don't like jail. That's the deal."

Boogie folded his arms and clammed up. Joe Amos drove another ten minutes wrapped in motor growls, exhaust, and a bumpy silence. In England, Boogie had not been like this, so edgy. This negative, sad-sack stuff started yesterday. Joe Amos waited a while, then told his partner so.

Boogie studied the grass fields dotted with abandoned vehicles. The wreck of a crashed bomber rose out of a marsh like a jumbled island, a bent propeller jutted up in the shape of a palm tree. Boogie said nothing. In a field, a cart was tipped over, a dead horse lay in the traces. Joe Amos watched Boogie's eyes linger on the bloated animal until it was behind them. Placards beside the road read: *Danger! Shoulder Not Clear of Mines!*

Joe Amos realized: Boogie's scared. Damn a'mighty, he thought. So am I.

He felt better and let the talk dry up. Being scared doesn't make you a coward, he decided. It means you've got eyeballs in your head, and some sense. Boogie John ran away from his fear; he, Joe Amos, walked toward his. Both were valid and human. Joe Amos privately smiled, because Boogie's reaction probably made more sense.

On the other side of the road, a long convoy roared by, headed back to OMAHA. He couldn't see the cargos under the canvas tops. A few soldiers stood in the truck beds looking over the gates. Other than them, the trucks seemed empty.

The column entered the outskirts of a larger town. The sign read: *Carentan.* The truck in front slowed and the gap narrowed. There were no brake lights on any of the Jimmies, only cat's eyes, two ruby slit lamps on the rear and one clear lamp in the front, lights that would not be visible from the air. Joe Amos tapped his brake. The convoy came to a halt. Joe Amos and Boogie leaned out their windows to find the reason.

The leading jeep had reached a bridge over the Aure River, into Carentan, a dozen miles from OMAHA. The jeep pulled off the road at the foot of the bridge and waited until all thirty trucks were idling in line. Then the first Jimmy motored across. The second truck waited, then sprinted over the stone span.

In a few minutes Joe Amos rolled to the head of the line. A sign next to the bridge said: *Welcome to Carentan. Courtesy of the 101st Airborne.* Below this placard was nailed a hand-painted poster, warning: *One vehicle at a time. Bridge under fire.*

Lieutenant Garner stood beside the road, his hand up to Joe Amos. He watched the Jimmy on the bridge trundle across. Without looking into the cab, he asked, "How you boys doin'? Boog, you lettin' the pup drive?"

"Boy got to learn sometime, Lieutenant. Y'all sure as shit didn't teach him nothin'."

The white officer chuckled. With the ninth truck safely across, he set his elbow in the driver-side window and looked past Joe Amos. The platoon CO was a tall Louisianan. The word was that the Army believed Southern officers knew best how to handle Negro troops. Garner spoke with a drawl, rubbed his bald head a lot. He was twenty-three, just two years older than Joe Amos.

"Boogie, if I can put up with you, why can't you put up with me?"

Boogie's chest jiggled with laughter. "I'm doin' what I can, Lieutenant."

Garner nodded at the parity of their situations. The lieutenant didn't want to command colored soldiers, they didn't want to be under him. That was the U.S. Army, and all agreed war was not the time or place to change it. Garner waved them onto the bridge.

"Don't worry, boys," he called after them. "I hear the German artillery takes about nine trucks to get their timing down."

Across the span, Joe Amos laid on the gas. He charged the Jimmy over the narrow river, into the ruined town of Carentan, and put his truck back in line to wait for the rest of the platoon. He didn't expect an enemy barrage on the bridge, but the 101st Airborne hadn't put that sign there as a joke; the banks were gouged with craters. Joe Amos sensed he'd crossed something more than a river. These were his first moments within reach of the Germans.

Carentan was a beat-up mess. The fighting here had raged house-to-house. Now that the town was taken, soldiers moved into every crevice. Gun barrels bristled in windows, fieldpieces behind sandbags pointed south. No soldier carried his weapon on his back, but in his hands.

"I reckon we don't give much of a damn about homes and such," Joe Amos observed. "I mean, Jesus. Look at this."

Boogie snorted. "What you want 'em to do? Be careful? I'd of knocked everything down, too."

"That's if you were to fight."

"Which I ain't."

The truck platoon re-assembled on the west side of the bridge and got under way. To the rear, another convoy halted at the bridge, read the Airborne's signs, and began their crossing.

Moving west of Carentan and the Aure River, the convoy was now a few miles from UTAH beach. The terrain around the road began a slow change, away from low hills and marsh. Bit by bit, the land closed around the road, a greener embrace of thickets along the shoulders, rimming the meadows and orchards rolling away south.

"Hedgerows," Boogie said, baring his teeth.

Joe Amos nodded. "The bocage."

The hedges gave the land a patchwork quality. Each field was bordered on four sides by a fence of bush, vine, and bramble, all woven together in a wall of leaves and exposed roots. Each ridge was three to six feet high. Dirt lanes diced between the hedges. From the truck cab Joe Amos could see mile after corduroy mile of the bocage, held by the Germans.

"Man," he said, "goin' in there . . ."

"Like pickin' ticks," Boogie agreed.

"Off a real mad dog."

Boogie whistled. The two drivers could add no more, the rest would only be imagination. Joe Amos drove steadily in his place in the convoy. Boogie never turned his face from the south, the immensity and tangle of the bocage as a battleground.

In another ten minutes the convoy entered Ste. Mère-Église. This town, seven miles inland from UTAH, had been the target of an airborne assault by the 101st Screaming Eagles the night before the beach invasion. Ste. Mère-Église was now the rally point for American forces on the Cotentin peninsula.

The convoy slowed and rumbled into the town square. A high-steepled church stood at the west corner, its roof punched in. Burned and busted shells of shops rimmed the rest of the cobblestone. Ste. Mère-Église had been pummeled.

Quartermaster soldiers scrambled to the truck beds as soon as the wheels stopped. Jerricans and crates were off-loaded and stacked everywhere in the square. Joe Amos and Boogie climbed down. At the head of their column, Lieutenant Garner spoke with several officers and a medic.

Wounded men lined the sidewalks, many standing, many on stretchers. They waited, swathed in gauze in every way. Joe Amos tried not to
stare. He glanced at Boogie. The big driver's eyes were riveted on the
wounded.

"Look how many of 'em," Joe Amos murmured.

Boogie winced. "Couple hundred, easy. Man oh man. This is just one
day's worth."

Joe Amos shook his head. "The hedgerows. The fighting's gotta be
bad out there. For this many."

"I know what you're thinkin'," Boogie said. "Can I tell you somethin'? You gonna listen?"

"Yeah."

"You remember the Kraut POWs back at Fort Lee? They were chop-
pin' wood and clearin' brush?"

"Yeah."

"You remember on Sundays they could eat in any restaurant in
town, long as they were with the MPs? They got to go to any church.
They got to take a crap in any bathroom in town. They got to sit anywhere on a bus, in any seat in a movie house. And you and me?"

"Yeah, Boog. I know."

Boogie John aimed a quick gesture at the lines of wounded. Some of
them, accompanied by armed guards, were German infantry, gray-clad
and wrapped like the GIs in bandages.

"Those Kraut sumbitches right there got to put on the uniforms of
their country and go fight. You ain't got that right. You ain't got as much
freedom as a goddam Kraut POW."

Boogie spat on the cobblestones.

"So whatever you got in your head, College, get it out."

Boogie John turned and climbed into the Jimmy's driver seat. Joe
Amos stayed on the cobblestones until his truck was off-loaded and the
bed was empty. From the head of the column, Lieutenant Garner waved
to the medic. A whistle blew. The lines of bandaged soldiers shuffled for
the convoy. The sighted guided the blind, the walking buttressed the
lame. Stretchers floated over the cobbles, hoisted by orderlies and chaplains. The procession had a scary, zombie-like feel, groaning men stumbling for the trucks across the square. Chaplains and buddies murmured
encouragement. Joe Amos did not want to be one of these unfortunates.
He didn't want a wound, a hole in his body, taped shut, and needing

help just to get across a courtyard. The thought made him cringe. He
hoped none of the soldiers saw his shudder, then realized no one was
looking at him at all.

The truck beds filled for the ride back to OMAHA. One soldier patted a comrade on the shoulder after helping heft his stretcher.

"Goin' home," the soldier chirped. His friend on the litter gave a
thumbs-up, then laid his bandaged head down. And for what? Was
Boogie right? Was he on the money? If you're going to pay with an eye
or a hand, you ought to get something in return. These white soldiers
got America. What was waiting for Joe Amos and Boogie if they arrived
home on a stretcher or with a cane, or in a box? It damn sure wasn't the
same America.

If he was this upset just looking at clean, dressed wounds, Joe Amos
figured he'd surely be no good in the wicked bocage itself, where the
bullets and bombs were flying, where these gashes were made and the
blood wasn't yet wrapped away.

Best face it. He was no fighter. Fine. His country didn't want him
to be.

The wounded were loaded into all but the last few Jimmies in line.
Once the bandaged men were in the truck beds, the orderlies and chaplains disappeared behind one of the slumped, ruined walls along the
courtyard. Some unseen bell tolled a hush over the square. Joe Amos fidgeted, watching.

A procession of orderlies carrying stretchers emerged. On every litter lay a corpse, torso covered head-to-ankle by a tucked-in olive blanket. From the laces on some of the boots, a yellow tag dangled. Helmets
and weapons lay on the stretchers with the warriors, these would not be
taken from them until the last. The corpses were hefted onto the last
trucks. The number of bodies—there must have been fifty—stunned Joe
Amos. He thought back to the Jimmies that passed him on the way to
Carentan, the ones that appeared empty. They must have been trans-
porting dead.

The platoon revved. Joe Amos climbed beside Boogie. The big driver
gestured to the maimed, bandaged, and killed that were now their
cargo.

"Yeah, College," he said. "You're right. I reckon you could do just as
good a job as them. You could get your ass shot off, too."

Joe Amos wanted Boogie to stifle. He set his elbow in the cab window and laid his chin in the crook, looking away from his partner.

Boogie crept forward in line, gentling the Jimmy, not rattling the wounded in the bed. He double-clutched gently into second. With a less tender touch, he poked Joe Amos in the back.

"I'm not gonna tell you this again," he said. "No matter what you do, they ain't ever gonna call you a hero."

Ben Kahn sifted through the sounds he knew, culling them from the ones he was hearing for the first time.

Rifle cracks and the dull *whumps* of artillery and mortar fire he recalled from the trenches of the Great War. These reached him from the fight a mile away west. The bangs tried to transport him backward, decades, yank him to the old bloodletting, but they could not because they were trumped by the louder, newer machineries of war. Bombers, air-to-ground attack fighters, wing-mounted rockets, strafing cannon fire, tanks, self-propelled artillery—the woof and howl of these weapons were new and fearsome. Ben could not picture what they were doing there, beyond the tiers of hedges. The Germans must have these things, too, he thought, listening. He felt old, an ancestor of this war, unsure of so much. He did not have a map and he did not know where he was. He knew only the name of the decimated town where he'd been dropped off. Gueutteville. He knew the fighting in the hedgerows was close.

"Soldier," he asked a passing doughboy, "where can I find Division HQ?"

A dirty, hurried hand aimed Ben to a barn at the eastern rim of town. Outside, several jeeps were parked. The fenders of one of the vehicles bore starred flags.

Ben picked through the rubble of Gueutteville. This brand of destruction, too, was different from the other world war. The fighting then was more static. Armies had dug in and squared off in the great fields, river valleys, and forests of France. They'd circled and pecked at each other for weeks and months and let attrition win battles. Only a few cities, like Verdun, had been laid low. But this street fighting and blasting of homes, churches, businesses, antiquities . . . Is the new war going to be so voracious in every town and village, will it smash every wall so thoroughly? Has it become necessary to stage so much demolition along with the killing of armies?

We didn't have this kind of firepower, he thought. Who knows what we would have done with it? The same. Worse. We were men at war, too. I used bayonets and shovels to kill. Can I say I would not have used rockets?

A guard waved him inside the barn. This private wore the shoulder patch of the 90th Division, two red letters, a tall *T* standing in an *O* against an olive background.

Ben rapped a knuckle on the soldier's arm. "You know, years back, I used to be in the 90th. I was a Tough Ombre, too."

"Yes, sir," the soldier said, mustering an uninterested smile. The boy needed a razor and a cot.

Ben nodded at the patch. "You know where that T-O comes from, Private?"

"No, sir, I don't."

"Well, you ought to. Texas and Oklahoma. That's where the original division was raised for the first war."

"You in that, Chaplain?"

"Yes, I was. I was a dough just like you. Right here in France. We're the ones who made up the name, Tough Ombres. And we were."

Ben squeezed the boy's arm, palm over the patch.

"Just like you, son."

The young soldier blinked in confusion. Ben saw in him the twin desires, one canceling the other, to talk and to be left alone—the foot soldier's urge to go noticed and unnoticed. War does this to you, leaps you out of your skin and shoves you into your guts, all at the same time. You don't know which way to jump, so you stay in the middle, alone and not alone, surrounded by men feeling the same, men counting on you, the next guy. Scared soldiers wanting only not to be scared, needing you to never be scared. And you watch and find out when everyone else does what you're made of. That's the soldier's question, more important than fate, more than life and death. What are you made of? Looking at this dirty, smooth face, Ben remembered the weight of the rifle across his own shoulder where he wore that patch. He thought of his son, Thomas, the first time he ever saw him in his Army Air Corps uniform, snappy in his waistcoat and wings.

The soldier guarding the door looked at his boots, seeming a little ashamed. Ben stepped into the barn.

The building was big and undamaged, an oddity in Gueutteville. No farm animals lived in the stalls but their aroma remained in the straw and clapboard. Field desks stood on rickety, fast-assembly legs; upturned barrels served as stools. Captains and colonels skittered from one to another, carting papers, aiming fingers into maps. Most smoked, an ill-advised thing in a barn full of straw, and haze hung in the bare rafters over these men and their talk. There was something else in the fusty air: Urgency? No. Frustration.

"Chaplain."

A Lieutenant Colonel waggled fingers, beckoning Ben into the stall where he stood. Ben rounded one of the old wooden posts holding up the barn.

The officer stretched his hand to Ben. The man was remarkably tall, maybe six and a half feet. His arm was so long, the hand reached across the desk before Ben was ready. The officer's uniform was neatly tucked, his chin strap was buckled. The only weapon Ben saw on him was a .45 at his belt.

The two shook hands. The Lieutenant Colonel gestured to a large milk pail.

"Grab a bucket, Rabbi."

Ben arranged himself on the pail. The officer sat behind his table on an upturned feed trough.

"Tom Meadow, Division G-2. And you are . . . ?"

Ben had his orders in hand. He held them out.

"Late!"

The word was barked from behind, outside the stall. Meadow, the personnel officer, rose from his trough. Ben stood also.

A short, thick General stamped up. He appraised Ben up and down, hands on hips. He snorted, making Ben think of a bad-tempered pony.

"Where the hell you been, Chaplain? We were expecting you six days ago."

"I know, sir. I was—"

"Wait. I've seen you before."

"Yes, sir. Captain Ben Kahn."

"You were on the *Susan B. Anthony.*"

"Yes, sir. Same as you."

"Aw, hell. You got on the wrong boat. You followed some of my dummies, didn't you?"

The General clapped Ben on the shoulder. He glanced at Meadow.

"You know this story, Colonel?"

Meadow shook his head. "Not the whole thing, General. I know we're still missing about a hundred men out of the 359th."

"Billups. Assistant CO." The General thrust a mitt at Ben, then burst into the tale for Meadow.

"Typical SNAFU. Morning of the 7th, mile off UTAH, our transport hits a mine. The *Susan B. Anthony*. She takes two hours to go down. Before she slides under, two British destroyers pull up on the port side and save our asses. Right, Chaplain?"

"Carry on, sir."

General Billups took up residence on Ben's milk pail. He short-armed the air, building tilted images of the doomed ship.

"She's sinking by the stern, see. We manage to get most of the 359th and everyone else off and up on the first destroyer, about three thousand total. But somehow, half of G Company figures they'll run all the way across the deck . . ." Billups shook his head and rubbed his brow under his helmet. ". . . and go climb onto the second destroyer tied outboard of the first one. The first destroyer pulls away from the wreck and transfers everybody to landing craft. These men all make it to shore. But the second ship . . . Tell him, Rabbi."

Ben winced at the floor. "Went back to England."

"Back to England," the General repeated heartily. "But here you are, Chaplain. Glad you decided to make it. I assume the rest of my boys are somewhere behind you?"

"I don't know, sir. I got here as fast as I could on my own. I got my orders to report to the 90th this morning."

"I see. Well, sad to say, we can damn well use another chaplain."

The personnel officer agreed. Ben figured there was something going unuttered between these two, the same black, hovering air he sensed when he walked through the barn door. Ben recognized and understood the strain in these men's voices, of thwarted control, slipping hope. He felt kinship; he was the father of a downed, missing pilot, and there was always that thing wrong with every moment, something he could not fix or end, no matter how hard he wished, prayed, or tried. What was he getting into here? What was wrong in the Tough Ombres?

He had come back to France for one reason—to push the war, make it conclude as fast as it could. He believed that was the only way his son's fate would be known. If the boy had been captured, he'd be set free. If he was dead, he'd be accounted for. God had returned Ben to his old division. But was this nervous-Nellie bunch, the new 90th, going to lead him to his son?

Propped on the milk pail, the General read Ben's orders, tapping a boot toe in the straw.

Nerves, thought Ben.

Billups handed the sheet to the Colonel. He addressed Ben.

"Alright, Chaplain. Welcome to the 90th. We're going to keep you with Division. I want you assigned to Headquarters."

"General, I was hoping to be given a unit. My own unit, a battalion. I'd like to be up with the infantry, sir."

Billups shook this off.

"No. We've got three regiments of infantry, one of artillery, seven battalions of support troops. I got Jews all over the place, Chaplain, but not enough in any one unit to warrant their own rabbi. I need you to be able to get to all of them. You'll work out of Division for a while. Then we'll see."

"Sir."

The General threw Ben a baleful eye.

"What, Captain?"

"Sir, I'm a chaplain in the U.S. Army first. I'm a rabbi second. My training is to minister to every soldier, whatever religion or none. I respectfully request assignment to an infantry battalion."

The General rose from the milk pail. He was half a head shorter than Ben, and stocky.

"Chaplain, I'll tell you straight: You are not a young man."

"No, sir, I am not. And this is not my first war."

Billups hooked his thumbs in his pockets. He glanced at Colonel Meadow. "Tommy, you might have said something."

"I didn't know, General."

Billups gave Ben another appraisal. "The Argonne?"

"And St. Mihiel."

Billups whistled, looking back to Meadow before crossing his arms and gazing at Ben.

"I missed those. I was stateside."

"I wish I had been, sir."

"Yeah. Tommy," the General spoke without taking his eyes from Ben, "the chaplain here is an old doughboy. You're a bloody man, Chap."

He said this as though it were flattery.

"Don't take that the wrong way. We need men like you right now."

There it was again, something urgent and unsaid.

"So what are you doing back here, soldier?"

Ben could have shown him. He carried the reason. But he only reported to this general. He was answerable elsewhere.

"There's a war on, sir."

"Okay. I'll buy that. Have you been briefed?"

"No."

"Alright. I'm not going to give you your own unit just yet, Padre. I'm going to wait on that. See how you do. But I will give you the dope on the 90th, since you're an old Tough Ombre. Maybe you can do some good. Lord knows somebody's got to around here. Tommy?"

"General."

"Give the rabbi your seat. Get my map."

Ben walked over the straw to the opposite side of the desk to sit on the upside-down trough. Colonel Meadow returned and unfolded Billups's map across the table, then moved aside. The General tapped a knuckle on the blue lines of the map.

"Alright, Padre, here's the situation. One week ago at 6:30 A.M. we landed here and here, on OMAHA and UTAH beaches. The night before the invasion, the 82nd and the 101st Airborne Divisions dropped behind these swamps at UTAH to screw with the Krauts and cut off the main roads from the Cotentin to keep reinforcements out. They got plopped all over the place in the dark and ended up lost in the damn hedgerows. Even so, those paratroop sumbitches pulled off every one of their missions. Incredible. The morning of D-Day, we got lucky over here at UTAH. The first LCs taking the 4th Division ashore hit the surf two thousand yards south from their target beach. Turns out this part of UTAH had a lot less resistance and fewer fixed defenses than if they'd landed where they were supposed to. The whole UTAH assault was moved here, and after a few hours the 4th had the beach secured and had units moving a mile inland."

With his finger, Billups dotted UTAH beach, satisfyingly thumping the table. He drew the finger east over the map, to OMAHA.

"Now, the deal over here was a lot worse. Piece of bad luck, really. We landed two infantry divisions, the 29th and the 1st, here on OMAHA. Just the day before, the Krauts transferred in their 352nd Division, a crack unit up from St. Lô, for a training exercise on our invasion beach. The 1st ran right smack into them. To make matters worse, once our boys got onshore, it turned out the big naval and air bombardments had landed too far inland and didn't do much to soften up the Krauts along these bluffs. For most of the morning, all along seven thousand yards of open beach, OMAHA was a shooting gallery. We lost twenty-five hundred soldiers before they ever got off the sand."

Billups looked up from the map. His tongue prodded his lower lip, his eyes batted. He seemed to fight back emotion.

"But, as you can see, Padre, they did."

Ben and Colonel Meadow gave the General a moment. Billups swept a knuckle into both eye sockets and continued.

"Today marks the seventh day we've been in Normandy. So far we've landed nine divisions over our beaches, the Brits and Canadians have brought ashore six on theirs. We've got a hundred and thirty thousand GIs in our beachhead and six thousand vehicles. More are coming every hour. To date, the Krauts haven't mustered a decent counterattack. Our guess is, they still don't believe this is the main Allied invasion. They think we're still planning on hitting them up there in the Pas de Calais."

"That's why Patton's not here," Meadow said. "He's still in England, running a ghost army."

Ben guessed at the massive deception. "You're making the Germans figure we're holding Patton back. For something bigger."

Billups nodded. "That, and for slapping those two kids down in Sicily. Don't worry, old Blood 'n' Guts will be here soon enough. For now, Rommel doesn't know whether to shit or go bowling. In the meantime, we're exploiting the situation as fast as we can until he and Hitler figure it out. The Krauts have stiffened here at Caen against the Brits. That's draining the Kraut positions against us here on the Cotentin peninsula. And because we own the skies, every tank the Krauts move had damn well better move at night or he's not gonna make it. Even so, they're putting up one hell of a fight. This morning, the Krauts fired their first V-1 rocket at London. They're not throwing in the towel, that's for certain."

Meadow piped in, pointing. "Montgomery's keeping the pressure on the Krauts at Caen. We're trying to break through to the west coast of the peninsula and seal it off. Up here at the northern tip is Cherbourg. We need that port real bad. Until we capture the city and get the port up and running, all our logistics have to flow across the beaches, and that just isn't going to cut it if we're going to support a big enough army in France to kick the Huns out."

"It looks like Montgomery's going to take a while to break out through Caen. Too much resistance," Billups said. "The Krauts figure

Caen is the fastest way to Paris and the Seine, and they're right, so they're tossing the kitchen sink at Monty. Eisenhower and Bradley have made up their minds that we can't just sit inside our bridgehead and wait for the Brits to get a head of steam. We need elbow room. We've got another twenty divisions in England waiting to land. So instead of going right for Cherbourg, we're going to cut off the peninsula first."

Meadow slid a finger west across the map, from Ste. Mère-Église to the Atlantic. The gesture looked like a man slashing a finger under a throat.

"That takes us through here. Right into the bocage."

"General," Ben said, "that's the worst-looking place I've ever seen to have a fight."

The General hissed a palm across his stubbled chin.

"Yeah, well, Chaplain, we're not getting to call our shots just yet. Monty's lack of progress at Caen means we've got to fight our way through the bocage if we're ever gonna break out of Normandy. It's not anybody's first choice, I assure you. We didn't exactly plan on this, to be honest."

"How's it going so far?"

Ben expected Billups to dissemble, to keep invisible whatever was wrong in the 90th. But the General did not hesitate.

"We're getting our asses kicked, Padre. And if you came through Ste. Mère-Église, you saw the casualties we're racking up."

"I saw them."

Silence followed this statement, as if the wounded and dead were here with them and respect was being paid. Ben glanced at the map under Billups's elbows. Two-thirds of the Cotentin peninsula remained to be taken. All of it to the ocean was dense, enemy-held hedgerows, fortified villages, and troop-swallowing swamplands.

Billups moved from behind the table. "Tommy, get back to work. Chaplain, come with me."

Colonel Meadow folded the General's map, inclining his head to the new chaplain. Ben followed Billups out of the stall, then through the rear door of the barn.

Outside, the road leading into Gueutteville dodged away into the maze of hedges. Soldiers dug foxholes in the fields or burrowed into the root walls of the hedgerows. Late-afternoon clouds predicted a damp evening. Billups led Ben several steps from the barn.

"I figured it was better if you and me talked out here, Chaplain. You're not a priest, I know, but we're talking in private, right?"

"Of course, General."

"Alright."

Billups removed his helmet, displaying a pate of gray thistles. Ben guessed the man was only a few years older than himself, maybe early fifties. Billups had the directness and flat accent of a Midwesterner.

"Son of a bitch," he muttered.

Ben waited the General out.

"Sorry, Chap. It's just . . ." The General lifted a hand to indicate west, where Ben caught more sounds of warfare.

"We're getting our hats handed to us out there. And if we don't take the peninsula, we can't expand the bridgehead. That keeps us vulnerable to a German counterattack that, frankly, at this point might stand a chance of shoving us right back into the water."

"How bad is it, General?"

"Bad. Over these first three days I reckon it could be worse, but not a lot. You want to hear this?"

"Yes, sir. I need to know everything."

"Alright, then." Billups swished his tongue over his teeth, deciding to speak.

"Two days ago the 357th and the 358th moved into battle. For every one of those kids it was the first time they'd been under enemy fire. I assume you remember what that was like."

The fear whisked through Ben's gut before Billups could finish the sentence. He recalled shock, at the rustle of bullets like whispering women, the blasts of artillery, and the agony of seeing wounded and dead, the finality—the reality—of death and dismemberment as common as trash on the ground.

"You know as well as I do," Billups continued, "you can't drive green soldiers into that." He pointed again to the west. "They got to be led. You got to have commanders who can coax them in. If you don't . . . well, they just get killed."

The trucks of bodies flowing out of Ste. Mère-Église.

"Where's the 90th right now, General?"

"Right now, we've got all three regiments in a line, the 357th, 358th, and 359th, from Amfreville down to Pont l'Abbé."

Billups jabbed the air, locating each of his regiments beyond the green mask of the fields and hedges. For Ben this underscored how close the fighting was to where he stood, and with each stab of the General's finger, he heard muted shooting. He wanted to walk away from this assistant division CO. In a mile he could be there, with the guns and the men.

"Since June 10th, the 90th has grabbed about a mile of these hedgerows. That's it. And already, out of fifty-five hundred infantry, we've taken fifteen percent casualties. In two and a half days of fighting. And he just sits there."

Ben followed Billups's accusing arm. Another man, older, lanky, sat in a chair he'd rocked back on its hind legs, smoking a pipe. Ben hadn't noticed him out front of the barn. He'd walked past the 90th's commanding General.

"Sulking," Billups spat.

"You want me to talk to him?"

Billups ignored the suggestion. He spoke with eyes fixed on his superior officer.

"Problem is, he's not infantry. He was the division's artillery chief. He got the CO job in January, right when we left the States. Our old CO got bumped up to corps."

Billups lowered his arm. He shuffled in the grass.

"I don't reckon it's his fault. Aw, hell, maybe it is. Yesterday, I found him hiding in a ditch next to the road. There'd been some shelling and he and his adjutant got caught out in it. I walked up and nearly kicked the sumbitch. I told him to get the hell out of that ditch. You can't lead a division lying in a damn hole. Get back to the CP, for Christ's sake, and walk, man, don't run, or you'll have the whole division wading in the Channel. That's what I told him. The man doesn't have a Chinaman's chance of knowing how to lead soldiers into combat. He knows logarithms, and that's it."

"Do you want me to talk to him?"

"Huh? No. No. I got the word, he's being replaced. And none too damn soon."

Ben turned from the commanding officer, so quietly frightened in his chair. War does this, he thought. It doesn't break just the green recruit, the clean-cheeked boys. Death visiting the lone soldier swings one scythe, but for field commanders, the numbers are a harvest. War is not for every man.

"What do you want me to do, General?"

Billups screwed his helmet back on his head. He pounded on top to mash it down.

"A few things. First, pray the new CO can lead this bunch, because if he can't, the 90th might be done for. There's already talk of breaking the division up for replacements. They're calling us a 'problem' division. We're not going to have that, you and me. Second, you get out in the field and show my boys what a man is. I figure you can do that, Chaplain Kahn."

The pang of Ben's doubt was fleet but sharp. Did he know anymore what kind of man he was? Regardless, he and Billups shared the same intention.

"Yes, sir."

"And what can I do for you, Rabbi?"

Ben was the one pointing now, at the crackles of fighting. An air raid had started over a town to the south.

"I want to go there, sir."

White Dog stalked the cobblestones.

The ten o'clock curfew loomed less than an hour away. This did not concern him. He knew Montparnasse better than any Gestapo or Kraut policeman. He'd hidden in these alleys and doorways for a year and a half now. When he needed to disappear, White Dog could become a shadow unstaked from the ground. Paris was a city made for a thief.

He let his heels click on the cobbles, echoing in the narrow way, off-gray walls and dirty windows. He passed a woman hauling a small wagon stacked with sticks for her cooking, an old man who needed a shave and a meal, and no one else.

The street ran long, curling past shuttered shops. He found the turn, a grim tributary off the wider, untrafficked road. The address he'd been given was in the middle of the block. He let loose a curse and a sigh of disgust at the chore.

"One thing's for sure," he muttered in English, "this is the last time."

Before knocking, he glanced over his shoulder, at the dark way he had come. Paris under the Germans was not the City of Light. The sickly hues of kerosene glowed in only a handful of windows. The rest made do with the flickers of wax or nothing at all. There was no electricity. White Dog saw none of the ones who'd followed him.

He rapped on the door.

In a window, a heavy curtain shifted. Lantern light framed a slice of a big head and a thick hand wearing two rings. The curtain fell back in place.

Behind the closed door, a man's gruff voice demanded, "Yes? Who's there?"

White Dog leaned close to the wood panels. He lowered his voice. *"Chien Blanc."*

A pause followed. Behind the door a woman's voice hissed, the wife. A chain was pulled off, the door opened inches. The same wedge of the big head—one eye and a grizzled cheek—slipped into the gap.

"Tell *Monsieur Acier* I will speak with him tomorrow."

White Dog slid his fingers into the rift between door and jamb. The big man could slam the door and mangle his hand. He would not dare.

"Monsieur Acier will not see you tomorrow. You will see me now."

White Dog pushed on the door. It gave way. The large head retreated, the door widened to show shoulders and midriff, broad and smelly in an undershirt. The French, White Dog thought, they never bathe.

With one hand closing the door behind him, White Dog whipped a Luger pistol from his belt. The door clicked as he advanced on the big man in his own small hallway.

White Dog held the pistol head-high. The man backpedaled clumsily, spilling an unlit lamp off a table, jarring a mirror. His shoulders struck a wall beside the stairs where his wife stood. White Dog glanced up to her. She, too, wore undergarments in the Paris summer. Both her hands muffled her mouth.

White Dog lifted the gun to tip the barrel into the man's eye.

"Chien Blanc, Chien Blanc," the man uttered, recoiling into the wall. Through her fingers his wife whispered, "No, no, no."

"Shut up," White Dog told them, "both of you. Shut up."

The man and woman in their stained underclothes froze. White Dog listened to the wife, she did not breathe. Her husband panted and gaped out of the one eye.

"Alain?"

The man nodded.

"You know me?"

"I know about you, *Chien Blanc.* Yes."

"Then why didn't you let me in when you heard who I was?"

The large man shuddered. He didn't know the answer, didn't know why he was being asked this with a gun to his head.

"I'm sorry, *Chien Blanc*. What can I say?"

White Dog leaned closer to the man. He tilted the gun higher, as if to pour a bullet into the man's socket.

"Tell me who I am."

The wife gasped through her hands. To this odorous French couple, it might have appeared like White Dog was rabid, not making sense. But the question seemed simple enough.

"Who am I, Alain?"

"You . . . you are *Chien Blanc*."

"And who is *Chien Blanc*, Alain?"

"Number two in . . . in the *Acier* gang."

The wife whimpered, terrified her husband had given the wrong answer. White Dog pressed his own belly into the man's undershirt, laying on him like a scorpion. He raised the gun to shoot straight down into the eye.

"Exactly. Number two."

White Dog eased off. The sweaty oil of Alain's undershirt clung to his own black coat and silk tunic. White Dog would have them laundered when this night was done.

"I see that the number two does not get an invitation into your home."

He put away the Luger under the hem of his coat. Alain remained jammed against the wall, unsure if White Dog's distemper had passed.

White Dog lifted one hand to the wife on the stairs.

"Come, *cher*. I want to talk with you, too."

White Dog made room for the wife to descend. She clung to her husband. White Dog followed them into the parlor.

A lantern yellowed the room, the wick turned low. Doilies splashed every table, spread under cheap glassware, pastel collectibles. White Dog pointed at a sofa of worn ruby fabric. The man and woman sat close. White Dog studied the sepia photos of relatives before he asked:

"Alain?"

"Yes."

"What is your wife's name? I forgot." White Dog planted himself on a tasseled hassock.

"Marie."

"Good. Marie? Alain?"

The couple looked at each other, frightened by the change in White Dog's tone. She gripped her husband's heavy arm.

"I understand you are both Communists."

Neither on the sofa moved or spoke.

"I don't care one way or another. It's just that I don't have to shoot either of you to get what I want. All I have to do is put a whisper in the wrong ear. If you get me."

"We get you," Alain said.

"Good." White Dog set his elbows on his knees and steepled his fingers. "Now, you and *Monsieur Acier*. You have made an arrangement, yes?"

Both heads bobbed. Under the shortages, the woman's figure had gone gaunt, this was visible in her slip and brassiere. The man's waist and bullfrog neck had not suffered, though. And both rings on his mitt were gold.

"The arrangement was pretty clear, I believe. You steal. We buy from you. We sell to others. Is this right?"

The man raised a palm. "*Chien Blanc,* wait. I didn't—"

White Dog countered with his own raised palm.

"Yes, you did, Alain. And Marie, you, too."

The man dropped his protesting hand. He looked to his wife with surprise, that she, too, had tried to swindle the biggest black market gang in Montparnasse.

"Marie?" Alain asked.

She lowered her eyes. "For the cause, Alain."

"Marie." White Dog insisted both keep their eyes and attention on him.

She shifted her gaze to him.

In English, he said, "The fuck do I care."

"*Qu'avez-vous dit?*"

"I said I don't care. We pay you to go out to the country and smuggle vegetables into the city through the train station. We don't expect to see you selling them yourself. We call that competition. We don't like competition."

"No," she said, scolded, though she was at least twenty years older than White Dog.

"Alain. Where are the cigarettes?"

"I have only a few. For myself, for my own smoking."

"Where are they?"

"In the kitchen, *Chien Blanc*."

White Dog stood. The big man rose from the tatty sofa. Marie stayed put. White Dog drew his Luger and laid it to the man's nape, in case he had more than cigarettes in the cupboard. White Dog hated this errand, putting the squeeze on two small-time scammers, for cigarettes and cabbage.

Alain opened a cabinet door. Inside, with very few cans of food and a mouse trap, was a knapsack.

"Alain," White Dog said, still behind the big man, "the next time you bring us a light load of anything—cigarettes, candy, socks, anything at all—this will not be what I give you."

White Dog swung the butt of the pistol into the man's temple. Alain crumpled, clawing the icebox on his way down. White Dog hit him again to drive him to the floor. This man worked in a warehouse for the Krauts. He was thick and strong, with sticky fingers, likely a bully to others; he had that ugliness. He ate well while his wife starved for the Red cause she thought was her husband's, too. He stole crates from the Krauts in the warehouse and the rail yards and sold them to the *Acier* gang, skimming what he thought he could get away with. He was part of his own little gang in Montparnasse, just a source, one of hundreds *Acier* had cultivated. Alain was a bastard and a cheat. White Dog had been dispatched to the man's home to show him a more dangerous bastard and cheat.

White Dog spoke to the cowering man on the floor. Blood dribbled between Alain's fingers.

"The next time I knock on your goddam door, Alain, open it."

White Dog lifted the knapsack out of the cupboard. Its weight told him what he knew already. Marie stood in the kitchen doorway, her hands again masking her mouth.

White Dog shouldered the pack, tucking the pistol into his belt. He brushed the woman aside.

Closing the front door behind him with a soft touch—a quiet counterpoint to the sobbing couple on the other side—White Dog looked left and right. The narrow street was empty. He set out over the cobbles, waiting, tensed. Eyes locked ahead, he walked half the murky block. He made sure his pistol was well jammed in his belt, then slid the knapsack off his shoulder, into his hand.

A whistle blew, high-pitched and two-toned, a police whistle. The stones of the street clacked with running boots. White Dog leaped to the sidewalk and ran, tracing the blackened shops and curtained homes. He ran on his toes to mute his footfalls.

The police whistles blared for a time, swirling echoes on all sides. The running boots spread into the alleys. German shouts barked in quick staccato. The language was perfect for pursuit; it was fearsome to hear such a bitten, snarling tongue in the twisting warren of Montparnasse's streets. White Dog ran in the alleys through a night that seemed to grow blacker; Parisians did not look outside when the Gestapo pounced, they shut their curtains and retreated into obscurity, trusting it as their only protection.

The curfew was not in effect yet. Others were on the streets with White Dog. He heard the Gestapo grab someone behind him, then let him go. White Dog dodged in and out of the jumbles of fire escapes, trash bins, inky stoops, and cars that had not moved from the curb in years. When he slowed, he was far from Alain's front door and breathing hard. He ducked through a wooden gate between two row houses and sideslipped down the narrow crevice. He stopped before emerging into another dark side street, then set the heavy sack of cigarettes down. Alain had grifted maybe a dozen cartons. At street value, one hundred fifty francs a pack, which was about fourteen thousand francs for a guy who probably made twelve hundred francs a week humping for the Krauts and another thousand stealing for *Acier*.

White Dog sucked his teeth at the profits. Paris, he thought. What's not for sale? Pretty soon, when the GIs get here and the Krauts are replaced by America, it's only going to get better.

He pulled a wad of francs from his pocket, three thousand in cash, and stuffed it into the sack.

He waited minutes, pressed between the walls of the alley. He disturbed nothing of the night, with shallow breaths and not a creak of his shoes.

White Dog heard what he waited for. More Gestapo whistles blared, like little trains in the tunnels of the alleys of Montparnasse. Boots and guns clattered, hobnails and metal rattles hustled, more whistles blurted. The sounds all herded to a spot two blocks away, right where they were supposed to be. Shouts rose. Even the hard sounds of rifle bolts raced over the cobbles to White Dog's hiding place. He poked his head out of the alley. A few windows in the upper stories awoke in tilted curtains and slivers of curious light, then blinked out.

No shots were fired, a disappointment for White Dog. It would have been easier, for everyone, if there had been shooting.

The tumult up the dark street subsided slowly. The Gestapo always liked to make a show, a statement that they remained a force in the occupied city. White Dog faded into the black embrace of the alley. One set of boots came his way. He crouched and took his pistol in hand.

A figure halted at the head of the alley.

"Is this the way you wanted it to go?"

The question came in English.

White Dog rose and hid the Luger. He tossed the sack of cigarettes through the darkness at the feet of the man who'd spoken.

"Yes. Here's a present for you."

"Another present tonight? *Vielen Dank.*"

The man knelt to lift the knapsack. He asked, "Did we give you good chase?"

"Good enough."

"I think it was believable, *ja?*"

"Sure."

White Dog heard the rustle of the backpack hoisted to the man's shoulder.

"We have him. He was exactly where you said."

"Good."

"*Gut.* Then our business is concluded. We will not speak again."

"Hey."

"*Ja?*"

"The Americans are gonna kick your ass."

"*Ja.* We know. But I think this is a problem for you when they get here."

"Not me. I got big plans."

The dark figure chuckled, an admiring smirk daggered in the laughter, and walked off.

D+9

JUNE 15

Joe Amos stared into the bottom of his truck. Enough starlight glanced off the ocean and sand to see the Jimmy's makings, the transmission linkage, brake cables, springs. He touched the long exhaust pipe: still warm. The Jimmy had run twenty of the last twenty-four hours.

Beside him in the sand, Boogie John snored and pitched to his shoulder. They and the rest of the hundreds of drivers awaiting cargo on OMAHA slept beneath their trucks. This was safer than lying in the open and risking being hit by falling American rounds after one of Bed-check Charlie's low, spoiling runs. Joe Amos did not sleep at all this morning. He could not rid the tremble of the wheel from his hands. Even behind closed eyes, the landscape of Normandy rolled and rolled. For three days now, he'd driven or rode while the sands became brush and the brush became trees, the trees mounted on hedges around fields that rose to the south in a green tide. He and Boogie found their combat depots, drank coffee while fast hands off-loaded their cargos, then ran back to OMAHA for a fresh load, and the land changed back, from bocage to beach. That was all Joe Amos did, all day, until he was given a few hours to lie beneath his truck, hours this morning he could not spend emptied enough to rest.

The sounds across the beach were incessant, mechanical, despite the early hour. Landing craft ferried supplies from the ships offshore, deep grindings bounced over the water from the assembly of the titanic Mulberry harbor. Closer to his truck on the beach, the noises turned human. Soldiers grunted unloading rhino ferries and amphibious DUKWs, the waiting wounded moaned. Some of the chatter was laughter, more was curses. Joe Amos lay motionless, and this was not what he wanted.

He scooted from beneath the truck. Boogie didn't wake. Joe Amos took a seat on the Jimmy's tailgate, dangling his boots. He struck up a cigarette. All the activity on the beach worked in a narrow sliver close to the bluffs, away from the ebbing water. Joe Amos imagined himself in the assault that had swept over these dunes. He saw himself rush them, take them, do some hard killing, join men doing the same, and share with them those frightening, vulgar, grandest moments in war. High behind the dunes, the morning flashed an orange dome, then another, then the grumble of artillery.

Joe Amos blew plumes of smoke. He watched the sparking sky and thought about what he knew, what he'd learned in his three college years at Virginia Union. Black men had fought for America. Black men were heroes. They were in books and newspapers. Crispus Attucks, the first man killed in the Revolution, a former slave who in a crowd outside a Boston customs house swung a cordwood stick at a redcoat. Attucks knocked the soldier's gun away and shouted, "Kill the dogs, knock them over!" and was plugged with a musket ball, a shot heard around the world. In the Civil War, 200,000 blacks fought for the north, 38,000 of them died. In the Wild West, the 10th Cavalry, the Buffalo Soldiers, galloped the plains, Indian fighters to beat the band. In World War I, regiments of black soldiers fought, the 369th even won a *Croix de Guerre*. And everyone had heard about the Tuskegee Airmen, the 99th Pursuit Squadron. They'd shot down German planes over North Africa and Italy, and hadn't yet lost one bomber they escorted.

Joe Amos tossed his cigarette. It landed in the sand and snuffed. The sky shook again, a passel of trucks somewhere close revved. A quartermaster soldier jogged up, bone-colored like the sand, with a clipboard in his hand. He saw Joe Amos seated on the tail of the Jimmy. He stopped long enough to motion beneath the truck.

"Wake that other boy up, y'all got drivin' to do. Let's go, Sambo!"

The man loped away. He did not stay to see Joe Amos's raised middle finger.

Joe Amos shook his head and spit into the sand. A hundred yards away, little waves stepped ashore, inevitable and tireless as history. He kept his seat on the tailgate, a defiance, but he knew it was small.

Silly, Joe Amos thought. Silly as hell to try and ignore it, even for a moment.

After the Civil War, all the Negro troops were disarmed, including the blacks in the Yankee states; reunited America didn't want thousands of Negroes carrying guns. The Buffalo Soldiers got their nickname because their nappy hair reminded the Indians of the nape of a buffalo. In World War I, colored soldiers had to fight under the French, the United States didn't want them as combatants. No matter how successful they are, the Tuskegee Airmen get called "the Spook-waffe." Only Crispus Attucks has been left a hero, and he was a mulatto.

Boogie stirred and woke.

Dawn dribbled gray over the hedgerows and hills. Boogie spoke to his rearview mirror.

"Come on, boys. You wanna keep up."

Joe Amos moved his head to see in his passenger-side mirror. He faintly made out the single blackout slit light of the truck next in line. The light struggled a hundred yards back, a low star. Then like a star it blinked out, disappearing behind a bend. Joe Amos felt the Jimmy heave to one side, then balance. Boogie John gunned the motor.

"I never told you I was gonna be a shitty driver. This stuff's got to get to the front and that's where it's going. Who's behind us?"

"Grove, I think."

"Old lady," said Boogie John.

"Maybe you want to slow down."

"Naw. I'm good and damn tired of driving like molasses. I got an open road and a heavy load and I'm gone. Grandma Grove and the rest can keep up."

The road ran narrow and winding, cloistered by hedges left and right. Overhead, branches wove to form a cathedral. The trunks and shrubs went zinging by, ghosts of abandoned tanks scabbed darkly in some fields, but there was no time to imagine the fights that had left them behind, Boogie drove so fast. Straight off the beach big Boog impelled the deuce-and-a-half like a scalded dog, bolting far out front. There was no jeep in the lead on this run; the convoy was small, only ten vehicles loaded with clothes and rations. Boogie got to drive the lead truck this morning. This was their first time at number one, and Boogie was making it memorable. The manifest had them hauling due south, their target was a town named Ste. Marguerite d'Elle, where the 29th Division's 115th Infantry had set up a depot on their way to take on the massive Kraut garrison around St. Lô. Joe Amos held a map in his lap under a flashlight. He was afraid that at this pace Boogie would drive them right past Ste. Marguerite d'Elle and into a German mess tent.

Boogie slowed. Joe Amos looked up from his map. They'd entered the outskirts of one more Norman village, ramshackle and busted by American guns. The name was another tongue twister: Cartigny-l'Épinay. Joe Amos checked it off on his map. Ste. Marguerite was next, about a mile and a half. Cartigny stood like fifty other burgs Joe Amos had seen in five days of bouncing around the tight American beachhead. Even without the destruction, Joe Amos could tell the town was dull, as country and simple in its way as anything in rural Virginia. He had come to Europe thinking of the French as elegant, somehow his betters. That was just how they always got played back home, with talk about Joan of Arc, Paris, wines, Napoleon, and perfume. But not anymore, he thought, not after seeing how the French lived, just like anyone else, on farms, with cattle, orchards, barns, and fences. Behind the villages, dirt paths led to the same kind of bare fields Joe Amos had run mules over beside the Dan River. Apparently the GIs fighting the Krauts through these dumpy towns felt the same way. They didn't give two shits in a handcart for the old buildings, stone fences, or for perfume or fancy snails. There wasn't one Frenchman anywhere better than an American soldier. The holes in the buildings and the bricks blown into the streets of Cartigny showed that to be the truth.

Boogie displayed his own lack of interest in France with the speed he poured on. The Jimmy exited the town, then crossed a tiny bridge on the south side. Boogie hit the brakes.

A six-by-six cab-over-engine cargo truck blocked the road. The twin cat's eyes in the rear—the red ones that looked like a sleepy driver's half-drawn and veined eyeballs—were blank. The truck was dead in the road.

"The hell," Boogie muttered. "Get out, College, and see what's up."

Joe Amos clambered down from the cab. He walked around to the silent grille of the COE. A pair of white drivers stood smoking, their cigarette gleams the only lights.

"Fellas."

"Alternator's shot," said one. "Battery's out." He took a seat on the bumper, crossing his boots.

"Okay," said Joe Amos.

"Go around," said the other driver.

"Where's the rest of your convoy?"

"Went on ahead. They're sending back a tow truck."

"Go around," repeated the standing driver.

Boogie tapped his horn. Grove and the other Jimmies arrived. The idles mounted, growling in line.

"The road's a little narrow through here, fellas. Maybe we can give you a push off to the side."

The seated one said, "No. I ain't putting this rig on the shoulder. No way to tell if there's mines around here."

The standing driver dropped his cigarette. Grinding it underfoot, the white man blew smoke. "I said go around. Now go around."

"Okay," Joe Amos told him.

Joe Amos walked away, back to the rig where Boogie waited. Grove stood pudgy below Boogie's elbow in the cab window. Boogie stared at the tail of the dead truck.

"What's up?" Grove asked.

"Man says their battery's out. Tow truck's coming."

"They can't sit in the damn road like that." Grove pointed south. "Soon as traffic starts comin' the other way, this road'll snarl up for miles. Then everybody's fucked."

To illustrate Grove's point, the grumble and dimmed lights of an approaching convoy sifted out of the south.

"You tell 'em we can push 'em to the side?"

"Yep. Man says he's scared of mines."

Boogie's door opened. Joe Amos had to dodge out of the way. Boogie leaped down, a big and nimble dark shape.

"Get in," he said, passing Joe Amos.

Boogie strode to the driver's door of the stilled COE. Joe Amos scrambled behind the Jimmy's wheel. He edged into first gear and crept ahead.

Boogie was in the cab of the truck before the two smoking drivers could move. Joe Amos heard the brake cable release, the gearshift clank, and knew Boogie had her in neutral. Joe Amos gassed forward, lightly kissed bumpers, and pushed the dead truck steered by Boogie John off the road. No mines detonated.

As soon as the truck was gone from the road, Joe Amos jerked up his parking brake and leaped out of the cab. Boogie was already on his feet and in a fight.

Ben Kahn thanked the ambulance driver. He stepped away into the ditch. The van U-turned in the tight confines between the hedges. Ben patted the fender when the ambulance pulled past.

He looked west along the skinny road, down the green tunnel that canopied the track. A few hundred yards off, soldiers trudged in a dust-kicking column, headed north. Ben jogged to catch them. Noon light spangled the lane rutted by tank and jeep tracks. He looked to see signs of battle through here, but the hedges rose too high and the fields were hidden.

Running toward the 358th Infantry, Ben felt light. This was where he belonged, with the infantry, where God insisted all their dealings be settled. Ben came now empty, armed only with penitence. The running was easy and this fit Ben's belief, that when you go the direction God intends, even the hardest of ways is smoothed.

He approached the column and slowed, to catch his breath and marvel at the sight of several thousand American soldiers in a line, marching four abreast. Since his arrival five days ago, he had been kept in the rear areas, aiding the wounded, visiting artillery batteries, praying with staff officers at headquarters. This morning, General Billups had released him to the field. The General was in no better humor now that the 90th had a new CO. The Tough Ombres were still behind schedule for every objective, and losses stayed high. The new CO was cleaning house, but Billups worried he was not going deep enough into the ranks, to replace hesitant and poor officers all the way down to the battalion level. Ben asked many times, until Billups sent him forward with, "Alright, get the hell out there, Padre." Ben climbed into the first vehicle headed to the front lines.

He moved alongside a sergeant walking in the center of his squad. Up close, he saw how dirty the men were. No chin was shaved, every fingernail was a grimy crescent. Their boots scuffed the dirt road and their weapons were carried like freight across their backs. Five days of fighting had dog-eared their bodies.

"Sarge," Ben said.

"Chaplain. You new?"

"Yep."

A voice from the squad, a burly soldier lugging a Browning automatic rifle, cracked, "You don't look so new."

Ben grinned. "I been around."

"Around what?" A few men chuckled. Ben spotted the soldier who'd made the jibe and shook a fist at him in play. One of the men said, "Oh, oh, look out."

"Where you boys from?"

Cities and towns cropped up: Des Moines, St. Louis, Ponca City, Lubbock, Shawnee. Ben pointed and each man called out his home, most of them from the middle of America. One soldier cried, "Youngstown, Ohio," and Ben answered, "Go, you Brownies." Another said, "Cleveland bites the big one." The sergeant let the squabble build, then told his squad to pipe down. Ben had stirred the pot. He felt fine about this. These boys aren't beat, he thought. They're tired and far from finished, and, sure, they're scared from what they've seen and done. They know that nothing will protect them from the bullet that's got a name on it. They've fought hard in their first five days and they've run away, too, according to Billups, who'd carped hourly. But no one ever said the Tough Ombres were cowards. These boys, this fifteen out of the four thousand tramping down the road, would prove themselves good fighters. They would take their bullets when they had to. And though he carried no rifle or mortar, no heavy pack, his own task—to see that these new sons went through with it—weighed across his shoulders.

It took him a half hour to work his way to the front of the regiment. He hustled beside the column as if beside a green river, waving to men who greeted him as he passed. A few spotted the Ten Commandments pin at his collar and hollered, "*Shalom*, Rabbi!" To these he shouted back, "*Shalom! Vee Geyts?*"

The Army had given each infantryman a weapon, a shelter half, blanket, mess kit, gas mask, folding shovel, raincoat, hand grenades, and bandoleers of extra ammo. Their uniforms were chemically treated to make them resistant to gas attacks, and looked to breathe no better than a burlap sack. The men slogged in the heat, and one by one, they cast off extra weight, keeping what was essential. From the GI litter, Ben judged the men put the most faith in their rifles, ammunition, trenching tools, and spoons.

Finally at the front of the column, Ben located the regimental com-

mander, Colonel Paar. The man shook hands with a firm grip and narrowed eyes. "Good to have you, Chaplain."

Up here in front, the momentum was heady from the treading thousands behind. There were less dust and smell than in the ranks. Colonel
Paar squeezed Ben's shoulder, putting on his leadership show. He
yanked a thumb behind him.

"Chaplain Allenby will fill you in. Welcome aboard."

Behind Ben, a smallish man broke ranks, pressing forward. His helmet rode low over his ears. On his collar was the cross pin of a Christian
chaplain. He lacked the Red Cross armband, and his helmet, which
should also have been marked with the cross, was obscured by dirty
tape. His uniform was not a bit cleaner than any soldier in the regiment.

"Phineas Allenby." Chaplain Allenby was not out of his twenties.
His cheeks glowed. He drew Ben away from the column to walk beside
it. "Baptist." The young man's voice was high-pitched and honeyed by
twang.

"Ben Kahn." Ben's name sounded threadbare next to Phineas
Allenby's.

"Welcome, Rabbi."

"Reverend. That's quite a name. Phineas."

"It's Egyptian." Chaplain Allenby shrugged. "It means 'serpent's
mouth' in the old Hebrew. You probably knew that."

"No. That's a new one on me."

"Phineas was the grandson of Aaron who killed an Israelite because
he married a Midianite. I've never been able to figure out if this was a
good thing or not." Allenby shrugged again. "Anyway, it's Phineas.
Kahn. Does that come from the Israelite priests—the Kohain?"

"Yep."

"A descendant of Aaron."

"That's right, Chaplain."

"So if it turns out my folks're wrong and y'all are right, I reckon
what? You'll be carried on the shoulders of the nearest Levites to the
temple, where you'll dispense wisdom and mercy. Have I got it right?"

"On the nose."

"So between us we got it covered."

"Yep."

"That's a relief. What class were you in?"

Ben smiled at the careering topics and protocols of this chatty little chaplain. They walked in a war zone less than a mile from an immense enemy, and Phineas Allenby wanted to talk names, Judgment Day, and the U.S. Army Chaplain School at Harvard.

"November '43."

Allenby brightened. "I was just in front of you, September '43."

"They didn't make the rabbis do the September class."

"That's right," said Chaplain Allenby, recollecting, glad to be back at cool, green Harvard, away from this hot and foreign road for a few seconds. "Rosh Hashanah." He was proud to display his knowledge.

"And Yom Kippur."

"Yes. Yes." Chaplain Allenby was disappointed not to have recalled this autumn High Holy Day, too.

"Where are the other 90th chaplains?"

Allenby shifted his stride to guide Ben farther from the column on their left. He wanted to speak without the men overhearing.

"The division has thirteen chaplains. Got all kinds. Latter-day Saints, Catholics, and pretty much all your major Protestants. Most of 'em stay at HQ with the aid station, ministering to the wounded and such."

"And you?"

Chaplain Allenby glanced over his shoulder at the long phalanx of soldiers, still molting away bits of hardware onto the road. "I reckon I'm fine here."

"Mind if I join you for a while?"

"Great. Is Ben okay?"

"And you're, of course, Phineas."

The chaplains shook hands afresh.

"Little Rock, Arkansas," Phineas said.

"Pittsburgh."

Ben told Phineas he'd been instructed by General Billups to float between the three regiments, the 357th, 358th, and 359th, to reach all the division's Jewish soldiers. He intended to stay with these infantry units and not go back to headquarters.

"I know a lot of the Jewish boys," Phineas said. "They'll be glad to see you. I can't ever pronounce the *Shema* right. I don't think people should laugh during a prayer."

Ben and the little chaplain smiled. In that moment it was a sunny day in France, a stroll with a colleague on a backwoods lane. In the next, the war asserted itself beyond the hedges. Artillery thundered and small arms spurted under the boot-march of the column. Every man cringed and looked up; some soldiers unstrapped their rifles into their hands. Phineas Allenby jerked his eyes to the ground, searching for somewhere to dive. Ben held himself in check, walking erect. He'd grown accustomed long ago to reading the telltales of incoming and outgoing artillery. These boys will pick it up, he figured. The shelling and gunfire droned, clearly aimed elsewhere. The thousands on the road firmed more slowly than they'd come undone. The column plodded on. Phineas grimaced, sheepish.

"We're a little jittery, I suppose."

"It goes away."

Remaining outside the column, the two walked side by side for a time without speaking. Phineas's face was flushed. Ben watched him walk, eyes turned down. Thousands of marching boots thumped on their left. Phineas Allenby appeared to want to recede back into the column. He had come unnerved in front of Ben and he seemed to need to deal with the sting of that.

"Tell me about Colonel Paar."

Phineas slowly raised his head.

"He just got the job this morning. The other CO was killed yesterday at Pont l'Abbé, and the assistant CO got wounded. Paar came over from 9th Division. There's been a big shakeup all across the 90th. New CO at the top, new commanders in almost every regiment and battalion. Them that didn't get hit pretty much got replaced. So we don't know much about Paar yet. Or much of anybody, except the men."

"What do we know about them?"

Phineas lifted his face full to Ben. He shoved the sinking rim of his helmet off his brow.

"Ben, you don't mind me asking—"

"Go ahead."

"You're a vet, aren't you?"

"Yes."

Phineas nodded and looked straight up the road where the column headed, into the dirt and green unknown for all of them.

"I figured that, the way you handled yourself back there a few minutes ago when those shells went off. So since you're an old Army man, I can tell you straight. Without the . . ." Phineas leaned closer. He whispered, which was charming and naive. ". . . bullshit."

"Please."

"I don't know if you know. It's been a rough start."

Ben made no mention of Billups. He wanted to hear from this pint-sized frontline chaplain what had been happening with these troops.

Phineas put his hands in his pockets. He glanced over at Colonel Paar and the staff treading around the regiment's CO, appearing to measure the distance so he would not be overheard.

"The 358th jumped off the morning of the 10th. We crossed the Merderet River causeway at Chef-du-Pont before dawn. That went okay—there was some resistance, but we made it over. We got to Picauville pretty good and pushed on to Pont l'Abbé. Right outside that town is where the first German artillery hit us. I've never . . . Lord forgive me, Ben, I have never been through anything like that in my life. The .88s. They're like some kind of nightmare, you know, but not inside your head. Right there blowing up in your face. I . . . we, all of us, we hit the ground and we stayed there."

Phineas spoke apologetically. Ben knew about trying to cram your whole body into your helmet when the explosions start. He understood that every man comes up sorry for what he learns about himself from his first artillery barrage.

Phineas pressed on.

"Afternoon of the 11th, we went after Pont l'Abbé. We made good progress behind our own artillery, but we got stopped by machine-gun fire outside the town. That night, we still hadn't taken it. Next day, we went after it again. That's when the CO went down. The whole attack fell apart."

Phineas dropped his gaze again. He seemed to search the road for something, glancing side to side, until Ben realized the little chaplain was slowly shaking his head.

"The casualties. Two days of fighting. There must've been a couple hundred. It was . . ."

Phineas lifted his head. He stared back at the soldiers tramping along, jangling. Ben looked back, too.

"They're good men," Phineas told him. "They need good leaders, is all."

"They need you, too, Phineas. You're a good man. And you're in the right place."

Phineas's cheeks pinked and he smiled.

"Thank you, Rabbi. I really hope that's so." He gathered himself to continue the story, to bring Ben and the 358th up to today.

"On the 12th, our 1st Battalion tried to get into Pont l'Abbé and got stopped again. So the brass gave up and called in an air raid and artillery both. That evening we walked in, kind of embarrassed, you know, about needing to blow the town to smithereens like that. All we saw alive was two rabbits, and they were none too spry. And the way I hear it, the 357th and 359th haven't done much better. Everybody's behind schedule, and everybody's getting beat up."

The next day, on the 13th, Ben recalled, the 90th got a new CO. The message was sent through the entire division: *You failed.*

"So now with Pont l'Abbé secured, or what's left of it," Phineas said, "the brass told us to double-time it eight miles north, to take up position on the 357th's right flank. We're heading west, all three regiments side by side. We're going to choke the Cotentin peninsula like a chicken neck. Then the rest can get to Cherbourg. I reckon we're heading into the hedgerows."

"A fresh start for the Tough Ombres," Ben said. "Might raise some spirits."

"Raise some hell is what we need to do."

Ben surveyed the little Baptist chaplain, and cataloged him as a gamecock. He tapped the covered Red Cross emblem on Phineas's helmet.

"What's with this?"

The preacher snickered at some private memory, either a brave moment or another revelation of the poor clay men are made of. "Kraut snipers. They seem pretty PO-ed that God's on our side. So I've kind of changed my own tactics."

"Yes?"

Phineas lifted the hem of his jacket. Tucked in his belt was a Colt .45 pistol.

He asked, "You carrying a gun? Look, I know we're non-combatants and all, but there's nothing in the Geneva Convention that absolutely says we can't."

Ben raised a palm, rejecting the weapon. Phineas covered the gun with his coat. He hoisted a finger.

"You think about your Old Testament, alright? Your Moses held his staff up on a mountaintop while the Jews conquered the Amalekites. Shucks, one time he even held his hands up for so long, he needed help to keep them up. Ben, I'll tell you, there's nothing says we can't carry a gun for our own protection. Not in the Bible or the regulations. Sniper wants to shoot at me, that varmint best hope I don't see him first."

Ben could have snatched the Colt from Allenby's web belt and clicked off every round into a man at forty meters. With a rifle he could hit a head at three hundred, a torso at five hundred. He knew this ability lurked in his hands and eyes. He could not flush it out of his body, but he could barricade his heart, his soul, and his fate.

Ben said, "I need to get through this war without a gun."

"Well, alright."

The young preacher's pace had quickened while showing off his pistol. Ben kept pace with him.

"I noticed you showed up without an assistant. You don't have one yet?"

"No."

"Well, he'll carry a gun for you. We'll find you a good Jew soldier."

Ben didn't react to the coarseness of this language, any more than he'd jumped at the artillery fusillade earlier. You need to know always when something is aimed at you. And this comment was not.

"Thanks, Phineas."

The two had walked a mile together. Out of sight, more small-arms fire sizzled, other units were engaged in the hedges.

"I got me a brother in the 82nd, out there somewhere."

"Airborne."

"Yeah. When we were kids he was always afraid of heights. So I was surprised when he went into the paratroopers. Last Christmas, we were both home in Little Rock and I asked him about his first jump. He said when he got to the door of the plane, the sergeant pointed down to the ground and yelled, Go! And my brother froze up, right there."

Ben asked, "What happened?"

"The sergeant told him he was either going to jump or he'd stick his boot twelve inches up my brother's bee-hind. So I asked him, 'Did you jump?' And my brother, he said, 'Well, a little at first.' "

Ben wanted to guffaw but would not beside the somber column of soldiers. Phineas loosed only a low chortle. Both men trudged on. Ben skirted a lump of blanket flung onto the road.

"Do you really have a brother in the 82nd?"

"Naw. Just joshin'. You got any kin in the war?"

Ben hesitated. He wasn't sure right now how God was working in his life. He couldn't tell if this Phineas Allenby was God's extended hand or if it was His foot to trip him. Moses had indeed held his fists high while the Hebrews battled and won. Moses had been given a burning bush. Moses was so fortunate, so certain.

Ben said, "A son," and left it at that.

The MP pulled the jeep to a brisk stop.

"Right in there, Private," the MP said. Joe Amos swung his legs out, then stood in a dust swirl behind the gunning jeep. He dabbed a fingertip on his tender left eye socket and cheek.

Another MP stood in the door, waving him over. The building was the remains of the city hall of Isigny, the inscription over the door read Hôtel de Ville. This is no hotel, Joe Amos thought. This is the town's jail.

In the doorway he gave the MP his name and battalion. The policeman checked a clipboard in his hand, then said, "Follow me."

Joe Amos expected to be led inside the building, a tough old structure of stone and mortar, pocked but still standing. He figured he was headed straight for the stockade. Instead, the policeman strode into the street, glancing to make sure Joe Amos followed.

The two moved down a block of buildings that bustled like some Main Street in America, except everything that moved was olive drab. The cramped conditions in the beachhead were stuffing the U.S. force into an area too small for it. Joe Amos was in trouble, but with so much Yank strength packed around him, he at least felt safe.

The MP dropped him off at the entrance to what had once been a bakery. Empty shelves were still dusted with flour, mingled with plaster from holes in the roof. Glass cases had been denuded of pastries, but the panes were miraculously unbroken. Joe Amos shouldered his way inside. Soldiers flowed past with folders and stapled bills, handing them off on the fly. He entered the stream and walked through the shop portion of the bakery to the rear, where the ovens and tables were. The room was big and full of white men, white as dough, all of them officers. Joe Amos recognized a few, the general staff of his 688th Truck Battalion. Only a handful in the room were black, all privates, like him. Joe Amos snagged the sleeve of a colored boy darting by.

"Hey. I need to see someone."

"Brother, what happened to your eye?"

"Little scrap."

"Oh, yeah. Then you got to see the man. Right over there."

This soldier turned Joe Amos by the arm and gave him a shove. In that direction was a major in a tie. He was seated at a table that had standing beside it a cooling pie rack festooned with files. The Negro soldier sped off with his papers, looking to swap them for new ones.

Joe Amos advanced, unsure. He'd seen this officer before, Major Clay, the personnel officer with the 668th, but rarely. Down in the hustle where Joe Amos and the rest of the guys operated, in the cabs, on the roads, the staff officers didn't come around much. If you didn't wrangle a wheel or a wrench, you typically stayed out of their way and did whatever the Major and this hive of clean soldiers did. Joe Amos watched the Major swirl pages on his desk as if he were stirring dough. He looked up after Joe Amos had been near for almost a minute.

"You're the other one in the fight, aren't you?"

Joe Amos had not looked in a mirror, but his eye must be pretty swollen to keep getting this attention. One of those white drivers on the road had snuck in a punch and it had been a doozy. Joe Amos staggered, then waded right back in, on his toes, one-two, jab and roundhouse, the way his club-boxer uncle Carlos showed him, but sloppier because this was a real dustup. It was the first fistfight Joe Amos had ever been in, and he hadn't been scared; he marveled at it while slugging away. It pleased him to see his makings, his own fists defending his friend, the way a man ought. Boogie roared and rammed the white boys, and got himself pummeled until Joe Amos jumped down to join him. The fight got broken up by Grove and some others after just a few seconds, but there was enough time for some good swats. The convoy that came the other direction had a white officer in the lead jeep. Boogie and Joe Amos were carted back up the road in separate empty truck beds. The white drivers got told to stay with their truck and calm down. From the back of the Jimmy, Joe Amos watched while his own convoy continued past the dead truck pushed out of the way like it should have been. He was handed off to the first MPs the convoy passed—Boogie, too, and then Joe Amos lost sight of him. He had no idea where Boogie was, but he sure wasn't in this big bakery room. Boogie John would have stood out like a house afire against all this flour.

"Yes, sir. I'm sorry, sir. But they started it."

"Really?" The Major settled back in his chair, knitting his fingers over his belt. "That's not the way I heard it."

The Major's scalp showed under slicked-down hair—not the slick from sweat, but some pomade. The Major had a gap in his front teeth, and for all the world he looked to Joe Amos like a gas station attendant.

"It doesn't matter. Have a seat."

The throb in Joe Amos's cheek and eye told him squarely it did too matter, but he kept his peace. He took the chair the Major indicated.

"Private Joe."

"Joe Amos Biggs, sir."

"Alright. My name is Major Clay. Battalion G-1. We've seen each other around."

Joe Amos knew the accent. Tidewater. Virginia or Carolina. More than a cracker. Less than a loaf.

"Am I going to the stockade, sir?"

The Major smiled, and while he talked, Joe Amos watched the pink bit of gum snugged between the man's front teeth.

"No, I reckon not, Private Joe. But I'm afraid Private John is going to spend a few weeks behind bars."

"You mean Corporal Bailey, sir?"

"I mean Private John Bailey. He left one of his stripes on my desk about twenty minutes ago."

Again, Joe Amos bit his tongue, and did not mention that Boogie John Bailey would gladly have left his entire uniform on this Major's desk.

"Sir, what about the two white drivers? They started the fight. I just got in because they jumped on my partner."

"I know, Joe. That's why you're not in the hooskow with Private Bailey. I'll tell you, that one is as hardheaded as a Swede. As for them other two, they're not from my battalion and they're not my problem. And what are you doing getting in a fight with whites, anyway? We do everything we can to keep you fellas apart so this sort of thing won't happen. But I reckon some of it's inevitable."

The Major wriggled his fingers resting over his belly while he leaned back farther in his chair. Joe Amos dispelled the image that this was a gasoline alley redneck and elevated the Major to backwoods county judge.

"You may have noticed, son, that the 668th, along with every other transportation unit in France, is busting hump to move supplies off the beach and into the hands of the combat troops. Pretty soon we're going to bust out of this bridgehead and kick the Krauts' tails all the way to

Berlin, and the Army's going to need our trucks to do it. To be honest, with that in mind, we can't spare good drivers."

"John Bailey is a good driver, sir."

Major Clay sighed and sat forward in his chair. He laid his palms flat on the papers littering his desk. "You're a good boy, Joe. Everybody says so. You keep your dress neat, you handle your duties. Lieutenant Garner tells me you're not a troublemaker. Now, I don't want to make trouble for you, either, but I can't have you making trouble for me. Do we understand each other?"

Joe Amos could only say yes to this. The officer had nicely summed up relations in the U.S. Army between blacks and whites. The whites were relieved when blacks did not make trouble for them. This man, this gap-toothed Major, was why Boogie could give a damn and Joe Amos longed for a gun to go fight Germans. Neither of them wanted their worth measured by how easy they were to get along with.

Major Clay tapped a finger on his desk. "Where you from?"

"Danville."

"Family?"

"Mom, four sisters."

"They must be real proud. No Pop?"

"Passed on. The cancer."

"Too bad." The Major seemed genuine about this. There were three kinds of white folks in the Army, Joe Amos knew. The ones who hate you, the ones who let you be, and the ones in the middle like the Major, who think they know best.

"I hear you got some college, Joe."

"Three years at Virginia Union University."

"Yeah, I know it. Good Negro college. Founded right after the Civil War."

"Yes, sir."

"Why didn't you finish?"

"I enlisted."

Major Clay cocked his head. Joe Amos read the questions on the officer's face as clear as the sheen in the man's hair. Why would a young Negro quit college and join the Army? Why would he put on a uniform and put up with the shit the Army had to hand out, why be a truck driver, a porter, stevedore, an orderly, a cook, when instead he could be a college graduate and the cock of the walk in his own neighborhood?

And why in hell would he voluntarily come to Europe to defend freedoms he was not given at home?

"My country, right or wrong, sir."

Major Clay grinned. "I like that, Joe. What'd you study?"

"History."

"That's good. You know, I went to college. William and Mary. Right down the road from you, in Williamsburg. Oldest college in America."

"I thought that was Harvard, sir."

Major Clay hummed to himself.

"Okay. We're just about done. You're going to be getting a new partner in a few days. Private John will be reassigned in the battalion when he gets out. Don't worry about him, you move on. Now, I got one more thing to ask you. You feel like you're ready to be a leader? I know you jumped into that fight to stick up for one of your own, and I admire that. But we need role models in this battalion. Got to give the men good images to live up to. You up for that?"

"I reckon, sir."

"That means keeping your nose clean. Folks'll be watching."

"Yes, sir."

"I'm going to be looking for big things from you."

From his desk drawer Major Clay pulled a white cloth stripe. Threads hung from it. He tossed it on the papers in front of Joe Amos.

"Private John said I ought to give it to you. Dismissed, Corporal."

The march lasted another three hours. Twice, the dirt track led the long column of the 358th to the edge of swamps. The regiment had to snake through fields that as recently as yesterday had been in enemy hands. Now German corpses began to appear in the pastures and ditches. Ben watched men break ranks to run up to the bodies. No officer or non-com prevented them. They rifled through muddy pockets, checked under sleeves and inside tunics, but found little of value—no pistols, watches, pins, or patches. The dead Krauts had already been looted.

Colonel Paar led the regiment on a path less than a mile behind the rear of the 359th and the 357th. He intended to take up position on the right flank of the 357th north of Amfreville. Out of the west, beyond the hedges framing the road, gunfire bursts popped the air, but nothing sounded menacing enough to make the soldiers break stride. Ben supposed the other regiments were waiting for the 358th to get in line before making a concerted move tonight or tomorrow. He faded back into the column, telling Phineas Allenby he wanted to get to know the soldiers. This was true. Also Ben wanted to move away from the inquisitive young reverend. He'd liked Phineas right off, but was not going to open himself up like a clam just because Phineas pried at him. Ben chalked it up to Chaplain Allenby's youth and his Christian training to ferret out sin and guilt. Ben, a Jew, kept his transgressions closer to heart. He believed he wouldn't be shed of them just by asking forgiveness. The Old Testament required more—remembrance, sometimes struggle, or blood.

Down the line, Ben spread the word that, once the regiment stopped and had dug in, he would conduct a sundown service. Anyone was welcome to attend, but he encouraged every soldier to tell their Jewish buddies about it. Phineas Allenby sprinted past, dipping into the line and racing out like an excited collie, barking about the new rabbi and the first evening service coming up for the Jews in the regiment. Ben watched the young chaplain head down the long file, hopping and tireless.

Ben had no *tallit* to lay across his shoulders. That had gone down with the *Susan B. Anthony*. He had no velour cloth or small scroll to spread over the hood of a jeep, no menorah or candles to glitter and make this corner of a field a sanctuary at dusk. He left his prayer books and Old Testament in his backpack. He kept his helmet on his head so the two hundred men would, too. The Merderet River burbled behind him. Every man standing before him knew this creek flowed not far before it murmured past the enemy. The doughs were clustered in a group the size of a company, many of them were officers, and they were inside German mortar range. They should be spread out, it would be safer, but they had gathered to hear Chaplain Kahn. Solemnity was among them with the gnats, the danger, and the missing faces from the battles already fought.

Ben lifted both hands.

"*Shema Yisraeil, Adonai Elohenu, Adonai Echud.*" Ben sang the Hebrew with inflection and meaning. The English translation he intoned. "Hear, O Israel, the Lord is our God, the Lord is one."

Voices chimed in. Close behind, Ben heard Phineas Allenby utter the

Hebrew and English. Phineas was right; he butchered the Hebrew. Ben looked over the assemblage. They were not all Jews, many did not know the words, or looked uncomfortable. But they were here with Ben and each other, and for these minutes, for as long as he held them, they were held, too, by God.

"*Baruch shem k'vod malchuto l'olam va-ed*. Blessed is God's glorious majesty, for ever and ever."

Half the men responded, "*Ah-mein*." The rest caught up, sputtering the word.

Ben pushed his hands down. The soldiers sat.

He opened his mouth to speak. In silence, he cast his eyes over them. Some heads had bowed, others blinked at him with expectation. Ben did not see his son replicated two hundred times in this dimming pasture of war. That would have been too simple. That would have been too comforting. These soldiers were not his son. They were alive and in front of him.

He felt the quiet grow unwieldy, he'd looked on them too long. Behind him, Phineas whispered, "Chaplain?" Ben pushed aside the veil of his memory and grief, but it did not part fully, it draped over his shoulders where the *tallit* should have been.

"In Leviticus, a man with an Israelite mother and an Egyptian father got into a fight with an Israelite. During the fight, the half-Egyptian blasphemed God. The people who heard this took the man to Moses for judgment. Moses appealed to God, who told Moses to take the blasphemer outside the camp and have the whole congregation stone him to death. Moses was told to speak to the people of Israel, that anyone who blasphemes shall be stoned, aliens and citizens alike. Anyone who kills an animal shall make restitution. Anyone who maims another shall suffer the same, fracture for fracture, eye for eye, tooth for tooth. Anyone who kills a person shall be put to death."

Ben let this sink in. He walked along the line of the seated front row.

"We Jews do not have a gentle God. He is jealous and He is vengeful and He is strict. He insists we live in peace among other nations, and commands us to make war on nations who will not. That's why you're here. Because the Germans will not live in peace."

"Amen," someone said. It was Phineas Allenby. No one took the Baptist chaplain's cue, the gathering stayed quiet.

"You are not here as Jews and Christians," Ben continued, "you are here as soldiers. You are in this land as tools of the one God. What Hitler and his people have done to the Jews is blasphemy. What he has done to the peoples of Europe is a shame, and God will not let these things stand. You are here as justice, as God's strictness and His vengeance."

Ben stood still. He opened his fists. He spoke from a deep place. A long journey brought his words to the surface, and they would not be slowed nor cooled.

"Men, you are not alone. I am here. Chaplain Allenby is here. The United States Army is here. God is here."

A voice in the back said, "That's right!" and this was taken up. Ben let the nods and agreement fever the soldiers for many seconds. He raised both hands to hush them.

"We say to the Germans what God said to the kings of Judah who turned their backs on Him."

From memory, Ben recited the verses:

"Your country lies desolate, your cities are burned with fire;
In your very presence, aliens devour your land;
It is desolate, as overthrown by foreigners.

"When you stretch out your hands, I will hide my eyes from you;
Even though you make many prayers, I will not listen;
Your hands are full of blood."

Ben held both hands outstretched to the soldiers, for their inspection. They did not see what he could see on them. He looked at their hunkered faces and saw only his son. Thomas Kahn sat dead in his pilot's seat, in the twisted wreck of a shot-down bomber on a cold, foreign ground. Ben watched German hands root through the boy's jacket, slip his watch off the wrist, steal a letter from his tunic, snatch tags from around his neck. The boy was stripped, he became just another body, not Ben Kahn's son. Then, in a shift, powered as always by hope, Thomas was not dead, but in a German camp. The young man wrapped his hands around barbed wire, gazing through the strands. Ben had trouble seeing Thomas's face like this; though painful, he could more clearly envision his son dead than tortured and starved. Ben did not know which fate was his son's. Either way, he'd come back to France to find out. If his boy was dead or imprisoned, the faster the war ended, the sooner he would know, and the sooner his boy would be mourned or freed. Until then, he could find Thomas only in his heart and in the air, the way the boy appeared right now, perched above these soldiers waiting for him to speak.

"Let me tell you all something, and I want you to remember this. When Jericho fell, the Israelites were forbidden to profit from the bodies of the slain. It is a sin to loot the dead. War is not for gain. War is a plague on every house. Respect the dead. They are taken from their families and from this world. They belong to God. And that means their watches and their guns and their wallets . . ." Ben tapped the pocket of his own coat over his heart, ". . . and their letters."

Heads hung at Ben's rebuke. He caught several pinched looks, too, men who weren't so ready to give up their lucre. Quickly, Ben realized he'd spoken from wrath. The thing had its own tongue.

He inhaled and brought a hand to his brow. Who was he to talk to these men out of his own pain like that? What did it matter to them? No one here had volunteered to be Ben's absolution. He'd chosen them for that role, not the other way around. He was a rabbi who'd been with this infantry regiment only one afternoon. In the shuffling silence, he heard one voice mutter, "Y'all Jews go ahead. Not me."

Ben turned to Phineas Allenby for his reaction. Phineas shrugged and laced his hands in front of his belt, guilty. Ben noted again how filthy the little Baptist was, as dirty as the men. Phineas had crawled in their places and shared their misery and fright. Yes, he'd failed to stop them from looting, perhaps he'd even taken a souvenir himself. Ben Kahn stood in front of them a clean and shaved stranger, the red cross on his helmet not blanked out because he had not yet faced the peril of snipers aiming at it. The 90th was a problem division, and Phineas Allenby and others had been their chaplains since landing at UTAH, probably since England. Ben had not earned his place among these Tough Ombres, not in this war, anyway. He could not help them, Jew or Gentile, until he gained their respect, the way Phineas had. Ben was wrong to reprove any of them.

He finished his service with a prayer in Hebrew, then translated in English. No one joined in.

"*Baruch atah Adonai, ga-al Yisrael.* We praise you, O God, Redeemer of Israel. *Ah-mein.*"

Ben changed his posture to let the soldiers know the service was over. Phineas Allenby came beside him. The two men waited for the last of the Jewish soldiers to come and welcome Ben to the regiment. Not many came forward, and Ben was restrained with those who did.

When the two chaplains were finally alone in the field, the first tints of darkness had descended. Along with the sliding river and distant pot-shots, the sound around them was of shovels. The men of the 358th were digging their holes for the night.

The little Baptist held a grave look on his face. There was so much compassion in Phineas's eyes. Sheepish, Ben looked to the ground.

Phineas took Ben's two wrists. He turned them over, facing palms up. Ben looked into the white plains of his own hands, gripped in Phineas Allenby's grubby fingers.

Phineas spoke, a depth in his voice that Ben had not heard until now. "The rest of it goes like this, Rabbi:

"When you stretch out your hands, I will hide my eyes from you;
Even though you make many prayers, I will not listen;
Your hands are full of blood.

"Wash yourselves, make yourselves clean,
Remove the evil of your doings from before my eyes,
Cease to do evil.

"Learn to do good, seek justice, rescue the oppressed,
Defend the orphan, plead for the widow.

"Come now, let us argue it out, says the Lord:
Though your sins are like scarlet, they shall be like snow;
Though they are like crimson, they shall become like wool.

"If you are willing and obedient, you shall eat the good of the land.
But if you refuse and rebel, you shall be devoured by the sword;
For the mouth of the Lord has spoken."

Phineas Allenby did not release Ben. The chaplain held out the rabbi's hands, like a gypsy reading the lines.

"David wasn't allowed to build the Temple because his hands were full of blood. The job fell to Solomon."

"I know. *Ein Kateigor Naaseh Saneigor.*"

"What is that?"

"It means a prosecutor cannot become a defender. Someone who's killed cannot bestow a blessing of peace. David killed thousands. Moses killed an Egyptian, and because of it God kept him out of the Holy Land. They were both Kohain. So am I."

"Is that why you feel God took your son, Ben?"

"I didn't say he was dead."

"You didn't have to. It's all over your face. Is he dead?"

"I don't know. Thomas was the pilot of a B-17. He was shot down over Verdun."

"Why're you so sure he's dead?"

"I don't think God will spare him."

"Why not?"

"I've killed men, Phineas. Plenty of men."

"That was in war, Ben. A righteous war. I don't think—"

"God doesn't make an exception. Moses killed that one Egyptian to save his own people. David killed whole tribes in wars. Didn't matter. God didn't tolerate either. He decides for each man how much is too much. I've killed more than He allows, even in a war."

The Baptist chaplain let go. Ben's hands stayed aloft, as though carrying the weight of the lives he'd collected twenty-six years ago.

"Well, God did say, 'Come, let's argue it out.' "

Ben nodded.

"So, I reckon you came, huh?"

Phineas said nothing more. Ben lowered his arms.

"Come on, Rabbi. Let's get us some chow."

Ben followed. He set a hand on his new friend's shoulder.

Phineas said, "And some tape for your helmet."

SECOND

The peasants, from time immemorial, have raised a bank of earth about each field, forming a flat-topped ridge, six feet in height, with beeches, oaks and chestnut trees growing upon the summit. The ridge or mound, planted on this wise, is called a hedge, and as the long branches of the trees which grow upon it almost always project across the road, they make a great arbor overhead. The roads themselves, shut in by clay banks in this melancholy way, are not unlike the moats of fortresses.

Honoré de Balzac
describing the Norman hedgerows

Coming under hostile fire causes inertia to our troops . . . do not believe they are afraid, but bewildered . . . Prisoners of war say they can tell the direction we're coming from and how we're going, which indicates we've got to control our fire . . . and they say we bunch up . . . we should be able to control our men better in this terrain.

Notes from a speech given by the 90th CO
to battalion commanders
June 15, 1944

That goddam country.

Description by a GI of the Norman hedgerows

D+12
JUNE 18

Joe Amos thrust up his hand.

"Me, Lieutenant! Give her to me."

He raised his hand so hard, his feet moved through the sand and Joe Amos found himself standing in front of the platoon, sixty men behind him. Joe Amos noticed a few snickers, a few huffs.

"Me, Lieutenant."

Lieutenant Garner gestured for Joe Amos to quit, he could have the assignment. Joe Amos turned to the platoon. He found the pudgy face he was looking for.

"Grove, come on, man. Let's do it."

"Corporal Biggs, if you don't mind," the lieutenant answered, "I'll make the duty roster this morning."

"Yes, sir."

"Dismissed, everyone."

The platoon shuffled off. Inside a few hours, they'd be dispatched on another run. Three LSTs churned their engines in the shallows to dry their flat bottoms on the beach, then dropped their great ramps to off-load. Another wave of landing craft circled in the flattened tide inside the Mulberry artificial breakwater. Supplies and machinery teemed over the recently completed lobnitz pierheads. Out in the Channel, so many ships traipsed back and forth that Joe Amos caught only snatches of the horizon, dashes of planet between the guardian destroyers pacing and the Liberty ships and transports waiting their turn on the beach or at the pierheads. In Joe Amos's excited nostrils, diesel stink blended with sea salt.

Lieutenant Garner called out, "Private Mays, you stay behind."

While the others flowed past, a powerful-looking boy held his ground. Joe Amos first noticed him around dawn; the boy was new and Joe Amos had wondered if this was the replacement partner Major Clay had mentioned. Lean but with veined forearms and a waist that funneled up to shoulders like a mantel, Private Mays was dark-skinned. When he said, "Yes, sir," his voice was deep and strong.

"Private, this is your new partner, Corporal Biggs." Lieutenant Garner waited while the two shook hands. Joe Amos was quietly relieved that Mays did not use the handshake to make an opening display of his muscles. He looked to be younger than Joe Amos, nineteen or maybe twenty.

The officer led the two of them away from the platoon's Jimmies to a deuce-and-a-half. The truck stood loaded past any regulation, jam-packed with crates of small-arms ammo strapped high above the rails, easily beyond the five-ton limit. Joe Amos expected to hear the suspension creak just sitting there.

"Yes," Joe Amos uttered. Here was his truck, the one he wanted, with the .50 caliber machine gun mounted in a ring welded behind the cab.

"The two of you get this son of a bitch up to the town of Tamerville. Just beyond Valognes. Map's in the cab. 79th Division is on their way to Cherbourg, and 3rd Battalion's short on ammo. You're taking this right up to the front line. That's what you wanted, Joe Amos, so you got it. Just get it to them, get back, and catch up with the platoon. Go on with you."

The lieutenant set his hands on his hips and stopped talking. Joe Amos jumped for the rail, to scamper over the crates and into the machine-gun ring.

Garner stabbed a finger at Joe Amos. "Biggs, get your tail behind the wheel! Damn, son."

Joe Amos dropped off the rail. He flicked a hand at Private Mays, who'd headed for the driver's door. "Go on around. I'm driving."

Garner shooed them with the back of both hands, like sheep in the road. "Mays, get in there next to him and learn something. And dammit boy, Joe Amos, stay out of trouble and get back here."

Joe Amos fired the engine. He felt the chassis groan.

"Lieutenant?"

"You're still here, Corporal."

"When I get back, can I keep this one?"

The officer tossed his head, chuckling.

"Sure. Now git, they're waiting on you."

The Jimmy wanted a lot of clutch to get rolling. The wheels crushed into the sand, the load teetered. Joe Amos needed to pay attention to heave the truck off the beach and into the draw. He expected Mays to start talking the moment they climbed into the cab but the dark private kept quiet. Joe Amos snuck a glance at him. The boy watched Joe Amos's feet and hands working the truck, just like Garner told him to do.

The load swayed coming onto the bulldozed flats of the draw. The remains of blasted German bunkers spoiled the bluffs on either side, raw marks of the ferocious fighting through here. Private Mays didn't look at them, he watched Joe Amos.

"Where you from?"

Mays didn't answer right off. The question seemed to be submitted to some authority in his head before he spoke.

"Little town in Florida."

Mays didn't name the town. Joe Amos tried another question.

"What's your first name?"

The low voice replied, "McGee."

Eyes on the road, Joe Amos screwed up his face. "That's a last name. That ain't a first name. How the hell'd you end up with that?"

Another pause preceded the answer.

"Name of the doctor that birthed me."

"Well, hell. Didn't the doctor have a first name?"

"Yeah."

Joe Amos shook his head. The boy didn't appear dull-witted or anything, but getting him talking was worse than dragging this overloaded Jimmy up the hill.

"What was it?"

"Adolph."

Joe Amos rammed the gear knob into second and laughed.

"Your mama named you Adolph McGee Mays?"

"I go by McGee."

"I guess you do. Shit."

Joe Amos lugged the Jimmy up to the road and had to wait for another convoy to speed past. These trucks carried stacks of five-gallon jerricans. Every driver ignored the twenty-five-mile-an-hour limit. It didn't matter, the roadside MPs just waved you by. Now that the invasion was equipped with the Mulberry harbor, the pulse of arriving supplies, vehicles, and soldiers had quickened. The American beachhead grew more crowded, the Krauts gave up ground like misers. The GIs were packing in. The hunger for matériel grew with their numbers, the need for replacements rose with the fighting. From the orange blinks in the night sky and the chatter and boom of guns all day long, Joe Amos got the notion that battle commanders weren't skimping on ammo or manpower in combat. Feeding them all were the convoys, and only them, right off the beaches. The French rail system was a shambles after three months of hard bombing before D-Day by the Brits and the Americans and sabotage by the French underground. That's why this road connecting OMAHA to UTAH teemed with traffic twenty-four hours a day, and not just Jimmies. Now there were huge tankers and five-ton tractor trucks towing massive trailers or artillery. The road began to show the wear and tear of constant contact with rubber and weight.

The convoy passed the intersection. Joe Amos gunned the Jimmy onto the paved surface and built momentum. Another column closed fast and he had to step on it to keep from slowing them down. He shifted deftly.

"See," he said to McGee Mays, "go ahead and wind her up. Don't baby her or she'll stall. She won't break." The Jimmy whined high into second before Joe Amos released her into third. "Don't break, baby." Mays chuckled.

Up on the road now, accelerating in front of the Jimmy behind him, Joe Amos pronounced his own full name. He kept both hands on the wheel, which shimmied under the burden. He explained how he was named after Joseph, a son of Jacob, who got sold into slavery by his brothers and became a high official in the Egyptian government. Joseph interpreted dreams and wore a many-colored coat. Also, he was named after Amos, one of the twelve prophets of Israel, who preached about justice and the coming day of God. Amos started out as a shepherd, but once he became a prophet he really let the people have it when they strayed.

"I like my names. A dream reader and a prophet. Gives you . . . I don't know, some juice. Like a boost or something."

Joe Amos stalled his chatter. He was accustomed to Boogie always running the talk. It felt good to be the corporal now, the one yammering on. McGee listened hard, he watched hard. Joe Amos didn't want to take advantage of the boy's silence.

"Now, a doctor, that's good, too . . ." Joe Amos nodded. "McGee's a good name."

McGee made no answer. He watched the countryside slide by, checked out the dunes turning into hedges and trees. Joe Amos jounced behind the wheel, fixing on the road and the engine.

"I'm gonna bring you up to speed, alright?" If the new boy didn't want to yak about hometowns and women, then fine. But Joe Amos intended to talk.

"About what?"

"About the war, damn it. See them dead tanks out there? The war."

"Sorry. Go ahead."

"Are you dumb or something?"

"No."

"Well, you . . . Look . . . sorry."

"I ain't dumb, Corporal. I'm a good driver. I ain't afraid. And I can kick a man's ass when I have to."

"You talkin' to me?"

"I reckon."

Joe Amos laughed, lifted his hands from the wheel to make a surrender gesture.

"Alright, then. Gimme that." Joe Amos laid out his hand, and McGee, hesitant, slid his palm over the offered skin.

"Okay," Joe Amos said, "we got to get used to each other, that's all. I had a different partner for a while, and that's, you know, that's the way he talked. I was just doing the same thing. My fault."

"Okay."

Joe Amos took another glance at McGee Mays. The boy waited, quiet and still. This, thought Joe Amos, this is the real Negro the whites are afraid of. He's quiet and he may be simple-hearted. He comes from some backwater town in Florida where he's learned to still that deep voice. They taught him down there to be silent and undemanding, and he agreed to be so. They've got him convinced of his station. Joe Amos is different, he has some college, he'll get the rest when he returns home. They figure Joe Amos Biggs is playing the game their way, so they'll crack the door a little bit for him. But they badly fear McGee Mays in his iron-black and quiet millions. They're scared he might change his mind, not be so quiet. So they don't give him a gun, they don't give him the chance to prove he's as good as they are at anything they do, work, think, fight. McGee Mays, not Joe Amos, frightens the bejeezus out of them.

"How you know what's goin' on?" asked McGee. He waved a hand at the terrain. The first busted town came up. "I mean, man, it's a war. Lookit this."

"Same way you're gonna know," Joe Amos answered. He patted the dash of the Jimmy. "A week now, I been driving every inch of the beachhead. There ain't one division I haven't delivered to. Men, ammo, food, clothes, POL. Then I take back prisoners, wounded, and bodies. By now, I know this part of France better than the generals. And I know what's going on. I'm gonna show you. You're gonna know, too."

"Yeah," nodded McGee. This seemed to strike the boy as a challenge, and he liked it. McGee scanned the land outside the windshield, now risen and diced into the dangerous hedges and fields.

Joe Amos looked from McGee's shifting features back to the road. His hands tightened on the wheel, not because of any bump in the pavement, but from a temblor up his torso. Like Joseph his namesake, he'd felt a jolt, a dream he'd read on McGee's face. There's changes ahead, he saw their coming on this boy like flights of black birds, fluttering and common, turned into clever, squawking crows. There's change coming and it doesn't matter who likes it. It was coming like Kingdom.

Joe Amos snagged his thoughts on a hymn, one of his mama's favorites in their shanty Danville church. *Rise up, men of God! His kingdom tarries long. Bring in the day of brotherhood, and end the night of wrong.*

"Tell me," said McGee.

"Alright."

Joe Amos shoved a thumb over his shoulder, indicating east. "Behind us, you got the British and Canadians trying to take Caen. That's a big crossroads city, right on the highway to Paris. They got themselves stalemated there. Caen's where the big breakout is supposed to be, get us the hell away from these beaches, but it don't look like that's gonna happen anytime soon. The Krauts ain't giving up Caen. Over on our side we're getting more crowded every day. So we might have to break out in our part of France. The only place to do that is right through the hedges. And that ain't gonna be a party."

The Jimmy rolled with traffic through a tunnel of treetops. McGee, new to this place, said, "Damn," probably figuring how awful and blind it would be to fight field by field through the bocage. Every time Joe Amos drove over this land, five, six times a day, he felt the same twinge, the responsibility of hauling supplies to the men doing that fighting. White boys or not, he didn't care what color when he saw them limping or on stretchers, wrapped in gauze or mattress covers, when he was close enough to hear the guns blaze beyond the trees and hedges and wreckage. All he wanted was to be shoulder to shoulder and see, just see, if in the smoke another soldier might not care about color, either. For now, hauling was all Joe Amos could do. He tried to content himself with being channelled through ten thousand guns instead of just one in his own hands.

"South of here, a couple infantry divisions are working their way down to St. Lô. The 35th, the 29th, and the 2nd. They're bad news, every one of them. Every time I head down that way I get the shit scared out of me, the way them boys are fighting. Man, I have trucked some bodies up out of there. The Krauts are dug in real good. They're trying to keep us bottled up, probably for a counterattack. But that ain't going to be easy for them, because our planes flat own the sky. They move in reinforcements, least during the day, we're gonna see 'em."

Joe Amos pointed ahead and to the right, north.

"Now, up here, where we're going, we got two infantry divisions, the 79th and 4th, just starting their move up the peninsula to take Cherbourg. That's the biggest port in Normandy. Once we get it, we can start landing supply ships there. I mean, there's only so much that can be hauled over the beaches. And there's probably another million more men and everything waiting over in England to get here and bust us out into open country. So Cherbourg is key."

Joe Amos revved with his words. He missed Boogie John, sure, but this was good, driving and talking, knowing. He was the corporal now.

"We got to keep the boys supplied, got to keep taking it to the Krauts hard as we can, day and night. And that means supplies. Ammo, gas, rations, shoelaces, medicine, what the hell ever. Supplies, man, that's the lifeblood of war. Somebody said that. That's what we are. Every truck we drive, every load we deliver, the boys can't do a thing without what we bring 'em. Got to have lifeblood. So, see, we need Cherbourg.

Problem is, the Krauts know it, too. So they're probably gonna do everything they can to keep it."

McGee gazed out his window beyond his resting elbow, off to the northeast, building images of importance and battle.

Finally, Joe Amos cast his pointing finger west, straight ahead.

"Those three divisions heading north for Cherbourg got their backs turned to the Krauts. So to protect the rear, and make sure the Krauts don't slip out down the peninsula, we got the 101st and the 82nd Airbornes, and the 9th and 90th Infantries cutting off the peninsula, like a chicken neck."

Joe Amos drew his finger beneath his chin.

"Just last night I heard the 9th and 82nd got all the way to the ocean. So now that we got the south sealed off, the 79th and 4th can go whup some tail toward Cherbourg. The 9th'll be heading north, too, I hear tell. That's where we're headed, up into that fight."

McGee's big eyes stretched wide. "Right into the fight?"

"Damn close, lieutenant said."

McGee pointed down at Joe Amos's feet.

"Then step on it."

The Lieutenant Colonel dragged on his cigarette and flopped his heavy boots up on his desk. Leaning back in the chair, he crossed his ankles and blew smoke. Ben did not read relaxation in the officer's pose, but a grim determination to take one last sip of comfort out of the chair and the tobacco before rising.

"Okay," the officer breathed.

Ben said nothing, to allow the man his short idyll.

The officer dropped his boots to the floor. "What'd you say your name was, Chaplain?"

"Kahn."

"Chaplain Kahn. I appreciate you checking in with me."

"I like to let the COs of every unit know when I'm around. I'm sort of an itinerant for the time being. Until Billups gives me my own battalion."

"Sort of a wandering Jew, huh?"

Ben let the officer laugh alone, but smiled to let the man know he wasn't offended.

"You want to take a Sunday walk, Chaplain?"

"Let's go."

Lieutenant Colonel Trow stood and trod on his cigarette. Ben followed him through the remains of the shop to the open doorway. The door stood propped against a crumbling plaster wall, blown off its hinges when 3rd Battalion entered Gourbesville two days ago.

The officer strode into the street and headed west, Ben beside him. The town, like every contested burg so far in Normandy, had been laid waste by American artillery. Only imagination could describe it, fill in the interrupted lines of walls, and lift the colors from beneath the mortar dust and akimbo bricks.

Trow, a lean man with early-graying hair, slung his M-1 into his hands. The town was not large and they reached the outskirts quickly. Instantly, the bocage greeted them on both sides of the skinny road. The Colonel's pace slowed, his eyes scanning the green unknown.

"You're looking pretty gamey, Rabbi. Where you been? Not at the aid station?"

"I spent the last three days with the 358th, north of here."

"Taking an infantry tour of the Tough Ombres?"

"You could say."

"Now you're doing the 357th. How's the division look to you so far?"

"It was pretty quiet where I was. But so far I'd say troubled."

"Yeah, troubled." The Lieutenant Colonel tugged his ear. "That's a word for it."

Ben glanced over his shoulder to the rubble of Gourbesville. GIs shuffled between ruins. The spikes of gun barrels rose like bristles in the debris facing west. The Krauts might try to take the town back, though this was unlikely; the enemy strategy was a slow withdrawal into the hedges, to make every step forward for the doughs tortured and bloody.

"I got here on the 16th, just before they took it," Trow said. "I was reassigned over from the 9th when the battalion CO got waxed on the road leading in."

Ben kept his dismay to himself. Here was one more officer in the 90th who'd been on the job only hours or days, replacing commanders killed or wounded or evacuated for shock or demoted for ineffectiveness. No wonder the division was in disarray.

Trow told his account, keeping his eyes on the bocage. The scrub thickened on the hedges the farther they walked out of town, into a warm and windless embrace.

"The Krauts had the road pre-sighted with a battery of eighty-eights. That forced the battalion to go through these fields. But the battalion CO, he wanted the road, so he jumped in a jeep and blared right through Bloody Corner. One round took him out, and his driver, they fired that eighty-eight right down his throat. That's not leadership, Chaplain. That's plain stupid, getting killed like that. Then both the regimental CO and his assistant bought it, trying to get these men going. These fucking guys."

Ben had noticed how the men, officers and foot soldiers alike, did not curb their cursing around him. Maybe they sensed that Ben Kahn had been in their boots before, scared, in another country, in a land of dying. Ben didn't mind their language, it was sincere, and that's what any man of God wants.

Trow pivoted south, lifting an arm to indicate the acres of fields and hedgerows. Ben squinted in the afternoon light. He raised a hand as a brim to his helmet. He touched the tape wrapped over his red cross by Allenby. In the pastures he spotted the black-rimmed gouges made by 105 mm howitzers and the smaller scoops of 81 mm heavy mortars. The fields and town had hunkered under a downpour of American shells. The town melted away and the ground was grilled. Fat lumps lay in the fields. Butchered cattle. They, thought Ben, were stupid, too, the worst thing to be in a war.

"They ran, Chaplain." Trow lowered his arm. He resumed his walk west, with Ben beside him.

"We called in the artillery pretty close, about a hundred yards off the nose of the lead company. And they must have got confused or something, thinking the rounds were incoming from the Krauts, because they up and ran. Lit out right for the rear. I saw it. Some of them dropped their weapons. And I'm thinking, What the hell is going on?"

Ben listened. He was likely a decade older than Trow and already this officer sounded like an old father, burdened like all fathers by the price their sons pay for wisdom. Ben felt the urge to tell this younger man some story about his own son, share an anecdote of loss. But Ben had nothing he could say. He did not know and might never know if his son was either brave or stupid. He couldn't even say if the boy was alive or dead.

"A captain ran by me, then his whole company sprinted behind him. I screamed at him to stop. That's how it happens, when the men see their officers crap out. You put this silver on your uniform," Trow tapped his collar, "you don't run for the rear. Ever."

The Colonel spit in the road, cleaning his mouth from the story.

"I notice you haven't got a chaplain's assistant yet, Rabbi. Can't find anybody in the T-Os you trust?"

Ben grimaced. The Colonel's comment was scathing. The low morale in the 90th was already leaching into this good man. Ben wanted to defend the division. Tell Trow there was not a single officer or soldier of the 90th who, entering the bocage, had ever been fired at by an enemy before he heard that first round whistle through the leaves. These men, from officer to private, were as green as the bushes, and nowhere near as mature, facing battle-tested Germans at every turn, many of them probably veterans of the Eastern Front. The doughs had reluctant leadership combined with a fearsome assignment, to hack straight into the heart of enemy positions prepared years in advance of their coming. Other divisions in the hedges had performed better, yes, but the tension is so great in combat that one small spark of hesitation can spread like a wildfire if it spreads from top to bottom like it had in the 90th.

Ben answered, "No, that's not it. I figure since I'm assigned to all three regiments, I'd wait till I visited them all to pick somebody."

But Trow had stopped listening. He bent at the waist and slowed. Beside him, Ben did likewise.

Ahead, in the ditches on both sides of the dusty road, two lines of soldiers huddled. Every man gazed down the channel of the hedges. Trow moved off the road to a ditch, too. Ben followed. The officer made his way up to the closest kneeling soldier.

"What's going on?" Trow demanded.

"I don't know, sir. We just stopped, is all."

"What company are you with?"

"Lima Company, sir."

"Where's your CO?"

"He's up ahead somewhere."

"Alright. Stay put. Chaplain, let's go figure this out."

Trow stood to his full height out of the ditch. Men squatting on both sides of the road muttered while the officer and the chaplain walked straight down the middle. Ben noted that many of the soldiers in L Company appeared to be replacements—few wore the crinkling, impregnate anti-gas uniforms and many had yet to throw away their extra equipment. These boys were newly minted from the repple depple and marched out here into the green void. They didn't have a clue why they were in a ditch or why they should get out of it.

Lieutenant Colonel Trow shook his head.

"Son of a bitch, Chap, this is just what I'm talking about. I sent this Captain Valentine out here an hour ago to set up observation posts west of town. And I come out to find two hundred men lying in a goddam ditch."

Trow walked briskly, making every buckle, strap, and weapon on his person clatter as he stalked past the immobile company. Ben lengthened his own strides to keep up and found himself jangling, too, though just with his canteen and backpack.

The head of the halted column came into view around a bend in the hedgerows. A knot of men were gathered on their knees around an object on the ground that looked like a radio. One soldier held something to his head. Trow quickened his pace.

"What in the hell is this?"

Closing in, Ben narrowed his gaze at what the men had circled around.

It wasn't a radio. It was a helmet.

Ben ran forward.

"Colonel! Sniper!"

From behind, he dove at Trow's knees. He buckled the man at the instant a bullet buzzed past, followed close by a crack out of the hedges.

Trow barely had time to get his hands out to break his fall. Down, he rolled over, Ben still clutching him about the legs. The Colonel's unbuckled helmet spilled into the road.

Trow said nothing while he scrambled on his belly, retrieving his helmet, then rose to run folded over to the men clustered at the front of the column. Ben stayed on his belly and crawled, not as nimble as the younger Colonel. Beside his elbows digging across the dust, a ruby patch glistened and soaked into the dirt.

Ben scurried to the ditch, some soldiers helped him to his feet. He kept close to the bordering hedge and, doubled over, jogged to the front of the line. Lieutenant Colonel Trow did not keep his voice down, he was already scorching some ears.

"Goddammit, Captain, I don't give a hoot! You got a sniper in these trees, you damn well find him and do something about it and get your column moving! I didn't send you out here to set up your OP in the god-dam ditch! Now, what direction did the shot come from?"

The soldiers parted and let Ben into their ring. At their center on the ground lay a lieutenant. A medic pressed a gauze pad over the downed man's breast. Empty sulfa packets lay on the road. The lieutenant's face was shock pale, dark eyes blinking, clouding. He licked his lips, the thirst of dying. One soldier pressed the lieutenant's hand high to his own chest. The medic snapped red fingers on his free hand, impatient for something. Others in the circle dug in their pockets for more mor-phine spikes. The lieutenant gulped for air, his jaw and Adam's apple worked like pistons, but Ben knew this wound, the sucking hole in the chest and lung.

Ben lifted his attention now to the captain, Valentine, with the Colonel's teeth almost chewing on his ear. The young captain was white-faced, eyes in the dust under the Colonel's harangue.

"Get your company off this road, Captain! Spread them out across these fields, and tell 'em to watch for mines. I want these trees up ahead glassed by every pair of binoculars you got in your company. Then I want you to start blasting away at every damn thing that don't look like wood. You following me?"

Valentine nodded.

"I want that sniper's ass down and I want this company in position. You're letting one sumbitch in a tree and one casualty hold up an entire company. You better figure it out fast, Captain, men are gonna die."

The Colonel eased his voice.

"Men are gonna die, son. And you can't give up command of the rest of them because you got a man down. Now, I need you to get up and get moving."

Captain Valentine did not bound to action. He paused, still unsure. Ben guessed the captain was no more than twenty-three. He was a man and still so much a boy. His decisions carried life and death, but no mat-ter how much Trow needed the man in this captain to step forward, the frightened boy in him would not relinquish his hold. Thomas, also a captain, was twenty-three, he'd be twenty-five now. Ben told himself to stop this, he could not superimpose Thomas onto every scared young soldier's face.

Trow patted Captain Valentine on the back.

"I'll stay with the company till we get the son of a bitch."

Valentine looked at the Colonel, relieved. The captain glanced at a kneeling first sergeant. For the first time, Ben heard Valentine's voice. It was heartbreakingly pristine and plainly without resolve.

"Sergeant Moran, you've got first platoon for now. Let's get the men into these fields, like the Colonel says."

Valentine peeled out of the circle, taking four others with him. The soldier who'd held the lieutenant's hand had to go but didn't know where to lay the arm. Ben reached out and took the dying soldier's grip in his. With Valentine and his men gone, the medic watched the struggling lieutenant's face, to be sure the wounded man was not watching when he shook his head at Trow and Ben.

Trow grew solemn over the reddening bandage. He muttered, careful that the fading lieutenant didn't hear him. "I don't even know this shavetail. He couldn't have been here more'n a couple days. This is what I'm talking about. That kid captain is shitting his pants and everybody around him is ready to do the same. Zero morale. Goddammit."

With that, the Colonel swept away.

Ben leaned close. "Lieutenant, can you hear me?"

The soldier's face shivered side to side, chilled to the bone by his seeping blood, which took his warmth with it. He nodded. *Yes.*

"Mendelsohn," whispered the medic.

"Lieutenant Mendelsohn," Ben said, "I'll write your family. I'll take care of everything."

The young officer's lids fluttered. He tried twice before he swallowed.

Ben felt the grip slacken. He had no time for conversation.

The medic fixed his eyes on the Ten Commandments insignia pinned at Ben's collar and nodded. Mendelsohn was a Jew.

Ben brought his face closer above Lieutenant Mendelsohn and spoke into the man's gaping mouth.

"The Lord is my shepherd. I shall not want . . ."

The hand in Ben's became a weight. The lieutenant's head stopped quivering. The gaping mouth issued a gurgle, as if a stone dropped long ago had found water. Ben completed the prayer. From under the OD T-shirt, he tugged Mendelsohn's dog tags, with the "H" stamped in the right-hand corner for "Hebrew." He unclipped one tablet, slid it into his pocket, and reconnected the necklace, tucking it in place. The medic rolled up his kit, leaving stained and emptied trash behind. Nameless, the medic jogged off to join his company dispersing in the fields. From the hedges, Colonel Trow's urging and vulgar voice was the crow for Lieutenant Mendelsohn's passing.

Ben reached into the dead man's pockets, for letters and personal effects he would mail with his own letter to the family. He rested his palm across the face of Lieutenant Mendelsohn.

"Thy sun shall no more go down, neither shall thy moon withdraw itself, for the Lord shall be thine everlasting light, and the days of thy mourning shall be ended."

He closed his eyes now and raised both hands, alone with Mendelsohn, who could not seek vengeance for himself. Ben would spend the night with L Company, out here on the rim of the regiment beside the young man's body, watching, listening for the Krauts to move. He held his hands up, kept them up, did not let them fall even when his shoulders burned, until he heard several shots from the company to kill the sniper.

A dirty GI raised a hand. Behind a log, a machine gun swiveled Joe Amos's way.

Joe Amos slowed for the checkpoint. The brakes squealed to stop the overloaded truck. Gonna need new brake pads, he thought. Running two weeks and already falling apart. That's because we're running nonstop.

A corporal sauntered up to the cab window. The man's cheeks bore streaks of grime. He stank.

"Ammo?" he asked.

"You 3rd Battalion 79th?"

"Let's go, man. I got hungry babies to feed."

The corporal shouldered his carbine. He moved to the side of the Jimmy, hoisted one boot on the double rear wheels, and catapulted over the rail to the top of the crates. In his rear window, Joe Amos watched the soldier's boots drop inside the ring of the .50 caliber machine gun.

"Naw, man," Joe Amos grumbled. "Damn, what's he . . . ? That's my machine gun."

The filthy corporal checked the ammo belt, charged the gun's chamber, and clouted on the canvas roof of the cab twice, *pop pop!*

"Hit the road, buddy! Straight ahead. I'll tell you when to turn."

Joe Amos spun a griping and scrunched face to McGee. The dark boy grinned and said nothing.

"White boys messing with my stuff," Joe Amos muttered, and slid into first gear.

The Jimmy passed quickly into the town of Valognes. The Krauts hadn't put up much of a fight here, the streets were not strewn with the shards of buildings like most of the places Joe Amos rolled through.

"See this," he said to McGee. "This is a bad sign. The Krauts didn't make any kind of stand here."

"Why's that bad?"

"Shows they're pulling back into Cherbourg. Hitler does crazy shit like that. Picks a spot and tells everybody no one leaves alive. Calls 'em 'fortresses.' He did that last year at Stalingrad, and look what happened. Place got blown to smithereens. A million Russians and Krauts got killed."

McGee looked quizzical. "How you know all this?"

Joe Amos didn't want to say, Because I went to college and I studied and now in war I listen and learn. What a man knows is what he is. Joe Amos held his tongue because he did not want to draw a dividing line between himself and McGee, the student and the strong-back Negro. Joe Amos came to war for every black man, so he shrugged, as if to say, I just do.

McGee asked another question. Despite the boy's earlier remark that he was not afraid to be here, McGee appeared fidgety the more Joe Amos drove through the town, headed to the front line.

"How come them soldiers back there didn't check us for paperwork or nothin'? I mean, couldn't we be infiltrators or somethin'?"

Joe Amos chortled. "Come on, man. The Germans don't have no colored boys driving for them."

McGee didn't laugh. Joe Amos had guessed right, the boy was nervous. Joe Amos kept talking. "Besides, we don't even have paperwork. Shoot, writin' things down was the first thing COM Z stopped. Too much supplies got to get moving too fast to worry about paperwork. We get a load, we get told where to go, we fire up and go. Bang, baby, we get it on."

Joe Amos put some pizzazz in his voice, to rile McGee past his worries. He held out a flat palm, waiting for McGee to slap it with spirit.

"Hey, brother, we're in the shit now. This is where we want to be. Give it to me!"

Reluctant, McGee spanked Joe Amos's hand.

The road out of town narrowed as the Norman roads always did, a tar stitch between hedges. Branches and twigs reached into the lane, scraping the cab and rails. Clearly, the Germans had prevented the local folk from trimming these hedges, knowing at some point the Allies would come this way. The corporal knocked on the roof again. The canvas bulged down at Joe Amos's head.

"Turn right, up ahead. See that dirt road?"

Joe Amos guided the Jimmy off the road and down the lane. The earth was rutted from zero maintenance and recent tank tracks. From high in the cab, Joe Amos began to see in the fields the trail of American soldiers, their litter, and a few German bodies.

"Another couple hundred yards," the corporal bellowed, rapping again on the roof. This was aggravating; the corporal stood not only behind the gun Joe Amos coveted, but his constant rattling on the roof implied that Joe Amos wasn't paying attention.

Before he could shout out his window some curse at the corporal to stop banging, sounds of automatic fire slashed from the fields and bocage ahead. The corporal swiveled the machine gun. Answering gunfire burst out of the bushes, coming from the corporal's unit dug into the bocage. Joe Amos saw no muzzle flashes or smoke. He pushed forward as fast as he could without tipping the truck over in the washboard ruts. This was the first time he'd driven this deep into the hedgerows. It was blind, all noise and green.

"I can't see shit," he said without looking at McGee. "Man, how can they fight in here? You can't see a damn thing."

Another smack landed on the roof. The corporal ordered a left turn at a dirt crossing. Joe Amos negotiated the bend and wheeled the Jimmy down an even narrower lane another hundred yards, when the corporal pounded one more time.

"Right here! Stop!"

Joe Amos hit the brakes. Before the truck quit rolling, the corporal had tossed the first crate down to a soldier who appeared out of nowhere. In moments, a dozen men leaped out of the hedges wearing on their helmets cut branches stuck into webbing, all looking like the soldiers of a forest god. In a fireman's brigade, they tossed and hefted ammo boxes away into their hidden and erupting battleground. No one called Joe Amos or McGee down to help. Joe Amos made no move to leave the cab. McGee was out the passenger door before Joe Amos could react.

Strong McGee moved to the tailgate below another soldier who'd climbed up to pitch down crates. In his mirror, Joe Amos watched the boy catch the boxes, maybe fifty pounds each, like pillows and swing them to reaching hands. Joe Amos did not open his door, he climbed out his window, set his foot on the Jimmy's outside mirror, and clambered up and over into the machine-gun ring. Up here, with his hands on the handles, a finger scratching the trigger, he heard the fighting.

A hundred yards away, an assault raged. Joe Amos gazed into the thickness of the hedges and saw none of it, the leaves stopped everything but shouts and gunsmoke. He even heard German screamed above the tumult. His nostrils widened at the cordite stink and his hands tightened on the handles of the machine gun. If he caught sight of an enemy through the branches, he knew he would empty the whole ammo canister. McGee, a little breathless, called up to him, "Lookin' good, Corporal."

Edgy and alert in his perch, Joe Amos guarded the truck from an enemy he could not spot. The soldiers stripped the Jimmy's load in two minutes and carted the crates away into the brush without thanks. When the last box was gone, so were the soldiers. Joe Amos and McGee were left alone in the shade with the battle swelling behind the curtain of the bocage. Mortars coughed somewhere off to Joe Amos's right, the shells lobbed and landed to his left, the explosions sounded close. McGee stood mesmerized, looking up, and Joe Amos gazed down at him. The two stared while they listened, and imagined the combat on the other side of the hedge.

McGee awoke first.

"We're gettin' the hell outa here!"

McGee leaped into the driver's seat and flung the Jimmy into reverse. Joe Amos jarred his ribs against the machine gun. The Jimmy's engine wound high as McGee charged backward down the lane to reach the crossing where there was room to turn around. Joe Amos had to pull his hands from the grips and hold on to the steel ring while McGee raced for the crossing, then cut sharp, shifted forward to first, and headed back the way they'd come. McGee had the truck in third gear and flying in no time, bouncing along the uneven dirt road. The truck almost danced with McGee at the wheel. The boy could surely drive scared.

Joe Amos stayed tall behind the machine gun all the way to Valognes and through the town. He set his hands to the handles and left them there, so the soldiers milling around could see him with the .50 cal in his brown mitts. McGee drove the Jimmy like a scalded cat past the city limits and only slowed when he came up tight against another convoy heading east on the two-lane main road.

With the Jimmy in line and moving slower, Joe Amos leaned to shout into McGee's driver-side window.

"Damn, what you think of that? That's the closest I been to the fighting."

McGee raised a fist out of the window. Joe Amos made a fist, too, and they knocked knuckles. McGee shouted, "Whoooo-ee!"

"Man," Joe Amos said to himself. He wanted to squeeze the trigger, let off a burst. If they weren't in line with fifty other trucks, he would have, just to shuck the bark off a tree.

Another loaded convoy approached from the opposite direction. Too many trucks to count rode in echelon behind the lead jeep; the tail of the convoy was lost behind the trees. Joe Amos knew the makeup of a load just by looking at the way it was stacked and the type of cartons or boxes or crates in the beds. The first Jimmy whirred by, and Joe Amos thought, Lubricants. The boxes were cardboard, but the truck squatted low on its axles, the boxes were heavy. The second and third trucks whizzed past carrying the same, then in the fourth Joe Amos didn't need to guess; once it was past he saw the bed full of artillery rounds, the pointy shell caps arranged neatly in stacked rows, they looked like a fat bed of nails. Then the fifth truck rolled by, another load of lube. This deuce-and-a-half, like Joe Amos's new truck, had a machine gun welded to the cab. No one manned it.

Joe Amos pivoted his head time and again, watching the long convoy, enjoying the whizzing *voom!* each passing truck made. The column looked to be over two miles long. Riding in the empty bed, standing behind his gun, he had a fresh view of the power of the convoys, the immensity of the matériel they moved. Just minutes after being so close to the fighting in the hedgerows, he understood better than ever how those boys back there were fighting with the ammunition he put in their hands. He tingled with pride at the job he was doing. Black hands and pink palms humming by raised from the convoy to him, standing behind his machine gun. He waved back.

A new sound rushed at his ears. It was not the *burr* of truck engines and straining transmissions, not tires grubbing the road. This noise was leaner, an angered yowl that in the first moment he heard it pitched to a higher keen. Joe Amos saw it then: dark wings like a knife-cut in the blue just above the tree line, rushing at the convoy from behind. The wings of the Messerschmitt sparked, left and right of the cowling, blinking brighter than the sun. Geysers of canvas and chips of metal flipped off trucks in the opposite lane; three Jimmies dissolved under the fighter's cannons. A truck careened off the road, spouting flames. Others pulled to the shoulder. The drivers flung open their doors to bolt for the cover of the hedges. By the time the Kraut fighter made its first pass, the convoy was snarled in the road, some of it burning.

Joe Amos stood in the rolling truck bed and watched. The fantastic event of war had happened so fast, with screeching and bursts, trucks and men in disarray all over the road, flames spewing jets of smoke, he hadn't even thought of aiming his machine gun and pulling the trigger. He was stunned by how quickly the plane came and went, at how much damage lay sown in its wake. Joe Amos hadn't even noticed that McGee had stopped the Jimmy, but now he saw that all the trucks on both sides of the road were halted, over a mile of Jimmies and tractors in a dead straight line, a shooting gallery for the Messerschmitt. Most of the drivers had dived in the bushes, the rest were shouting and heading for the ditches and roots. Joe Amos scanned the havoc, wishing he'd fired his gun, damning himself for freezing. A single sound dominated the day. Joe Amos whirled behind him. The lone Kraut fighter wailed, banking steeply, returning.

Joe Amos pounded on the canvas roof.

"He's comin' back!"

McGee shouted from the cab, "What you want me to do?"

Joe Amos pressed the machine-gun grips. He bent at the knees to tilt the barrel up and revolved to press his backside against the cab. Dipping his head behind the sight, he moved the barrel at the swinging, silhouetted Jabo.

"Get out!" he yelled.

McGee wasted no time flinging open the driver's door and sprinting for the hedges. Joe Amos did not take his eyes from the leveling, coming Kraut. He heard McGee cussing while he ran.

Joe Amos glanced down the lines of immobile trucks. The convoy was a sitting duck. But, looking closer, he saw every fifth Jimmy, the ones with the .50 caliber machine guns, had a black man standing in the truck bed, two fists on the grips, pointing their barrels at the Kraut dropping altitude and zooming in flat and hard. Joe Amos puffed his cheeks, blew out, and aimed his gun at the German.

Someone in the convoy shouted, "Get ready!"

Another called, "Here he comes, y'all!"

The Messerschmitt pilot dared every one of these men. He made no evading moves but evened his wings low over the road and roared in, flaring blue and yellow fire out of his nose and twin hanging cannons. A quarter mile ahead, Joe Amos saw gouts of road and metal chucked into the air as the first trucks in line were shredded. Drivers on both sides of the road opened up now, machine guns squalled across the whole column. The Kraut matched his speed and firepower to the convoy's weapons, he headed straight down the line to keep his profile small, just cockpit and flashing wings.

Joe Amos waited seconds to let the Kraut close in. He got a bead on him and held it, refining his aim, sure he had the fighter between the eyes, and let loose. The machine gun kicked, harder than he was ready for. The barrel wavered away from his true aim. Without releasing the trigger, flailing rounds into the air, Joe Amos tugged the barrel back toward the Messerschmitt's path. The engine roar ballooned and now Joe Amos heard the yapping of the plane's own machine guns and cannons. The noise was like a rain of steel pots falling, clanging all around him, *bang, bang, bang!* Joe Amos went blind to everything but steel and sound and metal splinters and the pressure he put on the trigger and the machine gun pointed into the storm, flinching and clutching, firing and screaming until the fighter was past with a roar. A wash of oily wind kissed Joe Amos goodbye, did not kill him, left him standing in a truck riddled with holes.

"Vous rentrez à la maison?"

White Dog stood naked at the open window. A breeze licked across his bare privates; he was done and limp, contemplative in the afternoon heat. The chiffon curtain hoisted on both sides of him, framed him, and fell.

White Dog did not turn from the window to face the bed.

"No. I won't be going home. I'll go to Africa."

She shifted on the mattress, making a noise and a fuss. White Dog could tell she was fluffing pillows to sit against the wall, to talk. He kept his back to her, facing the street six stories below.

No one looked up at his white nude frame filling the window. The afternoon was hot, and Parisians did not notice an undressed fat man in an apartment building high above the sidewalks.

"*L'Afrique?* Why not go home to America? You are a hero, no? You were a pilot. You were shot down. Now you have come to Paris to work with the Resistance."

White Dog chuckled. The French, he thought. They can rationalize anything.

"I don't think Uncle Sam's going to agree with you on that one, *mon cher.*"

"Ah, *merde.* Come, *Chien Blanc.* Sit with me."

He heard her pat the bed. She patted harder when he did not turn.

"Come."

White Dog pivoted from the window, sighing over to the edge of the mattress. He sat. The cheap springs tilted the whole bed. He scooted more to the center. She made room for him, taking some of the pillows and arranging them for him along the wall.

"*Chien Blanc.* Perhaps after so long in Paris, you still do not understand what you are doing for the French people. *Le marché noir* is . . . what is it in English, *salut?*"

"Salvation."

"*Oui,* salvation for the French. Thousands of men and women are fugitives from the Gestapo. They are Resistance, they are Jews, they are soldiers who are hiding. They have no identification *papiers,* no ration cards. How will they eat if not from the hands of the black market, eh? How will they survive the Occupation? The black market, it is resistance against the Boche because it is to live, eh?"

She waved an arm too thin for peacetime, only during war would a woman this beautiful be so starved. The spars of her ribs, where they came together at her sternum, showed pale ridges between her breasts. Her blond hair, which should have been golden and strawberry, had only the wan luster of poor nutrition and rare shampoo.

"And me? The rest of us? What do I do with this, eh?" She rolled over to the bedside table, grabbed her purse, and stabbed a lean hand into the mouth of it. She yanked out a tangle of francs and held it up like a magician disappointed with the skinny hare she'd pulled from a hat.

"I wipe my *derrière* with these! I cannot buy from the regular stores anything! The prices, you have seen them. They are skyrockets! The Boche have stolen all for themselves. In four years they have picked France clean as a bone. Shortages, shortages, I cannot buy vegetables, butter, beef, more than a hundred francs. Eggs, bread, *pff*! I must be a queen to have a breakfast if I buy from the Vichy stores."

She stuck the wad of bills under White Dog's nose.

"But I bring these to you, *Chien Blanc*. Then I can eat. Then I can thumb my nose at the Boche and their Vichy *ânes* and I can live until your Americans throw them out on their ears. Bastards."

She stuffed the bills back into the depths of her handbag.

"The black market is *patriotique*. Yes, you steal, but you steal from the Boche. You sell to the people. You sell to the Resistance. So you put the money in your pocket, what do I care? *Bon*, better you than the Boche. You are a hero, *Chien Blanc*. I will tell the Americans that."

White Dog lifted a knee and scratched between his legs. He knew he did not cut much of a heroic figure anymore. He gazed across the room, out the bright window. He imagined himself a hero. He'd throw up his arms to greet the first American tank. Hey, buddy buddy, where you been, you finally got here! I been here the whole stinkin' time, hidin' out. I'm a pilot, got shot down and stayed behind to work with the Resistance, making sure they got everything they needed. Helpin' the French people out. Oh, this? This gigantic stack of francs and Deutschmarks? Yeah, I'll be takin' these home with me. Can I get a lift? Here's some cigarettes.

Nope. I'm heading to Africa.

A year and a half in the shadows was enough. He was tired of shadows, no matter that he was making a score in the black market. There was nothing to spend it on here, no cars, no steaks, no luxury, just cigarettes, booze, women, and jazz.

His days in Paris were numbered. The GIs had landed in Normandy. Adolf wasn't going to stop them. White Dog looked forward to the Liberation, the chaos and opportunity of it.

Then Morocco, he thought. That's for me. Or Algiers. Sunlight, warm stucco, palm trees. Just hang on a little longer, until Uncle Sam gets here. A few months after that, a few lucky breaks, then I'm hightailing it.

White Dog let the bubble of home burst. America was not an option, it would have no open arms for him, just a court-martial as a deserter and a criminal—a prison cell and shame. It was better if he stayed dead, a crashed hero to America and a rich *bwana* to some Africans.

He let his eyes range beyond the window, between the lilting curtains, searching for something else, Paris's mood. Below the sill, the city rustled. Every automobile sound was a German staff car. Who else had fuel to drive, or papers to go anywhere if they could afford the gas? Paris had been jumpy for almost two weeks, since the Allied invasion. Everyone could sense the Yanks and Brits closing in, even though the armies were still bottled up in Normandy. Not for long. White Dog knew from the beginning that Germany couldn't hold the Allies back. He'd planned for it. It's why he decided to stay.

But Paris was more than the Krauts. Streaming just below the surface, jockeying for position, were the French Forces of the Interior—the *fifis*—and the Commies, the *Maquis*, the mob gangs, the folks with vendettas, collaborators biting their nails, Vichy on the brink of collapse, more black marketeers, and again the Krauts. The Krauts were crowding at the back door, ready to make a break. The two questions on everyone's mind were: First, would Hitler's famous and terrible habit for defending conquered ground turn Paris into a battlefield? Second, would the Krauts take off instead without a fight, and blow the City of Light to bits on their way out?

White Dog didn't care. He was positioned to win on every count. At the moment his trade was brisker than ever. The Reds, the *fifis*, the regular *Parisiens*, all of them swarmed to the black market before the big event, the Liberation, stockpiling everything they could afford. You name it and White Dog's network was swiping it and selling it, sometimes even back to the Krauts themselves. Guns and ammo, food, spare parts, batteries, real coffee, booze, tires—his crews jacked it all from train cars, warehouses, depots, Vichy shops. Whether the Germans fought for the city or they just blew it up and took a powder for the Rhine, White Dog would make a pile just as he said he would. He'd focus his operation on gasoline. A martyred Paris or a spared Paris, either would be a good market. This wasn't his city and these weren't his people, just a means to an end. He'd be lounging in Africa three months after the shooting stopped.

He leaned to kiss the girl on the shoulder. He pressed his lips to bone-stretched skin.

"*Cher.*"

"*Ce qui?*"

"You know the Americans are coming. Yes? You know things are going to be different."

"Yes, of course. We all wait for them. It will be wonderful. No?"

"For some. Maybe not for others."

She scooted away from him on the mattress, to face him square.

"What do you say?"

White Dog tried to lap his hand over hers but she yanked her fingers from beneath. Instead, he rubbed his chin.

"I'm saying, in the liberated towns up in Normandy there's already an *épuration sauvage.*"

"A purge? Why do I care if there is a purge? What have I done?"

"I don't know, I'm just sayin'. So's you know. I heard that in St. Saveur le Vicomte, as soon as the GIs took over, a bunch of women got their heads shaved for *collaboration horizontale.*"

She laughed. "That is a funny way to put it, *Chien Blanc.*"

"I'm not being funny, *cher.* Those women got off easy. In other towns, they're stripped and painted with tar swastikas. I hear a few have been kicked to death. What do you think is going to happen when the Allies hit Paris? I just want you to be careful, that's all. Stay out of the way."

She sat bolt upright, indignant.

"I have not laid a finger on the Boche. No one can say this!"

"I don't care, okay? Just, you know, just be careful. It's gonna hit everybody."

"*Oui,* it is. And good!" she said, smacking the mattress. "The Pétainists, the intellectuals, the fashionable people, writers, actors, maître d's, all those *lâches* who lined up on the side of the Germans, looking out for themselves. *Pfff!* Yes, the *épuration sauvage* is coming, and I will be in the front line of it. Watch me. I pray for the day."

White Dog raised his hands in defeat and let the topic go. He'd stepped on a nerve. But he'd spoken plainly; he didn't care. He made money, regardless of how things turned out. He bought hijacked goods, then sold them to anyone with francs or marks. That wasn't going to stop because Paris teetered on the verge of a revenge spree. Everyone with a grudge or a suspicion was going to grab scissors, paint, even guns, and take to the streets. The Communists in particular were going to draw blood, since Vichy made a practice of selecting Commie hostages for execution. The Reds, the *Maquis,* the righteous folk, they're going to remind the collaborators of their own sacrifices while they're shaving heads, smashing windows, testifying at show trials, and emptying their gullets of every pent-up hatred four years of jackboots had stomped into them.

White Dog was positioned perfectly. In the shadows at the heart of it all, waiting, planning, he'd worked every angle. The Germans knew he was an American, he'd been betrayed a dozen times over. But the Gestapo never stepped in to stop him because, quietly, he'd made himself invaluable, trading goods, services, and most importantly, information. The Krauts rewarded him with tolerance of his presence, some business, and they'd taken *Acier* off his hands for a fair price. Besides, the French black market played into the Krauts' hands: It demoralized the citizens, enflamed disgust with Vichy. The French were kept hungry, desperate, and pliable, eating from the black market trough. The *marché noir* fed them just enough and made them hate themselves for it, even as they groveled in the shadows.

And the Yanks? Who's kidding who here? The Americans weren't going to stop him. They were going to join him. Who would be greedier than a poor, dumb GI his first time in Par-ee?

White Dog had made all the right moves so far, timed everything to a tee.

"I'm going."

"Back to Montparnasse?"

"Got to keep moving, *cher*. It's what I do."

He slipped off the mattress to take his voluminous trousers off the back of a chair. He stepped into them, leaving the braces dangling, and searched for his socks.

"*Chien Blanc?*"

He found his socks and sat on the bed again to slide them on.

"*Oui?*"

"Why do you dress like a zazou?"

These were the children of the well-to-do, the young ones who showed their contempt for collaborationist Vichy by wearing zoot-suit clothes and indulging their love for all things *Americain,* like jazz and dancing—banned by Vichy—and "potluck parties." Because of the German curfew, zazou parties usually went all night.

"Do you miss America, *cher*? Is that why?"

"Don't worry about it."

"*Chien Blanc?*"

"What, *mon cher*?"

"Are we cowards? *Les Français?*"

White Dog drove his arms into his starched white shirt and tugged his braces over his shoulders.

"Are the French cowards? No, *cher,* you are not. Why do you want to ask me that?"

"Because," she said, gathering the sheet over her own nakedness now that he was dressing, "when the Americans come, will they think we did not fight the Boche?"

White Dog found the packet of sugar in his deep coat pocket. He set it on the bedside table.

"No, *cher*, they won't think that at all."

He stood beside the bed, buttoning his shirt.

"Lookit, you got your asses kicked by the Krauts, no question. But it wasn't a fair fight. It's taking the Americans, Great Britain, Canada, the Soviet Union, all of 'em together to beat the Krauts. You never stood a chance. That's not cowardice, doll. That's *reality*."

He patted her dull hair and turned the doorknob.

White Dog could have left her more francs. But he closed the door, leaving her only the sugar. The cash in his pocket, White Dog's own salvation—his reality—went with him.

D+15
JUNE 21

Rain pecked at the shed roof. Ben leaned back in an old cane chair. He watched the dive of drops out of dark and ancient joists. The drips splashed into puddles, the ground could no longer drink fast enough, so soaked was it from the three-day storm.

He sat at a salvaged rickety desk. Phineas had made this dairy farm shed his little office while the regiment was stalled by the weather. The desk stood in the only dry circle inside the shed, the rest of the floor had gone muddy from leaks. The air in here thickened with the musk of rust. Tillers and tines jumbled in the shadows, mule harnesses grown moldy hung on nails. A long-handled harvest scythe, its blade unstained, slanted against the wall, alone, odd and ominous.

Ben tilted the chair forward. He set his fingers to the keys of the Underwood typewriter Phineas had secured.

He typed. The military made available form letters for chaplains, but Ben would not use one. The parents of Lt. 2nd Class Lawrence Mendelsohn would receive this letter, and even before the officer who brought it was gone from their door, they would ask God why. They'd weep and soon know how their tears would dry and leave only salt. The letter would tear a hole in them the way a German sniper's bullet did their son. The somber father might carry it with him in a pocket or the mother in her purse, until they framed it or buried it in a trunk in an attic. They would never forget the moment they received this letter sent from Rabbi Ben Kahn and, writing it, he felt the slap of every keystroke, the blows of ink against paper.

> *. . . I was with your son when he passed. His death was quiet and dignified. He was struck down at the front of his company, leading his men with courage. He received comfort at the last and the blessings of God.*
>
> *Please receive the thanks of a grateful nation and a proud United States Army. The sacrifice you have made and the gallantry of your son Lawrence will never be forgotten. The cause for which he gave his life will never be forsaken.*
>
> *Your son has been buried in France at a location I cannot disclose. However, in due time, a permanent, national cemetery will be established here and your son's grave site will be one with full honor as an American and a hero of war.*
>
> *With respect and regrets, I remain . . .*

Ben spread the letter on the desk—Lawrence Mendelsohn's first, thin headstone—signed and folded it, then typed the family's address on an envelope. He left the unsealed letter on the desk for Phineas's assistant to post, later to be read in England by the censors. Then to the Mendelsohns.

From beside the typewriter, Ben lifted another sheet, the letter he carried always. He didn't need to read it; he knew every jot on it. He folded it along well-worn creases and slid the page into his breast pocket, buttoning the flap. Absentmindedly, he tapped it there. A covetous moment twisted in his heart, that the Mendelsohns should know the ending of their son—they will know it was brave and quick—and he did not know the end for his. This was the way of it always, selfish, wanting it over. Was Ben wishing for Thomas's death even while the boy was out there somewhere fighting to stay alive? Was Ben praying for his son's life even after God had taken it for His own? Unsettled, sad, an endless burning fuse, Ben balled his fist and tapped his chest.

Thunder, not artillery, boomed. Every rusting implement in the shed shivered.

* * *

Water coursed down the folds of Ben's poncho. His boot heels idled in puddles on the floorboard of the topless jeep. Drops bit his helmet so hard, he felt them strike. The windshield did little to keep the spray out of his eyes.

Behind the wheel, Phineas Allenby intoned, "How long, O Lord?"

Ben winced and raised his head to the leaden, pelting sky.

"Three days of this," Phineas called through the rain. "Back in Little Rock we'd be sitting on our roofs by now. This is one of y'all's plagues, isn't it?"

The Baptist chaplain laughed. Inside the tunnel of his poncho hood, Ben looked into the tempest and the grim, wet road. Fifty yards ahead, the blackout taillights of a Jimmy glimmed red through the downpour. The truck's tailgate was up, and Ben could not see its cargo, buttoned in white sheaths.

The little chaplain paused, made unsure by Ben's quiet.

"Anyway, how were things up in the 357th?" Phineas would not let the rain and the corpses dampen him.

Ben licked drops from his lips. "Same as everywhere else."

"Yeah, this storm's put a stop to everything. Ammo, food, fuel—everything's rationed, nothing's coming across the beaches in this weather."

The jeep swept along behind the Jimmy. Ben surveyed the gray-green fields turning to bogs.

Phineas kept talking, loud into the rain and the grinding jeep.

"It's no wonder the men are all upset. They're glad for the rest, but boy howdy, their pride's mighty wounded."

Ben had heard the talk in the regiments. Every officer and dogface knew the 90th was originally scheduled to be one of the divisions making the move up the peninsula, to roll up the Germans and attack Cherbourg. Now that mission was no more, not for the 90th. The hedgerows had cost them that shot. When the whole division got snarled in the bocage, the 82nd and the 9th leapfrogged them. Those two divisions drove west side by side all the way to the Atlantic, to the applause of the generals, cutting the Cotentin and claiming the laurels. That failure had lost the Tough Ombres their reputation and their commanding officer. It also cost them three thousand casualties and their self-esteem. Now the 90th was on babysitting duty, watching the backs of other divisions speeding north to capture the biggest plum in Normandy, Cherbourg's port. Add in the storm and the cutback on supplies, and the soldiers of the 90th had little to do but squat in foxholes, duck under canvas, bail with their helmets, and gripe.

Last night at dusk, near Le Ham, a Kraut battalion attacked the 357th. They'd come through the rain, hidden beneath the sluicing drops. The firefight lasted only an hour. The 357th held their ground. The Krauts backed off, looking for an easier way south out of the peninsula. Again, a 90th regiment paid and got nothing in return, no victory, no captives, just the ground they started with. They ended up swinging at shadows and rain sounds, after taking fifteen wounded and nine KIAs.

Ben tested his own gray mood. "I think it's letting up," he said.

Phineas took his hands from the wheel in mock holy thanks. "Thank you for that weather report, Rabbi Noah."

Ten more minutes passed. The jeep crossed a bridge above a swollen stream. Without expecting it, they rode through the ruins of another little town. Ben had missed the name sign at the limits. Just the one street curled through here, the village was no more than twenty buildings. Rain tumbled into every interior, not a roof was left intact. Elderly French men and women wandered with goats in the ruins.

Outside the town, the sign read Reigneville-Bocage. Ben had no idea where they were. Phineas drove with confidence, guiding the jeep behind the truck, dodging into a break in a fat hedgerow, bumping through a ditch, and into an apple orchard.

The truck and jeep labored across mud between the trees.

"You know," Phineas narrated under the rain, pleased to be knowledgeable, "Normandy's the only region in France where it's too cool to grow grapes. So the old Norman farmers planted apples here. Instead of wine, they made cider. They called it Calvados. The hedges were planted to keep the winds from the Channel off their apples."

Ben looked into the dripping branches of the apple orchard. It did not lift his heart the way it did for Phineas to consider a thousand years of peaceful fermenting done in these pastures and hedges. Ben saw only rain and, through its curtain, the truck filled with corpses stop beside four soldiers in ponchos leaning on shovels.

Phineas halted alongside the truck. When the vehicles shut down their motors, with Phineas quiet, the hiss of rain was everywhere. The little Baptist jumped from the jeep to take control, and Ben kept his seat, hammered in place under the driving drops and by how trying it was to bury more children. He felt as ancient as the orchard, rutted and sunken as the Norman roads. No one here, not Phineas or the boys with shovels or the dead boys in their shrouds in the truck, was more than half his age. Again, and unbidden, Ben struggled to stay out of the trenches of the other war, when he was that young and there was rain and French mud and there were bodies and shallow graves. He grappled, too, as he had hours ago beside the Underwood typewriter, with the wish that one of these bodies would finally be Captain Thomas Kahn.

The hole was a broad rectangle, enough for all ten corpses. It had been sloppily dug in the rain and was only three feet deep. On a sunny day, this place had been chosen as the division's cemetery because it was in an orchard, a beautiful spot. This was not a final resting ground, just a temporary grave until the doughs could be moved later to a permanent cemetery in Normandy. White stakes throughout the sodden orchard marked hundreds more resting places for the Tough Ombres.

Three soldiers of the Graves Registration detail moved to the tailgate of the truck. The fourth dipped a barrel into the brown pool at the bottom of the hole, then spilled it out. Both Jimmy drivers, colored boys without ponchos, scrambled down into the rain to help unload the wrapped bodies, not their job. They grew soaked in an instant. Ben stood beside the hole, watching as the soldier bailed and the rain filled the grave at almost equal rates. Phineas came beside him with an armful of hastily nailed-together crosses, and one Star of David. He handed Ben the star. Ben held it by the post, like a scepter. Phineas had built them of lathe sticks pulled from some wrecked French building.

The bodies were hefted from the truck bed without reverence, the rain seemed to make for urgency. Each was carried over to the hole, gripped by shoulders and feet inside the white mattress covers. The bodies were lowered all but the last few inches, then dropped. They splashed in the murk at the bottom, smirching the pristine sacks.

Phineas had marked each cover with the soldier's serial number, for later when they would be dug up and transferred. Over each, he had scribed in black ink a cross, except on Lieutenant Mendelsohn.

The Jewish soldier was laid in the center of the row of white sacks in the hole, not by design but just where he fell. Mendelsohn had lain unburied for three days; this was unacceptable in Judaism, the law commands the dead be interred as soon as possible. But with the rain, and Ben the only rabbi in the division, three days had to do. Mendelsohn was laid to rest with brothers, shoulder to shoulder. Ben hoped this would count for something with God, and he swore to do better.

Phineas pressed a lathe cross into the damp ground at the head of the first soldier.

"We therefore commit this body to the ground. Ashes to ashes, dust to dust."

Ben knelt and drove the post bearing the star into the orchard, the first Jew he'd buried in France. It should not have mattered so much that this was a Jew. This was a boy, a man, a soldier, a son, like any other, he told himself, but he longed to stay with this fallen son, to linger until the sun came out and hearts had healed and war was done. Phineas came and laid a hand across the poncho on Ben's back. This brought Ben out of the star and to his feet again, back to the rain.

"No. Leave me alone. I'm eating."

McGee Mays tugged on Joe Amos's sleeve.

"C'mon, please. I told 'em you'd do it."

Joe Amos glanced across the crowded mess tent to the table McGee had left. Seven drivers leaned in their faces at Joe Amos and smiled as if he held a camera. They were all young and new privates, like McGee.

"C'mon, man. I'll drive an extra shift."

Joe Amos looked at his chipped beef and bread, his corn hash, and saw it would all cool into paste by the time he got back to it.

Three days, Joe Amos thought, and not one damn run in this weather. All the trucks stopped, nothing to move. Man, the troops have got to be starving for everything by now. Joe Amos wanted to get back behind the wheel, do his job, and quit talking about his shot-up truck.

The drivers slid aside to make room.

"Fellas."

"Corporal Biggs."

"So what'd McGee here tell you so far?"

One private, small and thin with gold caps on his front teeth, spoke first.

"How you two drove right up to the fightin' in the hedges. Took them soldiers all they ammo. And you was up in the fifty cal."

Joe Amos heard the rural slur in this soldier's speech. He sighed, thinking this colored boy probably had only a few years of country education between his ears. He had no business being in the military. This was the joke, that to be taken into the U.S. Army all you had to be able to do was see lightning and hear thunder.

"What's your name, Private?"

The skinny boy swallowed. "Charlie."

Odds were that Charlie here was living the highlights of his life right now in France. He might never again have this kind of responsibility or stage. But just in case Charlie wanted more, in case he was made of better stuff than some others when the shit hit the fan and wanted to show it, he wouldn't get much of a chance in this war, just the way Boogie warned. That was the big difference between the war the whites fought and the one set aside for McGee and the others at this table. Joe Amos was different, he'd had a streak of luck come out of the sky. But no one can count on that. So, Joe Amos figured, after Charlie here goes home to the life that's been set aside for him there, too, let him say he knew some heroes, some black heroes.

"Alright," Joe Amos began.

The boys wriggled their fannies on the benches.

"McGee and I were riding back from a run up north to the 79th." Joe Amos set his elbows on the table. "About a mile outside Valognes, we came up behind a convoy. McGee was driving. I was up in the bed with the fifty cal."

"I want to hear this, too. Keep your seats, gentlemen."

Major Clay and Lieutenant Garner stepped forward. The boys at the table shot upright and stiff at the officers' arrival. The whole mess tent quieted. The tattoo of rain on the canvas echoed off metal trays and plates.

"Relax, fellas," Major Clay said, "I haven't had a chance to hear this adventure from Corporal Joe himself. Joe Amos, go on. Let's hear what happened."

Major Clay set his rump on the edge of the table. Lieutenant Garner stuck his hands behind his waist, in parade rest. Joe Amos flicked a glance around the hushed tent, full of drivers and cooks, and now these two white officers. Major Clay announced, "Get back to your mess, everyone. Thank you."

The white officer opened his hand to Joe Amos. The gesture said: There, all taken care of. Now, proceed.

Joe Amos nodded. Moments before, the clamor of colored soldiers eating and cajoling, passing the rainy, useless time, was familiar and homey, a little raucous. Now the mood was stilted. Major Clay waited.

"Yes, sir." Joe Amos faced the boys at the table. He reckoned there were over a hundred in the mess tent, all from his battalion. Maybe it would do them good, too, like Charlie, to hear a brave tale from one of their own. Anyway, Major Clay had said he was expecting big things from Corporal Joe. What the hell.

"Okay," Joe Amos said, out loud but to himself, agreeing.

He told the story.

After pulling up behind the convoy outside Valognes, with McGee driving fast and Joe Amos at the machine gun, a huge convoy passed, heading west into the peninsula. Suddenly, a Messerschmitt knifed in tight over the bocage, barreling straight at the big convoy from behind.

"He strafed the trucks good on his first pass." Joe Amos used a flattened hand to illustrate the German fighter's initial swoop over the trucks, sweeping low over the salt and pepper shakers on the table.

"A bunch of them caught fire. The whole convoy stopped dead in the road. I didn't even have time to think about taking a shot, he was gone like *that*."

Joe Amos snapped his fingers. Major Clay folded his arms and nodded approval. So did the rest of the mess tent. Joe Amos had never been given this kind of attention. Not back in Danville, with four loud sisters, not ever in the Army beside blustery Boogie all the way from training camp. Joe Amos waited for something inside him to wilt, to stutter, dig a hole. Instead, he was jazzed.

He lifted his hand from the table and curved it, mimicking the German fighter.

"Then he came back."

He put both hands in front of him, making fists on the invisible machine-gun grips. He lowered his head, he saw the Kraut coming, hot and mean over the trees.

"McGee jumped out and dove for the ditch."

McGee thrust an arm at Joe Amos. "He *told* me to!"

Every driver at the table and many in the tent laughed. Joe Amos glanced up at Major Clay and Garner. Both officers grinned.

Joe Amos hunkered again behind the pretend .50 cal. He took aim on the streaming Messerschmitt. The Kraut's cannons and machine guns lit up. Bits of road and metal popped like corks going off.

"Next thing I know we're squaring off, me and this Kraut, both of us got our guns going. Pieces of everything were jumping around me, I could feel the truck getting hit and I just kept my finger on the trigger and him in front of me."

"You were shoutin'!" McGee Mays piped up. Joe Amos's partner cast a wild and happy gaze around the table. "He was shoutin', I could hear him."

Joe Amos shook his head. "All I remember is watching him go by, *wham!* and he was gone. Right over my head." Joe Amos took one hand off the imaginary grips and skipped it away, flashing like the fighter plane. "I spun the fifty cal around to keep after him."

"Yes, indeed," McGee concluded, reverent, churchly, "shot him down."

Joe Amos lifted an eyebrow at his young partner. The boy was suddenly full of talk.

"Yeah, well, he was trailing smoke. Some other drivers shot at him, too. I reckon we all took a piece out of him. Anyway, he was flying so low he hit the treetops."

With both hands Joe Amos made a rising fireball, then held them out, empty.

"And that was it."

The boys at the table looked to each other. Charlie glared straight at Joe Amos, the boy's narrowed gaze spoke of how much he coveted Joe Amos's story, he wanted to do this. Joe Amos gave the thin boy his own private nod, telling him to go get him a Kraut plane, too.

"I saw your truck." Major Clay spoke into the whispering approval in the mess tent. "It's pretty chewed up."

"Yes, sir. I'd like to keep it, if you don't mind, Major. She still runs good. The Kraut didn't hit anything important."

Major Clay rose from his perch on the edge of the table. He laid a hand on Joe Amos's shoulder.

"No, he didn't. Lieutenant?"

Garner strode forward. "Gentlemen, if you don't mind, the Major and I would like the table alone with Corporal Joe."

McGee and the others rose and left. Major Clay moved to sit on the bench opposite Joe Amos, Garner sat beside the Major.

"You shot down a Messerschmitt," Major Clay said.

Joe Amos waited to respond, sniffing for the Major's intent. "I might have, sir."

"Oh, you did. The report I got from the CO of the other convoy said you bagged the sumbitch. Stood right under his guns and let him have it."

"Yes, sir."

"So, Joe Amos. I know I told you I expected big things from you, but you've kind of moved a little fast for me."

Joe Amos made no answer. He saw where this was going and tightened his lips.

"Lieutenant, we've got ourselves a bona fide hero in the 668th," Major Clay said.

Garner nodded agreement. "Yes, sir. Bona fide."

"Now what are we going to do with you?" Major Clay never took his eyes away, as if Joe Amos were a new and thorny thing. "What am I going to do with a hero in a colored truck battalion?"

Major Clay untwined his fingers. He lifted one and waggled it at Joe Amos. He issued a small and ironic laugh through his gappy teeth.

"I'll tell you the truth, son. I don't have any real use for one, if you get my drift."

"Yes, sir."

"Alright. Just so's you know. You did a hell of a thing out there. You know it and I know it. But for right now that's got to be good enough. The Army don't need more combat soldiers. What it needs is for you and the rest of these boys to drive them trucks and keep doing your jobs. And, well, it would be a help . . ." Major Clay paused, selecting different words. "It would be better all around if you didn't stir up any hornets' nests."

The urge to tell the Major to kiss his ass was fleet and gone, faster than the Messerschmitt, and it crashed, too. Joe Amos was not raised in Danville to make trouble, he was not Boogie John Bailey. Joe Amos didn't need a medal, and he didn't need slaps on the back. He only wanted folks to know what he and the men of his color could do. That wouldn't happen because of a few explosive seconds in the back of a truck bed, and it wouldn't happen in a year or over the course of this war. Joe Amos knew what he'd done, so did the coloreds in this mess tent and the black hands in that convoy. And the Major said he knew, too.

"Yes, sir."

Major Clay clapped his hands softly and rubbed them, satisfied.

"Lieutenant?"

From his pocket, Garner gave Major Clay a cloth patch, another stripe. Major Clay handed it across the table to Joe Amos.

"Here you go, Sergeant. Congratulations."

Before Joe Amos could speak or react, Major Clay stood. He raised his voice to the whole tent.

"Everyone finish your mess. Then come outside and saddle up. Follow me. I want to show you something."

Rain dripped in the shot-out rear window. Three holes in the cloth of the cab roof had been plugged with strips of towel. A puncture thick as a thumb gaped in the metal dash. In the empty truck bed, the track of the German machine gun could be followed like connect-the-dots, walking right up to and past where Joe Amos had stood at the .50 cal.

Joe Amos drove in line with his whole company, one hundred and eighty trucks. McGee sat on the bench across from him, staring in awe at the third stripe he held in his hand. The convoy crept along, with none of the breakneck speed the colored drivers poured on when they were alone or in smaller units. This time Major Clay and Lieutenant Garner rode at the head of the column, heading back toward OMAHA. The ride was long and muggy. Joe Amos's wipers worked hard to keep in sight the road and the taillights through the smearing day. "Cut it out," Joe Amos told McGee.

"You movin' up right fast, Sarge."

"Yeah. Well."

Joe Amos had nothing to say. Major Clay had told him pretty straight to cool it, make no big deal out of shooting down the Kraut. Joe Amos figured it was alright to be an inspiration, just not a distraction. Besides, Joe Amos knew he ought to be dead. The bullet holes in the truck were testimony to how much luck he'd used up facing the Jabo. Telling the story to admiring faces, even to Garner and Clay, he forgot the danger. He wasn't reliving the moments, just playacting them. But every time he sat in the perforated truck and saw the punches in the metal, he felt a foreboding, like dew before a hot day.

McGee pulled his eyes off Joe Amos and faced the windshield. Joe Amos pushed the Jimmy along in third gear. No other convoys rumbled at them from the direction of the beaches. The battalion had the road to themselves.

"I'm from Chattahoochee," McGee volunteered. "Two *A*'s, two *T*'s, two *O*'s, two *E*'s, three *H*'s, two *C*'s."

Joe Amos had asked this question three days ago, the name of

McGee's little town in Florida. Now Joe Amos was a hero and a sergeant—one stripe more than Boogie ever had—and McGee was spelling the answer for him with a school rhyme.

"Whereabouts is it?"

"On the Georgia line. Near the Apalachicola River."

"Fishin's good?"

McGee's smile bore recollection, of ease and heat, stringers and guts and panfrying, water snakes chased off by paddles and pebbles. Joe Amos had a river back home, too, the Dan River. There were bream and bass in the current, and copperheads in the weeds.

McGee stared into the rain. "Yeah. I'm goin' back there minute this war is over. Gonna drop a line and sleep. See my girl."

"You got a girl?"

"Little girl. My daughter. She almost two."

Joe Amos smiled for McGee. Here was a young colored man drafted away from his child and river and plunked in a war. Here was a quiet fellow, an admiring sort, a nimble driver, a physically strong man, a follower, a hero in his own way. This is the man Major Clay wants a whole corps of.

Joe Amos asked no more. He resorted to what Boogie always did when silence seemed the best tack. He punched McGee in the shoulder and looked him in the eye, then did what Major Clay required. He drove for the U.S. Army.

The pastures and hedges thinned, and the beaches neared. A lone passel of trucks came down the road and spurred past, headed west into the bocage. Man, Joe Amos thought, there is nothing coming off OMAHA. No road crew repaired potholes and bomb damage, no MPs waved traffic along, checking speed, no recently landed soldiers tramped beside the highway, tossing off equipment. The rain and lowering sky had clamped everything shut.

The long convoy wended the familiar route into D-1 draw. Joe Amos downshifted to drive over the sand in the gulley, packed hard and brown by tractors and constant wheels. Charred German pillboxes remained sentinels here. Joe Amos looked up the bluffs and imagined again the fury of D-Day. McGee stayed quiet.

At the mouth of the draw, the column dispersed. Lieutenant Garner stood there directing traffic. Joe Amos crept up, riding close behind the canvas tarp of the Jimmy in front. That truck pulled right. Joe Amos reached Garner and the first sands of the beach. Garner motioned Joe

Amos to follow to the right. He turned the wheel and emerged from behind the high slopes of the draw.

His mouth went slack.

As far as his eyes could pierce the rain, stretching miles east, OMAHA was a junk pile of wreckage. Joe Amos almost slammed on the brake by instinct to stop and gander at the incredibleness of the damage wreaked by the storm. The Jimmy behind him beeped; Joe Amos pushed over the rain-sopped sand to park in line with his company and battalion ogling the ruined, tangled remains of the artificial Mulberry harbor and hundreds of vessels.

Whitecaps on the Channel slapped at the hulks of battered landing craft. Every kind of ship had been driven like spikes into the ribs and faces of every other craft strewn across OMAHA. LCTs tossed in the surf, snapped at the spars where the blunt prows of huge LSTs had crunched through. Rhino barges lay sunken, waves ransacked across their cargo flats. A coast guard cutter wedged itself into a nest of LCMs and wound up with its smaller sisters sideways on the beach, all of them alien and appalling out of the water.

Mangled and mingled with the boats were giant bits of the ruined Mulberry harbor. Concrete pontoons larger than some vessels batted the gunwales of downed craft with every pulse of the waves. Steel piers twisted like ribbons. Massive floating pieces, recognizable or not, rammed and rolled until they found enough of a crevice through the jumbled vessels to stumble up on the beach. Only the sunken blockships offshore seemed to have kept their places, and half of them were broken-backed.

Joe Amos jumped down into the rain, McGee with him. Three hundred and fifty drivers gaped at the carnage. A dozen bulldozers and tow trucks plied bravely at the bedlam, breaking embraces and pulling wrecks aside to keep paths to the beach exits clear. Soggy soldiers scrambled into the holds of rocking wrecks to salvage what cargo they held, loading crates into a trickle of trucks to speed them off the beach. Joe Amos almost tripped in the sand, aghast at the chaos on OMAHA.

Major Clay stood in the rain, looking at the busted dream of the Army's artificial harbor.

"What's this mean?" McGee asked, moving closer to the Major in the ring of stunned drivers. "What's gonna happen?"

Joe Amos shushed the boy.

Major Clay raised a hand for quiet. Behind the officer, the groans of pierced boats ground like broken bones. Bulldozers spit diesel smoke and struggled. The rain pounded.

"As you can see, gentlemen, this is one great big goddam FUBAR!"

The drivers nodded and dug boot heels into the sand.

"Not even the Krauts could do what Mother Nature's done here. She's fucked up our harbor and fucked up our plans."

Major Clay turned away to take in the Channel for another moment, as if drawing power from the churning water to help him choose words that might equal it.

He turned back to the semicircle of dripping, sober faces.

"You men! This is what happened here. The U.S. Army's Mulberry is gone. We no longer have a goddam pier to load our trucks directly from the ships! And from the looks of this mess we also have a hell of a lot fewer ships! So. That means we are going to continue, for the foreseeable future until Ike comes up with a better idea, to pick up every goddam thing the whole goddam army needs to fight this war right here off the sand like we've been doing!"

Joe Amos rubbed a hand over his brow. This was rotten news. The Mulberry harbor was designed to allow trucks to drive right out to the ships tied up to the pierheads, take their loads from cranes straight from the holds, then drive across the piers to the beach and on to the troops. Easy peasy. Fast and efficient. Now, the slowest and most backbreaking way to move cargo, the way they'd been doing it—ferrying supplies from ship to beach, unloading it, then loading it again into the beds of trucks—was going to stay SOP. His heart sank into the moan of the wind and the bashing of ships.

Major Clay lifted his hand again.

"Here's the good news. Mother Nature had you boys in mind when she pulled this stunt. You soldiers and your trucks just became a whole lot more important to the United States Army than they ever imagined you would be. We're gonna be going twenty-four seven as soon as this damn storm stops. For how long, I can't tell. You got any questions, don't ask 'em! At this point you know everything I know."

Major Clay broke off and stalked to his covered jeep, Garner at his heels. Most drivers filtered back to their cabs. McGee walked off. Joe Amos spit rainwater off his lips.

He fingered in his pocket for the new cloth stripe.

D+25

Cigarette smoke roiled against the ceiling, branding the room a jittery place. Ben Kahn was one of the few gathered officers who did not breathe the tension through burning tobacco.

At the head of the room, General Billups patted the regiment's CO on the arm, completing some private brief before addressing the seated officers of the 359th. The Colonel sat, leaving Billups standing alone. Ben cast his eyes around the room, a nursery for the damaged church in Beuzeville La Bastille. No more than a dozen of the thirty-five officers were faces he had seen the last time he was with the 359th just ten days ago.

Billups strode in front of an easel bearing a six-foot-high map. He lifted a long pointer from a table and clapped it against his boot.

"Gentlemen. Good afternoon. Before we begin, I'd like to recognize Chaplain Kahn here." With the pointer, Billups accused Ben of being that chaplain.

"The rabbi here is a veteran of the 90th from the Great War. He was at the Argonne and St. Mihiel. He has returned to the fight and for that we are grateful. I'd like the chaplain to offer a prayer for our victory in this great war, as well."

Ben, not expecting this, rose. Officers doffed their helmets and lowered their heads. Before he spoke, he gazed at the map; there lay the scribbled futures for thousands of lives. The smoke stung his eyes. He closed them to pray. In two days, when the attack drawn on that map begins, these young officers would have the powers of life and death. Most of these lieutenants and captains and majors were new, the hedgerows chopped down so many before them. The assault may be their first time in combat. The 90th had seen enough of questionable leadership. Ben beseeched this group.

"God. You have brought us all here for a mighty purpose. You have shown us the place for victory. You have given us the tools. And You have given us the strength. We ask now that You give us, too, the will. Let us not shirk from victory. Let us not turn from our mission. Let our courage be Your hand in the fight against darkness in the world. Be with us in life, as we will surely be with You in death. For this we pray. Amen."

Ben raised his own head, then sat. Heads bobbed. General Billups made an intense and pinched face at Ben, pleased.

"Everybody got that?" Billups asked the room. "God wants no screwing up. My apologies, Rabbi."

Ben inclined his head.

Billups moved beside the oversized map. The room settled quickly, as nervous men will, taking good hold of themselves.

The General tapped his pointer to the center, over a series of black X's.

"How many of you have ever heard of the Mahlman Line? No one? Me neither, not till yesterday. Patrols have told us that this is the meat of the German's resistance on the whole Norman peninsula."

He slid the pointer over a series of wobbly concentric circles, the topographic symbol for high ground.

"This is Mont Castre. Hill 122. It stands right in the middle of the Cotentin, halfway between Carentan here . . ." a smack on the east, ". . . and La Haye-du-Puits," another to the west.

"Mont Castre is the commanding terrain feature of the entire Norman peninsula. From up here, the Krauts have a good look at every damn thing we do."

Billups laid the pointer just to the east of the hill, to a round spot of small, wavy lines.

"Right here is a giant bog called 'the Prairies.' The combination of this swamp and the German presence on Hill 122 has blocked all military traffic down the center of the Cotentin. On the western edge of the swamp is the town of Beau Coudray. The Boche have concentrated their arms and men on a salient stretching from the west coast of the Cotentin, anchoring its center on top of Mont Castre, down the eastern slope, to the edge of the swamp and the town of Beau Coudray. This is the Mahlman Line."

Billups swung the pointer to the hazy room, indicating the officers.

"Gentlemen. The Tough Ombres are going to chew the Mahlman Line up and spit it out. That is our assignment, and like the rabbi says, we are not going to shirk."

Billups went to parade rest in front of the officers. The long pointer wagged in his hands.

"I guess you all know the last resistance in Cherbourg fell two days ago. The Krauts lost four divisions in that battle, and more than twenty-five thousand were captured. The Germans repaid Uncle Sam for our efforts by destroying the entire port. Every damn thing they could blow up, they did. Piers, cranes, bridges, power stations—everything has been dynamited or burned. The harbor is strewn with scuttled ships and mines. It's going to take weeks if not months to sort that mess out and get supplies flowing out of there. Nonetheless, it was a splendid victory. Many of you in this room know that it should have been a victory for the 90th as well, but it wasn't. We've been left down here to guard the line across the peninsula, picking our way across the hedgerows a field at a time. This has been a lousy duty, no question about it. But now the Tough Ombres are being given another shot at the brass ring, gentlemen. We are being hurled against the hard center of the German force on the Cotentin."

Billups wheeled to slap the pointer flat across the map. The report was like a pistol shot, the first round fired in the fight for the center. The officers jerked in their seats.

"The Krauts are up on their hill watching the 90th. Eisenhower, Bradley, Montgomery, the rest of the big shots, they got their eye on us, too. I swear by God, gentlemen, we are going to put on a show for all them sons of bitches watching the Tough Ombres."

Ben observed the effect of this talk on the officers. They were not moved by this sort of cheerleading. Billups cast a glare over the men. He took a breath and pursed his lips.

"Alright. Now that COM Z has cleaned up the beaches after that damn storm two weeks ago, and with Cherbourg finally under wraps, we're back to full supplies and ammo. And more good news. We're getting some help for this operation. We're gonna get twelve extra battalions of field artillery. We're also getting the 712th Tank Battalion attached to the 90th. That's a lot of guns, and it tells us this is going to be a tough one. But this time we're going in with firepower, boys."

These statements hit home. The 90th had been overmatched slogging through the hedges. Heading into the forest on Mont Castre without big guns would have been suicidal. The mission looked difficult enough even with the extra cannons.

Billups spent the next fifteen minutes explaining the strategy and alignments for the assault. Pointing to the tall map, he located each regiment of the 90th and presented their objectives. At dawn on July 3, the 358th would commit on the left through St. Jores, the 359th on the right through Prétot, and the 357th would stay in reserve to pass through the 358th and seize Beau Coudray plus the high ground to the south. On the far right, the 82nd Airborne and the 79th Infantry, back from Cherbourg, would attack south against the Mahlman Line's coastal defenses. But the showpiece of the operation—the forest on top of Mont Castre—belonged to the 358th.

". . . and to you," Billups concluded, "the 359th."

Billups stabbed the tip of the pointer to the floor and stood behind it square and firm. Ben thought the General might have made a fine preacher, the brimstone kind.

"Any comments, gentlemen? Excellent. We jump off in two days, at dawn. Get your men supplied and in position. And one last thing. Save some of those cigarettes for your boys. They'll need them. At some point it might be all you can do for them. Good luck. Dismissed!"

Ben stood with the officers. At the General's word, they pocketed their cigarette packs, stubbing the last of their butts. Ben began to file out with them.

"Chaplain," Billups called over the shuffling of chairs.

Ben turned. Billups came beside him in the emptying room.

"That was a good prayer, Rabbi. Thank you. The men got your message."

"With a little nudge from you, General."

"I'm not a subtle man."

"How's the new CO working out?"

"I'm going to answer that by asking you a question in return. How's the 90th look to you, Rabbi?"

"Still pretty scared. Laying back. The men are hesitant under fire."

With a nod, Billups took up this theme.

"That puts extra pressure on my officers to get them to fight. The result is the officers get exposed to more danger. More danger means more casualties, and I wind up with a room full of officers I've never seen before. And the cycle just keeps spinning. Fresh officers means no experience, and that means more hesitation. And away she goes."

"And the new CO?"

"Short. Dumpy. Uninspiring. Does all his commanding from an armchair in a cellar. He's gloomy and distrustful. Just what we need, a Chicken Little running the Tough Ombres."

Billups sighed heavily and stared at his boots. He sucked his teeth in disgust, then perked and patted Ben on the elbow.

"I'll give you a ride back to the aid station, Padre. We can talk in the jeep."

"Thank you, General. But I'm figuring on staying up here with the 359th."

Billups cocked his head. "You heard what I told those men. You saw that map."

"Yes, sir."

"What I didn't tell them was that a platoon of the 358th made a probing attack this morning, south toward Les Sablons. They got their fannies whipped pretty good. Rabbi, the Krauts are ready and they are thick as thieves on this Mahlman Line of theirs. This is not going to be pretty. You're an old soldier, you know what's ahead for these troopers. I've got to ask you to come back to the aid station. You'll be needed there."

Ben hefted his backpack up to his shoulder. The gesture was meant to tell the General he intended to walk, not ride, from this meeting.

"General, you're a *mentsh*. I appreciate your concern. But I've already spent too much time at aid stations and graves. For the two weeks I've been with the infantry, the 90th has been sitting still in the hedges. Now we're moving again and I think I know where I'm needed most, sir. These men are heading into battle. Their morale is in the latrine, you've said so yourself. But like you said tonight, this is a second chance for the whole division. Let me stay on the front lines, sir. I can help a man in a foxhole keep fighting, but I can't get a wounded soldier off a stretcher. And we need fighters, General."

For a moment, Billups considered Ben. The smoke in the room bled out the open door, clearing the air. The General dug in his pocket for a new pack of cigarettes. He opened the seal, shook a spike onto his lips, and flipped his Zippo lighter. He fired the smoke and blew a white tuft between them.

The General reached for Ben's breast pocket where the letter lived. He unbuttoned the flap and shoved the full pack in.

"For the boys, Rabbi. In case you need 'em."

D+27
JULY 3

"Hey. Hey, Sarge."

Even in the dark, lit only by the scarlet of the cat's eyes ahead, Joe Amos noted how bleary-eyed McGee was. Joe Amos sat up from his slouch on the cab bench.

"What time is it?"

"I dunno."

Joe Amos felt better and stiffer than he ought after just two hours of sleep. Had McGee driven more than his shift? Joe Amos let it go with an appreciative nod. He rubbed knuckles into his sockets and yawned.

"Where are we?"

"Dunno. In line. South somewheres, heading toward Couvains. We're crawlin'."

"Alright. You need me to take over?"

"Yes, I do."

Joe Amos began the slide left, McGee was lithe and out of the driver's spot in a flick. The truck had no one at the wheel for a moment but she ran straight. Joe Amos grabbed hold and settled in. McGee laid his head on his joined hands like a child and stilled.

The Jimmy rolled along in third gear, at twenty miles per hour. The column tonight was long, his whole company of one hundred twenty trucks hauled supplies to the 2nd Infantry driving south for St. Lô. Joe Amos didn't even know what was in the bed of his Jimmy for this run, he'd dozed while it was loaded at OMAHA around midnight with McGee at the wheel. The feel of the truck told him the load was light, probably food or more new uniforms to replace the chemical suits. Countryside slipped past his windows black and slow as pitch. Not enough light spilled from the convoy to offer any clue where he was, nothing in the terrain gave a hint, just hedges and barns, falling away to dark fields without feature.

After five minutes of McGee's deep breathing, the convoy approached a right turn. Soon after, the road crossed the Elle River on a one-lane bridge that had been propped and strengthened by Army engineers. Joe Amos recognized the road south to Couvains.

On the far side of the bridge, the convoy slowed, then stopped. Joe Amos gave the wheel a frustrated tap. He idled for minutes, inhaling the fumes from under the cat's eyes and bumper close ahead. The load in the forward Jimmy was labeled as ration crates. Joe Amos figured that was what he likely carried, too, though it made no difference at all what rode in the bed of his truck after ten straight days of twenty-hour shifts, loading and hauling and unloading. Not even the booms of artillery or rifle crackles at the ASPs close to the front shook him or McGee anymore. The drivers were tired and dumb from work under sun and stars and, according to Lieutenant Garner, more rain than France had seen in a century. Joe Amos no longer bragged about the holes in his Jimmy. Everyone knew how he got them and no one had the energy anymore to comment or pat him on the back. The Messerschmitt seemed years ago. Joe Amos hadn't even stood behind the .50 cal in a week.

The column inched south, never fast enough to leave third gear. After a long half hour of crickets, clutching, and more inky Normandy, Joe Amos reached a crossroads. There stood an MP with a lantern, directing traffic in white gloves, wearing big letters on his helmet and sleeve. The traffic cop flaunted white-handed movements, cocksure and almost clownish, busily blending the 668th convoy with other columns of military vehicles out of the east.

Before Joe Amos reached the intersection, the MP waved through a short column of trucks towing anti-aircraft batteries. This was followed by a dozen flatbeds hauling bridgework. Joe Amos's company was made to idle while the MP waved the bridgers through the intersection.

The first 668th driver held at bay by the MP's white-gloved palm took exception and gunned into the crossroads. The MP tweeted his whistle and waggled the Jimmy to stop and back out, gesturing the engineers' truck through. The Jimmy driver refused to budge. The tractor drivers jumped out of their cab, the black Jimmy drivers did the same, and by lantern light the MP separated them before a few shoves could turn into fists. Joe Amos listened to the threats from all parties, from kicked butts and whupped asses to arrest and the stockade. No one said anything about anyone's color. That was good because it let Joe Amos sit back and enjoy the early-morning show.

Once the Jimmy pulled aside, the engineers ran through the intersection, every truck of them flipping the bird. Finally, Joe Amos was motioned ahead. McGee did not stir.

Joe Amos forged into the night, not refreshed but awake. Dawn circled, hours distant. He laid his head out the window to dash some cool breeze over his face. More potholes jarred his driving. Twice the convoy diverted off the road into a flattened path through a field because a crater in the pavement remained unfilled. The roads of Normandy were wilting under the constant pounding of American wheels. Lieutenant Garner had said the bridgehead now held over seventy thousand vehicles, most of them trucks; this giant figure was still forty thousand short of target because of the storm and the destruction at Cherbourg. Every day, Joe Amos witnessed examples of how crowded the U.S. force was in the bridgehead, the ruination of the roads, traffic jams, accidents, even fistfights at intersections like the one back there. The word was that seventeen hundred vehicles per hour traveled the road Joe Amos drove now.

The expansion of the bridgehead had been torturously slow. The hedgerows, the seasoned German fighters dug in there, the inexperience of the GIs, all added up to an American slice of France that grew no more than a thousand yards on a good day, and just one hedge or orchard on a typical and costly day.

More and more men, weapons, and vehicles poured over the beaches. Cherbourg would come online in another month, and the flow would increase, with little extra space to deploy everything. Something, somewhere, had to pop.

The thing that did pop a minute later was the universal joint in the rear of Joe Amos's deuce-and-a-half. He cursed it the second he heard the wrench of cogs in the Jimmy's belly. A wretched grinding scraped the slow night calm. Joe Amos looked in his rearview, saw sparks flying under his chassis. The drive shaft had cut loose from the rear end and dragged, spinning over the pavement. The rear wheels of the truck were now severed from the engine. The Jimmy coasted in a noisy shower of sparks. McGee sat up only when Joe Amos poked him. He braked to the shoulder.

"Universal's gone," he said to a blinking McGee.

"Dawg."

Joe Amos clambered out. The Jimmy behind followed him to the shoulder. The little light from the one white cat's eye in front glowed enough to see the drive shaft hanging dead. The smell of hot, ground metal stank up the country air. The rest of the platoon powered by; one downed truck would not stop them.

The driver of the following Jimmy, a black Latino from LA named Morales, ambled beside Joe Amos. McGee was already on his back under the truck, prodding.

"Universal," Morales said. "*Chingar.*"

Joe Amos stuck his hands on his hips. He kicked a tire.

"Man, this is what happens. They make us drive till we're cross-eyed, then there's no time to keep the damn things maintained. Truck's as tired as we are."

"Lube, man." Morales nudged McGee's boot protruding from under the Jimmy. "No lube, right?"

"Yep," grunted McGee. "Dry as Grandpa's pecker."

"See?" The truck Joe Amos had ignored the past week in his fervor to drive and deliver was again turned precious, reminding him how the holes in the cab and bed were his proof and medallions.

McGee clambered to his feet, sure of the diagnosis. Joe Amos walked to the rear to examine the load. He'd been right about the crates of clothes, and a quarter of the cargo space was filled with jerricans of gasoline.

"Morales?"

"Yeah, man?"

"Get as much of this off here as you can. Leave some jerricans for the tow truck and me to get back."

Wordless, Morales stepped into the road, flagging down the next several Jimmies in the platoon. McGee climbed over the rail to stand on top, to toss crates down.

Ten minutes later every box and container was transferred to other

Jimmies and put back on the road to Couvains, except for six full jerricans snug in a corner.

"McGee, go with Morales. Send me a tow. I'll wait here."

"You gon' be alright, Sarge? You know, out here by yourself and all?"

Joe Amos opened his driver's door. He slid his Garand M-1 from beneath the seat and handed the other rifle to McGee.

"Go on with you. I still got my baby up there." He stubbed his chin at the machine gun. This was raw bravado. Morales the Latino chuckled, but McGee gave Joe Amos a thumbs-up.

Morales said, "Hasta luego," and climbed into his cab with McGee and his assistant driver. McGee waved goodbye in the lean cat's eye light.

Joe Amos set the butt of his rifle on the road. He knelt beside the double wheels to smell the dry fittings of the ruined universal joint. He clucked his tongue, thinking how much his Jimmy had run the past two weeks. He patted the big, cool tire, sorry she was hurt but glad she'd get some attention. He nodded a silent pride at his truck, his bullet-punched Jimmy, tired as a tobacco mule. He thought, You take a break, gal.

The sky would not purple for another few hours. Joe Amos figured his situation was not that bad. A tow would come for him as soon as one was available, surely not before sunup. Plenty of traffic plied this road. The front lines of the 29th and 2nd Divisions were two miles south. He looked that way and saw no flashes, heard none of the clap of combat. Everything looked quiet. This was a chance to catch up on some shut-eye.

Joe Amos stowed his M-1 under the cab seat. He climbed in and closed his door. The stars of France gleamed, vivid without the taint of electricity anywhere around. Another convoy rumbled up and past; he waved them on. In minutes, while more Jimmies and tractors strained in lower gears just outside his open window, Joe Amos fell asleep.

Gears, exhaust, and the odd horn kept him from a deep rest. Joe Amos opened his eyes to an overcast morning. A raven cawed somewhere in the hedges. No trucks rumbled past in the moment he woke, though the front lines to the south made testy morning barks. Joe Amos licked his lips for coffee and other things that were back in America. Yawning, it occurred to him how little he thought of America lately. His life had gotten centered here in Normandy, on the job and the other boys in his company. There was danger, if not in his path, then lurking. He was a sergeant and responsible for others. He missed Boogie and worried about him in the stockade, hadn't heard a peep from him since the fight with the white truckers. But without Boog around to remind him all the time they were both black and Jim Crow was white, Joe Amos had lately formed a better taste for everything. Maybe it was the shot-down Kraut plane that was in his chest forever, or it was the twenty hours a day of work. Maybe it was the fact that most of the GIs in the infantry units were coming to understand it didn't serve to call the man a nigger who was bringing you rations, clothes, ammo, fuel, and replacements. In three weeks Joe Amos had seen enough of the white boys' blood to grant them his respect; an ignorant cracker can call you a spook and still be a hell of a man. Maybe the whites were beginning to see Joe Amos and his drivers in somewhat the same light, the spooks hauling everything the crackers needed all damn day and night. Same hours they fight, Joe Amos drives, and that's something for both of them to think over.

He didn't hear the tow truck pull up behind him. Footsteps trickled from the pebbles on the road shoulder. Someone inspected the rear of the Jimmy. Joe Amos sat up from the bench, wishing for coffee, hoping for a thermos on the tow truck. He looked out his busted rear window. A man, not a soldier, had one leg up on the Jimmy's tailgate, starting to climb on.

"What the hell you doin'?"

The civilian started, losing his grip and tumbling off. Joe Amos flung open his driver's door and landed, sweeping his carbine from under the seat. At the rear of the Jimmy, the man brushed grit off his pants.

Joe Amos put the rifle in both hands. "I asked you what the hell you doin'?"

The man lifted his head but continued brushing.

"*Pardonnez-moi, monsieur.* I was going to take one of your canisters of gasoline. I did not know you were asleep there."

He appeared unarmed and a little old. Joe Amos relaxed his grip on the M-1. The man wore a satin jacket and dark khaki pants that showed the dust of his tumble even after all his cleaning. Gray streaked his hair, worn past his collar. A long, sharp nose pointed at Joe Amos once he gave up on his pants and straightened. He stood half a head taller than Joe Amos.

The Frenchman showed no shame at being caught looting a broken-down truck.

"I apologize."

The rifle held down one of Joe Amos's hands. The other fluttered up on its own, flummoxed, a little amazed.

"Just like that. You apologize. You're gonna steal from the U.S. Army and all you got to say is you're sorry."

"No. I will also say I need the gasoline, and may I have it?"

"No. No, man, you cannot have it. What are you thinkin'?"

The civilian motioned across the empty road, the closeting hedgerows, the early day.

"No one will see. You will not get in trouble."

Joe Amos looked away, as though there were in fact some audience watching this comic routine. "No, it don't work that way. You just . . . no, is all. No."

The Frenchman put out his hand. The fingers were clean and round-nailed, his wrist very white. The bare cuff of his shirt had frayed.

"I am Marquis Jacques Chastain Villecourt de Couvains. And you?"

This was the first Frenchman Joe Amos had spoken with. The man's language was buttery slick, like he'd greased up every hard piece of English before he put it on his tongue. He stood ramrod straight in some kind of housecoat, he fussed over dirt on his drawers, he wanted to shake hands. Joe Amos took the offered grip.

"Sergeant Joe Amos Biggs. U.S. Army."

"*Enchanté.*"

Joe Amos released the handshake. "You speak pretty good English there."

"Many years ago, I have studied in England. Cheerio."

"Did you say you're a Marquis or something?"

"*Oui.* I am below an Earl and above a Duke. My château is down the road one kilometer. It is large and quite dark with the Germans gone and the electricity off. Your bombers are very good at what they do."

The man tugged at the hem of his jacket, bouncing once on his heels.

"May I have one of your canisters?"

"What's a Marquis do? You steal shit?" The first noises of a convoy sounded from the far bend in the road.

"No, Joe Amos Biggs. A Marquis does not do such things unless he must. I will trade some of the gasoline for kerosene. I will light my house until your Americans can turn the power back on. I may pour a bit of the petrol into my old car and start it for the first time in two years. I may trade for some food. I do not know what bounty I will enjoy with one canister of your gasoline, Joe Amos Biggs."

The lead jeep of the coming convoy cleared the trees a half mile off.

Behind it, a green column rumbled into view. Food, fuel, clothes, five hundred tons of everything moved for the GIs.

Joe Amos leaped onto the bed of the Jimmy. He stepped over the bullet holes to grab a jerrican.

He set it on the tailgate and jumped down. He hefted the can, then set it at the Frenchman's feet.

"Here. Go on."

The Marquis lifted the container with some strain.

"*Merci, mon ami.*"

The Marquis struggled away from the Jimmy, south along the shoulder. The weight of the canister tilted him to one side.

"Marquis, man! Get your ass up in the bushes. That convoy sees you, they gonna take that gas away."

The nobleman stepped across the ditch and shouldered into the shrubs without replying. Joe Amos watched his silvery head turn.

"Joe Amos Biggs! You will come this way again, yes? You will visit! I will thank you better."

Joe Amos waved. "Yeah, man. Marquis. Whatever. Go on."

The convoy approached. The Frenchman vanished into the thicket. Joe Amos heard him mewl at the brambles and mud. Joe Amos chuckled, thinking, he's probably getting all kinds of crap on his pants now.

The convoy came on, miles long. Embedded deep in the column, maybe the two hundredth vehicle, was a tow truck.

Ben stopped crawling. A whisper jetted out of the dark.

"Halt!" The voice hissed, plenty of pressure behind it. "Who goes there?" Ben did not see the gun but he knew an M-1 was trained at his shape on the ground.

He whispered back, "Chaplain Kahn. It's alright, I'm coming up."

A metal jangle expressed the re-aiming of the rifle.

"Okay, Chap. Come on."

On his belly, Ben skittered across weeds and stones. He found the foxhole after a low *pssst* from the soldier. He almost butted helmets with the dogface.

"Hey, soldier. Sorry. Didn't mean to sneak up on you."

"Better you'n some Kraut. Come on, there's room."

Ben lowered into the foxhole. The crouching GI hadn't lied, there was space for two, but barely. Their shoulders and hips touched.

"What're you doin' way out here, Chaplain?"

Ben shrugged, a subtle gesture likely unseen but felt by the dough.

"Not much call for me anywhere else at the moment. Too late for a service. Everybody's dug in for the attack. I couldn't sleep. I figured if anybody was awake for a chat, it'd be you boys out here in the listening posts."

The soldier rubbed his chin. Ben heard the stubble sizzle. "You been in the other holes, too?"

"You're the last one, Private."

"You came all the way out here to talk to me."

"You came all the way out here, didn't you?"

The private considered this. Ben could tell little about the man in the dark, hidden up to their necks in the dirt hole, but certainly he had the smell, the bad breath and pits of a foot soldier. The private bore a dark, week-old beard. This marked him as one of the company's "old men," a veteran who'd survived more than three days in the bocage. His orders tonight were to hunker in this LP dug fifty yards in front of his platoon. If he heard movement in the orchard ahead, he had a radio to call in fire support. He'd been chosen for this rotten, lonely, scary job in his unit by rotation. Somebody else would do it tomorrow night.

Ben whispered a few questions. He listened past the soldier's replies, into the woods and hedges. The enemy waited in the orchards only a hundred yards away. He sensed them with a timeless cringe that did not know a quarter century had passed since the last time he crouched this close to Germans.

The soldier's name was Previtera, from Rhode Island. He'd grown up "sort of Methodist." His father was a plumber. That's what he'd be, too, when the war ended. Ben admitted he was no good with tools smaller than a pickax or a shovel. He'd grown up around the coal hills of Pennsylvania and the slag heaps of Pittsburgh.

"Yeah? Go Pirates," Previtera whispered.

"Go Red Sox."

The two sat quiet for minutes. Nothing chirped in the bushes, not crickets or Krauts or the GI battalion to the rear. Thousands of men on both sides kept their peace on this black morn of the fight for the Mahlman Line. Ben did not press more talk on Previtera. Combat soldiers often took comfort simply from Ben's company, without chatter.

The dogfaces seemed to think that talking to the chaplain was talking to God. While glad to have Ben bring God close, they figured it was best to clam up lest they cuss or say anything God might pay them back for. The more bloodshed they experienced, the more reluctant they became, suspecting God might not approve. More and more, when Ben spoke to the frontline boys it was of baseball or hometowns or their girls, common topics to show he was a man like them, and God did not come and go with the chaplain. Ben meant for them to understand that God was already there when he arrived and stayed behind when he went away.

Ben let Previtera's shoulder settle against his in the foxhole. Together they listened into the woods and sky. Ben sensed rain for the opening battle.

Without prodding, Previtera did what soldiers on the verge did. He asked.

"What about the commandments?"

"What about them?"

"Thou shalt not kill. That one."

"The sixth."

"Yeah. How do we do this? I mean, holy smokes, man, you know?"

"I know, son."

"Do you?"

"Yes."

Previtera fell silent, listening to the darkness. Ben joined him, both held their breaths to listen. There, in the orchard, a voice coughed. The Germans had their own listening posts out, right there, so close the enemies could call to each other. Previtera gazed into the night, not seeing the man he would try to kill tomorrow morning, the man with a cough.

The GI faced Ben.

"What d'you say, Chap? What's God got to say?"

Every man of the cloth had to wrestle with this, or he could not come to war. Most, like Phineas Allenby, accepted the sword ideal, that one may kill the wicked, or those who threatened you or defamed your God. The Bible was a great friend to the man who sought righteous reasons to kill another. Ben had killed many in war, and never once felt right. He felt only victorious. That, he believed, was among his sins.

"You want the Christian answer?"

"Sure. Anything'll do."

"Alright. In several places the New Testament talks about centurions, the Roman soldiers, as men of faith. One soldier admitted at the foot of the cross that Jesus was the son of God. Another was the first to be baptized as a Gentile. Far as I know, the Bible accepts soldiering as an honorable profession."

The private snorted. "That's it?"

"I'm a rabbi, Private. That's all I got for you out of the New Testament."

"Alright. Tell me something out of the Old Testament. What do you hand the Jewboys?"

Ben did not flinch at the rough term. A foxhole, hours before an assault, was not the place to preach tolerance. He had to do what he'd promised Billups, find ways to keep these young men fighting.

"It's just another book, son."

Previtera looked again to the orchard where the cough came from. He seemed to visualize dawn.

"Gimme something, Chap."

The German foxhole lay close enough to slither to and slit a throat. Ben had done this in his life, many times. Those deeds hung on the tree of his time. He wanted to tell Previtera how in his war the trenches were so close they could hear the Germans' teakettles, or a sneeze, just like now.

"In the Talmud, Jews are taught that all people are descended from a single person, Adam, so taking a single life is like destroying an entire world. Saving a single life is like saving an entire world."

"What is that supposed to mean? I shouldn't take a life? Then why the hell are we out here? Why should I go and kill a German?"

"Because they're wrong, Private. You kill them because they're wrong down to the bone. What they've done by starting this war, conquering and killing innocents, what they've done to their own people and the peoples of other nations, no God, not mine or yours, could approve of. That's why you'll do everything you can to stop them and, yes, punish them. I swear I do not know if God wants it that way. But I do know your family back home does, and so does your country. They want these Germans beat."

His voice had risen above a whisper. He stopped himself. The private mulled Ben's words.

"What do *you* want?" Previtera asked him, confused.

"I want them beat, too, Private. That's why I'm here."

Previtera paused again, then answered with a voice also no longer a whisper.

"Let me tell you something, Chaplain. I'm no big thinker. I ain't fighting for no apple pie and no flag. No offense, but I ain't fighting for you or your Jews neither. And I don't give a hoot about the Bible. I'm here 'cause my country sent me here. I'm just gonna shoot that Kraut son of a bitch tomorrow morning 'cause if I don't, he'll get me or one of my buddies. And I ain't gonna worry about killing a whole world when I kill him, that guy out there ain't related to anybody I know. Oh, and no offense, but if you were so frickin' sure they were wrong, you'd be carrying a rifle and not just me, know what I mean? Now, if you'll excuse me, I'm the one with the gun here and I got duty."

Previtera arranged himself and his rifle away from Ben, toward the dark orchard. Ben said no more. He crawled out of the foxhole for the rear. He had no reservations about Previtera's morale now. The private would fight all the way to Berlin if he lived to do it. Of all the reasons Ben heard and spoke tonight for fighting in the morning—scripture and even the claptrap he'd laid on about right and wrong—no soldier in any foxhole in France had better cause for slaying another man.

The morning loomed. Clouds knelt low, and battle neared. Ben Kahn watched the soldiers steel themselves.

Some checked and rechecked gear. They tugged on grenades to be certain each was securely attached, patted pockets for extra ammo clips, many sharpened bayonets and knives on whetstones, making an eerie susurration that harked back to massed broadswords and spears. Others smoked and fixed a thousand-yard stare at the cobwebs of dawn. Lips moved in prayer and secret deals. Some sergeants jacked up their squads, pounding shoulders and helmets, reminding them of lessons and assignments. One lieutenant ordered his platoon to turn their fatigue jackets inside out, because the innards of the coats were duller than the shiny, sailcloth outer shell, and made better camouflage. A captain rubbed mud over the stripe on the back of his helmet, hiding from Kraut snipers that he was an officer. He tucked his binoculars and map case inside his jacket, and told his men not to call him "sir" after the battle began.

The replacements in the battalion looked to the grizzled veterans and wondered if they themselves would be so transformed. The veterans watched the officers, many of whom were new, shavetail lieutenants. The officers stayed aloof, readying themselves for the burden of life-and-death calls. No one looked to Ben. This was right. He did not carry a weapon. In the ticking before the assault, only the fight and the fighters mattered.

Ben walked along a high wall of hedge, past all three rifle companies of the 359th's 3rd Battalion. Soldiers in the ditch lifted their chins. A few greeted him with "Chap" and "Padre." Into every eye that met his, he tried to drip some iron and faith for the day ahead.

Ben joined the one hundred and ninety men of L Company. Their orders were to seize the five hundred yards of hedgerows and orchards east of Prétot, then advance into the town and move southwest in echelon with the rest of the battalion to assault Ste. Suzanne. Their assignment was one platoon, one field.

At 0600, the first mortar shells lobbed overhead from the heavy-weapons company set up to the rear. Ben headed for the ditch, careful not to leap or cower. He was not only a chaplain but an officer. The men of 1st Platoon closed around him.

A hundred yards away, the opening bombardment plastered the enemy hedgerows. Ben snuck a peek over the scrub and roots to watch the far hedge erupt in flame. For five minutes the mortars battered the Germans along a thousand-yard front. Leaning against the hedge, Ben felt the thumps on his chest.

The mortars quit. The morning smoked to silence. No tanks clanked up the dirt road, no Thunderbolts dove in support of the GIs. The bocage accepted only men.

"Move out!" The call came down the line. Ben stood from the ditch with the doughs.

"Go get 'em, boys." His hands stayed at his side. He did not clamber over the hedge into the orchard.

Captain Whitcomb, Lima Company CO, stamped past, urging the men, "Stay spread out! Don't clump up. Fire and move!"

Seeing Ben, Whitcomb paused. The captain was in his mid-twenties. Ben marveled that he had once served under officers so young and had thought them old and wise, instead of boys with lives in their hands.

"Rabbi."

"Captain."

"I've heard tell it's gonna do me no good to ask you to stay back."

Ben smiled.

"Who told you that?"

"Four privates you crawled out to see last night. Previtera said he couldn't get rid of you 'til he talked mean."

"Previtera is a fine young man."

"Does the Division Chaplain know you're up here?"

"General Billups does."

"Alright. Stay low, Rabbi. I don't want my men worrying about you. They got other things to think about."

"I understand."

Whitcomb hurried along the hedge. Like his brother officers, his map and binoculars were stowed, and the stripe on the rear of his helmet hidden under smirch. Ben said his first morning prayer, then stuck his head over the scrub to observe the attack, the first actual combat he'd seen since returning to France.

He watched two squads of 1st Platoon clamber over the mound and into the orchard. He gripped the roots of the hedge, uneasy. In the Great War, the Allies and Germans rarely engaged in sunlit, front-on assaults like this; they preferred to wallop each other from vast, fixed positions, trading murderous artillery and night raids. When those armies did find themselves out of their holes and face-to-face, the numbers were great and the bloodletting horrific. This skirmish in the bocage was on a more intimate scale than Ben's war. Three dozen men launched themselves at an equal number of enemy. Each soldier was so much more naked in this fight, one of a few instead of many ten thousands.

Most of two squads were now in the orchard. The third held back in reserve. Hedgerows enclosed the field, except for each corner where the hedges parted for a narrow gate. The trunks of the apple trees provided scant cover. The soldiers bent low and walked under the first tier of branches.

A single Browning air-cooled machine gun opened up over the backs of the advancing doughs, firing blind into the far hedge to keep the Germans' heads down. In the field, two soldiers dropped and took positions with their BARs; the rest of the men hugged the sides of the field and eased forward. In the first minute of their advance, nothing came from the Germans.

Ben wondered if the opening mortar barrage had cleared the opposite hedge of Krauts. Had they retreated to Prétot? His answer, and the answer for every man on this field, because they all must have asked it, exploded with a rip.

The first GI fell. The men in the orchard dove and scattered for ground cover, skinny trees, rotting apple baskets; many leaped into the hedges. The far mound burst with noise, *brrrrp, brrrrp!* Someone in the orchard shouted, "MGs!" The buzz saw of bullets spraying from the shrubs and roots exceeded the single machine gun and pair of BARs the GIs brought to bear in return. The dug-in Germans had fire superiority from the opening moment. Ben heard the reports of enemy guns and saw the scrambling results in the orchard but caught no blink, no smoke from any Kraut barrel. The enemy used smokeless, flashless gunpowder! They were invisible. Ben bared his teeth at the puffs above every dough's gun with every bullet they fired. He bit back a curse and wondered how Allied generals could have ignored this detail for fighting in the bocage. The Germans certainly knew.

In moments, 1st Platoon's assault bogged down. Three soldiers were hit before they advanced twenty yards. Two lay still. A medic ran to the third and dragged him into the side hedge. The soldier yelped. Ben stiffened to climb over the hedge but a trill of stray bullets whipped into the roots near his chest and he fell back. Until the firestorm slackened, Ben could do nothing.

He watched the two squads slog and suffer forward, pouring every round they could into the hedge. They crawled, some ran to gobble up a few fast yards before diving to the ground again. Many did not get up, afraid; others were hit. Yelling, bellowed orders, screams, men's voices in two languages filled the bowl of the field along with the smoke and roar of weapons. Ben could not leave his place, the combat was too fierce.

The squads paid a hard wage for the orchard. The fighting was man-on-man, it had to be this way. Looking at the hedges, Ben saw the terrible limitations of this battlefield. Tanks couldn't operate in such close quarters, there was no way for them to get into the fields past the mounds; the millennia-old roots of the bocage would repel any effort to break through them. The Shermans would just climb over the top, exposing their thin belly plates to Panzerfausts. And close air support from P-47s was a no-go; tree cover was too thick and the distances between foe and friend too narrow. The doughs of the 90th had to take these fields with only the guts and guns they carried with them.

Thirty minutes passed before the platoon held half the field, leaving eight men down. Ben saw heroism and hesitance in full measure, sometimes in the same men. One soldier lunged flat as soon as he cleared the hedge and landed in the field, refusing to advance. Minutes later, when a buddy ahead took a round to the leg, this reluctant private surged from the ground, grabbed his pal by the coat, and hauled him under fire into the hedge, then lay protecting him with his own body until the medic arrived. Another scooped up a BAR from a wounded corporal, ran to the front of his squad to set up a firing position. He squeezed off a few rounds, then changed his mind and ran to the rear, until a sergeant blistered him with a tongue Ben heard above the clamor; the soldier sprinted again to the front, laying down fire while the squad groped forward. Ben gazed in awe. He did not see cowardice or disobedience or rotten morale in the 90th, he saw only boys afraid to die and kill, and that was as it should be, the sixth commandment.

But something else should not have been: how untrained the GIs were for fighting in this kind of terrain. In 1918, Ben had been only an infantryman, but frontline troops were always the first to spot poor strategy. His foot-soldier's eye told him how grimly misfit the fire and movement tactics were in the tight green bocage of this new war.

For four years, Germany had occupied France unhindered. They'd had more than enough time to design their defenses not just on the Channel beaches but across the whole countryside. They knew every hedge and crossroads in Normandy. The Krauts must have practiced war games in these fields, dug in their .88s, and picked apples in these very orchards. German commanders had put a spate of automatic weapons in their units just for this purpose. Lanes of fire were calculated. Ben guessed they had routes of retreat laid out and covered by pre-sighted artillery.

The American plan of attack relied on fire superiority to suppress the enemy while the riflemen advanced. That went out the window in the first minute of an assault because the Germans had more firepower. The GIs were scared to shoot from cover because their gunpowder instantly betrayed their positions, while the Krauts fired away like ghosts in the brush. Because no one had figured how to get tanks involved in the hedges, the GIs were sentenced to a murderous walk across the fields. The opening mortar barrage had clearly done little to sweep the Krauts out of the far hedge. They likely had excellent bunkers and warrens hewn into the network of roots. Watching the doughs struggle forward, Ben grew resentful. Every soldier knew the math of poor preparation. Always, it created a deadly cycle in the ranks. When one of them went down, a replacement arrived days later. This robbed the unit of an experienced hand and plugged in one more raw kid to nursemaid and prod until he became a fighter or another hole to fill. The casualty rate swelled, and the cemeteries ate well. Ben snapped branches in his fists while the dogfaces of 1st Platoon crept up, outgunned and wrongly trained. Surely the Generals had to be scratching for answers. They've got to know what they'd set out for these soldiers to do. How can they call the Tough Ombres a problem division? What else could the 90th be, with this task and these tools? Ben loved every one of the boys for this, and he rose over the hedge.

"Chaplain!" Captain Whitcomb's yell split the spanking sounds of gunfire. "Chaplain, get down, *dammit!*"

Ben landed and stumbled. From his fanny he gazed across the smoky field, surprised to be where he was inside the hedges. He'd made no plan before jumping in. He hurried to his feet and bent behind an apple tree.

"Third squad! Commit! Let's go!" Whitcomb belted this order behind the hedge. Another twenty doughs cascaded down the roots. The machine gun at the corner barked to cover them. Ben's elbow was swept by a bear of a sergeant who hauled him to the left edge of the field and crammed down on his shoulders, telling him to stay the hell put! The sergeant kneeled beside Ben, scanned the field, then lit out.

In the melee Ben spotted the medic. He sensed he would be needed most wherever this man went. He crept along the edge of the orchard, moving on instinct. The sounds and smells were familiar, gunpowder and bangs, throats in roar, then silence and a strange, great emptiness while the battle caught its breath and lone voices cried for help. Ben's hands hung bare, they curled for a weapon. His legs remembered, they powered him through brambles and kneeled behind sparse cover while German gunners picked at the assault. The Krauts could not hold the GIs back now. The first rung of dogfaces had crawled and shot their way within grenade range of the far hedge. They pulled pins and tossed explosives over the mound, then fired at point-blank range through the tangled roots. Ben pulled his eyes from the last bits of the assault and, bent at the waist, jogged to the center of the field where the medic squatted beside a wounded dough.

Twenty yards from the medic, a bayonet had been plunged into the ground. Ben did not know what this meant. He ran on.

"Chaplain, no!"

In mid-stride Ben was tackled and knocked over. He landed on his backpack, badly winded. Gasping, he saw Private Previtera unwrap his arms from around him.

"That's a mine, Chaplain. Watch where you're goin'."

Ben sputtered thanks.

Previtera gathered to his knees. "Bouncing Betty. You hit that sucker, you're singin' soprano in the Jew choir. Know what I mean?"

Previtera patted Ben on the shoulder and took off to find another purpose in the fight. In his first minutes in the field Ben had distracted two men from their job and probably caused Whitcomb to send in his reserves before he was ready. Ben resolved to be less careless, less proud that he was an old soldier. If he didn't, he or someone else would wind up hurt, or dead.

Reaching the medic, he found a young soldier shot through the thigh. The medic had tied a tourniquet tight around the groin and sprinkled sulfa powder over the wet hole. Ben's first-aid training told him the bullet had struck the femoral artery. The boy may lose the leg, if he did not bleed to death in the orchard. The soldier looked past the medic and saw Ben. He grabbed Ben's jacket.

"I want a priest! Get me a priest!"

Ben covered the private's grip with his own. The copper tang of blood curled in Ben's nose. There was no priest in this field. The 90th had thirteen chaplains, each one of them ministering to over twelve hundred soldiers. They could not be in every field, or aid station, in the hands of every reaching soldier of every faith, they could not be everywhere.

"Son, hold on. You're doing fine."

The medic's fingers fluttered around the wound, probing the severity and the bleeding. "That's right," he echoed, "doin' fine."

The soldier's head fell back in the trampled grass.

"I gotta confess," he panted.

Ben shook his head. The soldier went rigid with fierce eyes.

"You gotta get me a priest!"

Ben squeezed the boy's hand.

"Chaplain, you gotta hear me."

Ben cut his gaze to the medic. Under his Red Cross helmet, the medic thinned his lips and shook his head.

Ben could not hear the confession of a Catholic, that was not allowed. The soldier's hand began to quiver in his, and Ben thought, This is allowed, boys dying in a foreign field. What is not allowed after this?

"Alright, soldier."

The medic stuck two morphine spikes in Ben's hand. He patted the downed soldier on the chest, and said, "Hang on, a litter's on the way." Rolling to his heels, the medic glanced at Ben, then took off.

Ben lifted a flattened hand to shield his face from the GI. Behind his hand, he said, "Give me your confession."

"Bless me, Father, for I have sinned. . . ."

Ben stayed until the litter bearers found them. He could not be with the other three soldiers who died in the orchard. He remained with Private Eddie O'Kelley, who'd picked up VD from a whore in England three months ago and had not been treated, and lied to his parents and gal in letters. Ben stuck him with both morphine needles. He recited the Act of Contrition in Eddie's silence, had crossed the soldier's hands over his chest. On the boy's forehead, with a bloody thumb he made the sign of the cross. Then he said the *Shema*, to thank God for allowing him to comfort this son.

The fighting at the far end of the orchard ceased. Ben rose when the stretcher bearers were gone. He walked through the apple trees to the far hedge, to see where the Germans had been. He saw tunnels scooped in the thick roots, where the enemy could hide from reconnaissance planes and weather almost any kind of bombardment. Machine-gun nests had been set in the corners with crossing firing lanes that peered even into other hedgerows. Ammunition, food, and medical supplies were stockpiled and abandoned, implying there was no German supply shortage. Empty shell casings spangled the ground and the leaves. Ben guessed the men defending this hedge had as many as five machine guns and a dozen submachine guns. The Germans left behind only five dead. The rest were gone, dissolved into the bocage.

A drizzle began. Trees stalled the first drips.

1st Platoon arrived through the hedge and assembled again into three rifle squads. The soldiers collapsed in the lane and lay in the ditch. Ben sat with the men and listened, assuring them he would stay. He prayed with some, until the flight of mortar shells overhead crashed into the far hedge and Captain Whitcomb marched past shouting orders, announcing the next hour, another hedgerow.

D+29
JULY 5

Joe Amos jabbed his shovel into the floor of the pit. He took his hands off the long handle and left it standing. McGee beside him did the same.

"No, no, no, you keep diggin'." Joe Amos swept the back of his hand at the boy. McGee tugged his shovel out of the dirt.

Joe Amos climbed from the hole, waist deep now. He sat with legs dangling and wiped his brow on his sleeve over the sergeant's patch, wondering how three stripes could not get him out of digging a latrine.

"Man," he mumbled his disgust. "This ain't right. We get one damn day off in two weeks and we got to spend it diggin' a hole. This is some shit."

McGee chuckled, thinking Joe Amos had made a pun. "Got that right."

Joe Amos watched McGee add to the growing pile of dark French dirt. The soil here was better than the stubborn red clay he split with a mule back in Danville. France was grapes and apples, Virginia was tobacco and beans. Joe Amos was a boy then, a man now, a college man, a sergeant, and this was a latrine. It was his day off.

McGee stomped his boot on the blade to drive it deeper, then levered up a heap. "I thought the Major liked you."

So did I, Joe Amos almost said. He bit the thought back, branding himself a dimwit for believing, for giving up his role of hero because Major Clay asked, trading his dignity for a stripe, and now a shovel. Someone had to dig this shithole, alright, but that someone shouldn't have shot down a Messerschmitt.

Joe Amos watched McGee carving at the dirt, then cast his eyes around the growing bivouac area.

Tents and mess kitchens sprouted over a dozen adjoining fields. Trucks waited for maintenance crews to peel off flat tires, change oil, belts, brake pads, and plugs, lube trannies, fill radiators, or cannibalize the most worn trucks and toss the sucked-out hulks into a spreading junkyard. Jimmies and tractors pulled in, drivers stumbled out, blind from wheeling so much. They snagged food and collapsed on hard cots under humid canvas. Coffee poured everywhere, the liquid admission of fatigue. Word went around that a movie projector was coming soon. This new tent city held over ten thousand drivers and support crew, flowing and mingling by race far more than any military base in America or England. Exhaustion and a schedule thinner than a Petty pinup poster kept the men occupied, enough to prevent most trouble.

A half mile away, the ruined town of Ste. Mère-Église rumbled day and night with comings and goings, fresh vehicles and soldiers from the beaches reporting for duty, bulldozers plowing fallen bricks into red piles. Non-stop work was putting Ste. Mère-Église back in order and setting up this COM Z bivouac on the outskirts. But so much labor without a break was tearing the drivers down, Joe Amos Biggs included. His back and arms blamed him for their ache. Joe Amos blamed white officers who figured a Negro didn't need a day to himself.

He pushed off the rim of the hole and yanked his shovel out of the earth.

Before he could ram the blade down, four German POWs rounded the corner of a tent, guarded by two GIs with M-1s in hand. McGee quit digging. He and Joe Amos looked up out of the hole, heads level with the soldiers' knees.

A dirty sergeant raised his hand to halt the prisoners beside the pit. The soldier looked haggard, with several days of beard, and a crust of dirt on his uniform. The GI with him wasn't much cleaner.

Joe Amos had not seen a living German until now. The four prisoners didn't look like what he'd imagined, a blond and icy-eyed race. These men were young, like him. Two were pale and two were ruddy and dark-haired. Each of the Germans was neater than the GIs, and shaved. Joe Amos figured if you rolled them around in the mud for a few days and changed uniforms, they'd look just like the two doughs guarding them.

The sergeant glanced down to Joe Amos. His eye snagged on the three stripes on Joe Amos's sleeve.

" 'Scuse me there, Sarge. I need to borrow your hole for a sec."

Joe Amos set his shovel against the dirt wall.

"For what?"

The sergeant snorted. He made an indulgent grin.

"Well, what do you think?"

Without waiting for a reply, the sergeant stepped behind his two prisoners. He set a hand to the shoulder of one and walked him to the lip of the trench. The other guard shoved his own prisoners forward. The fourth POW stepped to the ledge on his own. This one, the darkest of the four and seemingly the youngest, looked ready to weep.

McGee dropped his shovel and sprang out on the opposite side of the pit.

Joe Amos stayed put.

The young Kraut whimpered. Joe Amos flung his gaze at the sergeant.

"What the hell you think you're doing?"

"Don't mind him," the sergeant said, "he's been whining since St. Lô. Fucking crybaby. Thinks we're gonna shoot him." He narrowed his eyes at Joe Amos. "You might want to come out of there now, boy."

The sergeant undid his fly and shook his penis into his dirty hands. Joe Amos backed against the dirt wall and jumped out before the man's piss stream struck the bottom of the pit.

Joe Amos stood across the hole, glaring. The sergeant lifted his streaked face and moaned over his yellow arc.

The three older Germans undid their own trousers and joined the sergeant just as his urine was waning. Joe Amos stood beside McGee, staring into the soaking, smelling floor of their hole. The young, sniffling prisoner blew out a breath of relief. He swallowed and color returned to his features. He turned around and unbuckled his pants to slide them around his ankles. He squatted and hung his bare ass over the hole. The sergeant and the three prisoners buttoned their flies after their piss had made a disgusting mud, then the first turd from the squatting Kraut smacked the dirt.

"I ain't gettin' back in there," McGee told Joe Amos.

"Shut up," Joe Amos snapped.

Quickly he regretted speaking to McGee that way, but he couldn't express his anger at the sergeant. There was nothing he could say or do. These soldiers—even the captured Krauts—were fighting men. Joe Amos had dug them a latrine. Watching the Kraut's crap plop, humiliation swamped his heart.

The sergeant stepped in front of the squatting German.

"All done?" the sergeant asked. "*Kaput?*"

Without standing, the boy nodded up to him.

"Good." The sergeant backed a step and raised his rifle. The German boy stiffened when the sergeant laid the barrel against his forehead. Joe Amos froze, unbelieving.

With the gun, the sergeant pushed the boy backward into the pit. The German landed awkwardly, his pants still strapping his ankles. He missed the shit pile but landed in the damp urine muck. The sergeant laughed. The other guard backed the three Krauts away from the hole while in the foul bottom of the pit the boy struggled to get to his feet and raise his pants.

McGee took a step forward. Joe Amos gripped his sleeve and held him back.

Joe Amos moved to the edge of the hole. He reached down a hand to the soiled boy. On the opposite side, the sergeant, still laughing, called out, "Leave him alone. He'll be alright."

Joe Amos ignored him, reaching for the German. The boy's face had gone crimson, hot with shame.

"Come on, man," Joe Amos said over his extended hand, "I'm sorry."

The boy finished with his belt, tails untucked. His knees and elbows were stained with the foul mud. He glared at Joe Amos's hand. Then he spit at it and clambered out of the hole. The sergeant gathered him in.

"Sorry to interrupt your day," the GI called across the pit. "*Sarge.*"

Joe Amos watched the six walk off among the tents and shifting trucks.

"Don't that beat all," McGee said, beside him. "You was just tryin' to help that boy."

Joe Amos wiped the Kraut's spit off his palm.

"Get cleaned up," he told McGee.

* * *

Joe Amos walked along a line of Jimmies outside a maintenance tent. He knew by instinct to leave most of the trucks alone, they'd been driven to shreds. He studied wear on the tire treads, some slick, some with holes showing the fiber belt under the rubber like in a hobo's shoe. Some he skipped over by smell, catching the stink of overheated blocks and dried-out radiators. He strolled past thirty trucks until he found the one he wanted. The front grille was twisted, the cat's eye plucked out, the bumper missing. Joe Amos hopped on the running board and glanced in. The key hung from the ignition.

He slid into the driver's seat and turned the key. The engine cranked, three-quarters of a tank of gas registered. To the rising needles in the gauges, he said, "Perfect."

Careless of being caught, he pulled the Jimmy out of line. The sound of the motor and feel of the suspension told him he'd chosen well. In a minute of dodging through the bivouac, he stopped in front of the latrine. McGee waited there, his uniform brushed of dirt and his face and hands washed.

Joe Amos said, "Get in."

McGee ambled, plainly tired, to the passenger door, inspecting the wrecked front end. He climbed in. Joe Amos shifted to first and rolled.

"Where's Lucky?" McGee asked.

"We're not driving Lucky today."

"How come?"

" 'Cause if Lucky's gone, they might figure we're gone, too."

McGee worked with this and came up empty.

"Ain't we gone, Sarge?"

The road lay a hundred yards off. Jimmies limped in; others, refreshed, pulled out. Joe Amos put this dented, running truck in line with the others heading back to work.

"Nope. We ain't."

McGee settled in on the bench. An MP waved Joe Amos onto the road. The Jimmy was in third gear and in the heart of an empty convoy returning to OMAHA before McGee asked, "We gonna get caught?"

"Nobody knows what the hell's goin' on half the time. No, McGee, we ain't getting caught."

The convoy, with no loads in its beds, sped away from Ste. Mère-Église. Joe Amos shifted into fourth gear, a rare treat.

"Besides, yesterday was Independence Day. We're just a day late, you and me."

At the first opportunity, Joe Amos swung the wrecked-faced Jimmy south. He drove past emptied convoys heading the other way, back to OMAHA. At Isigny, he turned off the main road. A loadless truck should not be going this direction, toward the fighting around St. Lô, but he trusted the ruined grille of the Jimmy to be some sort of explanation, something out of the ordinary. He figured there was enough traffic on these roads to go on without curiosity. He found a loaded column and closed ranks.

McGee Mays did not ask where they were headed. Joe Amos let quiet fill the cab, enjoying it with the breeze and the blue-and-green world. The latrine was mostly finished. Garner would come along to check on them. He'd see just the shovels and the crap; he'd wonder about the crap but figure the two Negroes had decided the hole was deep enough. Garner would go off to tend some other business, thinking Joe Amos and McGee were probably sacked out somewhere in the sprawling bivouac, they weren't on duty until tomorrow noon. The business of their trucking battalion was huge and disorganized, moving far faster than records and files could keep up. The cracks to slip through were big.

With the wind whizzing in the windows, McGee began to hum "Amazing Grace." Joe Amos let the boy go for a verse, then listened while McGee sang the second. On the third verse, Joe Amos joined in, and their voices blended with the engine drone and the road.

> "Through many dangers, toils and snares,
> I have already come;
> 'Tis grace hath brought me safe thus far,
> And grace will lead me home."

"McGee."

"Yeah."

"We're AWOL. You know that, right?"

"Yeah."

"You okay with it? I mean, I didn't ask you first or nothin'."

"Where'd you get the Jimmy?"

"Out of maintenance. She was in line."

"We gonna put her back?"

"Yeah. Tonight."

"Alright."

"We're going to Couvains. I got a friend down there. Says he's got a big house and all."

McGee nodded, looking out the windshield. Joe Amos glanced at the boy who seemed to like and trust everything Joe Amos said. McGee stretched his arm out his window and made a wing of his hand, rising and dropping on the flowing wind. Elation hit Joe Amos, rose like a wind in him. He'd taken a truck and left his unit, he was out of bounds, breaking rules, thumbing his nose for the first time at the Army's command of him. That asshole sergeant had embarrassed him, having those prisoners use his freshly dug hole before it was ready, before Joe Amos had even climbed out of it. But right now Joe Amos was in a truck flying down the road, free and breezy, while that sergeant was still filthy and under somebody's orders. Not Joe Amos. No, sir, he was doing what he wanted this morning. He wouldn't get caught. Disobedience felt good. It was easier than he'd imagined.

"I grew up in Southside Virginia," he told McGee. "Town of Danville. We got a small farm. Papa left when I was a young'n. Mama says he was a no-good."

McGee said, "Uh huh."

"Got four sisters, too. Brenda, Linda, Glenda, and Edna." Joe Amos laughed. He loved saying his sisters names out loud. McGee tried to repeat them and fouled up. He laughed, too.

McGee asked, "How'd your mama come to have five chir'ren with a no-good?"

"Don't know. Never asked. I guess a fella can just become a no-good after a while."

"I reckon."

Joe Amos drove, contemplating his long-gone father and McGee's question, resolving to ask his mama point-blank when he got home. The query hung in front of him but the warm air rushing in his window blew it away.

"All my sisters have husbands. Everyone's got their own farms, but they go over to work Mama's land, too. She's growing tobacco on half, soybean on the rest."

"I like engines," McGee said. "I'm gon' be a mechanic."

Joe Amos sped on and kept speaking of his own home.

"I was the baby child, you know, so I got to do what I wanted a little more. My sisters' husbands took care of the place, so I got to go off to school. Three years. Then I joined up."

"You gonna finish college when you get back?"

"Oh, yeah. Mama said she'd hide me good if I don't."

McGee enjoyed this, the notion of a houseful of women telling Joe Amos what to do.

McGee said, "My girlfriend an' my little girl, they livin' with her mama. I'm gonna ask her to marry me when I get home."

Joe Amos let this nestle with the rest of the flowing afternoon. Home. We're all going to do the right things when we get home. But today was special because it was France and this was a war, and Joe Amos and McGee had the day to themselves.

Another convoy crept up on Joe Amos's rear. This put him in the center of a column several miles long, a thousand tons of supplies headed toward the struggle for St. Lô. Joe Amos relaxed at the wheel; in the heart of an immense column there was nothing to do but follow. He enjoyed a secret glee that he was not going where the other hundreds of trucks were headed. Today he had his own destination, of his own choosing. He saw France differently this afternoon with no load in his bed. Emerald hills swelled on every side, ridged with hedges and stone fences. Sheep and cattle grazed, shade lay sweetly by barns and streams. Joe Amos felt pride knowing he helped liberate this beautiful land. The emptiness of his truck bed tweaked him, riding selfish and bare when he might be full and useful for the fight. He passed the place where Lucky lost her rear end two nights ago. His regrets faded and he watched the next kilometer for the turnoff to the Marquis's château.

McGee made no comment when Joe Amos slowed and turned out of the convoy. The dirt lane did not reveal any home, just unpruned brush for a long, winding way. Then the shrubs gave over to grass and there was a palace.

Joe Amos caught his breath. The building was stucco and brick. Three chimneys stood high above a slanted roof. Wings extended left and right from a half-turret in the middle, topped by a *fleur-de-lis* wind vane. Windows and doorways showcased marble carvings in corners and cornices. All the mortar and frames looked weathered and grainy, just right for a home like a castle. Joe Amos entered a gravel driveway that rounded at front doors so wide he could drive through them if both were swung open. He stopped the Jimmy and shut the engine. He laughed, gazing at flowering bushes and a carpet of grass. A statue balanced on a pedestal in a dry fountain.

"Where the hell we at?" McGee asked.

"Man, I don't know. . . ."

The war was gone from this place, banished off the grounds. Joe Amos climbed from the cab and set foot on the gravel, thinking a change might come over him, too, only magic could do this. No one came from the great doors to greet them. With McGee, he walked along the facade of tall windows and scented bushes.

The sounds of rasping, a rotor, slipped around the corner. With McGee a step behind, Joe Amos ambled to the noise. He whistled.

Clearing the long wall, Joe Amos stopped. A man wearing slacks with no shirt pushed a lawn mower over a green sward. Brick walkways diced the wide yard, and in islands of dirt between the grass and brick, roses bloomed, fat and pink. The man wore his gray hair long down his neck, his back was white and soft. He was lean, likely from labor and hunger. He stopped mowing and bent for a large rake. He scraped at the clippings.

"Marquis!"

The man turned and let go the rake. He opened his arms. Against the pastels of the roses and the intensity of the grass, the Marquis seemed pale and unkempt, a boney gardener, not the royal magician who lived here.

"*Bonjour, mon ami. Vous êtes revenu pour me rendre visite, oui?*"

Joe Amos strode forward. McGee stayed a step behind.

"Joe Amos Biggs, you have come back to visit me, yes? And you have brought a friend? *Bon!*"

McGee uttered, "This guy knows you?"

Joe Amos let the question stand. "Marquis. Yeah, man, we had the day off. And you know, you said . . ."

"Yes! I said you should come and here you are!"

The Marquis embraced Joe Amos. He was careless about his sweat, his smell was green and part of the place.

Joe Amos patted him on his damp back. He'd never in his life been held like this by a white man. It seemed odd. Joe Amos squirmed.

"And your friend?" The Marquis bounded like a butterfly from Joe Amos to McGee, but with only a hand out. McGee clasped hands.

"This is Private McGee Mays, my assistant driver."

"*Bienvenue.* Welcome. Now, Joe Amos. Can you stay awhile?"

The Marquis rubbed palms, greedy for company. The man's ribs showed. The sun had pinked his shoulders, a small copse of white curls matted his chest. He seemed ready to bloom.

"Yeah. We can hang around."

"Excellent! I apologize, you have caught me in the middle of my groundskeeping. As your host, I can offer you some hours of work at my side, a glass or two of wine, and later a meal of mutton and potatoes I have purchased with your gasoline. McGee? What do you think of this?"

McGee screwed his face at Joe Amos. "What gasoline?"

"Forget it, it's nothing. You want to rake or mow?"

"Can we get the wine first?"

The Marquis clapped at this. "*Trés bien!* Yes, I have a cellar full! One moment."

He cupped hands to his mouth, calling to the giant rear of the house, "Geneviève! *Du vin!*"

The Marquis turned again to McGee.

"Come! Join me, take off your shirt and have some sun. We will work and we will drink, yes? You, Joe Amos Biggs, let's go! Up, up!" The Marquis hoisted his hands in a gesture to make them peel off their tunics. McGee complied and unbuttoned his shirt, then stood smiling in his OD sleeveless.

"You will mow first, McGee. You are a strong boy, I see this. We will finish the work in half the time! Joe Amos and I will rake and clip the bushes."

McGee shrugged and took up the mower. He shoved it and the blades spun, chewing grass. The Marquis watched after him, seeming to admire the dark American boy, a new color added to his garden.

Joe Amos unbuttoned his tunic slowly. He couldn't just throw himself in like McGee. Even AWOL, he stayed a sergeant.

"What's up with the house, man? How'd you keep it like this, with the war and all?"

"The Germans made a headquarters here. Officers took my house and allowed us to live in a corner. I have been the gardener. Geneviève was their maid."

The Marquis kept his face placid, mentioning the Germans. The man had lived under the heel of the Krauts for four years, serving them in his own home. Joe Amos looked from the Marquis to the ancient house, and thought the two were like this whole country, patient survivors. Not me, he thought, I'd spit, man, I'd spit every time I said the word *German*.

Joe Amos finished pulling off his tunic and OD. His color was lighter than McGee's but still many shades deeper than the Frenchman's. To him, their skins, their stations, seemed to pose no barriers. The Marquis had been the laborer in his own home, Joe Amos thought. Is that what changed him, shining the Krauts' boots so they could walk over his grass? What does that kind of change cost a man?

"Who's this Geneviève?"

The answer came out the door before the Marquis could reply. She carried a silver tray bearing a jug and three glasses. She was linen white and thin, long-armed and gangly, swaying in a cotton dress barefoot over the lawn. She wore her brown hair long, like the Marquis. She seemed at first glance Joe Amos's age, maybe a few years older.

Geneviève held the tray while the Marquis poured. She did not speak and her father did not introduce her, as though she were a maid. He lifted two glasses and turned to take one to McGee. When he walked away, she moved closer to Joe Amos, offering the tray. Her head inclined down, she looked at him under thick brows. Some instinct told Joe Amos not to speak but just take the glass and smile. The girl seemed to appreciate this; she returned his smile.

She set the tray on the grass. Joe Amos admired the way she moved, graceful, balanced. She backed away, looking at him before turning to the house.

"Rabbi!"

A captain lay only a yard from Ben, bellowing to be heard. Chunks of earth splattered their helmets and backs. Ben lifted his chin out of the dirt.

"Yeah!"

"You got a prayer for this, how 'bout sayin' it!"

Another shell brayed overhead to slam into the ground a hundred yards down the line. Ben felt more than heard the explosion; after an hour under the German guns, he was as deaf as every man in 3rd Battalion. Along with five hundred soldiers, he lay in the poor cover of high grass, weathering the worst Kraut barrage of the day. He set his chin on his forearm to glare at Hill 122, Mont Castre, a green welt in the flatness of Normandy.

American artillery answered the Krauts shell for shell. Orange bursts peppered the crest of Mont Castre, cracking and toppling trees. The difference was the big guns attached to the 90th fired blindly at the hill-top, and the Germans laid their rounds with lethal accuracy, looking from the high ground straight down the throats of the 359th lying in the fields.

It was impossible to know the casualties his battalion was taking ly-ing here. Every German shell was a lottery ticket, maybe you won, maybe you lost. Every soldier with his face dug in the dirt kept frenzy at bay while the concussions beat on him to flee, panic, beg for the earth to stop erupting. Every man on his belly with hands over his helmet plumbed his courage, reviewed his life, and fought not to pee himself when the explosions probed near.

Retreat from this field was out of the question. They'd just have to come this way again and pay for the same ground twice. The big shells weren't as deadly in an open pasture against an army on its belly as they were against a town, where they could knock down buildings and flush out defenders. But artillery could stop an advance, send the attackers to ground, and pin them there. Ben and the battalion could do nothing but lie exposed in the weeds, waiting for dusk, still an hour away. Once night covered them, they would move up to the rim of the Mont Castre forest.

He hid his eyes in the crook of his elbow, feeling the bombardment through his hips and chest. Though Ben Kahn was one of hundreds in these weeds and thousands at the foot of Mont Castre, the falling German shells, the muted shouts of men left and right, the stench of powder and cindered grass, made these private moments. Inside the lit-tle cave of his bent arm, memories of his home and his lost son and his other war dropped on him, too.

Ben said a prayer, in praise of God, not for the defense of his life. Of all the men in these erupting fields, he did not have to be here. So he would not ask God to preserve him. He asked only that God use him to end the war as fast as it could be stopped.

In the first two days of the assault through the hedgerows, the 90th had suffered a ten percent casualty rate, twelve hundred men. This was terrible and would worsen on the slope of Mont Castre. Ben would not pray that any American soldier be spared. The GIs around him and across Normandy were the instruments to rid the world of Hitler and the Nazis. No man could accept this mission and ask for his life, too. There would be no miracles of punishment, no plagues or crashing Red Sea. Here there were only men and guns: courage, sacrifice, and numbers would decide. Ben lay among the dogfaces to steady them, not to save them.

* * *

"You alright?" Ben asked the soldier. "Can you make it back?"

The private tapped his helmet beside his good eye. The other was swollen shut behind caked blood where shrapnel had cut his socket.

"I can see where I'm goin'."

Ben laid a hand behind the GI's neck. "God bless you, son. Go on."

The boy turned away, one hand extended. He wandered into the murk of night under the trees and was gone. He had almost a half mile to go north through the field and hedges to reach the collecting station. Ambulances could not come this close to the MLR. Those wounded who could walk were told to do so. The rest waited for litter bearers.

Ben did not watch the soldier disappear. He knelt beside the final stretcher. Automatically, his hand stroked the brow of the soldier lying there. He offered his canteen and noted it was almost empty. This boy had caught a shard in his calf. He was not in danger of bleeding out or losing the leg, so the medics triaged him to the end of the line of twenty wounded. The soldier didn't mind going last.

"Well, I'm outa here," he said under Ben's hand. The final light from the tail-end of dusk trickled into the forest. The soldier's face was a mix of pain and grin. "I got me the million-dollar wound."

"Looks like you did."

The soldier drank the last of Ben's water.

"I ain't ashamed, Chaplain. I did my job, I put my butt on the line. I just got lucky."

Ben made no reply. He would not discuss this soldier's pride in his luck. What if we all rode away and left the Germans on that hill, or the Japanese on their islands? Would that be luck, too? Victory was not close. There was a lot of fighting left everywhere. Ben could not congratulate this soldier for escaping with his honor intact and leaving the work undone. In this world, there were far greater issues than a man.

The last stretcher bearers came out of the gloom, hoisted the boy, and were gone. Ben stood, listening to the chinking sound of GIs digging foxholes for the night. The other two battalions of the 359th had taken positions on his battalion's right and left. Once the German cannons quit at nightfall, the doughs had all hustled forward to the base of the hill. The Krauts let them come, watching and prepared. Now two thousand riflemen were poised to assault Mont Castre, the anchor of the Mahlman Line, with the rising sun.

Ben needed water in his canteen. He wanted to wash out his distaste for the soldier's glee at going to the rear with a nick in his leg. The noises of shovels and hissed orders told him how close the line was to the Germans. The enemy hovered over their heads on the dark wooded crest. They loomed over tomorrow, filling every man's fate.

Ben turned to another chore. The row of dead. This dozen would not be evacuated but buried where they lay, in shallow holes marked on a map. Others would be put here beside them before Mont Castre fell. Then they would be upturned and taken north for better treatment. For tonight they were to be laid in the ground, out of sight where the harm they suffered would not be on display. It was the policy of the U.S. Army that a soldier may contemplate his death but he should not see it.

Ben did not determine causes, he did not probe wounds and conjure grim last moments for each body. He did not look in faces and imagine more than what lay before him. Ben was the reaper not for these boys but for their families. His duties were to collect identities and mementos, make certain nothing went with them into the earth that loved ones might cherish later. He delved into each boy's pockets, he harvested dog tags, letters, photos, necklaces, then put them in envelopes. He labeled each with the name on the tags. When Graves Registration came for the bodies he would turn over the envelopes. A few days would go by until Ben received a list of matching addresses of the KIAs from this battle. Then he would write each family and hate how little he knew of each boy, how little he could change each letter from the one before it. The dead were the same, that was why we cling to living. In his hands were the tags of Catholics and Protestants, a Jew, a Mormon, a Hispanic, two officers, a sergeant, the bodies were yellow teeth and fillings, bearded cheeks, mussed hair, each had his own wound and last expression, they were different and Ben despised that they were not. He knew this change from before, from the old time in France, when death became something to note more than fear.

Dropping the envelopes in the dirt, Ben sat beside the line of corpses, until the light withdrew from them and their deaths went dark.

The Marquis tipped a bucket of well water over Joe Amos's head. Joe Amos flapped in the cold cascade, swiping sweat and grass shavings off his chest and arms, out of his hair. Then the Marquis poured another. McGee came for his shower. The boy stood like black stone under the chill, his muscles glistened. The Marquis soaked him with three buckets.

Dark stopped them from mowing, clipping, and raking. Joe Amos thought it best to skip the mutton dinner and get back to the bivouac. The Marquis complained, pointing to his house and the flicker of kerosene light in the kitchen. Wood smoke coiled from the chimney and Joe Amos caught the smell of meat.

"Sarge," McGee implored. "We either caught by now or we ain't. May as well eat good."

"And drink," added the Marquis.

Joe Amos cast his thoughts to the bivouac. The mess tents were full now at dusk, hundreds of trucks passed bread-and-butter on and off the road, a thousand full cots, ten thousand cups of coffee, and in all that chaos he and McGee would not be missed. Every driver and mechanic had been worked to a frazzle; anyone noticing their absence must figure the two of them had slinked off somewhere to sleep every minute they had left. Joe Amos nodded. He walked, dripping, across the mown lawn behind the Marquis, who waved another empty wine bottle.

Before entering the house, Joe Amos dried himself with his tunic and put it on, tucking his tails. He told McGee to do the same, the country boy was about to go inside to sit for dinner with no shirt on. Inside the kitchen, Geneviève flashed past the window carrying a pot, her hands under her apron.

"My daughter is a fantastic cook," the Marquis said, buttoning his blouse.

"Where's Mrs. Marquis?" Joe Amos asked.

"Ah, *il est regrettable.*"

McGee asked, "What's that mean?"

"Sad, my friend. It is sad. My dear wife passed away two years ago. She had the influenza."

Through the window, Joe Amos watched the motherless girl set the table, whirling with confident hands. He imagined her mother, a pretty woman, old like the Marquis but odd like him, too, nice, with long brown hair and hands that were sure like the daughter's. He liked the Marquis and felt cheated that his wife was not here, a whole French family to be his friends.

"What'd the Germans do? Anything?"

The Marquis lifted a hand, waving the notion of the Germans aside. "What would the Boche do, eh? Help her? The Marquise was a pain in the *derrière* to them. My wife was a strong woman, she had a tongue, *vous comprenez?*"

"You miss her?" McGee asked.

The Marquis's joviality vanished.

"McGee, we are new friends. I am going to forgive that." The Marquis laid his hand to the doorknob to enter the kitchen. "Yes. All the time. Please do not mention her to my daughter. She still . . . Please do not."

Following the Marquis through the door, Joe Amos scowled at McGee. The private looked glum, until they entered the kitchen, where the aromas and warmth lifted all of them. Geneviève turned from the oven. A leg of lamb simmered in a pan. She set the pan on a trivet in the center of a lantern-lit table. Joe Amos forgot that he hadn't stood inside a home with a roof, a table, chairs, light, food, in almost a month. He ignored that he was AWOL. Looking at Geneviève he did not notice the Marquis had slipped away down a side stairwell. The man emerged holding three dusty, dark bottles.

"Sit," he instructed, pointing to the table. McGee grabbed a seat fast. Joe Amos had not once heard the voice of the daughter. He wanted to.

"Can I help?" he asked her.

The Marquis intervened.

"She will serve the meal. Sit with McGee. We will eat in one minute."

Joe Amos watched the Marquis instruct his daughter in the last phases of the food preparation. She basted the potatoes with the juice of the lamb while he retrieved clean glasses from a cupboard. The Marquis kept her separate, busy, an eye always on her. He seemed stern without being mean. Joe Amos had the pleasant sense Geneviève was purposefully not looking up at him.

Clatter and flurry filled the kitchen. Joe Amos knew nothing about cooking but could tell these two French folks took pride in the simple meal. The kitchen was clearly an old room. A fireplace rose head-high. The floorboards were worn, cut from the same red wood the small table was. A rough banquet table, large enough to seat a dozen, held the other end of the kitchen. Joe Amos figured this was where the house staff ate in the Marquis's better days. He envisioned the mother riding herd on the butlers and maids, and then, with her husband and daughter, becoming the staff themselves when the war hit. He imagined German officers seated in these chairs only a month ago. Then, because the room was bright and cheering, he imagined his own mother and sisters sitting here at the big table. The white Marquis and his pretty daughter served them all lamb and taters and French wine. He wished his mama could see this, see the sergeant's chevron on his sleeve. He opened one of the bottles and poured glasses for himself and McGee. Like two gents, the black boys dinged their glasses and drank an unspoken toast to themselves.

The mutton was set on the table, nestled in a ring of plums and baked apples. A bowl of steaming red potatoes was laid next to it. The Marquis took his seat. Geneviève pulled away her apron and spread it across the back of her chair. Joe Amos made to rise, to pull the girl's chair out for her, but the Marquis held out his empty glass.

"Pour the wine, Joe Amos. That is the honor of the guest."

Joe Amos relaxed in his chair. He didn't know French ways, didn't know if the Marquis recognized the chivalrous Southern thing he intended to do, so he let it go.

The girl spooned potatoes while the Marquis sliced and handed out portions of the lamb. Joe Amos emptied the first bottle into all four glasses. McGee seemed unaware of anything but the food, he tucked in before all the plates were filled. Backwater manners, Joe Amos thought. When the food was dished out, he raised his glass in a toast. McGee looked up, his mouth full, and sheepishly raised his glass.

"Here's to new friends. Victory and peace in France and around the world."

The Marquis hoisted his glass another notch. *"Très bien dit."*

The daughter raised hers, looking Joe Amos straight in the eye.

"Yes," she said, "that was beautiful. *Merci.*"

The Marquis cut his eyes at Geneviève and smiled. All drank.

The girl did speak English. Joe Amos, quietly, was glad.

The meal tasted better than anything he had put in his mouth in two years. Army cooking, English pub food, none of it matched the flavors these two French coaxed out of lamb, vegetables, and fruit. The wine, he suspected, was extraordinary but he had no way of knowing except to watch how the Marquis and his daughter savored it, with their nostrils and little lip smacks. Joe Amos tried to taste what was keen in the grapes, but the meat and potatoes were the show, the wine just made him tipsy and talkative.

For that reason, he told them how McGee's mother named him Adolph, after the town doctor. Joe Amos laughed alone until Geneviève joined, her laugh chirped behind her hand, shy. McGee, still chewing, glared at him; the Marquis knit his brows, indulgent but not amused. Joe Amos took a swallow, aware the wine might be to blame and thinking that he only needed a little more to get it right. He set the glass on the table and announced, "I shot down a German fighter."

This was the ticket. McGee sat bolt upright, the Marquis donned the face of an interested buyer, and Geneviève left her hand over her open mouth, making a breathless sound.

Joe Amos spilled the whole tale, from the fight in the bocage to the stripe on his sleeve. McGee, as he always did with this story, added punctuations, reminding that he was there for all of it, at the wheel in the hedgerows, in the ditch under the Jabo. Geneviève raised and lowered her hand to her lips at the exciting parts, murmuring, *"Mon Dieu."*

When the story was finished, the meal was done. The Marquis sat back from his empty plate and pushed it to the center of the table.

"That is a wondrous thing," he said. "Marvelous. Geneviève?"

Joe Amos thought he was asking for his daughter's reaction to the story. Instead, she rose and reached for the plates.

Joe Amos stood fast. He put out both hands toward the dishes. One hand touched the back of her wrist.

"No. No. Me and McGee'll clear the table."

"It is alright," she said, not meeting his eyes, both standing above the table and close. "I will do it."

"Joe Amos, sit." The Marquis took the third bottle, preparing to open the cork.

"No, Marquis. Geneviève." He was careful to pronounce her name this first time. "We'll do it. You two done enough. McGee."

"What?"

"Up, dammit."

"Oh." McGee stood and wobbled. He gathered in plates like they were made of tin, mess platters instead of china. Joe Amos grabbed the plates away from the boy.

"Go get some water out of the well."

"My friends, my friends." The Marquis pushed back his chair to stop them from squabbling and helping. Now the dinner was ruined, Joe Amos thought, everyone on their feet and tugging. The daughter moved in, to defuse it. Joe Amos looked down: her hand lay full over his.

"Please. I will do the dishes. It is my pleasure."

In the seconds he spent near her, under her hand, Joe Amos looked for stories in her skin and eyes—the years under the enemy, the death of her mother, her stolen home, her hunger. Joe Amos had never been so close to a woman like this, a life like hers that emerged in this gentle, brave shape.

"*Oui?*" she asked.

"Okay," he said, releasing the plates to her. He turned, not trusting anything now, the wine especially. "McGee, we gotta get back."

The Marquis moved behind McGee. "I will walk you to your truck, *mes amis.* Say good night, Geneviève."

The girl did not speak to make her farewell to Joe Amos. She gave him only a look that said she was satisfied with him and he should come again. Joe Amos did not believe what he saw on her face. He dropped his eyes and walked to the door.

"Good night," he said over his shoulder. The Marquis laid a hand on McGee's back and the two exited the kitchen. Joe Amos shuffled behind them, downcast that he'd been a fool somehow.

Her voice startled him.

"*Ah, diable.* Joe Amos, will you ever come back?"

He stopped on his toes and turned. The Marquis and McGee were out of earshot.

"You bet."

He sealed his words with a glance that felt electric. With one hand she gestured that he should leave now. They had a secret between them.

Joe Amos tore his eyes off her. He skipped out the door to catch up with the Marquis and McGee.

"I will not make you work so hard if you come this way again," the Marquis said to McGee.

"Ah, I don't mind. Shoot."

"Joe Amos, *mon ami.* Thank you again for the gift of the gasoline. It made the meal possible."

"No problem."

They strolled over the lawn to the drive where the truck waited. An hour's road lay ahead, maybe more if there was dense traffic or a snarl. Joe Amos had to drive, McGee was not sober.

"So," the Marquis said when they reached the Jimmy. "Perhaps we will see each other again."

Joe Amos kept his secret pact with Geneviève.

"Perhaps."

"Then, *adieu.*"

The two climbed into the cab. As soon as Joe Amos turned onto the main road, the white gleams of cat's eyes glittered a mile back, and ruby dots ran far ahead, the tail of another column. The road was busy as always.

Wind rushed in the open windows when Joe Amos wound up to third gear. McGee snorted. His head reared.

"What gasoline?"

Joe Amos ignored the boy, who fell back asleep in the next starry minute.

He glided down the steps below the Pont Neuf. There was no need to hurry: he could make an entrance. He chose this spot because it was damp and glittering. Gaslights from above fractured on the loitering Seine. The stones of the quay were large and old, damp always and mossy in spots. Paris was ancient right here, centuries of murder done beneath the Ile de la Cité. He imagined mist and overcoats, something from *Casablanca* or *The Maltese Falcon*.

White Dog looked over his six top lieutenants, aligning for his arrival at the bottom of the steps. In the dim light, theirs were desolate-looking faces, like moonscapes. All wore caps except White Dog, who liked to show off his hair combed high.

White Dog had considered buying them all dinner in Montparnasse before this meeting. It would be a nice touch, generosity with an air of authority. He decided against the meal, preferring the way the Jews buried their dead, fast. Once a man is done, you dig him a grave and put him in it. No waiting. Dinner would come afterward, for those with the stomach.

"*Bonsoir,*" he said to them all.

"*Chien Blanc.*"

He walked beside the river to spit in and see which way the current was flowing. The water swept west, away from Notre Dame. Good, he thought. This won't be a church burial.

"My friends," he said, walking to the center of their arc, "we make money, yes?"

Restive looks were exchanged. One man—Marcel, the oldest of the lieutenants—kept his dark eyes on the stones.

"In the three weeks since *Acier* was caught by the Gestapo, we have expanded. We are selling more food, more guns, more everything. We have found more suppliers, more customers, more profits. We have grand plans for Paris when the *Amis* arrive. Is all this I say true?"

White Dog knew his French was a little stilted for their thug ears. He didn't care. His jazzy clothes and hair, his accent, these reminded his gang he was American, not common like them.

"Yes," they shrugged.

"Then, why," White Dog asked, changing his tone to a lament, "why does one of you want to replace me? Why is one of you trying to start up his own operation behind my back?"

Heads snapped around. Marcel, whippet thin, dandruff dust on his shoulders, held stock-still.

"What have I done but make you all richer? Do you miss *Acier* that much?"

"No," the voices protested. White Dog made a shushing sound to remind them they were criminals in an occupied city. "No," they repeated, quieter.

A barge powered past on the Seine. White Dog waited until it was gone beneath the Pont Neuf. Greasy waves from its wake slapped at the quay.

"Marcel," White Dog said.

The skinny lieutenant stepped forward. He held his arms straight out from his sides, head down but his eyes on White Dog, a crucifix posture in a leather coat spilling dandruff flakes. White Dog nodded.

The sound of a click happened in one of Marcel's hands. The switchblade came out too fast to see the motion, but there it was, glinting like the spangles on the river.

Marcel spun on his toes, now like a bullfighter with his arms high, facing the five remaining lieutenants. Nimble and blinding he leaped to his left and drove the blade into the fat neck of Arnaud.

Marcel tucked his free arm under the traitor to keep him on his feet. The others stepped away, Arnaud spurted blood. Marcel drew the knife under the chin, widening the channel while staring into the red gush that struck him in the face. Arnaud's thick neck slowed Marcel's hand. White Dog watched him saw through the jiggling folds. Arnaud grew too heavy to keep standing so Marcel let him sink to his knees. He moved behind Arnaud and gripped his hair, pulling back his head, opening the slice. The pulses of blood sluiced like a toilet overflowing.

"No one leaves," White Dog said to his lieutenants as they backed away from the stone steps. "We're going to dinner."

D+31
JULY 7

Ben stepped carefully. The trail descended at a steep angle, and the moss floor had been rained on since sundown yesterday. In this hour before dawn, the path was trampled, dark and slick.

His hands ached around wooden stretcher handles. Both shoulders and knees threatened to give way.

He was surprised when he failed. His boots slipped. In a dozen or more trips up and down the trail, he'd lost his footing several times and always regained it. He expected to catch himself again, but the litter tore from his grip. The soldier holding the downhill end jolted forward with the sudden weight and dropped his handles, too. The wounded GI on the canvas hammock howled. Seated on the path, Ben gaped at the hurt boy, exhausted and shamed.

"Dammit, Chap!" The litter bearer spun on Ben. "Dammit!"

"Sorry, sorry." Ben got to his knees. In the dim light, he brought his face over the grimacing soldier. "I'm sorry."

"Ahhhh," the corporal let out through clenched teeth, "it's okay. Just . . . you know, watch it."

"Yeah, I will. I will. You alright?"

"What do you think? No."

"I'm—"

"Can we go?" The downhill soldier whirled a hand like a spindle, impatient. Small-arms fire crackled around the trail. The 1st and 3rd Battalions fought to keep the path open for the litter bearers and the Ammo and Pioneer Platoons. In an hour, when the Kraut spotters on top of the hill got their eyes back with dawn, the artillery and mortars would resume and this trail, with the rest of Mont Castre, would be very dangerous.

"Yeah. Let's go."

Ben got to his feet without confidence that he might not stumble again. He'd been muling on this rainy trail since dusk, with blistering hands full of wounded going down, medicine going back up. He knew in his bones he was done, but he was not finished. This tough, forgiving boy on the litter had a hole in his guts and needed to reach the collecting station now, not after Ben caught a rest. Ben flexed his hands, then coiled them again around the handles.

Another pair of litter bearers climbed the slope. Before Ben could stand erect with his end of the stretcher, his downhill bearer asked one of the others passing by to switch and help him to the bottom.

"Sure," the new carrier said. He handed to his partner the folded stretcher he bore on his shoulder. "Rabbi," he said, "take a break. You look *oysgeshpilt.*"

Ben released the stretcher to this boy, a Yiddish speaker.

"Thank you." Ben moved off the trail. He took a seat on a wet fan of ferns, there was nowhere on Hill 122 that was dry, or safe, just a place to be still.

Before lifting, the new carrier looked down at the wounded soldier. "Hang on, buddy. We're gonna sprint." He turned to Ben.

"Hey, Rabbi. Just wanted to say— The boys, they know what you're doin' up here on the line. They're talkin'. All of 'em, not just the few of us, you know? You're alright. And don't feel bad. I got this one for you."

Ben blew out a breath, nodding. "Where you from?"

"New *Yawk,* greatest city in the world."

"Go Yankees."

"Yeah." The boy grinned. "I hear I'm supposed to say Go Pirates." He hefted the stretcher, seemingly tireless. "*Biz hundert azoi ve tsvantsik.*"

Live till a hundred, like a twenty-year-old.

Ben lifted his chin; he didn't have enough energy to wave. "*Zay gezunt.*"

He watched the Jew and Gentiles descend Mont Castre. Yesterday's casualty count in the 3rd Battalion alone was eighty-three wounded and nine dead, a fifteen percent loss rate. For that fee, the three rifle companies had taken two thousand yards, crossing the field and road, then moved into the forest at the foot of the hill. The action took place out in the open, away from the bocage, accompanied by four Sherman tanks from the 712th TB. This was the first time the battalion had any effective support from the tanks, and all four Shermans were destroyed in the process. Once in the forest, the 3rd regrouped and fought through the afternoon for another five hundred yards of the slope. There, they dug in, and the stretcher bearers, A&P Platoons, and Ben got to work on the trail.

The big push for the north face of Mont Castre would begin at sunrise. Ben was so tired he didn't know how he could stay with the men through the morning. His hands ached, but not as bad as his legs and back. He thought to lay in the ferns but didn't, someone might see him and think he was hurt; that would interfere with the last flow of supplies and wounded. As before, the dead were not carted off the hill but laid aside and covered with tarps, out of sight until the objective was won. The dead had no role to play in the battle. That was the point of killing them.

Ben emptied his canteen down his throat. He felt guilty with every swallow, that the water was not given to a soldier. Ben drank, sorry for dropping the dogface on the trail, sorry that he was thirsty and needy and run-down. He stood, upset that his legs wobbled. He willed them onto the trail and plodded, empty-handed, upward.

He trudged for twenty minutes, thinking of a bed and clean, dry clothes. The morning shroud began to lift. Men passed him on the trail humping ammo and rations, the final runs until nightfall. Soldiers greeted him and Ben could not lift his face from the path to speak back.

In three days Ben could not recall sleeping more than an hour at a time. In combat he ran to the wounded to assist the medic, ran to the dying to ease their passage. The adrenaline squeezing into his veins under fire left him reeling and achy once the shots died down and he slumped to a ditch or a shaded patch, not to sleep but to collapse. In the aftermath of battle he hefted litters, held the hands of scared, wounded soldiers and prayed, dug through the pockets of corpses. He built a dam to hold in his horror at the wounds, the mangled limbs and missing pieces, the mortal holes in the soldiers. He could not ever recoil no matter how ghastly a man lay before him, but had to kneel close every time. Ben listened and calmed terror. He was the last ear for gasps, he tried hard to remember every face and every word said before the specter kneeled beside him. His tunic and pants were stained with the blood of a hundred men in those three days. He spoke beside graves and marked their place on a map for retrieval later. Letters to families piled up, waiting for him like debts. Men who'd not been hit but feared they were next asked him for prayers, chatter, attention.

Ben walked up the trail. He mustered the energy one at a time for each rising step, until he fell to his stomach behind a rotten log, beside Captain Whitcomb.

The young officer eyed Ben on the ground next to him.

"You look good."

Ben laid his nose in the dirt. His helmet tipped. *"Kush meer in toches, mamzer."*

"What's that mean?"

"To be honest, Captain, it means kiss my ass, you bastard."

"Nice."

"Sorry. It slipped out."

"You beginning to think a little better about staying back, Chap?"

"What time is it?"

Whitcomb rustled, checking his watch.

"Thirty minutes till showtime."

"Wake me."

In his dream, Ben was cold. He shivered. He awoke so abruptly he forgot the dream, recalling only the shivering. He cleared his head with a shake. Booms echoed in the trees and dripping brush, rolling downhill at him behind the rotted log. Captain Whitcomb was gone. The attack had begun and the shuddering was in the ground.

He sought the place of the explosions, up into the green nooks of the hill. A hundred yards farther through the woods showed the backs of scrambling soldiers. The five hundred remaining doughs of 3rd Battalion had moved forward—he pulled at his sleeve to check his watch—an hour ago. He'd slept through dawn and the opening mortar salvos that covered the surge.

Ben got to his knees. He was hungry and had to piss. Flakes and dirt clung to his cheek, he brushed them away. He peered up the slope into the morning, where gunsmoke hung like early fog. The blisters in his hands stung, the memory of exhaustion staggered through him. Standing, he took a few steps down the hill.

Behind and above him, the battle waged. He looped his arm around a thin trunk. Hanging on his elbow, he allowed himself the piss. When he was done, he couldn't let the tree go. He was surprised that he was failing. He'd never considered it, and saw how naive he'd been.

Ben's hand went to his breast pocket. Inside was the pack of cigarettes given him by General Billups. Tucked behind that lay the letter, the last written by Capt. Thomas Kahn. Ben patted the pocket and gazed down at his unmoving boots.

The battle sounds were vicious, at close quarters, against an entrenched enemy holding high ground. He could not stop patting his pocket.

Steps stumbled from behind. Ben whirled to see a soldier with one arm strapped to his waist in white gauze. A red stain marked the bullet in his biceps.

He saw Ben and stopped.

"Chap."

"Yeah."

The soldier shook his head. "Don't go up there."

The boy kept moving. The way was so steep it was hard for him to go without grabbing on to something. The dough grunted, disappearing into the green leaves. Ben turned to the battle, believing in the cunning of God to send him such a message.

Branches and trunks braced his climb. He headed straight for the steepness of the face, the shortest distance to the fight. His legs churned on a reserve he didn't know he had until he found himself mounting the slope in bounds. The letter in his pocket stoked his climb. Hitching and pulling himself up, slipping and retaking ground he lost, Ben accepted that the only way God had to stop him was death.

Everywhere, gunfire rang through the dripping, emerald forest. The trees and boulders pealed with machine guns, *zing*ed from richocheted rounds, and clapped with the thunder of lobbed mortar shells. Ben clambered past the first German bodies of the morning. Several were not dead but squirming. An Army medic skittered between them. Ben had no time for the foe, even for the call of *"Jude"* from one close by. He climbed past sandbag redoubts, silent machine guns, and draped bodies. He dove into the fray, to the side of Captain Whitcomb.

The officer had an SCR 536 hand talkie pressed to mouth and ear, shouting orders to a platoon leader in Lima Company. He did not acknowledge Ben's awkward landing. Ben was glad for a moment to catch his breath without explaining to Whitcomb what he was doing on the line again.

"I know, I know! But you gotta make 'em move, Lieutenant! Don't sit on one spot, fire and go, fire and go! That goddam hilltop has got to be ours tonight if it's only you and me. . . ."

Whitcomb snapped his head around to Ben. He grinned.

". . . and Chaplain Kahn left on top of it. Now move up! I want 2nd Platoon on that ridge in ten minutes. Call me when you got it!"

The young captain handed off the radio. He rolled to his stomach and surveyed the slope. The chainsaw bursts of Kraut MG42s spurted far to the right, as though lumberjacks were there chopping trees. These sounds were answered by the thumps of grenades and the distinct pops of M-1 rifle fire. Ben listened and envisioned the lieutenant that Whitcomb had just belted over the walkie, rousing his unit, tossing grenades into an enemy machine-gun nest, exposing himself to the worst dangers in order to be their leader. In his vision Ben saw this unknown boy with one silver bar on his collar mouthing a last and tragic plea for a prayer from the running rabbi.

"Good morning," Whitcomb said. "Have a good nap?"

"I'm not a vulgar man, Captain. But you push me."

"That's what I'm here for. Though keep it in English for me, will ya? So, you want to know what we got?"

Ben eyed the slope, left and right. Where doubts and exhaustion had been minutes before, military instinct took over.

Clearly, the Krauts were not going to surrender Hill 122. Ben guessed the crest lay another 100 to 150 meters away. He rolled to one shoulder and looked behind him. Even on a grim, clouded day like this, Mont Castre rewarded anyone gazing off it with a view for miles to the east, west, and north, the directions of the American advance through Normandy. The Krauts would defend this precious vantage point with every gun they could spare. Every German soldier who retreated southward in front of the Americans through the bocage would have come here. The enemy was not going to hand this mound over. The Mahlman Line existed for one purpose only: to keep Mont Castre.

Tanks were not coming up this slope. Close air support would be impossible under these trees. The trenches and forest of Mont Castre were being contested with rifles and artillery. These were the same tools the Krauts and Ben's Tough Ombres used in 1918. That made this hillside another piece of the eternal war, ugly, slow, and personal. Ben knew what Captain Whitcomb had got.

He had troops scared to advance into the gun sights of an enemy looking down on them. Under his command were as many green replacement soldiers and officers as there were veterans. Every dogface had a buddy in a shallow grave from the past forty-eight hours. He had a slim hold on his slice of the battlefield and on the soldiers who took it for him. Young Captain Whitcomb, L Company, 3rd Battalion, and the whole 359th Regiment were surely sharing this hill with a German force of equal and perhaps superior numbers. Lastly, all of the GIs had orders—to capture Mont Castre.

Ben scooted to his feet. He stepped over Whitcomb's rear and batted the young man on the helmet. Bent at the waist, he took off on oddly crisp legs to dash along the line.

He called over his shoulder, "Right now, Captain, I figure you got *bupkis.*"

Whitcomb raised a hand.

"Hey, I know that one! I got nothin'!"

"Right!"

"Where you goin'?"

Ben pointed to the gunplay.

"2nd Platoon."

Any reply from the captain was lost under the sawing of guns ahead. Ben ran behind a hundred doughs. Many of them popped up to fire a few rounds to cover the running rabbi. Some shouted, "Go, Chap!"

German bullets chewed branches and leaves several feet above Ben's head. He galloped through the cheers of the doughs and the slaps of rounds into the trees. The firefight of 2nd Platoon was easy to find, they were the unit farthest up the slope, the only ones close enough to the Krauts to fling hand grenades. He took cover behind a cool, mossy boulder.

Twenty yards uphill, a young lieutenant crept at the head of his forty-man unit. Ben lay at the foot of the rock to observe the assault.

Every man in 2nd Platoon was on the move. Sergeants waggled fingers and fists, battle hand-signs to direct squads to slide forward, fire, and move. Two corporals raked the slope with BARs, triggering in bursts to keep their long barrels from overheating. The platoon's machine gun railed tracers at the unseen Krauts above; the close confines of the forest multiplied this gun's howl. Riflemen creased at the waist to stay low, to grab a few more feet of Mont Castre, then take a knee or belly flop to empty a clip at anything that moved ahead. The lieutenant, a big man, under cover of his platoon's fusillade, hurled another grenade onto a ledge where the Germans had their best angle of fire. The grenade blew, men cried out on both sides of the burst, GIs screamed "Go, go!" wounded foreign tongues wailed somewhere out of sight.

Ben watched 2nd Platoon use their fire and maneuver tactic to perfection on this slope, a better fit here than in the knotted fields of the bocage. Thirty-eight rifles and the barking machine gun worked in tandem with the advance. Men gained ground in units, supporting each other in leapfrog fashion, fire, move, go, fire, move, *go!* The Germans, holding every card of firepower and placement, could not get their guns in action. If a head popped up, it was convinced to duck mighty quick. The doughs were inexorable, and this plus the lieutenant's grit kept them alive. Ben smacked a balled fist against the rock, joining the men's calls for "Get 'em, get 'em!" rising above the blasts. When he heard the shouts in German, *"Wir können nicht sie halten! Fall zurück!"* 2nd Platoon had the ridge.

Ben scurried forward then, with no reason or purpose other than to be in the midst of the doughs when they took the ledge. Remarkably, the platoon had suffered not one casualty in the action. Ben stayed low and jogged forward, catching up with a filthy sergeant. He tapped the man on the back. The squad leader touched Ben in return. Ben moved into the line of the platoon, forty men spread out, each walking a little taller. The lieutenant clambered over a shale shelf onto the lip of the ridge. Kneeling and leveling his rifle to his rib cage, he sniffed through the smoking barrel for trouble around him. He gazed into the woods up the hill. The Germans had melted away into other prepared positions on the slope. Now they were pushed closer to the crest.

The platoon assembled into the Kraut positions. Ben collected surprised glances.

"What are you doin' here, Chap?"

"Where'd you come from?"

"Hey, those Jerries took one look at the rabbi here and took a powder."

Ben accepted pats and elbow bumps, he smiled for the boys like an old mascot. Soldiers sidled past, taking firing positions facing uphill.

The two-man machine-gun crew grabbed their weapon and tripod and belts to hustle up the slope. The trench felt warm, the Krauts' absence in it was recent. The GIs breathed this in, happily, as if the slash in the dirt were fresh bread.

The lieutenant came to slump beside Ben. The man was broad, with a square jaw below Irish green eyes.

"Can you say some thanks, Padre?"

Ben nodded. He held out his hand. The lieutenant gripped it, and reached to the private beside him bearing the walkie-talkie. This boy took another in hand, and within seconds the forty men of the platoon linked themselves to Ben. He looked down the line. Each man kept his chest against the hill, the stock of his weapon propped at his shoulder, but all had put both hands in those of his buddies on either side.

Ben spoke loud enough for everyone to hear, even any Germans in range of their former trench.

"God, we are not finished. We cannot thank You for victory yet. We can only ask You to allow us to continue to fight until our job is done. We ask You to buck us up with Your courage. Protect these boys. Give them strength the way You've given them each other. Hold them in Your hand, too."

Ben squeezed the lieutenant's hand, wanting the young officer to feel it and send it down the line, a surge of spirit.

"Look at us, God. We've come. We're here. We're staying. This is our duty. This is our worship, and our thanks."

He was done. The lieutenant released his hand. Ben saw that the young officer's eyes were closed. The big man still held the hand of the private beside him. With his head lowered, he made the sign of the cross. He uttered, "In the name of the Father, and of the Son, and of the Holy Spirit. Amen."

Beside the lieutenant, the private did the same. Down the trench, soldiers crossed themselves and whispered. Others kept the hands of buddies in theirs and nodded, saying a quiet, "Amen." Two recited out loud the *Shema*.

When they were done, every eye turned to Ben.

"Okay," the lieutenant said. "That was good. Thanks, Padre."

The lieutenant took the radio in hand and clapped it to his ear and lips. Every dogface in the platoon clattered at his position, changing to fresh clips, charging chambers, the machine gun and two BARs set their sights up the slope.

"Lima Zebra, Lima Zebra," the lieutenant called into the walkie, "this is Lima Bear. We are in possession of target ridge. Do you read? Over."

Ben stayed with 2nd Platoon through the morning. The morning settled into a humid and dense blanket against the slope. Orders did not come for L Company to move up, they were far enough out front of the rest of 3rd Battalion. With eyes narrowed into the leaves and the choppy, rising ground, trigger fingers tensed, the front line of Tough Ombres rested and sweated.

Ben moved through the platoon. He talked with the doughs about homes, listened to funny remarks about the dirty fellow beside each of them, some habit of snoring or smell; these men were forged into brothers in the days or weeks under fire. Veterans cliqued with each other, trusting only the guy they'd seen in action. Green boys huddled together. A prayer rippled just beneath the surface for many of them; some asked for it from Ben straight-out, others seemed ashamed at the need but asked through their eyes, or silence. One soldier waved Ben off, sullen, eyeing the trees uphill.

"Everything alright, soldier?"

"Fine. I got no need, okay?"

"No need of what?"

The soldier turned his head to Ben. His hands stayed at his weapon.

"Talking to you means a man's gone weak. That's all."

Ben nodded. "Yes, it does."

The soldier laughed ruefully. He glanced at the dogfaces on either side of him. These other boys knew this sad sack and let the statement go. He was still a brother of the gun to them.

"The hell does that mean?" the soldier said.

"It means we're all weak, and we're all seeking strength."

"Yeah. Well, I'll tell you what, I got mine, okay?"

"Okay." Ben patted the soldier's boot. "Good. We'll all look to you, then."

Ben slid away to the next dough, but as he did so he heard the young soldier mutter, "Keep the fuck away from me, you Jew fuck."

Ben paused to look back. The boy's face was turned to the Germans. Ben moved on.

A grizzly corporal manning one of the cumbersome BARs lamented a Dear John letter from his gal back in Waco. She even wanted him to return her photo. Ben told the corporal to wait right there. He slipped down the line, asking dogfaces for pictures of their own gals and wives. He even asked the soldier who'd told him to get away. The boy dug in his tunic without a word and handed a little photo over. Ben returned to the jilted GI with twenty pocket shots of pretty young women. He told the soldier to send all of these back to Waco along with the girl's picture, and write her that she should pick out her picture and send back the rest, because he couldn't remember which one she was. The soldier teared up and laughed in the same instant, like rain on a sunny day. The platoon called down to the corporal, "Forget her!" "You're out here bustin' your hump!" "Good riddance to bad garbage!"

Ben duckwalked along the line, getting thumbs-up and chuckles from the doughs. In two hours he'd spoken with every man in the platoon, cheering and comforting all who let him, except the lieutenant. Now Ben settled next to him.

"Padre."

"Lieutenant. Where you from?"

"Texas."

"What part?"

The officer's eyes lifted, as though to think of his hometown, suddenly dumb. He made no answer. In another instant, Ben knew why the lieutenant looked skyward.

Beyond the leering branches of the forest, the sound of chariots arriving, neighing horses, screeched downward. The lieutenant filled his lungs.

"Incoming!!"

Every soldier clapped hands over his pot and burrowed his head as low into his knees as he could get. Rifles were left above the trench when the platoon doubled over at the first explosion.

Ben reacted with the rest, burrowing into the side of the lieutenant. The big officer wrapped himself around Ben, as the concussions slammed invisible fists, pounding the ground in a flurry so close one did not fade before the next landed. Ben snapped shut his eyes and felt the lieutenant quake with every shock.

The bombardment poured through the trees. Once a minute, another, fiercer blow hit the forest with an immense force, a supersonic shrill that could only be an .88 fired from miles back. These rounds turned the woods into a razor-storm of flying splinters, the shards whizzed down into the trench, leaving only a smoking stump.

The barrage lasted for a half hour. Several times Ben began to crawl away from the lieutenant to check on the men, but the burly officer clamped his hold on Ben and shook his head. Ben knew there was little he could do, he had no medical supplies with him, and the lieutenant was right to hold him back. Still, he chafed; through the roar of guns and ringing ears, the calls of pain were his summons.

When the final shell exploded, the men roused, unfolding from each other and the depths of the trench. The lieutenant again reacted the quickest. This time Ben moved at his pace. He knew the Germans did not simply fling artillery willy-nilly. They always had a reason. Ben and the lieutenant were of like mind; they peered up the slope through the wafting smoke, expecting to see the first wave of a counterattack. The lieutenant grabbed his rifle, bellowing down the line, "Man your weapons, get on 'em! Let's go!"

Uphill, the forest and ripped-up earth stayed quiet except for the crackling of embers in blasted trees and earth settling in new craters. The platoon nervously fingered triggers. Nerves boiled in the trench. Ben slid behind the lieutenant to move down the line.

None of the dogfaces was seriously injured. Many had cuts and gashes from the spikes of erupting trees. The trench bottom looked like the floor of a saw mill, with wood chips everywhere. A current of jumpy laughter flowed along the platoon, the men believed they'd dodged another bit of bad luck. Ben kept his doubts to himself while he again played the smiling mascot, the running rabbi.

Finishing his rounds, he settled next to the lieutenant. The officer kept eyes on his binoculars, peering uphill, looking for signs that the Krauts had made some move.

"Where were we?" the lieutenant asked, still glassing the slope.

"Texas. What part?"

"Dallas."

Ben had never been to Texas. He knew only that Dallas was a city that grew where two cattle trails crossed in the middle of an empty plain. He liked the thought of this, a wide-open place, not the steel confines of Pittsburgh, the tunnels of old Penn coal mines, and the wintry hollows of eastern valleys. He was about to say this when the sound of a bee zapped past his ear and plastered the lieutenant against the trench wall. A dot opened in the man's back, his coat ripped neatly in a red buttonhole. The lieutenant pivoted even as he slumped from the bullet.

"Goddammit!" he growled.

"Medic!" Ben shouted. "Medic, down here! The lieutenant!"

The officer was winded, the bullet likely pierced a lung. He grabbed at Ben's coat and gasped.

"Padre . . ."

"Medic!" Ben hollered again.

"Padre . . . downhill . . ."

The medic scrambled along the line. Men tightened against the wall to let him pass. He skidded to his knees on the trench floor. Ben said only, "Sniper." The medic nodded and got to work. Ben lifted the lieutenant's dropped binoculars and backed out of the way. The medic hauled off the lieutenant's coat, then rolled the man to his chest, tugging up his shirttail to view the wound. Ben set himself against the downhill wall of the trench and slowly lifted the field glasses, keeping low.

For a moment he saw nothing, thinking only that a sniper had been overlooked in the advance up the hill. The shooter was likely camouflaged, hanging in a tree. He'd taken a shot at the GI with the binoculars, marking that one to be the unit's officer. Ben intended only to glance for a few seconds downhill, he did not want to draw the sniper's attention. What he saw made him scream.

"They're behind us!"

On the floor of the trench, the lieutenant grunted his pain and dismay. A sergeant almost rammed Ben scrambling to his side, grabbing the binoculars. Ben pointed to where he'd seen the gray-suited Germans hustling up the hill, carrying a machine gun and belts of ammo. In a moment the sergeant saw them. He shouted orders to turn half the platoon's guns downhill.

The medic had needed only that minute to wrap the lieutenant's wound, swaddling the officer's torso in gauze. The bullet in his back did not keep him from hoisting himself to a sitting position against the trench.

"Radio. Ahh . . . damn, get me Lima Zebra."

The radioman got on the hand-talkie and located Captain Whitcomb. He gave the radio to the lieutenant.

"Zebra, this is Bear. I've got Krauts downhill from my position. Over."

He listened, eyes closed.

"Yes, I'm hit. I'll be okay. Over."

The sergeant knelt close. The wounded lieutenant sensed his arrival and blinked up at him.

"Roger. Will do. Out."

The lieutenant handed off the radio.

"Okay," he said. Ben could tell the man was marshaling his strength.

"Here's the skinny. The Krauts moved up under the bombardment. They've taken positions downhill from us. They've cut the trail. They're behind 1st and 3rd Battalions."

The sergeant leaned in closer, seeming to fold, not understanding. The radioman and the medic got the message faster. Their faces fell. They collapsed side by side against the trench wall.

The lieutenant held a shaky hand out to Ben.

"Hope you don't mind sticking around, Padre."

"Nope."

"Good. 'Cause we're surrounded."

The sergeant had little patience for his lieutenant's brave pose. His tone bore an edge.

"So what are we gonna do, Lieutenant?"

Even sitting still against the wall, the bullet must have twisted in the lieutenant's back like a dirk. Every word emerged gritted.

"Captain Whitcomb says to hold the ridge."

The sergeant spat. "That's smart. Where the fuck else are we gonna go?"

"Tell the men to hold fire unless fired on. We got to wait this one out, Sarge. I want discipline till the cavalry gets here. Everybody stays low till we get that sniper."

"Is the cavalry comin', sir?"

"Yeah. Just stay calm. We'll get through this."

Ben had spoken with this sergeant. He was older than the lieutenant, maybe twenty-six or -seven. He came from a small Kansas town. His family owned a bakery. His sister was a nurse. It was her picture he'd given up for the jilted GI from Waco.

Ben laid a hand to his wrist. "You remember how hard it was to get up on this ledge? Now we'll see if the Krauts can do it. I don't think they can."

The sergeant smiled and looked away. "Yeah." He turned down the trench to issue the lieutenant's orders to the other two sergeants in the platoon, then to the men.

The lieutenant struggled to move his right hand to his hip. With effort, he unholstered his .45. "Whitcomb says I should give you this. I won't be using it."

Ben let the pistol hover for a moment, until he saw how much pain it caused the lieutenant to offer. He took the gun.

"Don't say nothin', Padre. I can see it on your face, you got something to tell me and honest to God I don't have the strength to listen. Just shoot whatever sumbitch gets into this trench. Now go on. I won't need you for a while yet."

Ben's fingers closed around the heft of the weapon. This good young Texan was being taken from the world one crimson drop at a time. That was enough reason for Ben to seize this gun, to work a trade for a German should he get the chance. He had that, and so many more reasons, he had the letter in his pocket and a hole in his soul. Holding the gun it seemed he had nothing else in the world. The reasons crowded into his hand for the feel of the pistol. The Germans were on all sides of them. The battalion would need every man, Captain Whitcomb had sent that message.

Ben slipped the pistol back into the lieutenant's holster. He moved without a word, sparing the hurting officer his reasons and arguments.

"We'll get out of this," Ben said, his voice gentle.

He sat with the lieutenant until their own artillery barrage broke downhill over the Germans' heads. The sound of American shelling lacked the crystal crack of the Kraut .88s, but came with typical Yank power, concentrated, relentless, and indiscriminate. Some of the rounds lobbed long and exploded close to the platoon's ledge and the trench. The dogfaces cursed, nailing themselves into the floor of the furrow. The few trees left standing after the German fusillade ten minutes earlier were blasted now to sawdust and blades, the sniper was surely gone with them. The bombardment lasted just ten minutes and denuded the slope below the platoon and all of 1st Battalion. Ben crossed his legs to lay the lieutenant's head in his lap, then folded himself over the man. Listening to the lieutenant's heartbeat, he prayed to the heart, and to the God that made it beat, for the cavalry.

The Germans made their move at sundown.

Enemy mortars and artillery sowed fire across the north slope of Mont Castre. Ben and the trapped platoon crumpled again on the bottom of the trench. Ben clamped his hands over his helmet and felt the shivering shoulders of boys pressed against him. He knew the Krauts were moving up under the barrage. There was nothing anyone could do to stop them. You couldn't even watch them come. Fragments would have instantly shaved off any head lifted above the trench.

The shelling lasted only five minutes. No one was hurt in the platoon. The instant the rounds slowed, all three sergeants bellowed for their squads to man their rifles. The machine-gun crew hoisted their heavy gun to the lip of the trench and set it on its tripod, aimed uphill. Ammo belts were slung around necks for loading. Both BARs faced down the hill. Ben lifted his head to peer above the trench, turning first up the slope, then down. The bullet splash that sent him ducking came from one direction or the other, he didn't know. He dropped to all fours, and the firing began.

The platoon blasted in every direction, ignoring the lieutenant's order to conserve ammo. Ben crawled past boots and bended knees to reach the lieutenant at the end of the line. When he got there the man lay on his side, his legs splayed into the trench. His cheek touched the dirt and Ben knew he was dead. There'd been nothing the medic could do all afternoon but change his wrapping and keep him dim on morphine. Ben slid beside the officer whose name he never knew, even after the day's long hours in the trench waiting. The worried men, even the medic, referred to him only as "the lieutenant." Ben guessed he was a shavetail and that most of the platoon didn't recall his name, either. He arranged the body to lie in a straighter, more dignified manner. The man's wound was not so bad that he should have died from it, he could have been evacuated down the trail hours ago and saved, but the Krauts had closed the path with their counterassault.

Ben sat beside the body, looking down the length of the trench. The doughs fired and fought in two directions. Ben watched the first soldier take a hit, in the neck. The boy fell against the legs of the dough behind him firing uphill. He checked his wound with the flat of his palm. He looked at the blood on his hand, found himself only nicked, and roared something Ben could not hear. The dough took up his rifle, slammed himself against the trench wall again, and returned fire, yelling as the blood trickled along his neck, fearsome-looking and young, not fighting anymore for apple pie or France or anyone's freedom but his own vengeance and his own life. The medic slid behind the dough, tugged at this coattail for attention, and received a backhanded swat to get away.

Before full night fell, five men in the platoon were wounded and two more were killed. One of the sergeants had bullets in both shoulders. When the medic was done wrapping him the sarge looked like a football player on a white-clad team. One dying GI, a Protestant, passed quietly, giving Ben instructions for his mom and dad, accepting Ben's prayer to open heaven's gates. The other died madly, clutching and unbelieving. Ben could not hold this boy to comfort him; instead, he pinned him down while the medic dug into his pack for morphine. The boy died with fists on Ben's coat that did not release until the medic pried them off. The medic and Ben dragged both bodies to the end of the trench, where they were laid beside the lieutenant and Ben mumbled final words.

At one point in the pitched fighting a few downhill Krauts climbed close enough to lob grenades into the trench. Each was flung back in time: One exploded in the air only a second outside the trench. The doughs fired and fired. Ben eyed the pistol still in the dead lieutenant's hip holster. What would he do if the Krauts reached the trench and poured in? Would he grab the gun and shoot, dying in defense of his country and his life, spilling more blood, defying God at the last? Ben did not know. He sat sweating by the lieutenant, afraid and unarmed, still obedient. When the Germans backed down and the sergeants stopped the platoon's triggers with shouts of "Save it, save it!" Ben exhaled. He hung his head to calm himself, to push away the old soldier in him and restore the rabbi.

He peeked above the lip of the wall to see German bodies buckled beside smoking tree stumps. Some were wounded and crawling back down the hill. These broken ones drew fire from the platoon. Ben commanded the shooting stop. The call to war did not include killing the already maimed. The platoon let them go. The sight of bleeding, slinking men pulled dusk down on them all very slowly.

The forest grew too dark to see into. The shooting slowed. The face of Mont Castre slipped into night, an eerie, jagged ghost of a hill. Both remaining sergeants moved along the line, checking ammo, telling the dogfaces to save their rounds, water, and rations, this might be a long haul. Ben followed the radioman to one of the sergeants, the Kansan. The private held out the walkie-talkie.

"Cap'n Whitcomb's on the horn, Sarge."

The sergeant took the radio.

"Sir, this is Sergeant Pullin. . . . He's dead, sir. . . . Yes, sir, I am. . . .

Five wounded, three dead, with the lieutenant . . . Pretty low, we took a lot of incoming, it's been hot here, sir. . . . Yes, sir . . . I'll make sure . . . Sir? . . . Help's comin, ain't it? . . . Alright. Out."

Pullin handed off the talkie. The private scooted away a few paces but held his place near the sergeant, the new 2nd Platoon leader.

"How you fixed for batteries?"

"Got one more, Sarge."

"Damn it. Doc?"

The medic scampered up.

"How're the wounded?"

"One of 'em ain't gonna be alive tomorrow morning we don't get him off this hill. The other four'll likely make it."

"Can any of them fight?"

"Maybe two."

"Alright. Keep on it."

The medic peeled away to his labors. Sergeant Pullin knee-walked across the trench to Ben.

"Chaplain." He kept his voice low.

"Yeah."

"I'm not gonna tell the men this. Okay?"

"Alright."

"The cavalry don't look like they're comin' for a while."

Ben said nothing.

"Maybe tomorrow, Captain Whitcomb says. They're trying to find a battalion that can disengage and get through to us. For right now the Krauts have sunk their teeth into every unit we got around Mont Castre and Beau Coudray. It looks like 1st and 3rd Battalions are gonna spend the night right where we are. We got us a situation here."

"I understand."

"Good. I figure you do. Chap, I need your help with this one, 'cause I ain't no officer. The men got to stay frosty. No more trigger-happy fighting. No guzzlin' canteens. Everybody stays awake on the line. We're gonna take more attacks and we're gonna lose more men. We're gonna run out of food, medicine, and probably the radio and water. If we run out of ammo, that's my fault. If we run out of spirit, I'm gonna blame you."

The sergeant did not smile. Ben grinned at the Kansan. This baker's boy had been heated into a leader. His folks would be proud of what they had made, the doughboy, the son.

Ben unbuttoned his breast pocket and pulled out the pack of cigarettes given him by General Billups. He shook a coffin nail out for
Sergeant Pullin.

The sergeant took the cigarette. Staying low, he flicked his Zippo.

Pullin said, "You know, I can't tell if you're good luck or bad,
Chaplain."

Ben did not put the cigarettes away. He would ease down the line
and hand them out, telling the men to stay low and share the smokes.

"I'm hoping good."

"Yeah. Me, too."

Before the sergeant could pocket his lighter, a crackle pierced the
shattered woods out of the night, from the German positions uphill.

"*Amerikaners . . .*"

"Aw, Christ," the sergeant muttered, shaking his head. Now the man
broke a smile. "I change my mind. I'm thinking you're bad luck."

"*Amerikaners,*" a loudspeaker blared. The voice behind it arched
high, made tinny and almost girly by the little machine in the dark.

"*You are surrounded. You must surrender. We will treat you according to
the Geneva Convention. There is no need to die. Surrender. You have our word,
we will . . .*"

No one in the platoon made a sound. The Kraut's English was ser-
rated and ugly. The GIs with their chins and rifles on the lip of the trench
stared into the black scars of the woods. Dodging and returning bullets
with the enemy was one thing, that was battle; this was another, equally
harsh fight, not for blood but for the will. The platoon had no ammunition of that kind to fire back. They began to fidget and mumble.

Beside Ben and the sergeant, the private lugging the walkie-talkie
scooted close. He held out the radio.

"Cap'n Whitcomb for the chaplain."

The sergeant raised an eyebrow. Ben took the radio.

"Chaplain Kahn here."

The German loudspeaker kept whining across the trench, across all
the positions of 1st and 3rd Battalions on Mont Castre.

Whitcomb's voice asked, "Hey, Chap. That Yiddish you speak. You
talk Kraut, too?"

"*Ja.*"

"Good. Tell him to go fuck himself, pardon my French."

"Serious?"

"I got permission from Regiment. You're our man."

Ben handed off the radio. He stood to his full height, rising above the trench, standing for the first time in fifteen hours.

He pocketed the cigarettes, sliding them in front of the letter from Thomas. He cupped his hands over his mouth and bellowed.

"*Deutsche!*"

The loudspeaker snapped silent.

"*Deutsche! Die Vereinigte Staaten Armee erklärt Ihnen, zu gehen Bumsen sich! Dieses ist ein Jude der dieses sagt!*"

Ben listened to his echoes fly over the Germans in the dark. He hoped his insult slapped every one of them, the more thousands the better. He was sorry the lieutenant and Thomas did not hear him. But other sons, thousands, did.

The platoon stirred. Across the slope, hunkered-down dogfaces cheered.

"What'd he say?" the GIs muttered. "What was that? You hear that, the Chap speaks Kraut! What'd he say?"

Ben ducked below the trench wall. Sitting again, he spoke clearly down the length of the trench.

"Boys, I told the Krauts to go fuck themselves. I told them I was a Jew and to come fucking get me."

The three dozen living doughs of the platoon chuckled, and as one they set themselves to their guns aimed up or down into the night.

Sergeant Pullin patted Ben's shoulder. The cigarette limned his face red and hellish. He looked into the ruins of the forest.

"You're sure enough bad luck, Chap. I'm just hopin' it's for the Krauts and not us."

The MPs were a lazy-looking bunch. Not one of the four pulled their boots down from desks when Joe Amos inquired where John Bailey was kept. One hooked a thumb toward a door. Joe Amos glanced to the ceiling where a big sheet of plyboard had been nailed over a shell hole in the roof. Even swept and re-bricked, one month after almost being knocked over, this squat building in Isigny kept the ferrous smell of a jail.

Joe Amos passed into a narrow, unscrubbed hall. Black-barred cages lined both sides. An optical illusion worked here, the passage seemed longer and taller than it could have been. Just walking past two and three cells made Joe Amos self-conscious. Men looked out at him from unsheeted cots, through rusty rods and wafts of body odor and slop buckets. Every one of them beamed his story in his eyes, stories of anger, alcohol, stupidity. Joe Amos counted eight cells on each side. Out of sixteen prisoners, seven were colored. Joe Amos did not wonder how that could be, in an army made up of ten percent black men. Even in France, this was an American jail.

A few of the prisoners, black and white, called to him. "Hey, man, what's up? What's the news? Who's this now?" The others just stared at him as he walking past.

Joe Amos found Boogie John in the last cage. Boogie lay on his cot, arms crossed over his face to hide from the bare bulbs in the hall. The smell from Boogie's cell was no nicer than the others. A metal bucket stood in the corner, covered by a towel.

"Hey, Boog."

The big man dropped his arms and sat up. Joe Amos rejoiced the moment Boogie stood and came to the bars. The hard faces he'd seen walking through the cells had made him afraid that Boog would be bitter and harmed like these locked-up others. Boogie John smiled and his vast face was shaven, his eyes were untrammeled, and his laugh was giant.

"Brother, brother, brother," Boogie said, opening his arms wide. "College done come to see his old partner. Gimme some sugar, my man."

The two men hugged around the bars. Boogie's clothes were rank. Joe Amos squeezed his face between two peeling rods, and the inch his face entered Boogie's cell made him restive, to be inside even such a little bit.

Boogie backed off but kept his bearish hands on Joe Amos's biceps. "What's that I feel?"

He peeled back his hands.

"Three stripes. My, my, my, you must be playing the man's game really good, College. Look at you. Gettin' all high cotton."

Joe Amos felt the tinge of rebuke in Boogie's tone. He said nothing, tumbling back into his place beside Boogie John, playing the quiet, naive, book-smart one.

Boogie indicated a stool in the hall. "Grab that. Stay awhile. Catch me up."

Joe Amos walked to the stool and lifted it. The white man inside the bars there growled, "That's mine, boy."

Joe Amos backed away with the stool. Boogie shouted from his cell, "Shut your mouth, you cracker piece of shit. You're talking to a sergeant."

Up and down the metallic hall, cages burbled. Other springs squealed, other voices joined in, "Yeah, man," or muttered "Jungle bunny . . ." Up and down the hall, knuckles wrapped around bars. Joe Amos wished he'd been the one to bark at the cracker. He should have, he made up his mind that next time he would. He set the stool in front of Boogie's cell. Boogie took the corner of his bed, squeaking the cheap springs.

"You're lookin' good." Joe Amos started slowly.

"Smell like hell." Boogie laughed. "I look better'n you, anyways."

Joe Amos rubbed his chin, stubbled. "Yeah, they got us goin' day and night. I ought to be asleep right now, only got five hours off. I got another run after midnight."

"That's the only good thing about bein' in here with these assholes, I get to goldbrick and catch up on sleep. What's going on?"

"We're hauling mostly three directions. Back and forth to Cherbourg trying to get the port open up there. Down toward St. Lô where there's some big fighting goin' on. And over south of Ste. Mère-Église they're trying to take some kind of mountain the Krauts are hanging on to. Everything's still all cramped up across Normandy, same as before. Damn bocage is everywhere. Ground's coming real slow. But I hear the breakout is on the way soon."

"Still pickin' everything up off the beach?"

"Yeah. Man, that big storm beat the hell out of everything. You shoulda seen the mess at OMAHA, there were ships and pieces of the harbor busted up all over the place."

"You seen some fightin'?"

Joe Amos shook his head. "Boog, man, I seen some shit. Not a day goes by I don't wash out the back of my truck."

Joe Amos expected Boogie to use this against him, to gig him once more about his desire to fight, to remind him of the dangers and cost, and to tell Joe Amos again how the white folks are welcome to their war because they'll end up keeping all the spoils. But Boogie John just nodded over the undescribed red images of the bed of Joe Amos's truck. Joe Amos knew his friend was a hell-raiser and hard to govern, but Boogie loved life, and that was why he was always in trouble in the Army.

"Well, I figured you was busy, since you're just now comin' to see me."

"Sorry, Boog."

"It's alright. You're here, and I'm halfway done. They gave me forty-five days. Besides, I been wonderin'. Why ain't you in here? You were in that fight, too."

Joe Amos shrugged, glad to make light again. "Major Clay thinks you're the troublemaker. Not me."

"Yeah. Yeah, I heard all about you and Major Clay. I see you got the stripe I told him to give you. And I see that third one. He give you that 'cause you shot down a Jabo, or 'cause you shut your mouth after doin' it?"

Boogie smiled big as ever when he asked this. Boogie already knew the answer. He'd warned Joe Amos three weeks ago. *No matter what you do, they ain't gonna call you a hero.*

"Don't matter," he continued. "Those stripes look good on you, College. Try to keep 'em."

Joe Amos chuckled, relieved that Boogie meant no scold. Sergeant ain't enough, he thought, I'll have to make general before I stop listening to this big son of a bitch.

"You're stuck in here for three more weeks," he said. "I figure I'll be able to keep them about that long."

Boogie stood. He advanced to the bars. "I'll get you into somethin' else."

"I reckon. See you, Boog."

"See you, College. Thanks for the visit. Get some sleep."

Joe Amos stepped away, then stopped. He came back to the bars.

"Oh, hey, I forgot to tell you. I think I met a girl."

"Oh, man! I'm stuck in here and you're getting laid. Man, that is not right! Who is she?"

Joe Amos told Boogie about the broken universal joint, the thieving Marquis and his daughter, the latrine and the German POWs, the big house down in Couvains, the dinner, the secret look.

Boogie guffawed, enjoying Joe Amos's escapade. "Well, that's why I ain't gettin' no visits. Little brother is gettin' seriously busy."

Joe Amos spanked the bars in laughter. "Man, shut up."

Behind the steel rods, Boogie brought his face close. He lowered his voice.

"College, for real. You think this is a good idea? How often you gonna get to see the girl?"

"Hell, I don't know. Whenever I get the chance, I reckon."

"It's soundin' awful busy out there. How often you gonna get the chance?"

"Can't say. I like her, though."

Boogie cocked his head, in that troublemaking way of his. "You got a truck outside? You still got a couple hours off?"

Joe Amos laughed, backing away from the bars. He waved goodbye. "Always trying to get me into hot water."

"Ain't nobody gonna miss you. No one 'cept me, and I'm stuck in here."

"I'll see you."

"Shit, College, the rate you goin', you be in the next cell by morning."

Boogie called after him. "Better yet, you go shoot down another Kraut. Major Clay'll make you a captain next time. Then you might have a chance with that gal."

Joe Amos strode away from Boogie's catcalls. The rest of the cells held men watching him. The hall seemed just as long going the other direction.

"Hey, nigger."

Joe Amos stopped in front of the cell of the prisoner who said this, the white fellow whose stool Joe Amos had taken.

"What?" he asked, inviting it.

"You keep your darkie hands offa white girls. You don't touch 'em back home. You don't touch 'em here. You got that, boy?"

Joe Amos nodded. The rows of cells had gone quiet. Joe Amos walked back to Boogie's cell. He picked up the stool. Lifting it over his head, he hurled it against the bars of the cracker prisoner's cell. The legs broke off and flew into the cage. The stench of the prisoner wafted out when he ducked away.

"Here's your stool back."

Joe Amos didn't listen or look the rest of the way down the long jail hall, not even to Boogie's hoots from the far end.

Halfway to Couvains, McGee sat up. He blinked at Joe Amos behind the wheel, then gazed into the night out the windshield. A mile ahead, the cat's eye lights of a column climbed a dark hill. Behind rolled the slit lamps of another convoy. Occasionally off in the bocage a farmhouse window or open barn door glowed sallow from a kerosene lantern. McGee drew a deep, resigned breath through his nose and laid his head again on the back of the bench seat. In minutes he was snoring.

The sun had been down two hours when Joe Amos stopped in the circular drive of the Marquis's mansion.

Joe Amos climbed out of the cab. McGee awoke to swing up his feet and stretch out on the bench. Joe Amos closed the driver-side door hard, to announce his arrival at night. Behind the closed door, McGee sighed again.

Before he had walked out of the gravel of the drive, one of the wide double doors to the house opened. The Marquis leaned out, followed by a lantern. Joe Amos waved to him. The Marquis retreated behind the doors. Joe Amos watched the yellow light recede, but the door stayed ajar.

He stood in the drive, not sure what the open door meant. Should he let himself in, or was the Marquis coming back? Joe Amos waited until the shine of another lantern lit the doorway.

Geneviève stepped into the night. Like a ghost leaving the house, she wore pale sleeping clothes wrapped in a trailing white blanket. Her feet were bare.

He went to her and took the lantern. She gathered the blanket tighter.

"Sorry, I guess I woke you up."

Geneviève nodded, her face puffy, fresh from sleep. In the stark lantern light, she looked more than a few years older than him. But her long neck was pure white and smooth, and her smile was young enough.

"I don't get much time off," he continued, "and I'm not on shift until one o'clock. So, I figured I'd swing by. I'm sorry. Maybe . . ."

She shook her head. "It is late for a visit," she said. "But, *bon,* you are here. So we shall visit."

Joe Amos was flustered. He'd imagined he might find her in the kitchen or reading late in the living room. He did not know what to do with her in her bedclothes, barefoot in the driveway.

She saw his hesitation. "It is a warm night," she said. "We will sit on the lawn for a while. The stars and the moon are big tonight. And we have a blanket. *Oui?"*

A hand peeked out and softly closed around his. The girl led him off the gravel drive, stepping softly to the grass. Joe Amos lifted the blanket off her shoulders like a cape and spread it on the lawn. She stepped to the center and folded to her knees. She wore unbleached cotton britches and a faint silk top that left her shoulders bare. Joe Amos looked at the outlines of her breasts through the fabric while she turned down the lantern.

He sat beside her, feeling awkward and heavy in his movements, in his boots, beside her luminous feet and skin. He arranged himself with his legs out, ankles crossed, leaning back against his hands flat on the blanket. Geneviève shifted to mimic his posture, and they sat side-by-side like this, heads tilted back at the stars.

Minutes passed in vast quiet. Joe Amos was again befuddled, he felt pressure to say something very clever or deep. He might have an hour alone with her tonight, until midnight, maybe less. At dinner two nights ago, the two of them were at supper and the conversation was helped by the Marquis and the wine. Now, with only her beside him buttressed on her snowy arms, Joe Amos licked his lips and dropped his eyes from the sky to his dirty boots on her blanket.

"So, um . . . Geneviève."

She turned her face to him. "Yes?"

"What was it like growing up here? You know, in that big house."

"Oh . . ." The girl blew out her cheeks, searching for a description of her childhood at this mansion. "It was as you expect." She gestured across the grounds. "Running, playing in the fields. Horses and archery. Cutting the flowers and vegetables from the gardens. Not so interesting, I think."

Joe Amos snickered. "Yeah, not so interesting. Archery and flowers."

"But you, Joe Amos." Geneviève rearranged herself on the blanket, tucking her bare feet under her. "You have had a fascinating life, *oui*? You are young. You are very kind. You are a soldier. Tell me about your home in America."

Joe Amos started talking, eased by her bright manner and flattery. He told the girl about Danville. The big textile mill on the western edge of town. Truck farms and palisades of corn, alfalfa, and tobacco plots on the eastern outskirts. The Dan River, green in winter. Spring lightning bugs, summer bottleflies, autumn crickets. Cars on the paved roads, wagons on the dirt tracks. He bent to his boots and untied his laces. He pulled off one boot and sniffed it to make sure it didn't stink, then tugged off the other and copied her posture, feet tucked under his rump. Geneviève laughed charmingly at the funny bits of his descriptions. She asked questions to keep him going, and since none of her questions had anything to do with his blackness, he made no mention of what it meant in Danville.

"Tell me about your family," she said.

"Oh, my mama," he said, chuckling, "she runs the roost. I got four older sisters and they're all married. Then there's me, the baby. Now everybody's starting to have grandkids, too. Mama, she don't need a switch or nothin' to get her meaning across. She's God-fearin', but everybody says 'How high?' when she says 'Jump.' "

He told her about the mules he'd run over his mama's land, and the brothers-in-law who taught him to plow, hunt, and be a man. He didn't shy from telling her his father had run off when he was an infant, and was never seen in those parts again.

He paused to think of more to tell her now that he was rolling. In that still moment, he was struck by how pretty she was, how her dark hair framed her features. He knew her eyes were green even washed into gray by the stars.

"Geneviève?"

"Yes."

"Your father asked me not to say anything about it to you. And you don't have to, it's okay. But, I was wondering . . . can you tell me about your mother?"

Her eyes fell from his. Not like shooting stars, without the brightness, but just dark stones.

"What did he tell you about her?"

"That she died from the flu. And the Germans did nothing about it. Just let her go."

The girl played her fingers over her bent knees. Joe Amos wanted to reach for her hands but did not.

Without looking up, Geneviève told him, "Yes, she is dead."

"The Marquis said she was a real pistol. Gave the Krauts hell the whole time they were here."

"*Oui.* Even so, she died quietly."

"Really?"

"My *mère*, Joe Amos, she was a woman like your mother. Strong. But when the Germans were here for four years, she used all her strength."

"How about your father? What did he do?"

"He is a willful man. It was he who made my mother quiet, who made her bend her will to the Germans. He was correct to do this. If we would have resisted, they would have shot us or sent us all to a camp, perhaps burned our home. I do not know that we would have survived. I do not blame him. But it was silence that killed my mother."

With care, Joe Amos reached under her chin. He lifted her face. He imagined he saw there the vestiges of the brave mother, the years and sacrifice under the Germans, her fevered death. He saw no anger for the Marquis, so felt none on his own. Geneviève took his hand. Joe Amos squeezed her palm, then lifted it to his lips.

"We should go now. It is late," she said, "and I heard your McGee snoring in the truck."

She stood first, stepping lightly off the blanket. Joe Amos pulled his boots over his OD socks, then raised the blanket and shook it out. He wrapped it around her. He bent for the lantern and handed it to her. She did not turn up the wick but left it dim.

Geneviève stepped close. Her lips brushed his cheek.

"Come back," she whispered.

She turned away. The girl floated over the grass, the blanket a train behind her. Again, she was all in white, again a ghost, but now returning to the big dark house.

D+32

JULY 8

A milk of moonlight spread across the face of Mont Castre. The Norman summer night lay cool. Shadows and crater pools creaked with stepped-on sticks and shifting men. Each sound drew fire, blue gunpowder blinks from the GIs and the whiz of bullets from the Krauts above and below. When the shooting eased, they left someone hurt either in the doughs' lines or the unseen ranks of the enemy. Cries for corpsmen tolled the damage in English and German. For a mile across the surrounded positions of 1st and 3rd Battalions, the night and the slope of the hill snapped like a campfire with shots.

The Krauts called twice more for the thousand Americans to surrender. Between the loudspeaker assaults, they spoke with guns, mortars, and running boots. The GIs fired back their waning ammunition.

With dawn two hours away, Sergeant Pullin plopped next to Ben. The radioman private did not follow the sergeant around the trench any longer, the last battery was drained. Captain Whitcomb and the rest of Lima Company were out of touch with 2nd Platoon except for runners, and these rabbits ran under intense fire.

"Chap, you got any more of those cigarettes?"

"Gave out the last one two hours ago."

"Figures."

The sergeant licked his lips, perhaps wanting tobacco, or to moisten his mouth, with nothing in his canteen. Ben had no water or smokes to offer, just words, and he had none of them that were not stale. Somewhere to the east, shots rang. Pullin didn't turn his head that way. He kept his eyes down the hill.

"Why don't they just come for us?" he asked.

Ben knew the answer. The Germans hadn't changed their style of defense in a quarter century. Their Generals valued territory more than anything, more than the raw numbers the Americans used to yardstick success. Whenever the Krauts lost ground, they always counterattacked. They could lose ten thousand men and hold a fortress and call that victory. Americans would not bleed into the soil the way the Germans would. More than anything, more than any weapon or trait, that made them fearsome enemies.

"They're trying to wear us down first. They figure we'll get desperate enough to go after them downhill, to get out of being surrounded."

"Then they'll disappear into the woods. We'll swing and miss. I get it."

"And all we'll have done is give them back the hundred yards of this hill we already took."

Another yap of fighting erupted out in the fields at the north foot of Mont Castre. The sergeant nodded, comprehending.

"They're keeping the whole damned division busy," Pullin said. "No one can get to us."

"Someone will," Ben answered.

"He better bring me a steak."

Ben was hungry, too.

"When's the counterattack, you reckon?"

"Sunrise."

"You scared, Chap?"

"Yep. As much as anybody on this hill."

"Funny. The men don't think you are."

"What?"

"Yeah, they figure since you're older and you been in the other war, you've seen this kind of thing, being surrounded. And you got, you know, the God thing working for you."

Ben looked into the dark outline he made on the trench, wishing the shadow were a hole he could drop into, a tunnel leading away. He would not say to this sergeant how wrong the men's assessment was. He was more frightened now than he'd ever been as a fighting man. Ben Kahn the chaplain did not have the luxuries of a rifleman. He did not fix his stare into one place in the dark, uphill or down, guarding his station and doing his bit, he did not have comrades at his sides to whisper and confide in, no gun took up his hands with single purpose. His memories of the first war were no help, they only added to his burden of images in the dark and toted up the body count far more than what lay in the trench tonight. Ben was afraid and God was no solace because, godlike, he saw everything—struggle, life, and death. Ben could not look away, he, too, had to be everywhere and always selfless. And now that he was not even credited with fear by the men, he felt like God, alone.

The sergeant waited for a response but got nothing. Ben pivoted away. Keeping below the lip of the trench he walked to the far end, where the bodies were collected. Since nightfall another corpse had been added, another of the wounded had died. There were now three dead beside the lieutenant. Ben sat at their feet, his back to the platoon. He put his face in his hands. Should anyone come close, he would look to be praying.

Phineas Allenby arrived with the following dusk. The little preacher seemed to step out of a dream. The way dreams have coronas, Phineas glowed.

"Hello, Ben."

"Hello, Phineas. Get down."

Phineas stood too tall above the trench. He would be shot. The Germans shot everyone they could see.

"It's alright, Ben." Phineas came closer. He held out a canteen. "Have some water."

Ben could not take the canteen. His own hands were busy buttoning the pockets of Waco, the corporal who'd gotten the Dear John letter. Ben had rifled the boy's body, not looking for personal items, not trying to retrieve the twenty pictures of the platoon's gals, but scrounging for rations, cigarettes, water, anything the dead boy did not need, but the two dozen living men of the platoon had to have to go on fighting.

Sixteen bodies lay at this end of the trench, arranged in four piles. All the heads faced one way, boots the other. If Phineas asked, Ben could describe the wound that killed each, the last sounds from each mouth, the many kinds of prayers he whispered, the pressure of each hand before release. Deaths at dawn, daylight, sundown, or darkness, each had his own moment and parting light. He could tell Phineas how this one's from Houston, that one's got a gal who's a pinup model, this one wants to be a crop duster pilot. It was sad and wrong to stack them like this, to mingle them.

Behind Phineas, the tatters of the platoon were still there, squatting and staring up the hill. Ben could point at each of the twenty-four men still breathing and tell details of their living. Half of them wore the last wraps of the dead medic's gauze supply, scavenged by Ben from the medic's pockets and cubbies. All had bayonets fixed, out of ammo at last.

There were other figures in the trench, faces he did not recognize. Each dogface of the platoon had an angel with him, another soldier giving him things, settling beside him and aiming another gun up the slope. Sergeant Pullin spoke into his radio, someone had found him a fresh battery. The men puffed cigarettes, though Ben had given them the last of his pack a day ago. Phineas was Ben's angel. Ben cupped his blood-rusted hands under the canteen Phineas still held. Phineas poured. The water instantly became red, slippery with blood. Phineas stopped pouring.

Ben turned from Phineas. The boots of one of the corpses began to rise. Above the trench, where the Germans would surely shoot them if this were not imagined, three teams of litter bearers lifted bodies out of the trench to lay them on stretchers. Ben did nothing to stop them, dream or not. The dead had been his alone for thirty hours but he knew they would be taken from him. He watched the first boy carted off, and with the boy went the memory Ben held of him. He could not recall the boy's name or his town or what he'd found in his pockets. He watched another hoisted and hauled away. Ben had meant to mark every one of them. When a third was plucked from the trench, Phineas woke him with a firm touch. Ben's hands were cold. He looked up at the little chaplain and blinked.

"Drink some water, Ben."

His awakened body was a miser. The water in his throat stoked his need. Phineas would not let him drink as fast and much as he desired. Ben let the canteen go reluctantly, gasping as though running.

"I reckon you're hungry."

While Phineas opened a K-ration pack, Ben could not stop his fingers from waving like antennae. He devoured every edible thing. When he was done, he huffed, glaring at the knapsack for more.

Phineas sat in the trench. All the bodies were gone. Ben had not noticed the last of them ferried away. The trench was peopled again with living soldiers, their guns faced to the crest of Mont Castre. Where were the Germans downhill? Ben was not thirsty and only a little hungry. He looked at his washed hands.

"What happened?" he asked Phineas.

"We broke through to you guys."

"Who did?"

"2nd Battalion, 358th."

"When?"

"An hour ago. Didn't you hear us?"

Ben could not remember the last hour—or any hour—from the trench. Like sand in an hourglass, the bodies were how Ben had measured time with the dying platoon.

"No. There was just fighting."

Phineas said nothing for moments. His eyes studied Ben, seeming to measure him. Ben wondered how bad he must look and saw that Phineas wanted that experience for himself, the heroism of surviving, the haggard tale.

"Tell me about it."

Ben shrugged. The men of 2nd Platoon had not lived a tale on Mont Castre. There was no story to tell, just misery and terror. Phineas was eager for combat and proof. The bulge of the Colt showed at his waist. Ben wanted to sleep, not relive the trench. But Phineas had come for him, so he spoke.

"Sundown yesterday they started shelling us. They didn't let up more than an hour at a time. They had this awful little loudspeaker they used to ask us to surrender. The voice was the same every time, some high-pitched Kraut. You could tell by the sound of his voice in the dark they were getting closer. Then somewhere this morning before the sun came up they stopped talking. They shelled us for an hour straight. When it was over, that's when they hit hardest, from both directions. The boys were low on ammo, no one had slept a wink since I don't know when. The medic went down, the radio was dead, only one sergeant was left. It was . . . there was . . . some grenades got into the trench. We . . . I don't know how, we kept them back. There couldn't have been a hundred rounds left in the whole platoon. Then they just went back to shelling us. All day. A couple of the boys, they wanted to get up and hightail it, I guess they just ran out of steam. There wasn't anyplace to go. First one, then two more later on, they stood up. I couldn't . . . I wasn't close enough, I don't know. The rest, we just . . . I don't want to, Phineas. That's enough."

Ben shook his head, saying no. His head would not stop shaking side to side, the shake became a tremor, as if something were trying to hatch out of him. He gritted his teeth and could not look at Phineas. The little chaplain tried to wrap his arms around Ben, but Ben parried him off. Phineas held his ground and took Ben in an embrace, laying his nose to Ben's shoulder and clasping hard. Ben trembled, out of control. He closed his eyes and listened to Phineas pray for him.

Ben calmed. Phineas let go. Embarrassment stained Ben's breathing but Phineas blinked and smiled, certain that God had eased his friend. Ben saw that Phineas had allotted him heroism, and by being Ben's friend, by comforting him, Phineas Allenby had pilfered some for himself.

Ben turned at bootsteps above the trench. Even with Phineas and the 358th here for his rescue, Ben tensed until he saw Captain Whitcomb drop down.

The officer had faded in thirty hours, growing thinner and raven-eyed. He folded fast to his knees, not confident like the newcomers that a man could stay above cover.

He aimed a filthy finger at Ben.

"I don't want to hear one word out of you, Chaplain. This is an order. The trail's open again, and I don't know for how long. I'm telling you to get your butt down Mont Castre to the aid station."

Ben could not consider this. A little sleep, a meal, he'd be fine. But the look on Whitcomb did not invite cavil. The man had been pared down to a blade of a figure, perhaps because his whole company had been cut down by the Germans. Young Captain Whitcomb had lost bits of himself along with his winnowed command.

"If I see you up on the line in the next few days, believe me, I will hog-tie you myself and deliver you to the first boat back to England. You take me serious at this, Chaplain. Get out of here and get some rest. Your friend here will see you down the trail."

Whitcomb looked at Phineas.

"Thanks for coming to get us, Chaplain. Make sure you tell your boys that."

"Will do, Captain."

Ben felt Whitcomb's order release him, now he was finished with the trench. Phineas took Ben by the arm and stood, towing him to his feet. He stood in the trench on rickety, knurled knees. Whitcomb gazed at him.

"By the way. You probably haven't heard the word. It just came down. Colonel Melrose got the sack yesterday."

Melrose was the 359th's CO. Ben had not met him but by all reports he was a good, respected man.

Whitcomb licked his thumb. "Reckon somebody had to be the goat for us getting stuck up here. Man, this ass-coverin' merry-go-round is killin' us."

Whitcomb saluted Ben and Phineas, then stalked off across the charred slope. The assault up to the crest of the hill would continue as soon as supplies were hauled in and replacements arrived to flesh out the ravaged 1st and 3rd Battalions. Through a day and a half of incessant attack, no one had surrendered, no piece of this slope had been given back. Men had died here. Hungry, thirsty men had fixed bayonets when their rifles got as empty as their bellies. No matter. Once more the 90th was in turmoil, with blame flying like shrapnel. Every dogface who'd suffered through these woods and was alive to be thankful was now told with the firing of his regimental CO that he had not given, not bled, enough. That he was to blame.

The sun sank on Mont Castre. The Kraut loudspeaker had been shut up. The Mahlman Line would be broken tomorrow by these Tough Ombres, still the U.S. Army's problem division, with their morale again kicked into the latrine.

Phineas never took his hand from Ben's shoulder. They clambered up on the ledge. Ben did not speak to the men of the platoon who stayed behind. There was nothing he needed to tell them. They had a wisdom now beyond what he could impart.

He and Phineas joined a long line of soldiers and stretchers tramping down the trail in the fading light. Too many blankets on litters were pulled high, faces masked under the OD wool. On other litters wounded and exhausted boys, all of them veterans now, were grateful to be carried away. Dozens walked on their own. Some, like Ben, had no visible wounds. Ben was too tired to be amazed at the amount of casualties spit out by Mont Castre. Phineas clucked his tongue.

Halfway down the trail, Ben looked through the remnants of the forest to the flat fields at the hill's foot. There, a convoy of Jimmies with their shaded little lights began to pull up and form echelons. Soldiers jumped out of the beds. Through the stumps and charcoal trees Ben heard sergeants yelling at the soldiers to line up. These soldiers were replacements in clean uniforms. They milled like cattle in the field until voices prodded them to order.

Ben pulled his arm from Phineas's grip.

"Let's hurry," he said, speeding his pace down the slope.

"They'll be alright," Phineas insisted, "they're not your concern. Let 'em alone."

Phineas believed that Ben wanted to get down the trail to speak to the replacements, to maybe give them a prayer or encouragement. Ben did not say otherwise. He wanted only to get off the trail. He could not bear to see the new boys pass.

White Dog tapped a pen on the bistro table. Ersatz coffee steamed at his elbow. His legs were crossed. He brushed a crumb of *pâtisserie* off the knee of his baggy slacks.

A Gene Krupa drum solo nibbled in his brain, distracting his attention from the café. No matter. He had excellent security. Two men watched the front door; one, the back. A network of urchins, all on the candy-bar payroll, loitered in the alleys. A motorcycle waited stashed behind some garbage cans.

White Dog wondered if Gene Krupa was the best drummer in the world. The world seemed to think so, but they hadn't heard this new kid, Gaston Léonard. No one had heard Léonard play yet, not outside Paris. The Krauts didn't give a damn about jazz. Léonard could play his butt off. The day's coming, White Dog thought. A lot of stuff's going to start when America finally gets here.

White Dog had decided to wait only a few more minutes when his men stopped a fellow at the door. Except for White Dog, the café was closed. The owner, paid in meat, stayed in the kitchen and only came out to serve him a coffee and a sweet. White Dog liked this custom, where the French knocked off for two or three hours in the middle of every afternoon. The Frogs figured a long, leisurely lunch eaten at home was the best practice of a civilized folk. It was one of many things the Krauts had failed to stamp out about Paris. Besides, the chronic shortage of food and the high prices in restaurants made it cheaper for the Frogs to eat in their own homes. Everything's got two reasons, the one you say and the one you don't. White Dog smiled hello and stood.

"*Bonjour. Êtes-vous Voltaire?*"

The newcomer was short and stocky, thicker in the middle than White Dog. His jowls jiggled when he answered with a laugh and a handshake.

"*Je ne suis pas Voltaire. Je suis Hugo. Voltaire ne vient pas aux réunions personnellement.*"

White Dog and the man who said his name was Hugo sat. The owner, keeping a close eye if not an ear, appeared with coffee and another pastry. White Dog and Hugo waited for the man in his apron to bustle away.

"So Voltaire doesn't come to meetings personally?" White Dog spoke in English to keep his henchmen and the café owner from eavesdropping.

Hugo answered in English. "No. He sends others."

"Or maybe he just doesn't want to meet with me. Is that it, maybe?"

Hugo eyed White Dog. He cocked his head and answered carefully.

"I will carry your request."

"Do that, *mon ami*. I prefer Voltaire to Hugo anyway. Do you guys have a Balzac, too?"

"*Oui.*"

"Maybe send him next time."

The fat little man who went by the name Hugo slurped his coffee, amused and probably dangerous. He was an odd-looking gangster, not like the ones White Dog had grown up reading about. Dillinger, Clyde Barrow, Machine Gun Kelly—they were real tough guys. This bad-egg Hugo looked more like Capone, soft and mean. White Dog had grown soft, too, flabby from *beignets* and cognac, pale from shadows. He wondered if he had the same nasty eyes that Hugo had trained on him. White Dog considered making a jest, that he was thinking about renaming his own gang the White Dog Band, giving his men names like Dizzy, Basie, Duke, and Tatum. He eyed Hugo and figured the grim little shit wouldn't get the humor.

Hugo held his saucer under the cup while he sipped. It was a fey French gesture, annoying to White Dog. Americans just drink the damn coffee, he thought.

Hugo finished his coffee. He showed no distaste for the fact that it was not real, just chicory.

"I may ask you a question now?"

"Shoot."

"Where is *Monsieur Acier*?"

White Dog licked his lips, pausing to give Hugo an impious look.

"He's gone."

"Gone where?" Hugo asked.

"Gone. He got picked up. Last month."

"How unlucky."

"I almost got grabbed myself. The Gestapo did a crackdown. Chased the hell out of me."

"You were fortunate to get away."

"Very. Anyway, I'm running things now."

"Yes. So you say."

"Listen," White Dog said, "I got everything you want. And what I don't have, I can get. Is that gonna be a problem for Voltaire?"

"I think not. We would merely like to know you can be trusted."

"Let's just say I have ambition. You have ambition, Hugo?"

"*Oui*. We all must, or there is no reason."

The reason you say, White Dog thought, and the one you don't.

"Then we see eye to eye."

"Voltaire will be relieved."

White Dog uncrossed his legs. He pushed the hem of his silk jacket behind his hip to lean across the little bistro table.

"Let me tell you something, Hugo. When the Yanks get here—and they will get here—who do you think they're going to deal with? You and your Frog buddies, a bunch of gangland wannabes, or me, an American? A shot-down pilot, one of their own. Hmm?"

"You. *Certainement*. However, Voltaire is of the opinion the Americans might also have dealt nicely with *Monsieur Acier*."

"*Acier* didn't have a plan. He didn't think big."

Hugo ran a finger along the rim of his coffee cup. "You are a big thinker."

"You got that right. The Yanks are gonna be here before summer's out. I'm ready for them."

"*Comment?*"

"Here's what I'm proposing. I'm gonna specialize in gasoline. Everybody else will be running crap like chocolate bars, nylons, butter. Not me. I got it all worked out. I got a system, and I got the network. Nothing, I mean nothing, is going to be available in more quantity, and at a higher price, than gas. You know this. I'm talking about millions of gallons."

"I believe that will be so. You Americans love your machines."

"Paris is gonna explode. For four years, the Krauts have kept the whole city down. As soon as they're gone, the demand for everything, you name it, is gonna go through the roof. And how are all those goods going to move around? Got any idea? Trucks. And what do trucks run on?"

Hugo inclined his head. "Gasoline."

White Dog dug a thumb under his suspenders. He snapped the elastic against his linen shirt and sat back in his chair. "Gasoline."

Hugo grinned, enjoying this Yank showmanship. White Dog didn't care that this Frenchman might consider his suspender snapping, his thumb now pointing into his own chest, vulgar.

"I will inform *Monsieur Voltaire* of your big plan. Gasoline. It may help him forget his fondness for *Monsieur Acier.*"

White Dog pointed one finger like a pistol, to say: You got it.

Hugo asked, "*Chien Blanc?* Why is this your *surnom?* White Dog. I see the white, you are quite pale, you know. But why a dog?"

Hugo finished his poor coffee and dabbed his lips with a handkerchief. White Dog struggled not to loathe this man. Hugo was a saggy, jowly criminal with manners affected to be superior. I've got to get out of here soon, White Dog thought, or I'm going to shoot one of these Frog bastards.

He beamed toothily, unconcerned that he was making himself a lampoon in his roomy suit, spats, and skinny moustache. It was a way to spit some America on this sissy Frenchman.

"Because I'm your best friend," he answered.

THIRD

Gregarious, extrovertive, strongly attached to group and family. Easygoing—line of least resistance, not physically lazy. Very sensitive. Resentful of correction. Easily hurt by criticism in public. Mentally lazy, not retentive. Ruled by instinct and emotion rather than by reason. Has to be made to face facts, prone to escapism . . . Lies easily. Can only be led, not driven.

Excerpt from a War Department memo:
"Certain Characteristics of the Negro Which
Affect Command of Negro Troops"

D+35
JULY 11

Joe Amos opened his eyes to a white face leaning close.

"Joe Amos."

He sat up on the cot.

Joe Amos whispered back, "What you need, Lieutenant?"

Garner patted him on his bare shoulder and motioned to follow him outside. The air in the bivouac tent stank of exhaustion, drivers too wiped out to shower or brush their teeth. The smell of snores, farts, and socks added to the humidity leaching from the damp ground. Someone had griped that France got more rain in June and July '44 than in any month-and-a-half period of the twentieth century. But the last two days had been hot and dry and the earth seemed finally to be wringing itself out.

Joe Amos tugged on his OD undershirt. He eased from the flimsy mattress and headed for the tent flap held open by Garner.

Outside, he asked, "What time is it?"

"0500. I've got a detail I want you to head up this morning."

"Alright." Garner held three cartons of Chesterfields. "Those for me?"

Garner did not smile. He treated the question as ludicrous.

"No. These belong to Major Clay. At 0700, you'll lead a squad of ten trucks up to UTAH. You'll pick up a company of Airborne that's coming ashore this morning. Take 'em up to Cherbourg."

"No problem."

Garner lifted the boxes of smokes. He waggled them in front of Joe Amos like they were stacks of dollars.

"It turns out that the Kraut General in charge of defending Cherbourg, ol' Von Schlieben, he got himself and his garrison ready for a nice long siege. They stocked a bunch of underground shelters with everything they'd need. Apparently, that included the biggest collection of French wines, champagne, and brandy that anyone has ever seen on this earth."

Joe Amos thought of the Marquis and his wine cellar. How large must the Krauts' cellars have been to supply thirty thousand men?

Garner lowered his voice. "Von Schlieben had no problem smashing the whole damn harbor so we couldn't use it. But when it came to spilling good booze, he couldn't bring himself to do it. So." Garner rattled the smokes again for effect, coming to his point. "Major Clay would like you to do him a little favor while you're up in Cherbourg. He wants you to trade these for as much of that booty as you can get your hands on. He says you can keep two packs of the Chesterfields for yourself. What do you say, Sergeant?"

"Sounds fine."

" 'Course, if anyone asks, you're just working for yourself. The Major don't know nothin' about this. You understand?"

"Where'd I get those, just in case?"

"Same place I got 'em. From Mr. Nobody."

Joe Amos took the cartons. "Got it."

"Good. Go get another couple hours of shut-eye."

"Lieutenant?"

The officer turned impatiently.

"What?"

"I don't mind doin' this. But I got something I'd like to ask you back. Between you and me."

"Uh huh."

"Every chance you get to send me down to St. Lô, I want it."

Garner seemed tempted to ask why. But this was a man who'd just handed Joe Amos three cartons of smokes, far more than any single soldier, even a Major, should legally possess. An agreement struck itself between the two with Garner's quiet, simple nod.

* * *

"Wind 'em up!"

Joe Amos, lead driver and sergeant on this morning's route, hollered, walking down the line of Jimmies. He spun his arm in a big arc like a propeller. McGee Mays grinned proudly when Joe Amos climbed behind Lucky's wheel.

Joe Amos led the ten trucks out of the bivouac. Muddy ruts in the grassy field cut by a thousand tires had dried, and Lucky kicked dust. The muffler had sprouted a hole; the Jimmy sounded powerful in low gear. The day promised to be steamy and clear. McGee seemed raring to go. His breath smelled of coffee. At the main road, Joe Amos was waved onto the tarmac by an MP and quickly set the pace for his little convoy.

"McGee, look in my pack."

The boy finished rolling up his sleeves over sleek black forearms. Joe Amos noted again the muscle and color of this Florida Negro. There was nothing ambiguous about McGee, not in his heart or his skin.

"I be dogged." McGee whistled, gazing into the mouth of Joe Amos's backpack. "Where you get these?"

"Don't worry about it. Open a carton."

McGee did not pursue the question. He tore the side out of one long box and handed Joe Amos a pack of Chesterfields. Joe Amos tucked the flimsy pack in his shirt.

"Take one for yourself and stick the rest in the glove compartment."

McGee did what he was told and set away the backpack with the two remaining cartons. Joe Amos reached for the pack McGee held on to. He tore open the foil top with his teeth, spit a shred out the window, and stuck a fag on his lips. He flipped his lighter and dragged in the smoke. He returned the pack to McGee.

"You don't smoke, do you?"

"Never had no money for it. I always liked liquor better."

Joe Amos tossed his lighter and Chesterfields into McGee's lap.

"Give it a try."

In a minute, McGee was doubled over hacking. Between puffs, he looked to Joe Amos, who smoked stylishly without touching the cigarette with his fingers, he just stuck it to his lips and worked the tobacco, with his hands busy on the wheel. McGee labored through the Chesterfield with eyes watering from the coughs. Joe Amos held out his hand.

"Alright, alright, give 'em back. You're gonna kill yourself."

McGee held on to the cigarettes and lighter. "No, I'll get it, Sarge. Leave me to it."

At UTAH, the company of Airborne waited. Two hundred scrubbed soldiers milled in the sand with their trouser legs tucked into jump boots, even though they'd come across the Channel on a cruiser. Joe Amos pulled up across the broad beach. Behind him, the other trucks formed a fine straight line. Joe Amos was glad to see the discipline in his convoy, a good first impression for these green white boys.

UTAH was not strewn with wreckage the way OMAHA had been after the storm. And the invasion here had been less difficult, not defended as heavily by the Krauts. The dunes were flatter, access off the beach was not so limited as it was at OMAHA, with its four bunkered draws. Splashing through the skim of early-morning surf, a local in a beret trotted his sulky behind a beautiful chestnut horse. McGee grinned big at this sight. His fourth cigarette was snugged between fingers that pointed out his window at the clopping horse, the snap of a buggy whip, and the hiss of sliding waves.

"Mornin', y'all," he called out his good mood to the Airborne. "Ya'll see that buggy? That's somethin'."

Joe Amos did not hear the reply from the men climbing into his truck bed. McGee pulled back, his face stung and slack.

"What?"

"Nothin'," McGee said. "Let's just drive 'em."

"What? Somebody say somethin' to you?"

"Leave it, Sarge."

Twenty soldiers clomped into Lucky's bed, twenty into each Jimmy in line. Their jump boots made more clatter than regular Joes did. These Airborne troops were weighted with equipment and grenades, every one of them wore at least three knives and two cartridge belts, trenching tool, blanket roll, rifle, and pistol. They looked part soldier, part tractor. Every face bore a scowl, a tough-guy mien, though not a one of them had seen the first minute of combat. McGee had seen more, even from a ditch. Joe Amos had shot down a Jabo; these Caspers were standing now on the bullet holes a black man had won. McGee had just been trying to welcome them to France. Joe Amos ground his teeth.

"Gimme the cigarette."

McGee handed it over. An Airborne captain came to his driver's side and spoke up.

"Cherbourg, right?"

"That's right."

Joe Amos did not say Sir and he did not pull the cigarette from his mouth.

The captain glared up. Joe Amos bore down.

The captain said, "That's right, *sir.*"

Joe Amos took his elbow from the sill. He tossed the cigarette into the sand.

"That's right, sir."

The captain gave Joe Amos another moment to say more. Joe Amos did not. The officer seemed to consider this all the victory he had time for this morning over this uppity colored driver.

"Alright, then. Move out."

The captain leaped last onto Lucky's back. The canvas shells on all ten Jimmies were down. Joe Amos saw the company mounted in his rearview and gave the gas and clutch their nudges. The muffler grumbled and the Jimmy rolled easy. Men weighed nothing next to Lucky's normal tonnage.

Joe Amos led the convoy off the beach. He simmered alongside McGee, both sat quiet while the sand gave way to pavement.

Out on the road, Joe Amos's ten Jimmies got in line behind another column headed north from UTAH. Far back, more trucks closed the gap.

"Road's crowded this mornin'," McGee said.

Joe Amos didn't answer. The road to Cherbourg was always crowded, every road in the American lodgment was being choked and worn out. Since June 6, more than a million and a quarter Allied soldiers had been ferried from England, and more than 600,000 tons of supplies, enough to load up a freight train two hundred miles long. All this had been bottled for five weeks behind a front only forty miles long, chewing up men and matériel and the trucks to deliver them and the roads, too, just to gain a few hundred yards a day, especially down around St. Lô and south of Ste. Mère-Église.

Distracted, Joe Amos came up too close behind the rear of the last Jimmy of the convoy ahead. The truck hauled ration crates. He didn't see a pothole and clipped it.

The truck clouted on its suspension and shimmied, a spring was probably shot. Someone in the Airborne smacked a fist on the canvas roof, the cloth plugs in the bullet holes bowed in.

"Dammit, boy! Watch it!"

Joe Amos looked in his side mirror. Arms and faces lined the slat

sides of the bed. The soldiers arrayed their heads into the wind like riding dogs, mean, junkyard Danville dogs, Joe Amos thought. He'd been
chased by a few of them before. He wasn't a sergeant then. I ain't being
chased anymore, he thought. My men ain't, either. Not McGee, not any
of them in my convoy.

Joe Amos laid back from the bumper in front and waited.

The morning brightened. Without the military traffic roaring everywhere on conked-out mufflers, without the knocked-down fences and
char places in the earth, the air felt clean, blue, and sandy. Joe Amos ignored it the way a man in a sour mood dispatches a playful child from
his presence. He had something in mind. McGee sensed it.

"What?"

"Nothin'. Just watch."

The column passed through Ste. Mère-Église and slowed, so much administration of the American force in Normandy flowed out of here.
Northwest of town stood the village of Le Val. Some of the bombs that fell
on Ste. Mère-Église the night before D-Day had landed wide and tore up
the little burg and the road that ran through it. COM Z engineers were still
working on repairs. Traffic had been routed through the fields over a bulldozed dirt track, rejoining the main road a mile later at Edmondeville.

Joe Amos crossed his fingers that the trucks in front of him would
not turn off at Ste. Mère-Église. They did not. He nodded and closed the
gap again to the bumper.

He told McGee, "Roll your window up."

The last Jimmy of the convoy in front was put there for a reason. Its
muffler was shot. The thing spewed exhaust in smelly gouts. An oily
cloud backfired on gear shifts. The engine block was surely on its last go-
round, oil was mixing with the cooling water. Joe Amos held a fist out
his window. He opened and closed it several times, until he saw the
driver behind him, Baskerville from Philadelphia, do the same for
the truck behind him. The gesture was repeated truck to truck through
the ten Jimmies. Joe Amos had given the signal to close ranks tight. Now
he rolled up his window. Baskerville did, too.

Joe Amos moved ten feet behind the spitting exhaust pipe. Instantly
the stink of oil smoke thickened the air in the cab. In a minute, his eyes
began to sting. Over the muffler prattle, he heard coughs from the Airborne. Someone thumped the canvas roof.

"Back off, goddammit! Hey, boy, back off that truck!"

McGee, breathing through his shirtsleeve, showed Joe Amos a smile with his eyes.

"Sarge, you bad."

A great painted arrow outside Le Val turned the convoy off the road into the fields. The ground here was clay, red banks of hard earth plowed level by Army 'dozers. The Jimmies, each one twenty-six thousand pounds with load, rolling on ten tires slick or treaded, peeled over the dried rain ruts and powdered the ground like brown flour. Billows of dust boiled high and thick. Joe Amos stayed on the tail of the failing Jimmy, close inside its gray trail of exhaust. Behind him, vague in his rearview through the dust, Baskerville hugged Joe Amos's bumper, and the whole convoy did likewise. Apparently, the Airborne fellows had made themselves unpopular in every one of Joe Amos's trucks this morning.

Joe Amos endured poundings and curses on his roof, knocks on his window, for five minutes until the clay road ran past Edmondeville and rejoined the tarmac. Then he backed off the exhaust pipe of the leading truck and rolled down his window. His windshield and hot hood wore a jacket of dusky red dust. Joe Amos held out a fist, the signal to the column to stay in echelon, with the standard sixty yards between bumpers. Baskerville laid off. Windows went down. The convoy shed dust in the wind like comet tails. From the truck bed, more coughs and curses burbled from the Airborne.

"We gon' get in trouble?" McGee asked.

"Naw."

Joe Amos did a mental run-through of the jawboning he was going to get from the Airborne captain once they stopped in Cherbourg. He'd take it with a stoic face, as hard a face as any of these white boys who'd just seen their first trouble in France, which was dust and black men who wouldn't take shit off them. The captain would probably threaten to report Joe Amos to his battalion CO, Major Clay. Joe Amos had three cartons of black market cigarettes given him for trade by Major Clay.

"Naw," Joe Amos said again. He punched McGee in the shoulder.

The air in his window was fresh again, playful and blue clean. Joe Amos took it in and thought that a cigarette was no way to breathe this French air. He might quit, he decided, even as McGee shook out another spike for himself and asked for Joe Amos's lighter.

* * *

Cherbourg was as wrecked as anything seen in the war zone. For two weeks, VII Corps had sat outside the port city pummeling the holed-up Kraut garrison with artillery. Then the bombers hit, giving rise to a new phrase in warfare, "saturation bombing." The Germans sat under an incredible number of American bombs, each blast adding to the wreckage of the city. Driving through the streets, Joe Amos followed a winding path, pointed by MPs from detour to detour because of the destruction. Above the chuffing of Lucky's muffler, the Airborne soldiers whistled at their initial look at ruined France.

After a half hour straining in first and second gears, lurching through narrow ways between brick piles and dodging craters, Joe Amos spotted COM Z Headquarters. HQ was in a large brownstone facing a statue of Bonaparte on a horse. Beyond that sprawled the ruined harbor.

He eased the truck to a stop. The bad spring made the Jimmy rock like a boat on choppy water. He waited with his elbow in the windowsill.

The Airborne captain walked alongside. The man was red-clay grimy. A raccoon mask of white skin showed around mirthless eyes where he'd put on his jump goggles. Now he looked like a combat soldier.

Joe Amos handed him two fresh packs of cigarettes.

"Go get 'em."

The captain did not react.

"Sir."

The officer measured the smokes against giving this uppity colored a tongue-lashing. Then he took the Chesterfields and pocketed them, glaring at Joe Amos the whole time. Finally, he turned to yell for his troops to fall in. Joe Amos watched the Airborne soldiers jump down, filthy, patting dust off themselves like putting out fires in their clothes. McGee watched, too, then smiled admiringly at Joe Amos when the captain and his boys walked away without giving them trouble.

Once the Jimmies were emptied, Joe Amos led the column past the verdigris Napoleon into the sparking harbor. Everywhere, in the air and on the quays, engineers touched welding rods to metal bars and beams, cranes hoisted new trusses in place, twisted wreckage was raised dripping from the water. Acetylene lights twinkled deep in the rust jungles and tangles, and the shouts of men, the clangs of hammers and riveters, made that special echo of metal, what every American knew was an

American sound. Hot yellow stars tumbled from a hundred feet in the air, bounced, then disappeared. Every tool these men used, every sound they made except their voices, had come off the back of some truck. Lucky and the rest of the Jimmies and tankers and flatbeds and the black drivers inside them were here in the flashes and hammer shots, just like they were in the sounds of battle out in the bocage and fields. Joe Amos drove slowly into the port, leading ten trucks, feeling a pride he could never describe to Boogie, feeling that he with his .50 caliber behind him, his bullet-holed Lucky around him, and his little convoy following him were a parade for the men pounding Cherbourg back into shape. You guys get this port up and running, he said silently to the men putting the harbor back together, and 'til you do, we'll keep the supplies flowing off the beaches. We got you covered.

Deep in the harbor, Joe Amos stopped on a broad quay. Beneath the water, with hawsers still tied to gigantic steel cleats, lay a titanic cargo ship scuttled by the Krauts and resting on the mud bottom. The ship's rails were level with the platform when they should have been twenty feet in the air. Men crawled all over the boat like ants, chopping and slicing with flaring torches and metal saws howling. They whittled the great ship into shards that were lifted by a crane onto the back of a scow. The sight was tragic and remarkable. Joe Amos gazed up at a huge piece of deck floating almost gingerly at the end of the crane's cable. He watched it swing out over the water, then crash onto the solid back of the scow, the rusty old grave digger attending the dead ship. All that metal would be floated back to England, then America. It would return to France as rifles, cannons, and Liberty ships. McGee thrust his head and arms out his window, astounded at the scale of the operation to clear just this one berth in Cherbourg when there seemed to be another hundred to clear, too.

Joe Amos took up his backpack. He opened his door. McGee didn't turn.

"Stay here."

"Okay."

In the second Jimmy, Baskerville climbed out to meet him.

"What's up?"

"Gotta see a man. You keep everyone in line for a few minutes? I'll be right back."

Baskerville squared his shoulders. "You need me, man? You want me to come wit'choo?"

"Naw, 'Ville. It's cool. Just some business. You know."

Baskerville nodded and narrowed his eyes. He eyed the backpack dangling in Joe Amos's grip.

"Awright. Hey."

"What."

"That was very cool with them crackers."

Joe Amos didn't say they deserved it. This was assumed. And if they didn't deserve it from 'Ville, Joe Amos figured some others did some other time and got off light, so this squared it.

Baskerville glanced up and down the quay. "You go ahead. I got your back."

Joe Amos turned away, chuckling at the intrigue. It was just a couple cartons of smokes for some fancy French booze. 'Ville acted like they were on a mission from Ike.

On the opposite side of the quay ran a line of squat wooden sheds, too humble for the Krauts to blow up. The shingle sidings rotted in mint green. Screen doors slapped as greasy engineers went in and out. All of them carried some bundle or other. Joe Amos headed for the shed at the far right end.

Stepping inside, he set his backpack on a long counter. On the far side was a pair of desks clotted with papers, In and Out boxes, and yellow telegrams. Clipboards hung on nails below a filthy window. A tall bald fellow unfolded from an accountant's chair behind one of the desks. He made a show of slapping his ink pen to the desktop.

"Well, well, it's the Jabo killer."

"You heard?"

"Colored boy shoots down a Messerschmitt, yeah, I hear."

The sergeant behind the counter flipped out a big white palm, not for Joe Amos to shake but to slap.

"What you got for me today? You bring me my welder's mitts and goggles? I need gas canisters, more torches, Christ, I'm short of boot-laces."

Quartermaster Sergeant Thalhimer leaned around Joe Amos to see out to the quay through the screen door.

"Those trucks are empty."

Thalhimer looked down at the backpack on his countertop. "You drove a bunch of Jimmies to my front door to bring me this? I don't think so."

"I was hauling assholes today. Left 'em off at COM Z."

Thalhimer dropped his fast banter. "Aw, shit. Bad?"

"I've heard worse. Bad enough."

Thalhimer shook his head. "I don't get it, man. I don't get it."

"Yeah, you do."

Joe Amos shrugged and snorted, unable to say more. The Quarter-master sergeant fidgeted in the silence of their shared sympathy. His long fingers beat a bothered tap on the countertop. Joe Amos had never known any Jew to be comfortable with being recognized as one. It wasn't the same being colored. Then folks saw you coming a mile off. But Jews tended to keep their kind quiet, and who could blame them? At what time or place in history had it ever been a good idea to raise their hands and say, "Hey, we're Jews over here"? Never, that's when.

"Well, screw 'em," Thalhimer said.

"Screw 'em, Himey. I brought you somethin'."

Thalhimer slid the backpack closer and looked inside. "Cigarettes. Where'd you get two cartons of cigarettes?"

"Can't say. You know."

"Yeah. What do you want me to do with 'em? I don't smoke."

"Trade 'em."

Thalhimer gave Joe Amos a bemused gaze. "Trade 'em, huh? What makes you think I got anything to trade you for 'em?"

Joe Amos returned Thalhimer the same quizzical look. The quarter-master shrugged.

"For what? You want a welder's apron, I got one your size."

"Booze."

The sergeant snickered. He pushed the backpack across the counter to Joe Amos.

"I don't know anything about booze. I'm a quartermaster."

"A colored boy shoots down a Jabo, you hear. An underground cellar of wine and enough booze to get thirty thousand Krauts high, you don't hear about. Himey, come on, brother. Who you talkin' to here?" Joe Amos shoved the pack across the countertop again, like another move in chess.

The sergeant considered the pack, then looked at Joe Amos. "You on the level?"

"Straight and true. You know me."

" 'Cause it's trouble for a lot of folks if you're not. You included."

"It's cool. Honest."

"Close the door."

Joe Amos shut the rickety hut door. Outside, Baskerville and the other drivers stood ogling the hunks of metal flying overhead and the great *whomps* when the crane plopped them on the scow. When Joe Amos turned around, the backpack lay emptied on the countertop. Thalhimer had disappeared into the oily confines of his shack.

Joe Amos waited. He hadn't expected such drama just swapping some smokes for a couple bottles of Frog brandy. Major Clay must have known it would go this way, that's why he picked Joe Amos Biggs, a cool hand.

By the time Thalhimer returned with a cardboard box, Joe Amos felt some rite had happened, that he'd passed a kind of test to enter the secret world of alchemy, where cigarettes became booze. Thalhimer set the jingling box on the countertop.

"Alright. Pick two."

Joe Amos glanced over the lip. Six dark bottles stood with dusty necks.

"I dunno, man. You pick."

Thalhimer dug out a fat bottle. "Armagnac. Dupeyron vineyard, '34. Nice stuff."

He set this aside.

"Lafite Rothschild. Bordeaux, '23. You like wine?"

"It ain't for me."

"Okay. Whatever. Here you go, take this one, somebody will love you."

"Gimme one more."

Thalhimer already had his hands on the sides of the box to put it away, back into the hidden inventory.

"One more is for me. Come on, Himey."

"I give you one more, you owe me, sport."

Thalhimer grabbed a bottle with a cork held in by wire. The glass appeared older than the others, fat and dark. Its label had yellowed.

"Champagne. Veuve Clicquot Ponsardin."

Thalhimer held the champagne at an admiring arm's length.

Joe Amos asked, "What year is that one?"

"1899. Turn of the century."

"Man, that's old. Is it still good?"

"It's probably great."

Joe Amos reached for the champagne. Thalhimer handed it over, saying, "Funny thing, though. The folks who drank this stuff back then had no idea."

"About what?"

"That they were toasting the blood twentieth. You know, *Veuve* means widow in French. Lot of widows this century."

Joe Amos almost handed the bottle back for a different, less ominous sounding one. But he kept it, because Thalhimer said it might be great.

Ben Kahn put on his boots. He had not worn them in sixty hours, since Phineas left him at this aid station. He'd kept his uniform on, never took it off, slept in it. But three days ago, the moment Phineas had left, before he collapsed on the cot in a corner of the hot tent, Ben pulled off his boots, washed his socks, and hung them on the bed rail. He stayed barefoot, lying down or sitting upright to talk with the doctors or nurses who checked on him. He did not leave the cot, ate three squares a day, dozed, and stared at nothing. He did not say a prayer, no one asked him to. He sniffed his boots several times a day, to enjoy that they were airing out.

He tied the second shoelace knot and lifted his head. Sitting on a stool next to the cot, Phineas seemed to Ben very much the Christian, grinning his approval. Phineas had rescued him on Mont Castre, from Ben's own exhaustion and failing spirit. Phineas had come to France to do good, and found much here to do. This was why he never seemed tired or downcast. So much evil and death ran rampant that Phineas was having one long field day. Ben envied Phineas his mission more than his youth and energy.

"You look swell," Phineas told him now. The boots were ready, and the little Baptist had come to take him back. Ben glanced down at the wrinkled sheets of the cot.

"You sure you don't want to do a stint here?" Ben asked. "Got this bed all broken in for you."

"No, no, I'm fine. You just pushed too hard, is all. But you look great now."

"So do you, Phineas."

The young chaplain did. He propped on the stool like a bit of the bocage itself. Phineas was dirty as a path. Bits of sticks and leaves were caught in the webbing over his helmet. Looking at Phineas, an almost feral-looking boy, Ben did not want to leave the cot just yet.

"Any news? What have I missed?"

Phineas pulled off his helmet. This was the first time Ben had seen the top of his head. Phineas was strawberry blond, more saffron than his eyebrows revealed. His hair was cropped in a military flattop. He ran a hand over the bristles like a teenager, playing soldier in the mud of a farmer's field.

"Well, Monty and the Brits finally took Caen yesterday, a city everybody figured he would've gotten on D-Day. I hear the place is blown to Kingdom Come, but at least it's in our hands now. Down south, the St. Lô sector is heating up. Three divisions set off this morning on a big offensive. A battalion in one of them got raided by four hundred Kraut paratroopers after midnight, before the attack got under way. Krauts just ran right through their lines tossing grenades and firing into foxholes in the dark. That's crazy. The battalion took fifty percent casualties."

"The attack go off on time?"

"Yeah, but it's headed right into the hedges. You know it's gonna be slow."

Slow meant deadly.

"How about on Mont Castre? How'd we do?"

Phineas cocked his head. "You didn't hear?"

"No. I . . ."

Ben looked down, ashamed suddenly in front of Phineas. He had not ministered to any of the GIs flowing through the aid station. He'd kept to his cot, barefoot.

On the stool, Phineas shifted. He set his hands to his knees and leaned forward.

"Let me tell you how we did."

Ben lifted his gaze. Phineas beamed, eager and wholehearted. The little Baptist could do this, absolve a man with just the faith in his eyes.

"The 90th has got a new name for Mont Castre."

"What is it?"

"Purple Heart Hill."

Ben envisioned the blood and bandages, bark winging off trees, the gunfire through the forest, and the shouts of men knocked down.

"Did we take the crest?"

"Oh, yeah. And a lot more."

"What did we lose?"

"Two thousand for the first five days. A hundred or so yesterday and again this morning."

Phineas continued with enthusiasm. Ben pushed away the urge to remind the young chaplain he was talking about death and maiming in huge proportions. He figured he was no one to lecture Phineas Allenby. The boy knew the costs and dangers to the soldiers as well as any front-line dogface. Listening to the tale of Mont Castre's fall, Ben saw how caught up Phineas was in the uncomplicated themes of war, the simplicity of valor, the completeness of blood. Phineas, like Ben, urged the men forward. Ben's intent was to see victory and find his son. Phineas did it to see the soldiers go, and to go with them.

"The night we got you off the hill, all three battalions made it to the top. We took away the Kraut's OP and that made things a little better for a while. We hauled in four hundred fifty prisoners, to boot. Then the Krauts decided they wanted their hilltop back."

Phineas returned his pot to his head, reliving the incoming rounds of his story.

"They beat the heck out of us with mortars and such. Then they came after us with everything they had, grenades, hand-to-hand, you name it. It got so bad the 359th had to gin up a J Company out of every boy they could find in the Field Train. Truck drivers, clerks, cooks, mechanics, they handed 'em all a gun and got 'em up on the hilltop. Let me tell you, sir, them rear boys fought like banshees, like everybody else did. And they took their lumps like everybody, too."

Phineas carved images for Ben out of the warm air. He grabbed a steering wheel for the drivers, shoved a rifle in their mitts, and waved hands for the fighting of banshees. His voice took the tone of a sermon, and his passion for war and the Tough Ombres fashioned his words into a great clashing in the forest of Mont Castre. The wounded and killed did not burden his telling.

"Dang a mule, Ben, you should've seen 'em. Coming down the south slope of that hill, those Joes fought through five kinds of damnation. Went whoopin' after the Krauts. The closer they got to the bottom, the harder the Jerries tried to stop 'em. They had hidden machine guns and mines, trenches, everything prepared way in advance, and you couldn't barely see twenty feet for the trees and scrub brush all around. But yesterday we got across the Lastelle road and broke through the Mahlman Line. And while this was all going on, the 357th kicked the Krauts out of Beau Coudray. So this mornin' the Jerries are on their heels and backin' up."

Ben rested his palm on the cot beneath him. The bed had been his refuge for three days while the 90th slugged up and over Mont Castre, then chased the Germans down the back side of the hill. There was no reproach in Phineas's voice for the fact that Ben stood in a bed instead of the fight. Nonetheless, Ben wriggled on the cot, working his toes in his clean socks, uncomfortable with his own safety. He'd told the men in the trench he would stay with them, and he hadn't. Whitcomb had ordered him to come down. Ben was not at fault. But he'd given his word. He juggled these thoughts, guilt and blamelessness, while Phineas spun his heroic tale.

The young Baptist must have seen Ben's agitation. He quit his descriptions of the battles and outcomes.

Quickly, he said, "So I came to get you. Figured you'd want to be in on the last of it. You sure earned it, Rabbi."

"Thank you, Phineas."

Ben stood. He reached for his helmet, its metal was cooled and rested, too. Over two thousand casualties, he thought. What will be left of the Tough Ombres? Shavetail lieutenants nobody knows or trusts, exhausted veterans using up their luck, green boys with clean hands. The 359th's CO had already got the boot, more brass will follow him out the door. More high-up asses will be covered to explain the body count. The 90th's victory on Purple Heart Hill will do little to lift the division's morale. Who will be left to remember it? Barely more than half. Ben. And Phineas.

"Let's go."

Phineas did not rise from his stool. He pulled off his helmet again.

"Not so fast. Have a seat."

Baffled—he thought he was supposed to be leaving—Ben sat again on the cot. The mattress felt foreign now, with his boots on.

"What, Phineas?"

"You had a son."

"Yes. Have a son. Maybe. I don't know."

"I want to know."

"About what in particular?"

"About him, about the blood on your hands. Why you're back in France. What happened?"

"You're younger than my son. I never explained myself to him. I don't think I need to explain myself to you."

"I'm your colleague, Ben. And your friend."

Phineas's posture on the stool was firm. He held the power of belief, what a man can do when he knows he is right.

"Neither of us has got a single soul we can talk to out there, Ben. We get tight with a fella and next thing we know we're collectin' his things. Dang it, you're gonna go crazier'n you already are if you don't open up to somebody. I don't care if I'm no older than your last haircut, I'm here and I'm willing to talk. Especially if I'm the one who's gonna have to come and round you up every time you push too far. Now, talk to me."

Phineas crossed his arms over his chest and waited.

"Where do you want me to start?"

The suddenness of this startled Phineas. The little Baptist clearly expected more of a fight. Caught off guard, he lowered his arms. Ben lifted a palm.

"You're right, Phineas. Everything you just said. It's very lonely what we do. I hadn't expected that but it is. I wasn't lonely back then as a soldier, we were all in it together and we were so young. But I am now as a chaplain. I just spent three lousy days barefoot on this cot wishing somebody would ask me what's wrong, afraid the whole time somebody would."

Phineas couldn't keep his seat. He stood and began a step forward, perhaps to lay a hand to Ben's shoulder. Ben pointed him back to the stool.

Ben hid his smile at the little *nebbish*. He thought, the boy has such a good, Christian heart. And such a different one from a Jew. *Goyim* are so willing and quick to speak out their ills, to ask each other for grace and forgiveness. It must be so healthy for them. Jews, we endure. We're not a people inclined to ask for help, it has come so rarely. Perhaps like Phineas says, we're a bit crazier than we otherwise might be.

"Tell me about your home," Phineas said. "And the first war."

Ben knit his fingers and dropped his gaze to his lap. He caught himself being reluctant, looking away, his habit of avoidance. Then he brought his gaze to Phineas and spoke.

"My papa was a German, my mother was Hungarian. They lived in Berlin and left in 1904 when I was five. We settled in western Pennsylvania. Papa was a rabbi in Germany. Respected. He was an *eydel mentsch*, a gentle, refined man. In America he was a coal miner. I had one older brother, a *ganif*, a crook. He got killed in the mines in a fight."

Phineas said, "I'm sorry."

Ben carried on his story. The long-dead brother was so little of what there was to be sorry about.

"When the war came, Papa told me not to go. I was the only son. He told me to stay in school, to become an American rabbi."

Ben chuckled.

"Mama never liked the Germans. She said go, fight them. I couldn't do what my father asked, Phineas. One brother was a disgrace and he was dead because of it. I wasn't going to live a disgrace, that's how it felt when I was eighteen. Everyone was signing up. I wasn't going to live my father's life over for him. I joined up. And I never saw my papa again. He died while I was overseas."

"That must've been hard."

"I'll be honest, I didn't feel it really deep when I found out. There was so much else going on. Papa dying didn't hurt any more than the guy next to me. Later . . . later, when I came home and saw Mama without him. Then."

Phineas let a silent moment hover, a monument to Ben's papa and mama. This is something, Ben thought, a Jewish moment from the little *Goy*. Remembrance, a very Jewish thing.

"Tell me about the war."

"Back then, the 90th wasn't the Tough Ombres. We were the Alamo Division. I came in as a replacement. Almost everybody else was from Texas and Oklahoma. I joined them in England. On July 4, 1918, we put on a parade for the Lord Mayor of Liverpool. The whole brigade was given a banquet right in the city square. Then we shipped over to Bordeaux for six weeks of training. In mid-August, we got to the front lines at Limey near St. Mihiel."

Ben paused.

"Phineas."

"Yes, Ben."

"I wasn't the same man back then."

"It's okay."

Ben let out a long breath.

"I don't know if it is." He looked away again. "Right at the turn of the century, the guns changed. Quick-firing artillery, machine guns, the magazine rifle, this was the first time these things had shown up in large-scale battle. So the armies, we didn't know what to do with each other. We almost never fought the Boche out in the open, it was a slaughter both ways whenever we did. Instead, we dug in, sometimes a half mile apart from each other, sometimes fifty yards."

In the same way Phineas had done describing the fighting on Mont

Castre, Ben began unconsciously to build images with strokes of his hands. He swept the flat of his palm across a ruined vista he could still see. The land was stripped of vegetation down to soil and rock, every tree was snapped jagged. Even the fallen branches and leaves were blown away by bombs and their green bits burned or swept off by unfettered wind. The first trench in line was protected by a range of barbed-wire obstacles strung between posts. Ben recalled how the posts, arrayed for miles in meticulous order, looked like a vast black cemetery, and the wires made a dark mist that never lifted.

"The trench systems were pretty elaborate. Three lines in a row, a couple hundred yards apart, all connected by communication trenches. We had bunkers for sleeping and eating. Imagine digging enough trenches for twenty thousand men to live belowground. And the Boche did the same."

Phineas gasped, the way young men always have at the primitiveness of their elders.

Ben's hands felt blisters and calluses again. He remembered looking at his nineteen-year-old palms, thinking then how they were not the hands of a rabbi, how much they resembled his father's coal miner hands.

"For a month, we sat staring over no-man's-land. The Krauts dropped artillery on us every day, at dawn and dinner. We did the same to them."

Ben halted his telling. He stilled his tapping fingers. He'd reached the point in his story where his hands, like the guns of the new century, changed.

Phineas said, "Ben, go on."

Ben set his hands on his knees, to keep them out of the telling.

"Every night, we sent out scouts. They called us scouts, but we weren't. We were assassins. Phineas."

The little chaplain said and did nothing. Ben did not know why he'd said Phineas's name just then, until he felt the warm drops around his eyes, and knew he was calling to Phineas for help.

"I volunteered, you understand. No one made me do it. I was mad at my papa. I was mad at my German background. I didn't want to be anything or anywhere else in the world but a soldier in Germany. I was an American doughboy and I volunteered to crawl out at night and slit as many Hun throats as I could. I did that for two months. Two months. I don't know how many . . ."

"Ben . . ."

"No. I don't know how many throats I cut, a hundred, probably more. You want to know how it's done? You take your time and come up from behind . . ."

Ben lifted his left hand and curled it to muffle a hundred mouths.

". . . you draw the knife sideways like this. You pull the head back to stretch the gash. You cut one more time to finish the windpipe. That keeps him from screaming. Then you stab hard into the heart from behind. You got to lay him down easy, so no one else hears you coming."

Ben held both arms away from himself, done. He did not look at Phineas but into the crumpling air between his hands.

"Every night, I crawled back across no-man's-land under the barbed wire, me and a dozen others just like me. We left a few of us in the wire, but there was always another volunteer to take his place. In the dark we'd crawl past the ones laying out in no-man's-land, we'd pat them 'em on the helmets for luck. We used to say our favorite nights to go out were in the rain. We got to come back to the line washed clean."

"But you weren't."

The young chaplain's voice was not sympathetic. Ben saw Phineas was giving him what he needed, strength instead of coddling. God just said that to me, Ben thought, God through Phineas.

"September 12, at dawn, we went over the top. After that, we didn't stop for seventy-five days, every one of them under fire. Beyond St. Mihiel we were in the Argonne operation. When the Armistice came in November, we were still advancing. We took ten thousand casualties, Phineas. We were gassed, bayoneted, shot, blown up. The 90th never gave back a foot of ground. Not one."

Ben turned the tale to his homecoming. He went back to the coal mines, his old job was waiting. His sad mother sickened and died in his first year back. Ben was twenty, a veteran, a hero, and alone.

"Suddenly, I was an orphan. And I was a coal miner again. The two years before, the war and Mama and Papa dying, it was like I'd come through some sort of fog, and when I came out the other side I was by myself. All of a sudden, it seemed like I'd been robbed."

Phineas listened, saying nothing.

"I couldn't remember much, Phineas, not much except two years of death. That was the thing that stood out, all the dying around me. I know it sounds weird but that's how it felt. My parents, they . . . they were just two more folks who'd died. I couldn't feel them going away, not like I should have. I tried. After France . . . I used to play this game in my head. I'd count the people I'd speak to in a day, just to say hello or how are you, down in the mine or up in the mess shack. They never amounted to more than the number I'd killed. Once, I tried to talk to a hundred people in one day. It wore me out, but I did it. Then I imagined I'd stabbed or shot every one of them myself. I never went back in that mine, Phineas. I had no family left, no home really, so I went off to the city, to Pittsburgh. Got a job in a steel mill. It was like working on the sun, but it was better than a coal shaft. There were folks everywhere, noise and fires, and I liked it. It made me hard again, like the Army. In 1920, my first year there, I met a Jewish girl, got married. I went to night school at Pitt."

"You had a son."

"Thomas."

Phineas nodded, as if this were progress, having Ben say his boy's name.

The wife did not stay long, only six years, until she met a softer man, not one out of the mines and mills but a Ford car salesman. Ben made the steel that went into that man's cars, made the wife that clung to the salesman now, made the son the new man called his own. Ben, with no knife or gun in his hand, no mama or papa, no mate, child, or brother, was alone again.

In the mills, Ben stoked himself, trying to make his heart an ingot, the hardest he could. He finished his schooling at Pitt. On the nights he was not in classes, he drank. He did every stupid thing a young man out of war and love can do. The Depression took his job.

"But I couldn't leave Pittsburgh."

Phineas said, "Your son."

God did not come to Ben in one fell blow. Instead, Ben sensed God arriving in bouts, in the jabs and gouges he'd suffered since defying his father and going off to war, as though God spent fourteen years beating His way into Ben's spirit. God came also in the form of a run-down Ford coupe his ex-wife's husband gave him, perhaps out of pity, more likely as a way to show the contested son, Thomas, who was the better man. In 1933, Ben enrolled in the rabbinical school at Union Seminary College in Cincinnati. Every other weekend he drove three hundred miles each way to Pittsburgh to be with Thomas, never letting on that he slept in his car in warm weather and in a Squirrel Hill flophouse in winter. He worked nights in Cincinnati as a security guard. After four years, he re-

ceived his rabbinical degree and became the rabbi of a small conserva-
tive synagogue in Squirrel Hill, down the street from the flophouse.

Ben reached to his breast pocket. He undid the button and took out
the letter. It was too soon in the story for Thomas's final note but Ben
held it, turning the folded sheet like a slow pinwheel.

"Those were good years," he said.

Phineas nodded but did not smile.

Ben tried and became a better father. The boy grew into a handsome
lad, dark-haired and deep-eyed, lean and quick like his father, prudent
like his mother, and in the way of all young men, passionate. Thomas
came to Friday night services, where Ben watched the teenage boy *dahven*
when he prayed, rocking with the pace of the Hebrew under his breath.

Ben unfurled the letter. "When he was fifteen, I started to see some of
myself in the boy I didn't like."

"He had a mean streak," Phineas said.

"Yes."

A few times, Thomas got in scrapes at school and with the police. He
was in fights, he'd lobbed rocks into car windows, some drinking, some
pranks went awry.

"Teenage stuff," Ben said. "But underneath, there was something
else, I could tell, I knew him. He wasn't just rebelling. He didn't just fall
in with a bad crowd. There was a taste there. For trouble."

The demons that had chased Ben away from home and into no-
man's-land now pursued his only child. Thomas read everything he
could on the worsening situation in Europe. He listened to radio reports
of Hitler's speeches and Neville Chamberlain's appeasements of the
Nazis. On his eighteenth birthday, Thomas told Ben he intended to finish high school, then enlist in the Army. Ben said no, he would go to college, he would study.

"He asked me, 'What about the Jews over there? Don't you care?' "

"What'd you tell him?"

"I said what the Jews of Europe needed most from Thomas Kahn
was not another soldier but another Jew, a leader of their people in
America. I wanted my son to become a rabbi. 'You're Kohain,' I told him,
'like me.' Turns out he was more like me than I wanted. Nothing
stopped me. Why did I think I could stop him?"

Thomas's mother and stepfather begged the boy not to enlist. The
stepfather bribed him off with a new Ford. Thomas took the car and en-

rolled at the Carnegie Institute of Technology. He studied aviation for eighteen months. He sold the car, quit school, and enlisted in the Army Air Corps.

By this time, Churchill and England were fighting the Germans in Africa. Hitler steamrolled across Russia. U.S. troops surrendered on Bataan. Doolittle bombed Tokyo. War had again swallowed the world.

Ben fingered the letter, making it crinkle. He began to unfold it, peeling back the top portion slowly, like a parchment. The page was thin blue. A hole had sprung in one of the creases. Ben studied the rip, careful not to make it worse.

"The last thing I said to him, right before he left for Basic, was no. He just turned away. That was the last word I ever spoke to him, Phineas."

He unfolded the bottom half of the letter.

Thomas's handwriting never failed to fool Ben for a heartbeat that the boy was alive. Each inked word still bore the swirl of a pen. How easy it was for Ben to pretend that he could answer this letter, that he might still make right that moment when Thomas turned away.

He prepared the blue sheet to be read, spreading it. The rip in the crease lengthened just a bit.

Thomas was with the 95th Bomb Group, the pilot of a B-17. His twenty-second mission was over Hanover, February 25, 1943. On the way home, over France, a flight of Focke-Wulfs caught up with them and shot up his squadron. His B-17 lost a wing and exploded mid-air. The mission report said only three chutes from the ten-man crew ejected before the plane hit the ground. The tail gunner made it back to England. He didn't know who else got out. The other nine men were listed as missing.

"He could still be alive," Phineas said.

"He could be," Ben answered. "I don't know."

He held up Thomas's letter, the last known thing.

"I got the Army's telegram that he was MIA. A week later, I got this." He read aloud:

Dear Dad,

I have to make this one short. We're taking off before sunup. I've been awake for a few hours now. You can sure see a lot of stars here in England, was it like that when you were here?

I know I haven't written you much. I guess I should have. I'm sorry the way things have gone between us in the last year or so. But I'm writing you and I hope you'll write back.

Like I said, there's not a lot of time right now, so I'll get right to it. I've been doing a lot of thinking. I want to tell you that you were wrong to try and keep me from joining the war. I don't want to be a rabbi like you, I never did. Maybe I should have said this before, maybe it would have spared us both some hurt feelings and a shouting match or two, but I don't want to live your life for you over again. I don't want to end up in the coal mines and the steel mills when this war is over. I don't want to end up sleeping in a car. You didn't think I knew but I did. That's okay, I admire you for what you've done, but it's not my life, Dad. I want different things, bigger things.

We're different, you and me, and we're the same in a lot of ways.

There's still a lot I can learn from you and maybe I need to get better about listening to you. But you need to get better about listening to me.

With all these stars overhead, all this seems pretty far away.

For a month now we've been dropping bombs on German cities. We aim for the factories, but we miss, too. And all the shells the Krauts fire up at us fall on their own houses. We're killing people left and right, and while the generals tell us that's swell, I remember how you told me once you used to count the people you killed in France. I look at the night sky with the planes loading up and I think, We'll kill more than there are stars up there. Like I said, we're a lot alike, you and me. Bombing was easy at first, but it's started getting hard. You told me it would.

I got to go now. But when this is all over, we'll sit and talk about our wars. I bet when it's all said and done, they won't have been too different, either.

Everything else is fine. Don't worry.

Thomas

Ben folded the page. In his own voice he'd heard his son's, another fooling thing to make Thomas alive for one more minute. The boy retreated with the letter into Ben's pocket.

Phineas said, "He sounds like a handful."

Ben released a rueful chuckle.

Phineas spun his helmet in his hands. "A prosecutor cannot become a defender."

"No," Ben said.

"You're afraid God took him because of the blood staining your hands."

"Yes, Phineas. I am. And maybe the blood on his, too."

"Like he said, you're a lot alike. Except for one big difference."

Ben said nothing.

"Sounds to me," Phineas said, "like Thomas was a little quicker than you in regretting the blood on his hands."

"Ours isn't a Christian God, Phineas. He doesn't ask us for regret. He asks for obedience."

Phineas nodded, calculating.

"So that's why you've come back, isn't it? You've found a loophole. You've lost your wife and probably your son. You're angry. You can't fight anymore, or you'll lose God, too. But others can fight for you."

"Yes, they can."

Phineas held out his own pink palm, accusing Ben with a hand unbloodied in war.

Phineas said, "You came back for revenge."

"That's right."

"On the Germans."

"I can't take it on God."

Phineas stood from the stool. Even scorning, Phineas Allenby would not sacrifice compassion.

"You came back to war as a man of God. But you're not."

Ben stood also. He clapped his helmet on his head, ending the session with Phineas and his barefoot stay in the aid station.

"God wanted my son dead. I don't know if He succeeded or not. But I'm here to find out. Me, I want Germans dead. My reasons are as good as God's. He won't abandon me for that."

Ben pointed at Phineas's hip, to the bulge of his pistol holster.

"That's the great thing about God, Phineas. He's no hypocrite."

Alone, Ben headed out of the tent. The day was blue and clean, the last smoke of the battle coiled at a distance, rising from the far side of Mont Castre. Ben paused and gazed up, hoping for a clear night, an English night, to look at the stars.

D+43
JULY 19

Lieutenant Garner propped a foot on the Jimmy's bumper. Exhaling smoke, he set about answering Joe Amos's question: When's the breakout coming?

Yesterday, Garner explained, pointing the cigarette south, the 29th Division rolled into St. Lô like a cavalry charge and the Germans finally retreated.

Once St. Lô fell into the GIs' hands, those hands had to be cupped to keep it from sifting through. The entire town, a thousand years old, was beat to rubbish and remains. Little was left standing, barely more than the tower of a church, some chimneys. This was the worst devastation so far of any liberation in France. From his drivers, Garner heard reports of entering 29ers dazed by what they had done.

Over on the western side of the American bridgehead, Mont Castre was captured and the Krauts evicted from their best observation point. The 90th and 8th Divisions were rearming and refilling their depleted ranks, especially the Tough Ombres, who'd fought through the worst of it, over the top of the hill and down the back side. Garner's trucks had ferried over a thousand replacements to the 90th.

This morning, on all fronts, the American war in Normandy rested. Garner ground out the cigarette. Joe Amos extended another.

The lieutenant waved away the offer. "Something big is shaping up," Garner said, getting to the point. "I think the breakout's right around the corner."

The officer took a swig from his canteen. He'd been standing in the sun talking with Joe Amos for a half hour now, in the late morning. Garner, although he hailed from the Deep South, spent a lot of time in the shade. He had that bald head to protect.

Joe Amos asked, "Where you think it's gonna happen?"

Garner looked south again, squinting, pretending he could see the landscape beyond the hedges.

"Don't know. They pushed awful hard for St. Lô. The breakout's gonna be near there, I reckon."

Breakout. The word was magic. Joe Amos envisioned his trucks, cramped for so long, sprung free across the rest of France. Jimmies and tractors like a vast green swarm powering over the countryside. They'd spread America and freedom into every corner, the way light in a kitchen runs off roaches. Breakout. Then lookout, Germany.

"Even so," Garner said, still squinting into the distance, "we're a ways from being out of these hedgerows."

Joe Amos was eager to see the land beyond the bocage. He figured it was long, easy plains, green fields, vineyards. He'd arrived in France wanting to see all of it, run down every road, capture it and take it home in his memory. The desire for rolling down new highways, past new-named towns, really began to percolate when Lieutenant Garner walked up this morning and told Joe Amos the good news from the fronts, and that his company had a day to rest and repair. It was their first day off in eight days of solid wheeling.

Garner spat in the grass. Perhaps this was the way in Louisiana they ended conversations, Joe Amos didn't know. The lieutenant mopped his brow.

"Make sure your truck here gets some lookin' after. That's what the day's for, alright? Then pick up some cable at OMAHA and take it down to St. Lô. Go ahead. Major Clay don't mind. Be back by dawn. Then we go again."

The lieutenant nodded into Joe Amos's eyes like a man laying down a dollar to pay an old debt, with a *there you go* wink. He sauntered over the grass to find shade.

*   *   *

Joe Amos painted the last strokes, daubing black dots on a pair of white dice, a one and a six. Beneath this roll of seven, the name *Lucky* dried, a florid white script on his driver-side fender.

He set the brush in a jar of turpentine. McGee stood on the bumper, folded over the grille, bare torso across the engine block. His dark back gleamed like rain on coal. Both of McGee's arms were swallowed in the engine compartment. The sounds of a tool and a bolt fiddled up from the guts of the Jimmy.

"Jus' about done," McGee said, sensing Joe Amos watching. Joe Amos walked to the rear, inspecting his good tires, the welded patch on the muffler, and the new springs on his axles. Lucky was the best-maintained deuce-and-a-half in the 688th, because McGee was the top mechanic among the drivers. McGee said some of the men were even calling Joe Amos by a nickname, Sergeant Lucky. Joe Amos stuck a finger into one of the bullet holes in his truck bed, liking the sound of that.

McGee climbed off the grille. Grease coated his palms. He made a show of closing the hood with his elbows. No other trucks in the battalion, parked all around the bivouac this noon hour, had their crews attending to them, and only a few waited in line at the maintenance depot. Most of the Jimmies looked exhausted after a month and a half on the ruined roads of Normandy. The colored drivers, too, began to take on a gamey shell. They didn't shave or shower in these rare rest periods, maintaining themselves as badly as their trucks. They seemed to take pride in grinding their Jimmies down to wheezing engines and bubbling rubber. The drivers let this happen to their bodies, as well, growing rough and bleary. They wanted their deterioration to show for the white soldiers coming and going to the front. The colored men weren't earning stripes and medals like the whites, so they put on display the wear and tear of their own war.

Not Joe Amos. He kept himself, Lucky, and McGee running and looking sharp. The .50 cal in the bed had extra ammo belts slung visibly over the ring. He made McGee shave regularly and clip his nails to keep the grease from building under them. Two days ago, Joe Amos washed his and McGee's uniforms in the rain and dried them on Lucky's hot manifold. The winning dice painted on the Jimmy's fender was a nice touch, he thought. It'll look good running over France, maybe right into Paris.

He tossed McGee a turpentine rag. "How we doin'?"

"New plugs, points, cap, and rotor. I peeked at the starter, some rust on the brushes but they good now. Oil's black but I get that later."

"Take a shower. I'll see you at mess."

McGee swung his OD and tunic over his shoulder. He dug into the cab for his kit and ambled for the showers, trailing a short shadow in the midday sun. He turned.

"Look, if he's gon' make me do the yard or somethin', I'd just as soon take a shower later. Don't make sense, get all clean and have to work."

Joe Amos waved the boy on to the showers. "It's alright."

McGee batted the air. He walked off.

No one was going to be cutting grass anymore for the Marquis.

Joe Amos jumped from the cab to the hard sand of OMAHA. By now so many bulldozers and tracked vehicles had plied this beach, the sand was solid as tarmac, and smoother than most of the roads in Normandy.

OMAHA teemed. Landing craft bellied through the surf disgorging trucks and tanks, and men on foot wet from the knees down. The only remaining marks of the great storm were red buoys out in the water marking wrecks as shoals and some concrete pontoons washed to the sand that had not been hauled away.

Joe Amos walked off from Lucky, leaving McGee at the wheel. He wanted the boy to drive today. The 29ers were a division made entirely of Virginians and Marylanders. They'd fought through the worst of the invasion landings and some of the ugliest swamps and thickets of the bocage, to reach St. Lô, a city they blew to hell. They were known among the Negro drivers as a tough-tongued bunch. Joe Amos figured he'd keep McGee in the cab and keep his day rolling without problem.

He searched through the rambling vehicles, engineers, and arriving troops. Dodging rolling Jimmies, he gave the colored boys driving a thumbs-up. He found the man he was looking for, a Quartermaster sergeant, standing beside an acre of gasoline jerricans. The man held a clipboard and pointed at the jerricans, counting them. He stubbed his hand at the cans three, four times, then recorded something on a sheet.

"Speedy," Joe Amos called, approaching.

"Lucky man!"

The top of Speedy Clapp's head did not rise to Joe Amos's chin. From Queens, he seemed to be the shortest man in the Army, called

Speedy because he was no bigger than a jockey. He complained that somebody at the Draft Board hated him. Speedy made everything look big. The clipboard he waved at Joe Amos appeared to be a barn door, the rows of jerricans looked like a pasture in the middle of the beach. Joe Amos laughed to hear Speedy call him by his new nickname.

"What can I do to you, my friend?" Speedy put out a mitt, Joe Amos took it.

"How many jerricans you got here, Speedy?"

"I haven't got a fucking clue. What's it look like to you?"

"A hundred thousand."

"Funny. I wrote down one-fifty. Who fucking knows? What ya need?"

"A couple spools of cable."

"Over there. For who?"

"The 29th."

"Oh, yeah, my favorites. Half the ammo comes across this beach gets fired by those bastards. Trigger-happy bunch. What else?"

Joe Amos dug a fresh pack of cigarettes from his tunic. He was already halfway through the carton he'd skimmed off Major Clay.

"Think you can let me have a couple of jerries?"

Speedy examined the Chesterfields. He pressed the pack to his nose and inhaled. Speedy was a known connoisseur of barter. Joe Amos was getting a taste for this, toss a guy some smokes and walk off with whatever you want.

"Sure, sure. Take two." Speedy grinned. "Lemme mark 'em off on my chart here." The Quartermaster sergeant pretended to write something. "There you go. All accounted for. Pleasure doin' business."

Joe Amos bopped Speedy in the shoulder. "See you around."

Speedy hid the cigarettes in his trousers.

He said, "Oh, yeah. I think so."

Joe Amos grabbed a jerrican in each hand and tottered across the beach to McGee and Lucky. No one paid him any mind, the beach swelled with soldiers carrying stuff, full of colored boys, too. So much matériel flowed ashore and spewed out of LCs every minute that the height of the Army's record keeping was Speedy Clapp's make-believe accounting. Again, magic. You want it, you got it, no one's hurt and no one's the wiser.

Joe Amos hefted the jerricans into the bed. He climbed in the cab and pointed McGee to the storage area for the wire spools, high on the sand below the steep dunes. Another soldier waved the Jimmy to a stop and asked what they needed. The man did not even have the pretense of a clipboard, he just shouted, "Sure thing, boys," and padded away like a walking teddy bear. Joe Amos figured this one had his fingers into the chocolate rations. Everybody was taking a piece for themselves.

Five minutes later the cable spools were lifted by crane to Lucky's bed. McGee tapped on the steering wheel, anxious, looking at the glove compartment where the rest of the Chesterfields were stowed. Joe Amos did not let him have any more. He saw a greater value for the smokes than letting McGee hack away at them.

The afternoon road to St. Lô was choked. Now that the fighting had slowed, every division in the field was refitting and reloading. Just looking at the traffic, Joe Amos saw what Garner had alluded to, the coming breakout. Everywhere, on the main arteries and the side roads, in fields and blasted orchards, over dirt paths leading into the bocage, the beachhead seemed to be swelling, almost inhaling, before jumping off into the free spaces of France. Guilt again nagged in Joe Amos's breast, that he should be gallivanting off on his own today, hauling just a few spools of wire to make it look like he was busy. McGee was oblivious, along for the ride.

Awe replaced the guilt, though, when Joe Amos saw St. Lô. The road crested above green humps of fields. Joe Amos told McGee to pull to the shoulder as the convoy they'd tagged along with pulled away, continuing south. Joe Amos climbed from the cab. A few miles away, St. Lô lay inside the green hills, nestled on river flatland. But the town was blackened, something scorched and pulled from a fire; St. Lô, a town they'd heard about and followed the fight for, a town of twelve thousand before the attack, was gone, more gone than Cherbourg or Sodom and Gomorrah.

"My goodness," McGee breathed.

Joe Amos shook his head.

McGee raised a hand to shield his eyes in the afternoon light.

"We don't give a damn, do we?"

These were the first words Joe Amos had heard his assistant utter about the war that were not excited or bored. McGee stared at the ruins, at the tumbled stones of a high and ancient fortress wall, at a lonely Gothic spire missing its church. McGee appeared affected more by this ruined vista than anything he'd seen in France. Something had just snapped in McGee Mays, some belief in America that had survived this long.

Joe Amos again took the passenger seat, keeping McGee behind the wheel. They found the 29th depot a mile north of town. The compound was a chaos, a confusion of crates, barrels, boxes, stacks, and debris. All the mobile depots were this way; every armed unit sucked in supplies and moved on, leaving behind mountains of garbage and spills. McGee drove into the field where the 29th's supplies were staged, beckoned by a guiding MP. He pulled to a stop; within seconds, soldiers leaped aboard to shove the two wire spools off the truck bed. The spools hit the ground, and one soldier leaped down carrying the two jerricans. Joe Amos spotted him in his mirror and climbed out, telling him to put them back. The soldier refused. Before Joe Amos could curse or argue, McGee came out of the cab, saying nothing, just standing beside Joe Amos at the foot of the bullet-holed truck bed with hands on his hips and a look in his eyes that made them small and very dark. The soldier set the gas cans down and stamped off behind the rolling spools, glowering behind him at both colored boys.

"I put him over here."

Captain Whitcomb walked beside Ben without much chatter. The young officer had shaved recently and managed a fresh uniform. He looked now to be the sum of his years—maybe half Ben's age—instead of much older, the way he had on Mont Castre. Even so, his voice and eyes bore an edge only a much older man should have, but the young inherit in wartime. Whitcomb's mouth stayed drawn, his glances quick, never settling but searching for danger, in the trees and on the ground, used to watching for snipers and teller mines. That was the edge, the thin boundary between clutching your life close and letting it go, the line that older men cross at some point through illness and loss, and young Whitcomb traipsed daily under enemy fire. He will never lose this, Ben thought, sad and recalling his own youth following his war. The chasm between life and death should be wide for the young, they should not be able to see across it. But war makes the divide so narrow. Whitcomb and every combat soldier will never again see death as far away, they are done with being so young as that.

Ben laid a palm on the captain's back. He rubbed between the shoulder blades, for no reason other than to connect. Whitcomb walked under Ben's hand, looking down to skirt a crater.

Their steps carried them through a tank-punched gap in a low stone wall. In the center of the field stood an untouched barn, made like the wall of stacked stones. The building was likely five hundred years old, Ben marveled. America in this war was a bull in a china shop, breaking anything in its way, ancient or not, missing a few items here and there.

"How old you think that barn is?" he asked Whitcomb, to get some talk flowing.

"I don't know." Whitcomb glanced up from the passing weeds. "A thousand years. I don't know."

The captain didn't care. This barn represented nothing in Whitcomb's future, off where his fate lay. Ben dropped his hand from the man's back. They approached the barn in silence, until Ben asked about the breakout.

"What do you hear?"

"Not much. They're keeping a lid on it. But it's soon, I reckon. Nobody's moving up right now but us."

"So they're getting ready for one big shove."

"Looks like it."

"What are the orders?"

"Just a local action. The 358th is gonna cross the Sèves River south near St. Germain. There's some Krauts holed up on high ground there, surrounded by marshes. The rest of us are in reserve. Shouldn't take too long."

The 358th was Phineas's regiment. Ben had not spoken to Phineas in a week, since leaving him behind at the aid station. Phineas had pried too deeply, then judged Ben's motive for coming back to France. He'd said Ben was not a man of God because he'd returned for revenge.

The God of the Jews was a vengeful God. Count the miracles, Ben thought, and shook his head. They're mostly the visiting of death on Israel's enemies and those who broke God's laws. Mass deaths, by drowning, plagues, battle, killer angels. Phineas's Christian God was gentler, but even He made no bones about punishment for those who strayed. Either way you tote it up, the God of both peoples was no stranger to retribution. Ben's pact with God was only that he not kill again. But never had God commanded Ben not to be angry.

Whitcomb jerked a thumb toward the door of the stone barn.

"I don't know what to do with him, Chap. He was a good soldier. Now, I dunno. You talk to him."

Whitcomb moved to precede Ben through the door. Ben stopped him.

"Let me do it alone. Alright?"

"Yeah, sure. Let me know what you think, okay?"

Ben nodded. He stepped into the stone cool of the barn.

A skinny soldier sat cross-legged on straw in a corner. His rifle stood propped beside him, his helmet hung cockeyed on the gun barrel. His pack lay on the other side of him. The soldier seemed to have stripped himself of every protection except his hands, and they were tucked around him as though he were cold. When Ben entered, the soldier stopped rocking against the hard wall.

"Hello." Ben stopped in the doorway, listening behind him for Whitcomb to walk off. "I'm Chaplain Kahn."

The soldier released himself. He made to stand.

"Keep your seat." Ben approached slowly, as if walking into a cave, to spook nothing. "I'll join you."

Ben slid to the straw floor, pulling off his own helmet. He stuffed the pot over his bended knee.

The soldier knit his fingers in his lap, pressing the thumbs. His gaze strayed. He was no older than twenty, pimpled and faintly bearded.

"You're Private Sam Baum."

"Yes, sir."

"I hear you've had a rough time lately."

Ben gauged the young private, gathering what he could of the boy's story from his form, folded and agitated. Baum had quit. Or worse, he had broken.

"You want to tell me about it?"

"Nothin' to tell. I'm chickenshit."

"Maybe not, Private."

The boy raised his eyes to Ben, fiercely. "Yeah. And maybe so."

"Tell me what happened."

"I don't want to talk about it."

"I'm here to help, Sam."

Baum snickered, tapping his teeth with his thumbs. He did not meet Ben's look.

"Rabbi, I appreciate you comin' by and all. You want to say a few prayers, go ahead. I'll say 'em with you. *Shema Yisrael, Adonai Elohenu, Adonai Echud.* I know that one. But I ran away. Pure and simple. When you're done talkin' to me and you leave, they're gonna come get me and they're gonna court-martial me."

"Why don't you just tell me what happened."

"I don't want to think about it."

Ben kept silent. Baum tapped his teeth harder, closing his eyes.

After moments spiking himself with his thumbs, he lifted his head. He spoke into the empty barn.

"Captain Whitcomb says you're okay. He says you know what's up. That you were on Purple Heart Hill."

Ben nodded. "I was."

Baum's hands snapped from his mouth, his knees unfolded in the straw. He seemed to want to stand and run, some burst had gone off inside him and he needed to hide. With effort, Baum kept himself on the ground, under the onslaught in his brain.

"Then you know what it's like. The artillery. The . . . the . . ." He searched for a word, to contain the pounding, concussion, destruction of the shells.

". . . the shock."

Ben was close enough to lean and touch the boy's leg. He did not. Baum looked like he would bolt if one more thing in the world touched him.

"That's what it is, Sam. Shock."

"It just . . . The goddam Krauts. They wouldn't let up. It's like fingernails scratching . . ." Baum reached over his bare head and clawed the air, to invoke the screeching whistle of incoming rounds, ". . . then, then . . ."

He could not say, *the blasts*. The gouts of earth and man spinning in the air, splintered trees in a killing hail, the stubbing pressure in your ears, lungs, and eye sockets with every detonation. Hours at a time, day or night. No place to hide. Only two choices: burrow in and hold on, or run.

Baum's hands bent and faced each other, shaking.

"After a while, this pressure, it builds in your gut like it's gonna blow up your insides, right there in your chest. Every time another round lands close, it gets bigger, like you're gonna explode yourself. I didn't . . . I didn't want to. But we been under their guns for weeks. Up on the hill, in the hedges, every stinkin' day. It just . . . just . . ." Baum's hands quavered, as if pressing together a steel ball they could not collapse, although he squeezed with all his strength. He looked to Ben.

"I know, Sam."

"This morning. We was just sitting still, not even in a fight, just resting up, and they started again." Baum pointed outside the barn. "Two of my buddies, Owen and Hise, they got blown to bits, just ducking in their holes. That ain't right, Chap. To die like that, not even fighting, that ain't right."

Baum massaged the dark bristles of his pate, gazing into the straw.

"You ever want to run away, Chap?"

Ben considered this before answering. He knew Baum referred to war. Ben had never dodged combat. But he had spent much of his life in retreat. He thought of the Great War, how he ran to France from his father's demand that he stay. Then of the steel mills and coal mines of Pennsylvania, how he fled from them to alcohol and depression. From his failures he'd fled to God. When Thomas was lost, he'd come back here to France, to run away from his grief.

"Yes."

The current in Baum, rifling though his limbs and eyes, eased. He lifted his head.

"I ain't afraid, Rabbi. It's just my nerves couldn't take it no more."

"Captain Whitcomb said you were a good soldier."

"He said that?"

"Yes, he did. I'm sure he's right."

"How can you tell? After what I done? Rabbi, I deserted under fire. They can shoot me for that."

"You're not a coward, Sam. Anyone can see that."

"Then what am I? Honest."

"You're an ordinary man, being asked to do extraordinary things. You know what Ralph Waldo Emerson said?"

"No."

"He said a hero is no braver than an ordinary man. He just waits five minutes longer."

Baum raised his eyes to the dim rafters. He chuckled. Ben took hope.

"You believe in God, Private?"

"Most times."

"Well, look at it this way. If you can believe in God, who's invisible, you can surely believe in yourself. Where you from, Sam?"

"Pittsburgh."

"You're kidding me."

"No." The boy squirmed. "From Squirrel Hill. Why?"

Ben laughed.

Baum, in so much trouble, edgy that he might be getting into more, insisted. "Why?"

"You know Isley's Ice Cream Parlor?"

Baum coughed, amazed. His jaw hung slack.

Ben asked, "Waldorf's Bakery? The Hot Puppy Shop?"

Baum found his voice. The lines in his young face smoothed, the flitting of his eyes stopped and steadied on Ben, wide to take in this miracle of home.

"Yeah. Yeah, we'd go to the Hot Puppy for malts, then go to Frick Park . . ."

". . . to make out. I know."

Baum enjoyed this, the old rabbi knowing about Frick Park.

"And the old Manor Theater. And Hyman's butcher shop on Murray."

"Swimming at Kennywood Park."

"Yeah! Hey, did you go to Schenley or Taylor Alderdise?"

Ben paused. He swallowed.

"No. My son . . ."

He expected to stop right there but he did not. Private Baum was waiting for good words and memories, and if Ben did not shirk, he had them to give the boy.

". . . my son went to Taylor Alderdise."

Baum, eager, noted nothing. He saw only the high school rivalries in Squirrel Hill.

"I went to Schenley. How old is he, maybe I know him?"

"No, Sam. He was older than you. He was . . . he was gone before you went to school."

Baum sat back. He looked square at Ben.

"Rabbi?"

"Yes."

"Did he come over here?"

The boy's face was different now, long and solemn, though still nakedly young. Against the old stone wall, seated in the moldy straw, he took on another form from the twitchy, shell-shocked deserter. This was the soldier that Captain Whitcomb described. The good soldier, the steady dirty hand, a veteran of the bocage and Mont Castre, who'd only lost his nerve for a moment in all the fighting days he'd faced. This was a lad who knew war for its suddenness and impartiality, how it showed no favorites to buddies and sons. Private Sam Baum was another boy with a view across the chasm he should not have.

"Yes. He came."

"Is he okay?"

"I don't know. I don't think so."

Baum sighed again and furled his legs and arms. He shook his head. "There's a lot of them."

Baum was right, Ben thought. There were a lot of them. Not just yours, Rabbi. A lot of them—American, British, French, Canadian, Poles. Baum would not reach across the little space between them to comfort the rabbi and grieving father. He had his own losses. Private Sam Baum had even himself to grieve, the loss of his honor, maybe his life if a military court decided so. He was Ben's equal in despair.

Ben stood.

"Wait here."

The boy's arms and legs coiled again. He took up his rocking against the stone wall. He looked as if the rabbi had never come into the barn.

Ben walked outside. Captain Whitcomb was easy to find, sitting in a jeep not far away, smoking.

"What do you think, Chap? What do we do with him?"

"Give him to me."

McGee Mays stayed silent for the drive to Couvains. He simmered in the kind of funk Joe Amos's mama used to call a "coffee mood," black and bitter. Joe Amos ignored his sullen assistant except to tell him to drive faster. McGee's mulling over the destruction of St. Lô was not going to cost Joe Amos one extra second with Geneviève.

At the turnoff for the Marquis's house, Joe Amos told McGee to brake.

"Look. While we're visiting, cheer up, will you?"

"Yeah. Alright."

Joe Amos watched McGee change gears to travel the long wooded lane to the mansion. With a pouting violence, McGee slammed Lucky into second.

Joe Amos asked, "What's the matter? What you want?"

The boy glared through the windshield.

"You got a girl. You got them stripes. You got the Major sending you off to get him stuff. That's alright, I ain't mad at you, you shot down that Jabo fair and square. But all I got is the U.S. Army. And I ain't real happy about them right now."

The big house emerged from the forest. McGee wheeled Lucky into the circular drive. Joe Amos patted his assistant's shoulder.

"It's okay. I know what you mean. You stick with me. We'll get you somethin' else. I got a feeling about things. Alright?"

The boy was reluctant. Joe Amos poked him and McGee grinned for the first time in hours.

"Awright. You say so, Sarge."

Joe Amos laid out his hand for McGee to slide him some skin.

The two climbed out of the cab. The Marquis shoved open one of the great doors at the center of the house. The door was so large, he had to put his shoulder to it.

With lifted arms and a broad smile, the Marquis greeted them.

"What have you done to my daughter, Joe Amos Biggs?" he called, approaching.

Joe Amos shot McGee a glance, reminding him to be pleasant. The Marquis wrapped Joe Amos in a hug with busses to both cheeks, then he gave the same to McGee.

"I didn't do anything. I just . . ." Joe Amos did not know what to make of the Marquis's welcome.

"No, no, boy!" The Marquis laughed and waved away the concern Joe Amos put on his face. "I did not mean *what did you do?* I mean, what have you done in her heart?"

A tingle coursed in Joe Amos, that Geneviève had spoken of him.

"Is she inside?"

"Yes, yes, of course." The Marquis peered into the Jimmy's bed at the two jerricans of gasoline. "Are these more gifts from *mon ami* Joe Amos?"

"Yeah, they're for you. McGee, get 'em down."

"*Un trésor!*" The Marquis made a theatrical sweep of his arms, as if Joe Amos had brought him something magnificent. "Go, go. She will be happy to see you. McGee, you and I have work to do!"

Joe Amos gave his assistant one more look. "Marquis," Joe Amos said, "you know, one of those jerricans is a gift from McGee here. Maybe you can let him relax a while today. Show him around the place."

The Frenchman looked up to where McGee stood on the truck bed holding the twin canisters. He sighed and flapped his hands to his trousers, in charming defeat.

"*Certainment.* Come, McGee. Bring these cans around to my Peugeot. We will gas it up and go for a ride. We shall leave the lovers alone, yes?"

Joe Amos hustled his backpack with the champagne bottle out of the truck cab. Slinging it over his shoulder, he headed for the door before the Marquis could ask if this was another gift for him.

Inside, Joe Amos paused at the grandness of the house. Murals of hunting parties and tapestries framed the hall, a chandelier dangled over an ancient, giant rug. The furniture, the staircase of mahogany, everything was sumptuous and old, a survivor. Joe Amos moved into a passageway to call for Geneviève. He tried not to remember that Krauts lived here just weeks ago. He thought of St. Lô and the other destroyed places he'd seen, the ones not so fortunate as this house. Then he found her.

She'd come from the kitchen, wearing her apron. She dried her hands in it before holding them out to Joe Amos. They joined hands and he waited, to see if she would pull him in. She did. He kissed her.

The kiss poured over Joe Amos like cement. After she pulled away, he could have stood like this in the hall for a year, with hands and lips curled and empty but frozen in elation. Geneviève grabbed one hand and tugged at him to follow.

"Can you stay?" she asked, turning to him in the kitchen.

"Yeah, sure."

"Dinner?"

"Yeah. Maybe a little after, too."

"*C'est merveilleux.*"

"I brought you something."

From the backpack he handed her the champagne. She took the bottle with reverent hands, reading the label and gasping.

"Veuve Clicquot Ponsardin? This is forty-five years old. Joe Amos, where did you get this? It is . . . I do not know how to say."

"I can get more, anytime I want. It's for you."

"My father. He will not believe this."

"It's not for him, Geneviève. Just for you."

The girl pursed her lips, considering. She cocked her head. Joe Amos believed he had never seen a more dazzling gesture.

"Is McGee with you?"

"Your dad is showing him the Peugeot."

"*Parfait!* He will have McGee fixing it the rest of the afternoon."

Geneviève spun to a cupboard. She flung it open to retrieve two crystal goblets.

"Then this bottle, it is for you, *aussi. Oui?*"

Almost giddy, Joe Amos watched the girl unwrap the foil and unravel the stopper wire. Humming, she gripped the neck between her knees and let the cork sail up to the kitchen ceiling. The flight of the cork, forty-five years in place, popped them into laughter. Joe Amos took from her hand a glass of champagne from the last century. Those years gave their clinking toast an extra sweetness, and a hint of misbehavior, like icing on a cake. The two sipped the bubbles and kissed again.

Joe Amos had never tasted anything like the vintage champagne. Sweet and crisp, bubbling like laughter, their gulps drew them inching closer with each ping of their goblets, until they drank the last drops smelling the sweetness on each other's breath. They set the glasses together on the table and slipped into each other's arms. His hand rose to her, her nipple through her dress nubbed tenderly in the center of his palm. He tasted the champagne on the lid of her mouth and in the eager fencing of her tongue with his.

Joe Amos knew he was drunk, surprisingly quick. This made him hurry, before dizziness distracted or lessened him. He brought his other hand to her breast. Now he was not holding her to him but groping and kissing. Geneviève pulled her hands from behind him, to push at him, but kept her mouth engaged. Joe Amos sensed he'd taken a wrong turn in the depths of this kiss. Instead of easing his pressure against the girl, he stepped forward, to express the desire between his legs into her thigh, believing in his confusion that speed was important. Geneviève tugged his hands down from her chest and stepped back, breaking the contact at all but their lips. Joe Amos stayed put, leaning out over his toes to bridge himself to her. At last she released the kiss. Joe Amos stumbled forward. She dodged out of his way, giggling.

"Sit down," she snapped, but playful, pointing at a chair. "Joe Amos, sit down."

He sat, trying to match himself to the new rhythm in the kitchen. The champagne continued to slosh over his senses. His lips and palms buzzed, and his erection needed adjusting in his pants. He waited for her to straighten her apron with her eyes cast down before nudging it to lie along his leg and not protrude like a pup tent.

"Damn, girl. What was in that champagne?"

She waggled a finger in his face. "It is not the champagne that concerns me. And you know it."

"Sorry." But Joe Amos wasn't sorry. Geneviève stepped closer. She laid fingers under his chin.

"Do not be sorry. But this is not the way. *Vous comprenez?* You understand?"

"Yeah. I am. I do. I mean . . . I'm sorry. We'll . . . I dunno, we'll date."

"*Oui!*" She applauded. "We will date!"

Joe Amos kept to the chair for another hour while Geneviève prepared dinner. She chopped vegetables and split a chicken, wielding a knife and chatting on as if she had not drunk a drop. Joe Amos could handle any liquor or beer, but he cataloged champagne for the future as something to be careful with. She brought him glasses of water spiked with herbs. After a while he closed his eyes and lowered his head to the sounds of the girl blithe and quick all around him—at the counter, in the cabinets, and at the table.

He awoke with a snort, alone in the kitchen. He stood and stared out the kitchen window, through a sore haze that added to his respect for champagne. In the yard by the well, McGee washed himself from a bucket.

Joe Amos listened for Geneviève in the house. The place was a mansion and she could be deep in it somewhere. He walked outside to McGee.

Before he could reach the well, the snarl of the Peugeot rounded the house from the front drive. McGee looked up from splashing his arms. Seeing Joe Amos, he shrugged, admitting he'd been pressed into service on the car. The engine revved, the horn honked once, and Joe Amos headed around the building. McGee grabbed his tunic and OD undershirt, lagging behind.

Emerging past the shrubs, Joe Amos saw Geneviève step from the Peugeot. The Marquis left the motor running and sat rubbing the steering wheel, savoring what was probably his first drive in years. Seeing Joe Amos, Geneviève walked briskly to him.

Passing, she draped a hand along his waist.

"I'll get dinner ready. Go for a ride."

She spoke to McGee before she entered the house. The Marquis called from the driver's seat.

"Joe Amos! Your McGee is a wizard, a shaman with the engine. *Mon Dieu*, this car has sat so long and now she motors like she is a cat! Come! We will take her out!"

Joe Amos walked to the driver's-side window.

"No thanks."

"Yes, of course." The Marquis lifted a hand to mimic striking himself in the head. "You *live* in a vehicle. Why should you want another drive? Eh? McGee! I will show you what you have done! Come!"

McGee waved off the suggestion.

"Ah, well." The Marquis shut down the engine. He ran fingers over the steering wheel in a parting caress, contemplating something, lost time, a missing wife perhaps. Whatever it was, Joe Amos guessed the look on the Marquis's face was not in thanks but regret.

The Marquis climbed from the car. He laid a hand on Joe Amos's back. "Walk with me."

Joe Amos nodded, muzzy from his nap and the champagne. He hoped Geneviève had tossed away the bottle, to keep their interlude in the kitchen just between them. They walked past McGee. Joe Amos said, "Car sounds good."

McGee's shirts were a clump in his hand. He narrowed his eyes at the Marquis.

"It oughta."

The Marquis led Joe Amos onto the lawn, to the shade of a great oak. Cicadas whirred and birds on high branches chirped. Joe Amos imagined himself the heir of this manor, husband to the girl inside. The great house spread wide like welcoming arms. Joe Amos wanted to tell the Marquis how much he desired to belong here. He wanted to compress all the time that lay ahead, the time needed to know Geneviève and this man well enough and to earn their love and his place among them. He realized he was still rushing forward, the way he had with Geneviève in the kitchen, and that had been a mistake. He smiled at the Marquis.

"I see the looks my daughter has for you. Perhaps I think she is *amoureuse.*" The Marquis sighed, seeming to lament that Joe Amos required a translation. "She is in love."

Joe Amos thrilled to hear this. Instantly he composed a speech that in another second he would launch into, swearing to take care of Geneviève for the rest of her life, to be a good man and a good son-in-law, so help him God.

The Marquis lifted a finger, sensing the gush on Joe Amos's lips. "Let me be perfectly clear, my son. It is only fair to do this."

Joe Amos held his breath.

"Yes, sir?" He had not thought before to call the Marquis "sir." The man was a thief. Now he was the father of things Joe Amos coveted, Geneviève and this shady ground.

"I believe you care for my daughter, *non?*"

"Yes, sir. I do. I think she's the best."

"Yes, well. I can see in her eyes, I know her voice. She is taken with you, as well. However, I want to warn you."

Joe Amos stiffened. Where was there room in this shade, on this grass off the road, away from the war, for bad news, a warning?

The Marquis swept a hand.

"All this you see. And yes, I can tell, you admire. All this is not what it seems. Geneviève and I, we are not so much with money as once we were. The Nazis for four years were in our home. Everything has fallen down. We have no money, the land has grown over and cannot be farmed until it is cleared. There is nothing left to us but this house, a few chickens, and two cans of gasoline you have brought. We lived like beggars at the Nazis' hands, and like beggars we are still."

Joe Amos looked from the Marquis to the manor, across the groomed lawns. He knew all this was a facade, had realized it even before he saw this place, when the Marquis was caught rummaging through his truck bed like a raccoon. The Marquis and Geneviève were not the masters of this property. They were its servants, just as they were when the Krauts billeted here. The Marquis kept up appearances, mowing, sweeping, pretending he was still royal.

Affection surged in Joe Amos for the man and this place. The Marquis was admitting to him that everything here had indeed fallen, the Marquis and his daughter, too.

Joe Amos, from rural Virginia, a colored in the United States Army, understood how a man can be put down, and want most in this world to rise.

"So," the Marquis said, hands in his pockets, gazing into the mown grass. "I do not want you to come to my daughter because you believe she is with wealth. I would not want that for her."

"Marquis, no, man. No. That's not it at all."

"Say no more." The Marquis raised a palm, accepting Joe Amos's protest. "I believe you. I know the character of a man. And we are not so poor that we cannot cut up one more chicken for you and your fine McGee for dinner, *oui?*"

"Yeah. *Oui.* That'll be great."

The man linked his arm inside Joe Amos's. They walked behind long afternoon shadows, which led them like dark horses before a carriage. Passing the truck parked in the circle drive, the Marquis stopped. He stuck a finger into one of the bullet holes in the Jimmy's bed.

"Very brave."

Joe Amos waited, standing close. He retreated a step.

"So, Marquis. The truth."

"Yes? Truth of what?"

"You really don't care that I'm a black man?"

The Marquis tilted his head at the question. "No, no, *mon ami*. This is France, not your backwards America. I do not care at all that you are black, or purple. Why should I? I am a poor man. Who can I look down on, eh?"

The Marquis returned his attention to the Jimmy. The man sucked his teeth once and Joe Amos saw something there, a hesitance, then a flash that may have been too quick for the Marquis to catch and hide.

He doesn't care that I'm black, Joe Amos realized. That isn't the thing, what makes me not good enough for his daughter.

He cares that I drive a truck.

"Marquis," Joe Amos said.

The man looked up from the bullet holes. "Yes?"

"I can help."

D+46

The forest of Mont Castre left its mark on the Tough Ombres.

In the pre-dawn light, Ben walked Sam Baum along the lines of the 358th. In the ten days the 90th spent breaching the Mahlman Line, the division had been savaged. The slopes and crest of Purple Heart Hill split the 90th like light through a prism into three parts: the dead, wounded, and survivors. Among the survivors were the hardened ones, and the scared ones who would break or die next, and those whose damage twisted only their insides, like Sam.

The dead and wounded were gone, almost half the division. In their places stood green boys and officers who had not seen the bocage or Mont Castre. Since arriving in France, measured by casualty numbers, the entire division had been replaced more than once.

Ben could not take time out with each voice in the morning gloom that reached to him. 1st and 2nd Battalions, roughly a thousand doughs, waited along the LD for the signal to move up to the narrow Sèves River. Ben, with Sam at his side, kept a quick pace, speaking words of encouragement. When he caught a glimpse of a face he'd seen before, those men did not call to him for attention but simply nodded. Ben nodded back and continued to look for Phineas.

Ben wanted to find Phineas to wish him luck today, and tell him he was here to help. The 90th's action across the river at the village of St. Germain-sur-Sèves was the only operation in the whole American bridgehead today. Everywhere else, the troops geared up for the breakout, jumping off sometime in the next few days, though no one was saying exactly where or when. Ben asked a few soldiers if they had seen Chaplain Allenby. They all had, and each pointed a different direction where they'd seen him last. Typical Phineas, Ben thought, bouncing like a rubber ball among his men.

Walking beside the 1st Battalion, no one uttered a word to Sam. Ben wondered what kind of reception his chaplain's assistant would get, if the doughs would be jealous or somehow unkind to a soldier whose job it was to stick with Chaplain Kahn. Ben had never even seen Phineas's assistant, the poor private probably couldn't keep up with the little Baptist. Ben looked his assistant over. The veterans in the line saw instantly the vestiges of combat on the skinny boy, his dirt and beard, and the tired scuffle of his boots. The replacements lacked the nerve to question anyone as grim-looking as Sam Baum.

"Hey, Chap." A lieutenant jogged into the lane. "Chap!" The officer took Ben's elbow, pulling him to a stop. "You got a minute?"

The lieutenant had shaved, but his uniform was dog-eared and he smelled like smoke. Ben paused to determine if he'd seen this boy before, on Mont Castre. He decided that he hadn't, but that this young man had been there.

"I got a guy over here. Maybe you could say something to him."

"Lieutenant, I'll try to come back. I have to check in with the regiment CO. Can it keep?"

The young officer rubbed his neck, clearly intending to ask again. Before he could speak, Sam Baum moved from Ben's shoulder into the platoon. Ben and the lieutenant watched him step among the men, dodging fifty heads and shoulders popping out of foxholes like prairie dogs. Sam located one soldier alone at the rear of the unit, a boy cradling his rifle and squatting on his haunches. From fifty feet away Ben knew this was a replacement, fresh from the repple depple and the short jump from the back of a truck. This boy's first combat lay minutes away and across the little river. The soldier rocked from his toes to his heels, hiding his face behind the lowered brim of his helmet.

Sam kneeled beside the shaken dough. He laid his own rifle on the ground to free his hands. With Ben watching, Sam Baum wrapped an arm around the soldier's neck, pressing his own helmet close to touch. He whispered straight into the GI's ear. Ben turned away.

The lieutenant grinned. "Does he do the dishes, too?"

Ben returned the smile. "Well, I don't know yet. I expect he might."

The lieutenant looked east, across the hundred-yard grass pasture separating their line of departure from the river. He winced.

Ben followed the young officer's gaze over the field. "Doesn't look like much. Should be just a local action."

"Should be."

"But?"

The lieutenant blew a breath through puffed cheeks. He tilted back the lip of his helmet to squint into the morning's thickening mist. The day and the battle promised to be rainy and gray affairs.

"But I got fifty men in my unit, thirty of 'em I never seen before two days ago. I got two of my three sergeants I never met till yesterday. I got a company CO that I can't even pick out of a lineup."

He aimed a hand over the dewy stalks of grass.

"We're making a daylight assault across open land and a water barrier. I got no tanks for the initial attack. And we're doin' it all on a day when there's no other attacks anywhere in Normandy. Everybody's sittin' out today but us."

"I see your point."

"Hang on, Padre, it gets worse. On the south side of the Sèves it's like an island. See? My map shows the town over there is up on high ground about three clicks long and one click deep. On three sides it's surrounded by swamp. So there's only one way in. Right here, where we're headed. You think maybe the Krauts'll see us comin', Chap? They got nothin' else to do today."

The lieutenant gazed into the haze.

"And just for good measure, we ain't gonna get air support in this mess."

The lieutenant ran a hand over the back of his neck. Then he snapped his fingers, brightening.

"Hey, on a good note. Did you hear about Hitler?"

Ben started at this. There was good news about Hitler?

"No, Lieutenant. What has Adolph done now?"

"He almost got himself dead."

Ben's jaw dropped. He hadn't heard. But last night the lieutenant caught a snatch of news on the radio. Two days ago, a bomb in a briefcase had been snuck into a meeting with Hitler. The case was set under a table. When the blast went off, Hitler escaped only slightly injured. He broadcast to the listening world that a cadre of "ambitious, unscrupulous, and stupid" officers had attempted to kill him, but he remained very much alive.

"Churchill was on the radio yesterday. He said, 'They missed the old bastard, but there's time yet.' Ain't that a hoot?"

Ben shook his head. Without closing his eyes, he prayed that someone would try again. He asked God to stop dawdling and get the job done, to pick better confederates next time, with a bigger bomb and a smaller table.

The drops fattened and soon would become rain. The young officer looked at his watch.

"Best get down."

He laid on the ground beside Ben, who stared down on him. In foxholes up and down the LD and in the platoon where Ben stood, the helmets of a thousand GIs dipped below the earth.

The lieutenant said, "It's 0615."

Ben put his hands to his hips, remaining upright.

The *shush* of a locomotive whisked overhead, low and frightful. Ben looked up into the clatter. The shells were fired from the rear, they were American rounds aimed at the Germans on Sèves Island.

Three hundred meters away, the tree line erupted in fireballs. Shock waves pulsed across the river reeds, nodding them like wind. Ben felt the nudge of the explosions with the roar.

Hands still on his hips, he turned to find Sam and the frightened GI. He spotted his assistant sprawled beside a foxhole. Sam's hand reached into the hole, still connected to the scared dough. Sam's lips moved at the boy's ear.

"Those are our guns," Ben said to the lieutenant.

"Yeah," the young officer called up through the woofing din across the river. "They got replacements back there, too, you know."

To make his point, a round swooped lower than the others and blew on the wrong side of the river, no more than seventy meters away. Ben dove and crammed his helmet to his head, shoveling his nose into the crushed grasses.

The artillery preparation lasted fifteen minutes. In the middle of it flowering fire across the river, Sam crawled up to Ben.

"He'll be alright," the boy shouted close to Ben's ear.

Ben, on his belly, asked, "What'd you tell him?"

"Pretty much what you told me."

The explosions boomed three hundred meters away, dense and vivid through the mist. Ben had to bellow to be heard.

"What was that, specifically?"

"That a hero's just a regular Joe who waits five minutes."

Ben smiled, pleased.

"Right. The Emerson quote."

Sam winced at the erupting shells. Ben searched for clues in his assistant's eyes of how he was handling the barrage. The boy seemed on edge but under control.

"Yeah! Tell you, Chap. I left out the Emerson part. I just said it was something you said."

Ben patted the boy's helmet. Together, they lay beside the lieutenant and his platoon, waiting while the artillery softened up the enemy on Sèves Island.

The lieutenant had been right about one thing so far. Every American cannon in range was bearing down on the Krauts across the river.

Five minutes later, the detonations stopped. Echoes raced away. The doughs stumbled from their holes, officers along the LD ordered them to their feet. 1st and 2nd Battalions took their first tentative steps into the thistles of the meadow. Ben watched the lieutenant lead his fifty into the hazy field. Rain and smoke parted for their passing, then closed behind them to swallow the platoon and all thousand moving men. The boy Sam had coddled walked with his unit, no less sure than the rest but on his feet and headed forward.

Ben rose to his knees, flecked with grass and dirt. He brushed his uniform once, then stopped.

The two battalions in the mist froze, craning their heads upward.

Across the river, red and green flares seared high.

The German defenders of Sèves Island were marking their positions.

Ben listened, beneath the sizzle of the slow-falling flares.

Several men shouted, "Incoming mail!"

The GIs raced back for the pits they'd just left. Officers and sergeants screamed, flapping their arms to wave the men down, *down!* Sam's hand drove Ben to the ground.

The first German rounds smacked hard among those who'd been farthest into the field, several of them officers. Ben raised his head to see at least a dozen doughs twisting in the grasses. Under his ribs, explosions rocked the earth. The young lieutenant had been right again. Today, the Krauts, too, had nowhere for their big guns to focus but here.

Sam tugged hard on Ben's sleeve. Ben turned to see the boy pointing at an empty foxhole, big enough for the two of them.

Ben shook his head.

He scrambled to his feet, bent at the waist. He ran forward, into the field.

Ben skidded to his knees beside a corporal missing a leg. The GI's face furled in a howl Ben could not hear for the blasts. He shoved both hands onto the soldier's chest to push him to the ground. The boy opened his eyes to see Ben kneeling over him. He beat the dirt with fists, bared his teeth, and clamped his jaw.

Nodding to him, Ben unbuckled the corporal's web belt and slid it from beneath him, contorting the boy's face again. He strapped the belt around the stump at the groin and knotted it to form a tourniquet. The blast had ripped a jagged wound; splintered muscle and bone made Ben choke down a gag. Blood throbbed from severed vessels with the wild beating of the boy's heart and the pounding of his fists. Ben took the boy's shaking fist in his hands, checking that the tourniquet quelled the spilling blood. The leg was somewhere in the grass, Ben did not look for it. Concussions came thick and quick, flinging hails of dirt. Rain and grit blew against Ben's cheeks and neck, stinging him, scratching at his eyes. He kept low, fearing the whizzing shards.

The corporal lay exhausted and in shock. Ben scuttled around to grip under the boy's armpits. Through the haze he saw others had followed his lead, dragging comrades out of the blasting meadow. With hands under the dough's shoulders, Ben struggled to lift. He looked back to the platoon, hoping for help.

Ten yards away, Sam lay faceup, spread-eagled. He must have been right behind when Ben jumped into the field. Ben's heart plummeted.

In that instant, Sam lifted his head and shook it, woozy but alive. Relieved, Ben lay across the corporal's torso, waiting for Sam to gather himself and slither the rest of the way into the field. Another shell blew close, deafening, hammering.

"You alright?" Ben hollered.

Sam pointed to his ear and shook his head again.

"Can't hear, Rabbi!" Sam scurried alongside. "Let's go!"

Together they dragged the unconscious soldier to the platoon. A medic hurried from another wound to attend, immediately doping the corporal with morphine spikes and unraveling a plasma bag. Without looking up he shouted, "Thanks, fellas. He'll make it."

Ben and Sam skittered to the lip of a foxhole and fell in together. Blood trickled from Sam's ear. The boy took up drumming his back against the dirt wall. Ben sat pressed against Sam's shoulder. With every explosion he felt the tremor in the ground and in the boy, like stones falling in water.

By 0700 the German barrage slacked enough for the two battalions to jump off again for the riverbank. Officers hollered at their men, prying their shaken replacement soldiers out of the holes. The veterans moved first, and even they balked at each explosion. Ben watched officers tread backward into the field, bellowing and demanding the men to follow.

Halfway to the river, German machine guns opened fire out of the hedges across the Sèves. The GIs hit the ground again. Quickly, the MGs were answered by more American artillery, while German shells continued to fall on the advancing doughs. The world on every side of the GIs, on their guts in the grass, roiled in mid-air, blown there on gales of concussion and blinding smoke.

In their foxhole, Ben nudged Sam.

"Time to go."

The boy looked into the exploding field, at the soldiers cowering on open ground. He lowered his eyes. Ben was packed tight enough in the hole beside him to feel him draw a shaky breath.

The boy raised his face. He smiled, laughing in apology at how scared he was.

"Okay, Rabbi. You say so."

Sam eased first out of the hole, Ben in his wake. Sam took his rifle in hand and walked yards ahead, eyeing the grasses, moving into the midst of the men where they could be seen. A shell rocked them off their feet. Ben and Sam stayed flattened, crawling through the men. Under the explosions, several GIs beckoned Ben over, with hurrying gestures, as though they had only a little time.

The advance to the riverside was torturous. The weather stayed socked in, barring air support. Through the battle haze and damp mist, Ben caught no sight of Phineas. It seemed every ten seconds after getting to their feet the men dove back to the ground at the cue of another whistling incoming round or the crackle of a Kraut MG. Sam stayed in front of Ben, quiet and boring a trail through the mist and smoke for his chaplain to follow.

It took two hours for 2nd Battalion to reach the north bank of the river. E Company lost thirty-five men in the advance through the pasture, including their CO. Ben and Sam jogged back and forth at the rear of the assault, tending to wounded, giving comfort to three men dying, saying a fast prayer over four men dead. Sam lent what hand he could, sometimes pushing an agonizing soldier down so the medic could tend to him, or just laying a hand to a shoulder. Once, Ben heard him utter the *Shema*. Every explosion made the boy flinch.

At 1030 hours, E Company forded the river under cover of artillery. With no spotter planes in the air to direct fire, and difficult visibility on the ground, the big American guns, miles away, flung haphazard rounds at best-guess coordinates, unable to keep up with the shifts in the German defense on the island. Still, enough gunsmoke and dirt were hoisted out of the ground to cover a hundred and fifty doughs squeezing over the Sèves. On the German side, the Tough Ombres took up positions in a row of farm buildings.

Ben lay in sight of the river. Upstream arched the remains of a little bridge, blown by the Krauts. As soon as the GIs formed a bridgehead on the island, engineers would bridge the gap and send over tanks. In the meantime, just like in the bocage and on Mont Castre, this fight raged man-to-man under a blistering fall of shells.

Ben watched the doughs of 1st Battalion, next to wade the river. He caught sight of Phineas, up to his neck in water, in the company of two other chaplains. Ben chuckled: this was probably the first bath the Baptist had allowed himself in weeks.

Ben pointed for Sam to see. "That's my friend! Chaplain Allenby."

Sam said, "He's little."

"Only on the outside."

They joined E Company for their crossing. The water chilled Ben up to his armpits. A hundred and thirty boys waded with their rifles held high. A round blew in the water near the bridge. The GIs cursed and leaped sideways, as jittery at the underwater concussions as if there were a shark under the surface nipping at them. Before the spray and steam had blown off, the boys were out of the water and running up the south bank. Ben jogged with them into farm buildings along the riverside. Kneeling, looking out a window, he measured the next crossing.

Another uncut meadow lay ahead, maybe a half kilometer wide, bordered on the right by swamp. The land spread without cover of trees, structures, not even crops, just hip-high grass, and drizzle. The approach to St. Germain was a shooting gallery.

The soldiers in the barn huddled along the walls, staring into the empty center. Ben put his back to the stones. Beside him, Sam did his slow drumbeat with his back against the wall. A lieutenant moved inside the ring.

"Everybody alright?"

Nods answered, and only a few voices.

"Now, boys, what's the worst thing we can do out there? Huh?"

No one spoke, until someone said, "Get killed."

"No," the lieutenant said, patient. "The worst thing is to stop. 'Cause if someone does get hit and you stop, then others are gonna stop, and then all we'll have to show for the price we'll pay is nothin'. So we gotta keep movin' up, no matter what."

Ben figured, looking at the young, listening faces, that half the fifty or so soldiers in the barn were replacements. He saw it in their eyes, darting too much or fixed too long at the floor. The old men in the unit did the same as Ben, identifying the green kids and making up their minds to keep away from them. The lieutenant moved to his sergeants, speaking with each. Then he stepped to the center again and said, "Padre, good to have you with us this morning. 'Fore we head out there, you got any words?"

"Yes," Ben said, standing against the wall. "Fight."

The lieutenant smiled, rubbing his brow.

"Yeah, Chap. I kinda meant, words from God."

Ben did not pull his gaze from the young officer.

"God doesn't like to repeat himself, Lieutenant."

Ben cast his eyes around the barn, and like a taper lighting candles, where he looked the doughs stood. The lieutenant turned, watching his reluctant boys rise. He walked over to Ben, and struck out his hand for a shake. Ben granted it. Every one of the wet GIs came to shake or pat Ben's arm. The medic was the last of them, then Sam, too. No one made a sound until they were all done, and the lieutenant, squatting by the door, said, "Follow me."

The officer stepped out under a dribbling eave. The platoon left the shelter of the building tepidly, Ben in their middle. Left and right, other units of the two battalions walked with them into the meadow. Two hundred soldiers advanced, bent at the waist in the light rain. Ben walked empty-handed, though he laid his hands to the shoulders and ribs of the slow marchers, the reluctant ones. Ben prodded with a firm voice, "Move up, soldier. Come on."

The only cover in the field was the soldiers themselves. Every man moved exposed from the belt up. When a Kraut MG opened on the left flank, the doughs around Ben froze. The lieutenant gave them a vulgar lashing. He strode forward, determined to lead his unit across the field, widening the gulf between himself and his unit while shouting to drag them along. The soldiers balked, casting crazy glances across the field, unable to find an enemy in the tall grasses to shoot at. A few of the men laid down right there.

Ben moved through the platoon, to walk beside the lieutenant. The officer turned a sour face to him.

"Thanks, Rabbi. But you better fall back."

Ben did not answer, tramping on pale stalks alongside the lieutenant. He walked, listening to the guns firing elsewhere but close. Behind him, someone said, "What're we doin' out here?" but Ben kept his back to the unit, plowing forward, sensing this was all he could do. The lieutenant pivoted, watched, then announced, "Let him go." Ben heard the running boots fade, one soldier hightailing it for the rear. The rest of the unit kept walking forward, another hundred yards into the damp meadow.

The blare of two MGs did not send Ben to the earth while every soldier around him plunged. He kept his feet for the first moment, smitten by the sight of the meadow grasses ripping, weeds sliced off in straight lines. The bullet trails from the pair of guns crisscrossed, drawing a cat's cradle in the grass.

Ben knew he'd waited too long. He tensed to get down, when the first bullet hit him.

Before the pain of the bullet could fully strike Ben, he was bowled over. He landed on his rump, Sam's arms wrapped around him, a hard tackle. The two lay below the palisade of weeds, face to face. Ben looked up past Sam's nose to the shredding grass inches above his back. The meadow was being whipped into a froth by the Kraut machine guns. Beneath the fizz of the bullets and the hiss of rain, Ben heard the falling whine of artillery.

Sam stayed on Ben's chest, pressing them both to the dirt. The explosion quaked in the ground and in Sam's chest. Ben pushed him off.

"Sam . . ."

"Rabbi! Damn it! What the hell!"

Ben rolled to his stomach, ignoring his assistant to listen for more incoming, and for the sounds of wounded.

"Rabbi!"

"What, Sam? What?"

"You're hit, damn it!"

Ben felt the sting now, in his right hip, just beside his pocket. He reached a hand to his pants, felt a rip over his buttock. He flexed the leg, the sting did not worsen.

"Flesh wound."

"Yeah, this time."

"Thank you, Sam."

"Yeah, I know. Look, Rabbi, right now might not be the best time, but are you out of your mind?"

Ben wiped his blood on the grass. The platoon lieutenant bellowed through the curtains of the weeds, for the unit to move up and stay down. Boys slithered past, headed deeper into the meadow. A voice cut through the weeds and the rain, in the pauses of the machine guns, crying, "Medic!"

"Rabbi, listen. You get hit, you know what's gonna happen to me? I'm gonna get court-martialed. You're the only thing stoppin' 'em. So, for God's sake, do you gotta be out front all the time?"

Sam shook as if he were cased in ice. Ben marveled that this scared boy had the balls to stay upright when the machine guns fired, to knock down his chaplain just ahead of the worst of the bullets. Shaking or not, Sam was no coward. Ben patted his hand, to calm him.

But why did Ben hesitate when the MGs opened up? What made him move to the head of the men beside the lieutenant, not the place for a chaplain? Not even Phineas walked out front into battle. Ben wondered, looking into Sam's disapproving face: did he have to admit he was so distracted over finding his son's fate, so driven to end his worry and this war that he'd begun to lose sight of his own life? Was his carelessness, his brave posing, really a wish to atone through his own sacrifice?

No. That wasn't what God wanted from him. Not Ben's death.

He crawled forward, moving with the rest of the unit. The bullet gouge in his hip was little bother.

Sam took a grip on his pants leg to hold him back.

"Rabbi, hang on. Let me get in front. For Pete's sake."

Sam edged past, muttering into the ground.

"The white boys are gatherin'."

Joe Amos hung an arm out the cab window. His Jimmy eased to a stop on the narrow road, another drab link in the long traffic jam north of Amigny.

Beside him, McGee nodded. "That's always bad for someone, sure enough."

Joe Amos snickered. His windshield wiper squeaked, not enough water to ease its swipe now that they were idling in line. Joe Amos cut off the wipers, letting the gentle rain patter on the glass.

The girl's kiss was just three days old on his lips. He put his fingertips there.

"I reckon now's a good time."

"Okay." McGee shrugged.

Joe Amos opened his door and hopped down to the road. More trucks arrived behind him, lengthening the backup. Ahead, probably two hundred Jimmies and tractors waited to move forward. Their cargo was men.

Joe Amos walked around Lucky's grille while McGee slid behind the wheel. He strode off the road, gazing south down the traffic jam. Hedgerows bristled the backs of green hills in the rainy haze. Joe Amos thought again about winning the war and the freedom that would follow, to drive up and down those hills anywhere he wanted, but this time it was not a Jimmy he drove in the daydream but the Marquis's little car, and not McGee next to him but Geneviève.

Several steps off the road, Joe Amos took a leak. He paid no notice to the two dozen soldiers from the 2nd Infantry Regiment in his truck bed, keeping his back to them. Before he was done, traffic inched forward. Joe Amos walked alongside his own truck. Saying nothing, he took from his tunic a pack of cigarettes and lit up. He had two cartons in the glove compartment, gotten in trade from Speedy Clapp for two bottles of the Marquis's wine.

Joe Amos exhaled smoke, strolling close to the wooden slats of the Jimmy. Several soldiers leaned and looked down on him. Joe Amos knew from seeing a hundred thousand white boys come and go that these had not been in combat. It's that white skin, he thought, it shows every mark like a piece of paper. You can read the days on a white boy's face. Not like a black man. You don't see a beating so fast on a dark face.

"You fellas gettin' ready to go kick some ass?" he called up with a billow of tobacco smoke. "The big breakout, huh? Man. Y'all look ready!"

"Yeah," replied a few voices. Joe Amos looked into young eyes confused by the slow momentum sweeping them into battle, envious of the black fellow walking happily below them with a cigarette, not going off to fight and die with them, not allowed to go do this and lucky for it, but still black and unlucky.

A company of Sherman tanks clanked up from behind, rolling over the shoulder of the road. Joe Amos jumped on the Jimmy's running board, out of the way. The tanks rolled past and Joe Amos saw something new and odd on them: a pair of steel tusks welded low on the front chassis. Instantly, the tanks created a stir among the soldiers in the truck bed, buzzing with guesses at the purpose of the innovation. Joe Amos listened while one old man explained his theory, grinning at the simplicity and inventiveness. Those steel horns would allow a Sherman to ram a hedgerow and, instead of bouncing off, the tank would dig into the roots and plow through, keeping its tracks on the ground and its vulnerable belly down.

The doughs agreed. Another soldier bet the beams had been cut from the obstacles the Krauts had set off OMAHA and UTAH.

Joe Amos found this exciting, to see a secret weapon moving up, on the way to get its baptism in the breakout, and to see that the Generals who ran the war were adjusting, trying new ways for the fight. Soldiers in every truck cheered the passing tanks. Joe Amos shouted to McGee, "You see that?"

The Shermans and their tusks shot forward in tight formation, like circus elephants. They did not kick dust out of the wet earth but chewed corduroys beside the road and spit a nasty exhaust. With their black puffs, Joe Amos blew more cigarette smoke over the crowded, staring soldiers. He saw a few nostrils lift.

He dropped off when the tanks were past and walked beside the creeping Jimmy, keeping up his chatter.

"What y'all think? War's gonna be over in a month? Two?"

A voice knifed out of the truck bed: "Tell that nigger to shut up and get back in the truck and drive."

Joe Amos made no reaction. Many of the young faces looking down at him grimaced. They wanted to apologize for the mean voice in their bunch and did it with their eyes. Joe Amos took one more drag on the cigarette and handed up the unsmoked half.

Soldiers reached for it. One GI grabbed it, swallowed a hit of tobacco, and passed the butt along. A boy asked, "Hey, Sergeant, you got any more smokes?"

Joe Amos appreciated the mention of his rank from a white boy. In that moment, he sensed the same kind of confusion he figured these soldiers felt looking down on him. He wanted to go with them, to fight in the big breakout, be right there when America kicked down the door out of Normandy. At the same time he was glad not to be going, glad to have a French girl here and not just a perfumed letter from home like these crackers going off to get shot at. He thought of Boogie in jail, the Jabo in flames, the .50 caliber rattling in his hands, Geneviève's touch, and the bodies he carted back from the bocage day after day. In the last month and a half, more had happened to him than in the rest of his whole life. He couldn't be mad at Uncle Sam for letting him have this adventure, even if it meant he wasn't going off with these boys to win the war with a gun.

"Yeah," Joe Amos answered, "I got a few packs."

"Hey, how 'bout lettin' us have a couple. We'll pay for 'em. Come on, Sarge. Be a pal."

Joe Amos pulled off his helmet to scratch his head, to mock thinking it over.

"I don't know, y'all. They were pretty expensive for me."

"Shit," one soldier said, "what do we care? We're goin' to get our asses shot off anyhow. How much? Gimme a pack."

Joe Amos stuck his helmet back on his head.

"Okay, I'll sell 'em to you for what I paid. How's that?"

"Good enough."

Joe Amos lifted a hand to the open passenger window. A carton of Chesterfields sailed out of the cab. He caught McGee's toss, opened the box, and held up a fresh pack.

"Two bucks each."

"Two bucks?" Faces curdled. "That's a night on the town in Paris. Christ."

"Sorry, boys. It's what they cost me."

The ugly voice from the far side of the truck bed cut in: "Where'd a coon get that kind of money?"

The Jimmy jarred to a halt, jostling the soldiers. Joe Amos scowled at McGee, jerking his head at the boy to get the truck moving again.

One of the GIs turned around to snap, "Hollywood, shut up." He dug in his pocket and handed down two bills. "Here you go, Sarge. Gimme one."

Joe Amos sold the whole carton. In the truck bed Zippos flipped, cigarettes fired up. He could have sold some from the second carton but thought it unwise to break that one out. Then he might have had some explaining to do.

Climbing back into the cab, he peeled off three dollars and handed them over. McGee stuffed the bills in his shirt.

Joe Amos glowered. "You never been called nothin' before? Huh?"

McGee stared ahead, driving slow.

Joe Amos pulled the last carton from the glove compartment. He took a pack and spun it into McGee's lap, then stowed the rest.

"This ain't your little town in Florida. This is business now. Don't you screw this up for me."

McGee pursed his lips. He set the cigarettes on the dash.

Joe Amos rolled the bills and strapped them with a rubber band. He stuffed the wad in his pants.

At 1800, under a gray drizzle, sounds of the German counterattack sheared across the open ground.

Rumbles of mortar fire and crackling shots pitched from far ahead. The CO of 2nd Battalion reached for the radio almost flung at him.

Ben listened. He watched the Colonel spit his frustration into the grass and shake his head at the tinny shouts in his earpiece. 1st Battalion was under attack on their flank. There was nothing anyone could do to help them.

During the afternoon, while he and the rest of 2nd Battalion had crawled and crept forward drawing fire, 1st Battalion on their right advanced too far, a half mile from the river. 2nd made it only 350 yards beyond the Sèves, and was stopped in the meadowland, deep to 1st's rear. 1st Battalion was up there alone, exposed on three sides.

Watching the Colonel clutch his radio, Ben saw the blows the 1st was taking by itself.

Phineas was up there. Ben waited while the Colonel assured his counterpart on the radio everything possible would be done, but for now he was stuck in place, with a significant Kraut force pinning him in the grasses.

When the Colonel handed away the radio, Ben asked if any units were being sent forward. If so, he'd like to go, too.

"Sorry, Chap. We're both stuck where we are for the night. Besides, I'm afraid soon enough they'll be back here in bits and pieces."

By nightfall, the Colonel was proven right. Wounded and stragglers by the dozens stumbled over the field to the rear. Ben ran into the dusk and the fast-fallen misty night to take soldiers by the arm, help them limp to the river. He walked beside stretchers, murmuring comfort. A few of those coming in from the dark were not hurt, just green boys who'd seen their first day of battle and could not stand to see another. One soldier had a bullet shot cleanly through his hand, a wound Ben suspected was self-inflicted. He stayed silent to these quitters and let them go on, they were nothing he could salvage.

D+47

At 0300, Ben walked the last of the wounded to the river. He guessed close to a hundred men had staggered back in the night. Almost one in six from 1st Battalion had been hit on just the first day's action. Ben had no idea how many dead there were.

He lowered himself into a foxhole. Sam left him alone, finding his own shelter nearby. Before seeking sleep, Ben gazed into the dark sky, starless and quilted. A couple hundred yards back, the Sèves swelled from the rains. By morning, bridging the river was going to be impossible. That meant no more tanks on this side beyond the four already here. The sky showed no intention of breaking, once more ruling out close air support. 1st and 2nd Battalions were marooned on Sèves Island, tangling with a determined and clever force of defenders.

Ben's last thoughts before closing his eyes were of the lousy leadership the 90th was getting. How could all this happen in a single day, almost two hundred casualties in two battalions, in what was supposed to be just a local skirmish while bigger forces primed for the breakout? How could everything keep going wrong for the Ombres?

The night was quiet and Ben did not dream. When he woke, he looked out of the hole into fog so thick it swirled in the hole around his knees. He moved, stiff, not young in any part of him. His mouth tasted vile. He rubbed his chin, over an itchy beard. His hands were so dirty he thought of his papa's hands, the coal miner.

Ben rose out of the foxhole. He caught the sounds of fighting, again from the 1st Battalion, now fully lost in the fog. Sam came with a plate of hash and a mug of coffee. The boy's face still had bits of dirt clinging on one side of his own growing beard where he'd slept against a dirt wall.

Ben ate without talking. No one in 2nd Battalion was readying to push forward, to ease the pressure on 1st, up there alone and under assault. The fog clung too tightly to the meadow, artillery cover would be dicey. A pair of tanks by the battalion CP tent did not even have their motors running. Finishing his breakfast, Ben figured the Germans on Sèves Island might be a smaller force than everyone reckoned. The Krauts seemed only able to deal with one GI position at a time.

At 0800, the reports and explosions flared again out of the mist. The Krauts were staging another counterattack against 1st Battalion. No one around Ben moved from their foxholes. Supply trains on foot began to pass by, laden soldiers soaked from crossing the fattening river, hauling crates of ammo and medicine forward.

"Let's go," Ben said.

Sam unshouldered his weapon.

"Go where?"

"Up there."

"I swear, Rabbi." The boy shook his head. "If I could go back to the infantry without gettin' court-martialed, I'd do it. It's gotta be safer."

Ben put fists on his hips, disapproving. "See, that's the problem with you Schenley boys."

Ben turned into the mist. Sam moved in front, saying, "Get behind me, Alderdise."

They caught up with a pair of A&P soldiers and took over the handles of a heavy ammo box. The A&P boys returned to the river for more.

They walked with the weighty crate hanging between them. Ahead, the sounds of battle faded. 1st Battalion had beaten off the second counterattack. Several times Ben and Sam stopped and listened, sometimes dropping the crate and diving for the ground when artillery or tank fire whined out of the haze. Gauzy forms of soldiers headed through the fog past them, more wounded making for the river.

By 0930, Ben had followed the supply line to 1st Battalion's CP, a collection of folding tables and chairs beneath a rare tree here on the meadow's edge. The mist had begun to thin. Ben and Sam laid the ammo with the stacks of supplies seventy yards from the CP. Sam waited there while Ben approached the officers at their desks and radio sets.

Beyond this rim of the field, Ben noted the ridges of hedgerows, and behind them the first roofs of the village of St. Germain, the nests of the Krauts on Sèves Island. Several hundred riflemen were gathered in a knot around the battalion's commanders and their tree. Few foxholes had been dug; the CP must have been forced to move several times in the night and dawn.

Ben looked at the gathered officers, leaning on flattened palms over tables or holding field radios to their ears. He hoped to spot Phineas, knowing it was more likely the little chaplain was crawling from boy to boy in the last of the reeds. He wondered if Phineas had fired his pistol yet, or if he'd taken a wound himself. Ben looked forward to showing off to Phineas the rip in his pants and the sore red stripe on his tail.

Halfway to the CP, Ben sensed the wariness of the officers. Everyone under the tree moved too fast, urgent and unsure like water popping on a hot skillet. Others stood, hands in pockets, waiting. Waiting for what, Ben wondered? He strode forward, eager to get the feel for what was happening up here.

Closer now, he surveyed the officers. Phineas was not among them.

Ben stopped. The eyes of every man under the tree lifted from their maps and dials into the still branches, looking beyond them, into the rising gray haze. Five hundred GIs clumped in the field raised their heads, too.

Artillery was on the way, American guns. The officers and doughs shook their fists to each other under the keening shells.

The first shells blew behind the hedges two hundred meters off. These blasts grew into a curtain of blows, slamming the ground between the village and bocage like an anvil. Ben felt the shudder in his boots and each *whump* and fireball on his chest.

Somebody must have figured the Krauts were laying there, behind the hedge mounds. Probably these officers called in the artillery because they were concerned about another attack. They'd already been hit on the flanks twice this morning, maybe they saw enemy movement straight ahead. Clearly officers of 1st Battalion were nervous on the trigger.

The artillery began to creep forward, rolling the exploding curtain closer to the soldiers in the grass, to scour German positions on both sides of the hedges.

Ben stepped ahead toward the CP, then stopped dead again. This time the sound that snagged his ears was not the whistle of shells overhead or the pounding in the earth. He narrowed his eyes toward the last of the high grass before the hedges, and saw helmets rise, then gray camouflage battle dress. The noise he heard over the explosions came from German throats.

A skirmish line of Kraut paratroopers ran straight at the GIs, firing and screaming. The artillery had flushed the Germans out of their hiding spots on the edge of the field. They couldn't go backward, that meant death under the shells. So they ran at the Americans, a suicide charge.

Ben took another step forward, expecting a slaughter of the outmanned Germans. They came out of the grass, maybe sixty of them, shooting and running full tilt. The firefight would be over in seconds when the GIs got off their bellies and returned fire.

Sam's hand gripped Ben's shoulder, stopping him.

"Hang on, Rabbi."

Out of the burning and blasted hedges, somehow intact, two German Mark III tanks clattered forward. The rushing Germans let out a roar. One tank followed suit, its turret flashed and a gout of earth beside the CP scooped high on a black blast. The officers dove to their stomachs. The tanks rolled into the field and the running Krauts shot their way forward.

"Get up," Ben muttered at the officers.

Sam's hand pressed on Ben's shoulder, urging him to kneel or lie down. Ben pushed the boy's arm away.

"Sam."

"What?"

"Fire."

The boy dropped a knee, drew a bead on a rushing German, and shot at him. Sam missed. Ben watched the Kraut assault with dread, and listened in awe to the pops of only a few answering guns from the Tough Ombres.

The Mark IIIs came unchallenged across the field. None of the GI officers under the tree was on a radio telling fire command to adjust the shells. Artillery rained chaos on the emptied hedge, behind the Kraut attack. Out in the field, at the running cusp of the Germans, several hundred doughs did nothing to stop them. Ben saw the first American hands go high.

The Germans fanned out ahead of their tanks, weapons leveled, but no longer firing furiously. GIs stood without their rifles and thrust their arms in the air. Handfuls of Krauts took entire platoons prisoner. Under the tree, a battalion officer stood, hands up. With a German machine pistol aimed at his head, he shouted for his men to cease fire.

Ben took one step forward before Sam stopped him again, this time with a bear hug.

"No, Rabbi, no. We gotta get outa here."

Ben could shout, Shoot! Shoot them! He would run into the field and get the doughs fighting again. He couldn't believe what he was seeing, a hundred GIs with their hands up, hundreds more scuttling to the rear, their backs turned to just sixty Germans and a pair of tanks. Sam's grip tightened around his chest. He could scream, Don't quit, don't quit! Don't disappear!

Sam hoisted Ben off his feet and yanked him from the surrender. Facing the rear, the boy set Ben down but did not let go, and began to run, churning his boots, pushing. Ben tried to gape over his shoulder, unwilling to tear his eyes from the scene, not ready to run away. Sam did not release him, and Ben, to keep from tripping in the tangle of their boots, began to run, too. Behind them, German guns snapped, bullets whizzed past, buzzing in the grass and damp air. On all sides, soldiers sprinted for the river, to the safety of the rear. The sounds of their jangling gear and heaving lungs, their frightened whinnies, churned the morning into a stampede. Frenzy filled the meadow. Brave shouts and harsh commands could no longer rally the doughs. Ben ran with them, shamed and shocked, and for the first moments since he arrived in France, abandoning his son.

The tatters of 1st Battalion, maybe three hundred boys, dashed over the meadow. 2nd Battalion was dug in another eight hundred yards off, across the featureless field these doughs had fought through yesterday. They shouted while they ran, warnings for the approaching A&P boys still ferrying supplies: Germans! Tanks! These soldiers dropped their supplies and joined the panicked retreat.

Ben pumped his arms and legs, Sam at his side. He glanced at the white, wide-eyed faces bounding around him. Replacements and experienced hands, all running alike, the same, scared, leaderless boy.

Ben heard firing. He thought the Germans might be chasing them, shooting at their backs. He saw GIs at the head of their running pack crumple, shot down. He pulled up, breathing hard, confused and frozen in place with the rest of the battalion.

Out of the grass, hidden and flashless, two German machine guns cut loose.

The MGs had been secreted into the high weeds, they'd been there all morning. Five minutes earlier, unaware, Ben and Sam had walked past them. Now they ripped the open field, killing the stock-still boys of 1st Battalion. Ten, fifteen, twenty went down before someone hollered, "Hit the damn dirt!" Soldiers spun as bullets tore into legs, arms, and torsos. Sam dove. He looked up at Ben and screamed, "Rabbi!"

No, Ben thought. I do not stop here.

"Sam, get up!"

Ben did not wait to see if the boy followed. He took off running for the river. The machine guns pivoted for him, rounds clipped the reeds at his legs, but he did not slow or go to ground. He ran until the guns turned elsewhere, searching out better targets in the meadow, motionless ones. Then he looked back.

His decision to risk the guns and escape had been taken up by half the doughs in the field. The others, badly wounded, dead, or petrified, were left behind. Far back, one of the Kraut tanks closed on the surrendering officers, leveling its guns at point-blank range at the men under the lone and undefended tree.

Ben spun around to run with Sam and the last hundred of 1st Battalion, almost every one of them shouting, "Go, go!" Ben shouting, too. Exhausted, disgraced, they staggered to the river. Soldiers from 2nd Battalion jogged over the grass to meet them in the eroding mist.

Wounded overflowed the two aid-station tents. Doctors and medics of the 358th were bloody as butchers moving between men sitting up, lying on the ground or on litters, many just standing with confusion and hurt. The medical staff had no time to tend to anything more than the physical damage to these men. Ben followed behind the sulfa sprinkles and bandages, walking through the red copper stench of the men who'd run from battle. No one called to him and Ben offered no consolation. Shame bent every neck. The boys suffered their wounds quietly, as though they were welcome punishments that evened the scale for running.

A Catholic chaplain strode among the cots. He wore a white stole over his shoulders and carried a Bible. Ben watched him kneel beside soldiers who turned their faces. The priest laid his hand on chests and the backs of heads and moved on. He saw Ben near the door and approached.

The priest was younger than Ben, softer, with a narrow face and wire-rimmed glasses. He extended a pudgy hand.

"Chaplain," he said.

"Chaplain."

The priest looked back at the wounded. "You were out there with them. What happened?"

They turned tail, Ben thought. A whole battalion run off by a platoon of Krauts. And these boys had made him run with them, had spattered their guilt on him.

"A small German unit got flushed out of the grass by artillery," Ben said instead. "They attacked straight at the CP. No one shot back. The officers surrendered. Then half the battalion put their hands up. The rest tried to make it back to the river. A couple of MGs were waiting in the field. We got cut up pretty bad. Some of us kept running, the others stayed behind, one way or another."

"That's terrible."

"Yeah."

The priest noted the dingy tape and dirt covering the Red Cross symbol on Ben's helmet.

"I'm Edgar McGwire, from Sacramento. You must be a friend of Phineas's. He wears his helmet like that."

"I've been looking for him. Is he here?"

"No, I haven't seen him."

A raven chill landed in Ben's gut. Phineas had not been among the wounded at the aid station. There were only two places left: either he was lying in the field in no-man's-land, or taken prisoner.

Leaving McGwire behind, Ben hurried from the tent. He found the CO of 2nd Battalion. With three other officers, the Major stalked the front lines of his five hundred riflemen, barking at them in their foxholes to keep their heads up, stay ready.

"We gotta pick up the slack!" the CO hollered, striding tall. "You see what happens? Goddammit, you men keep focused!"

Ben followed the Major, waiting to catch him between bellowed breaths. Ben stayed out of the way while this officer did what every leader must, lead from the front, be visible, show resolve.

When the Major had gone to the farthest reach of his line, he turned to the rear, to head back to his CP. Ben held up a hand.

"Chaplain. I'm really busy right now. Can it wait?"

"No, sir. It can't."

"Alright. Walk with me. What?"

Ben fell alongside the Major's long strides. Before he could make his request, he saw McGwire and another chaplain coming at full tilt. The Major halted until all three chaplains were around him. He waved his staff to go on yelling at more soldiers without him.

"What do you want, gentlemen?"

Ben spoke first.

"Sir, there's dead and there may still be wounded out in the field. I'd—"

McGwire interjected, "We'd like to see if we can go get them." The chaplain beside him nodded. Ben shot McGwire a grateful tip of his head.

The Major took in the three faces, all men older than him by at least a decade. He pulled a rag from his pocket to wipe the nape of his neck.

"Gentlemen, by my count, we got two hundred and fifty riflemen and eleven officers captured this morning. We got over a hundred wounded, and no idea how many dead. For all intents and purposes, 1st Battalion has ceased to exist. If you can go out there in that goddam meadow and get us back even a few of those boys, I and God Almighty with me will be beholden to you. What do you need?"

While McGwire explained, Ben peeled the tape from his helmet, to expose the bright red cross.

With Sam, two medics, and six litter bearers at his side, Ben lifted a Red Cross flag and stepped into the open field. A hundred yards to his left under another flag, the priest, McGwire, and his crew headed along the rim of the swamp. To Ben's right, the other chaplain, Jay Bolick from the Salvation Army, waded into the tall grass. Their three red-and-white banners fluttered in the clear noon.

Before they walked fifty yards, a triangle of P-47s flew in low and fast, strafing the German positions. The planes were looking for the twin

MGs that had gunned down so many doughs two hours ago. The racket from the fighters' rockets and machine guns made every man under the white flags cringe. Then the planes banked in formation and circled hard to come in again. Overhead, more artillery whined, to thunder on the hedges far ahead. The battle for Sèves Island carried on.

Once they were deeper in the field, Sam moved to walk in front of Ben.

"Sam?"

"Yeah, Rabbi?"

"Get behind me. I don't want a rifleman in front. This is a peace mission. Let me lead. Put your weapon up."

"Rabbi—"

"Do it."

Sam shouldered his M-1 and faded behind the litter bearers. Ben stepped to the lead and held the little flag high. He looked across the trampled grasses, feeling the disgrace of fleeing freshen in his heart.

"1st Battalion!" he shouted over the reeds. "1st Battalion! We're Americans!"

To his right, the three P-47s dropped low and flattened their wings. The fighters rushed the ground and fired long, ripping bursts into the marsh grass. Ben and his unit stopped until they were gone with a terrible roar of speed and smoke. Ben held the red cross as high as he could, to make sure the planes and any Germans hiding in the grasses or any wounded GIs saw it.

"Spread out," Ben ordered his men. He told Sam, the only one carrying a rifle, to stay close.

Off to the right, close to where the fighters had plowed the field, Chaplain Bolick's team stopped. They'd found a GI down. Ben's steps quickened.

In seconds, one of his litter bearers shouted, "Over here!" Before Ben could turn, he saw more dreadfulness of the morning strewn at his feet, a tangle of bodies, littered boots, limbs, and helmets. He waded in, bending quickly to each, tugging and rolling boy from boy. These soldiers had been hit bad and, left to die, had crawled close to each other: some lapped arms over others to give succor before their own deaths. Ben wept and did not make himself stop, looking for breath among these lost boys.

One soldier shocked Ben when he moaned. His wounds were the grimmest in the jumble, his left arm was shot away at the shoulder and his torso shredded. Ben readied himself to bring his face close and ask the boy how he could pray for him, but first took his wrist and felt a strong pulse.

"Medic! Medic!"

Looking up for the running medic, Ben noted the Thunderbolts were not banking for another pass. The planes circled over the river, holding off. There had been no small-arms fire in the meadow since the chaplains entered.

Beside Ben, the medic skidded on his heels. The wounded soldier coughed. The medic glanced at Ben in wonderment at this clinging life, then shouted for a stretcher.

The boy was not conscious enough for Ben to speak to him, shock and blood loss kept him limp. Ben stood, lifting the Red Cross flag. Across the meadow, all three teams tended to wounded, or located and lifted bodies. More soldiers from 2nd Battalion headed up from the river to help carry stretchers out of the meadow.

Ben tromped through the field, hoping and afraid to find Phineas. He walked to the other two chaplains to ask if they had recovered him. A half kilometer away, artillery pummeled the hedges, and beyond them, St. Germain. But in the meadow, a truce seemed to have taken hold.

The three chaplains ranged across the grasses and far into the swamp. Every step, Ben knew, was taken under the gun sights of crouching Germans. In the first hour, ten seriously wounded GIs were taken from the field. A dozen bodies were carted off, three times that many were found. Ben's chest tightened with each dough found in the grass, dead or still alive. He saw the medics run, and ran behind them, ready with a prayer or a soothing word, he gripped GIs' hands hard to instill life or gently to whisper goodbye. He stood over one boy, riddled and gone. He turned to look south, toward the hedges and village, and thought this island should have been taken by now, by these dead and maimed boys on the ground.

Then he blinked, to be sure his vision was correct, to make sure he really saw the Kraut soldier walking across the field.

Ben raised the Red Cross flag and walked toward the German. Seeing him, Sam jogged to catch up. Ben lifted a hand to stop the boy.

He approached the German. When they were twenty yards apart, both of them stopped.

The German called, *"Wir lassen Amerikaner verwunden. Lassen Sie irgendwie Deutsches verwunden?"*

Ben answered in German. "Yes, we do have some of your wounded."

The man was tall and wore round glasses. He seemed by his insignia to be an officer. He carried only a holstered pistol.

With gray camouflaged pantaloons tucked into his boots, Ben took him to be a paratrooper.

"Good," the German said. "We should like to make an exchange, yes?"   .

"Yes. Thank you. We will bring them here."

"We will do the same. Your German is very good, Chaplain."

"One half hour." Ben had no desire to swap pleasantries.

"*Ja*. One half hour."

The officer pivoted to walk away. Ben called to him.

"Sir?"

"Yes?"

"Among the prisoners—"

"Yes?"

Ben expected the German to smirk and mention they had taken quite a few. He did not.

"Did you take a chaplain?"

The paratrooper paused to recall, or perhaps to consider something else.

"*Ja*," he said.

The German paratroop captain checked to see that Ben carried no weapon, then led him through the hedgerows. Ben saw now how ineffective the blind American artillery had been. The earth was scorched and the old mounds had been hacked at, but machine guns nested in the dense bush kept their eyes on Ben and his escort.

The captain made no conversation. With a raised eyebrow, he noted the Ten Commandments pin on Ben's collar and walked on.

Many times in the Great War, Ben had been behind enemy lines, but always crawling at night with other Yank serpents on an assassin's mission. He tried to dredge up some of the courage of those young days and could not; he was older now, frailer, in daylight, and protected only by the red cross on his helmet. In that first war he'd been a killer, not a Jew. Now, striding past five hundred hidden, watching Germans, he was only a Jew.

The captain led him to the edge of the village, to a squat stone farm-house. No trace of the shelling showed here, the house was unscathed. On a lawn beside the building, horses in the traces of wagons grazed. Ben saw no other vehicles.

The gray captain took him to the foot of the porch. A paratrooper snapped to attention.

"Von der Meer," the captain told the guard. To Ben, he said, "I'll go get your wounded. Good luck," then turned away for the village.

Ben stepped through the doorway, the guard at his shoulder. Soldiers filled the kitchen and den with talk and tobacco smoke, poring over maps. This was the German CP on Sèves Island. No one turned to notice.

The guard motioned to the stairs. Ben climbed. At the top, in a broad loft, an officer sat bareheaded at his desk.

The man stood, not tall, trim at the waist, and very white-skinned. His thin hands looked more to be made for the piano than battle.

"*Was ist los? Ein anderer Amerikaner?*" the officer called to another room, "Bergen, *kommen Sie hier!*" To Ben he gestured one of the pale hands, indicating he would speak with him in a moment when this other arrived.

"It's alright," Ben said, "*Ich spreche Deutsch.*"

"*Ja?*"

"*Ja.*"

The officer indicated a chair for Ben. "Bergen," he called, "bring tea!"

Sitting, he asked, "You will have tea, Chaplain?" He leaned over his desk to peer at Ben's collar. "Excuse me. Rabbi."

"Yes. Tea."

The man leaned back in his chair. He tapped his lips with a long finger. "You are?"

"Captain Ben Kahn, 90th Division chaplain."

"Major Fritz Wilhelm Freiherr von der Meer, 6th *Fallschirmjäger* Regiment." The Major inclined his head, polite and cool.

The tea tray arrived. Von der Meer waited for his adjutant to pour both cups. The young man did so, then left the loft.

Only after the Major had taken his first taste of tea did he ask, "Where were you captured, Captain?"

"I wasn't captured, Major. I was escorted across the lines under a white flag."

The officer pursed his lips, seeming to approve. "And what do you wish to speak with me about, Rabbi?"

Ben set the china cup on the saucer with a click. Unsaid, Ben heard the word, *Jew*.

He said, "Thank you for allowing us to pick up our wounded."

"It seemed not too much to ask."

"Today, you took several hundred prisoners."

"Yes, we did. Quite a surprise."

"One of them was a Baptist chaplain. His name is Phineas Allenby."

"Yes, I met the chaplain this morning. I had him and the other ten officers from your 1st Battalion for tea. I remember, he was extremely red-faced all through our meeting."

"Where is Chaplain Allenby now?"

"Nearby. Waiting with the rest of the prisoners to be sent to the rear, to a prisoner-of-war camp."

"Major, I must ask you for Chaplain Allenby's release. He's a noncombatant."

Von der Meer shook his head.

"No, he is not. Unlike you, Rabbi, your Baptist friend had the red cross on his helmet obscured."

The Major slid open a desk drawer.

"And more importantly, he was captured carrying a gun."

From the drawer, the paratroop Major lifted a .45 pistol.

"In fact, he was carrying this gun. The sergeant who took it from him gave it to me as a souvenir."

The Major removed the magazine and slid the Colt across the desk.

"I give it to you, Rabbi, to remember your friend."

Ben did not take the pistol from the table.

"Major, look in the magazine. It's full. I'm certain Phineas never fired it."

Von der Meer glanced at him in surprise, then pressed on the spring-loaded rounds in the clip.

"Yes, you're right."

"Then . . ."

"Then that is our good fortune. Not his. I'll tell him you stopped in."

Ben stood. His chair legs screeched on the floorboards.

"You can't do this."

"Are you in any position to tell me what I cannot do? Rabbi Kahn?" The Major kept his seat.

Ben glared at the man. Von der Meer sipped his tea again, then set it aside with distaste for its loss of heat. When he returned his eyes to Ben, they, too, had lost their warmth.

"May I tell you something, Rabbi?"

"What?"

"Please have a seat."

"I'll stand."

The Major was displeased. He took Ben's measure, then nodded, affirming something to himself.

"I understand your hatred of me, Rabbi. You do a poor job of hiding it. Now let me tell you something of my loathing for you."

Ben linked his hands behind his back at parade rest. He spread his feet to shoulder width, to firm himself. "Feel free, Major."

Von der Meer put his chin in the air. He drew a slow breath before he spoke, leaving Ben to stand rigid and waiting. He tapped a fingernail on the desk.

"Twenty-five years ago, we were fatherless children, we Germans. You killed our fathers. Yes, yes, I see it on you, you were here and you did your share."

Ben glared back, soldier to soldier with this man, thinking, Yes, I did. The Major saw the look, noted it, and continued.

"After the war, we had only mothers. Our women worked in the mills and factories, they were the ones put to labor to pay you for Germany's humiliation. And though we had no fathers, millions of us young ones became brothers. Hitler came forward. He told us he wanted to become our father."

"Lucky you," said Ben.

The Major waved this off. "*Ach.* At first, no one took him seriously. He was mad, he was brutal. But slowly, he became the only voice left to Germany. He became the new head of our broken family. He spoke to us as one. He gave us pride, gave us hatred, and after enough time the two became inseparable. Together they were new life for Germany. Before we knew it, before we could stop ourselves, we were a mad and brutal people. Now, in the middle of a war, fighting for my life, I find I am angry to be such a thing. I know what the world thinks of us, Rabbi. And the world is correct. But make no mistake, you did this as much as we did. You shamed us after the last war. You tried to crush Germany. You gave us Hitler. Now sit."

The Major pointed to Ben's chair. Ben wished for the bullets to Phineas's gun.

"Sit, Jew, and let me tell you what we have made."

Von der Meer gestured again at Ben's chair, insisting. Ben sat, both hands squeezing the wooden arms.

"There are too many bodies," the Major said. "So they use ovens."

D+49
JULY 25

Joe Amos and McGee sat on the Jimmy's hood, smoking. They had orders not to smoke around the ammunition. Their convoy was two miles long and crammed with shells of every caliber, plus a million jerricans and enough lubricant to fill a pond. Lucky strained on her springs under five tons of 75 mm tank rounds. No one walked along the line of motionless trucks and tractors to tell the colored drivers not to smoke. Every eye was trained on the sky. Joe Amos and McGee lit up and leaned back.

At 0936, the air attack started. Joe Amos and McGee heard the first pistons beat out of the north behind them. They waited for the first planes to zoom overhead, guessing what they would be and how many. They sat with heads tilted and fixed, like watching a movie at a Saturday matinee.

Joe Amos offered the first guess. "P-47s." This one was easy, the fighter-bombers always came in fast and at treetop height, their roar erupted and they were on you and gone in a snap.

McGee puffed. He said, "Yep. A shitload of 'em, too."

Yesterday Joe Amos and McGee sat right here, smoking, their backs against Lucky's windshield. Smoking was a way to advertise they had cigarettes to trade. Lucky was becoming known in the 668th as Lucky

Strike. Their convoy waited at Pont Hebert behind the 2nd Armored Division, ready to roll in the tanks' wake. First would come the bombers, smashing or dazing everything German along a four-mile rectangle south of the St. Lô–Périers road. Then fifteen thousand infantrymen would pour through the gap, protecting the shoulders, keeping the hole open. Next, the Shermans. Then Joe Amos and his supply trucks, and at last the American Army would break out of Normandy and boot this battle for France in the ass. But the weather yesterday stayed gloomy. The air assault was canceled, but 350 bombers failed to get the word and dropped their payloads by mistake. In the soupy visibility some planes missed the blast zone and dropped short, killing a couple dozen GIs in the 30th Division and wounding over a hundred. After that, a gloom as fat as the weather spread over the entire breakout force. So did a fear that it could happen again today. That was why neither Joe Amos, McGee, nor any of the Negro drivers reclining on a thousand tons of ammo and gasoline worried about smoking.

Joe Amos pointed up, with a Chesterfield between two fingers, at the speeding bellies of at least five hundred P-47s. Like great locusts crowding wing-to-wing, the planes flashed past, headed for the opening strafing run on the zone four miles away. Joe Amos shouted, "Whoooo-ee!" into the rushing of the planes and kicked up a leg, he couldn't sit still with that much sound and power storming past to make war just down the road. McGee tucked an arm behind his head against the windshield, unmoved by the opening spectacle. Joe Amos dug an elbow into the boy's ribs.

He shouted, "I bet they can hear that all the way over to Couvains!"

McGee shrugged, and shouted back, "The Marquis hear this, he prob'ly think it's a big lawn mower or somethin'. That's all he cares about."

Joe Amos chuckled. He settled back and listened to the first explosions arching over the treetops and hedgerows. For ten minutes the P-47s ripped into the dug-in Krauts with rockets, bombs, and napalm incendiaries. In that time, Joe Amos sold four packs of cigarettes, pocketing seven dollars, and tossing a buck to McGee. Some of the drivers offered trade, like rations or clean socks, things they'd bartered for or stolen themselves, but Joe Amos was a cigarette-and-cash man only.

When the P-47s were done over the bocage, they fled north above the convoy, climbing to cross the Channel. As the blue-and-white morning grew still, the fields smoldered four miles off. Joe Amos dropped his half-finished Chesterfield over the edge of the hood and listened. McGee heard it first, saying, "Holy cow." Joe Amos only nodded, but his gut jumped.

An army marching on the ground cannot compare to one in the sky. Wheels are not wings, and the drone of boots and trucks is not so terrible as the approach of waves of angered angels. This time the full air assault was on, and the sound was like nothing Joe Amos had ever heard. He gazed into the swelling din, holding his breath for the sight of the leading edge of the first flight of heavy bombers.

The B-17s' roar was full-throated, miles high. The bombers came in a swath, packed tight because the blast zone was only seven thousand yards wide. The lead formation inched ahead, scratching white contrails behind them. Around them popped the first black dots of anti-aircraft fire.

This was a promenade of power and determination that every German, Frenchman, and American in Normandy could see. The English over in their sector probably got a good gander, too. Joe Amos imagined Geneviève on her front lawn, gazing up, whistling and moved that her colored soldier's country had come like this, across heaven for everyone to see, to rescue her and her father and their home. He wished the girl could see him here, sitting on Lucky's hood, nonchalant, ready to roll behind the tanks right into battle. Then he thought maybe she shouldn't see him with his truck, him and McGee just hauling the ammo for the goliath tanks and not fighting in them, just ogling the beautiful bombers aloft and not flying them. Tomorrow, when 2nd Armored whipped through the gap, two companies of riflemen would ride on the tanks, holding on and ballyhooing, each man and his buddies charging right out front, the best that America had to throw at the Krauts, while Joe Amos will ride into the breakout on the comfy seat of a Jimmy. His rifle will likely stay stowed beneath his bench, miles to the rear.

But she knows all this, Joe Amos thought. She could have any of these white boys, and she picked me.

Joe Amos shook himself another cigarette. A dense wave of heavy B-24s slid in behind the B-17s. He looked north, down the long conveyor of bombers stretching into specks. "Fifteen hundred," he said.

"More," McGee said.

"Two thousand?"

"Whatever," McGee said, giving up his count. "It's still a shitload."

Joe Amos sat back against the windshield. He crossed his legs at the knee, lounging on the hood like he was at the beach. He felt good again, sensing himself lifted and ready for the next phase, the one beginning this very moment, with the whine of the first sticks of heavy bombs plummeting on the Krauts' heads. Something big lay ahead, changes, in the roads and fields outside Normandy.

D+57
AUGUST 2

The German soldier dug into his wallet. He held out a fan of francs to White Dog.

"Did you hear the rumor," the soldier asked while White Dog took the bills, "Patton is here now?"

White Dog gave the soldier a paper sack. Inside were three pairs of nylon hose, for one hundred fifty francs each.

"I heard. It was a bluff, you know. Keeping him in England. It was to make you think the real attack hadn't started."

The soldier let this answer hang, to appreciate the irony.

"Well, I think the real one has started."

He peeked into the sack, rummaging a finger to check the hosiery.

"A goodbye gift," the soldier told White Dog.

The German boy's smile was sad, to be leaving Paris just when he'd found love. A week ago the Allies had broken out of Normandy. They'd pulverized a stretch of land west of St. Lô and swarmed over it. Nothing the Germans could do would stuff that genie back in the bottle. Now the unofficial word was that Patton was in France, and in charge of the newly formed Third Army. Already the Third had bolted thirty-five miles south to Avranches. It was about to turn the corner into Brittany.

This young Kraut knew his days in Paris were likely on their last page of the calendar.

"I guess you'll be going home soon, eh?" the soldier asked White Dog, the hiding American.

"Sure."

"Maybe me, too."

"Sure."

"Well, *danke.*"

"*Kein problem.*"

White Dog pocketed the francs. The soldier turned to walk away into the alley. White Dog didn't move. The Kraut's high, polished boots clicked on the old cobbles, he was tucked and clean, going on a courting call this evening.

Out of a doorway, three thick Frenchmen in leather coats jumped the German. The first wrapped the boy's arms so he couldn't get his MP 40 off his shoulder. The second bulled his comrade and the German to the ground, clapping a hand over the tackled boy's mouth. The third raised a bludgeon and smacked the soldier in the temple below the helmet. He pounded a second time, and his cohorts stood from the cobbles. The Kraut alone stayed flat. One of them lifted the machine pistol off the downed boy's arm, another took the sack with the nylons. The third mugger kicked the German's ribs savagely, stepping back and coming in like a football kick, before melting into the twists of the alleys. White Dog muttered, "Oooo."

He walked to the German. The boy wasn't dead, he was breathing, but he'd have a lump the size of a potato. White Dog stepped over the body. Out of the doorway, a voice called, "*Chien Blanc. Merci.*"

A man stepped into the alley, to walk with White Dog. This one was squat like the first three but older, with wide black rims to his glasses.

He said, "So you see. This is how we must do it. One gun at a time."

White Dog chuckled.

"I've got to hand it to you Communists. You're patient."

"Oh," the elder man swept a hand through the alley's gloom, "revolutions aren't all they're made out to be. Yes, there's a few days or weeks of fighting and flash, lots of history in a short period. But for the most part, minds are changed and hearts are won only a little at a time. Revolutions are more like a tide than a flood."

"When does the revolution in Paris start?"

"Unofficially, it started last week, when the *Amis* broke out of Normandy. Now that we are certain they are coming, we are gathering for the storm. Paris will come first. The power is in Paris, so this is where the battle will be. Then the rest of France."

White Dog wondered why all politicos talked like this, in sentences peeled out of pamphlets. The Commies, the Gaullists, the Nazis. Whenever they tried to sway him one way or another, he became glad he was a businessman, without sympathies. The only thing they all had in common, him included, was treachery. At least White Dog had something to show for his. The man handed over two hundred franc notes. White Dog tucked them away.

"We have plenty of money, *Chien Blanc*. Can you do a little more to help us get guns?"

Last week, the day after news of the breakout swept like wind through Paris, thirty-five Frenchmen tried to buy weapons from a man who turned out to be an *agent provocateur* for the Gestapo. All thirty-five had been lined up and shot.

"No."

The man nodded, elegant in his silence. White Dog didn't know his real name, only that he was called *"Chef"* and that he ran the Red cell here in the 18th *arrondissement*. The Communists were the strongest faction in the FFI. The closer the Yanks came, the harder time De Gaulle was going to have reining them in.

"Too bad. It might have made a nice arrangement for you."

"I have arrangements."

"Yes, you do. With the Boche, the Party, the Republicans. With hunger, lust, and greed, as well. You seem to be truly a man of the people, *Chien Blanc*."

The *chef* stopped, White Dog alongside. Ahead through the fading alley, a thoroughfare buzzed with traffic, headlamps on. The Germans were restive, many had begun their exodus out of Paris. Neither White Dog nor *Chef* would walk to the road, into the open. Instead, they would both remain here in the alleys, where there was work for them.

The Communist asked, "Have you thought of becoming a man of principle? Or are you too much of a capitalist to consider this?"

White Dog remembered a time when he would have been irked at this man's insults, when he might have bothered to defend his dignity, with a word first, or a fist. Something inside him flicked, some attempt to light a response. But nothing took the flame, the fuse was powderless.

"Wait for the Americans to get here," he said. "Then I'll get you anything you want."

FOURTH

In the months succeeding the conclusion of hostilities, I had many opportunities to review various campaigns with the leaders of the Russian Army . . . They suggested that of all the spectacular feats of the war, including their own, the Allied success in the supply of the pursuit across France would go down in history as the most astonishing.

Gen. Dwight D. Eisenhower
Crusade in Europe

The armed men went before the priests at Jericho who blew the trumpets; the rear guard came after the ark, while the trumpets blew continually. To the people Joshua gave this command: "You shall not shout or let your voice be heard, nor shall you utter a word, until the day I tell you to shout. Then you shall shout."

Joshua 6:9–10

D+60

Ben pulled Phineas's Colt from his waistband. He'd worn it like this for two weeks, the way Phineas had, hidden under his jacket.

Gun in hand, Ben approached a lieutenant waiting in line for breakfast. The young officer watched him. Dawn came clear this morning, blue and hot.

"Padre," the lieutenant said, "that's quite a hand cannon you got there."

Ben held out the .45. "It belonged to a friend."

Others in the lieutenant's platoon holding mess plates turned to see.

The lieutenant patted the holster at his own hip. "I got me one just like it."

Ben rolled the gun over, to show the empty magazine slot. "I wondered if you could spare a clip."

Every day, Ben had waited, like these men in line for chow. He held out his hands for God to plop something in them. His hands were empty like the gun, like the mess plates, waiting to be filled. At night, in foxholes, in the beds of bumping trucks, under a tarp out of the rain, slogging on dusty dark roads, Ben closed his eyes, always feeling the Colt press against his side, a prod from Phineas. The gun joined with the last letter from Thomas, prodding at his chest. Ben did not sleep anymore. He waited for God to feed him and take away his hunger, which was fury.

Ben accepted the full magazine from the officer's web belt. The bullets were copper-tipped and weighty. He fed the magazine into the butt and slapped it home with his palm.

"Careful with that thing, Padre," the lieutenant warned.

Care, Ben thought. He was far, far beyond taking care. Other forces were at work now, none of them cautious.

He thanked the lieutenant and turned. The officer spoke.

"Hey, Chaplain, stay in line. Get something to eat. You look hungry."

Ben tucked the .45 away and stayed in line. He made innocuous talk with the platoon, accepting a hearty portion of eggs and sausage. He slammed the food in.

Once he had eaten, he wished the boys luck, then walked to the convoy of thirty deuce-and-a-half trucks. Soldiers of the 357th, on their way to attack another town, helped him climb onboard and found space for him on a bench. Sam followed close behind.

Ben looked at the two dozen GI's seated in the truck with him, their two dozen rifle barrels pointed up. Sam lapped his arm around Ben's shoulders.

Maybe it was Ben's first full belly in two weeks that woke him up. Maybe it was Sam's arm around him and his face close. Ben thought it might have been the load of bullets finally in Phineas's pistol that brought him around.

He sat up under Sam's arm. The boy took down his arm. Ben gave him a wan smile.

He could not remember where he'd been since leaving Sèves Island. The last thing he could recall was the German Major ordering him to sit, then shattering him in the chair.

A new book of the Chosen People was being written in Europe, the Major told Ben. The seas here had parted not for Israel, but for Pharaoh.

Von der Meer spat at Ben what he had seen. In the Major's eyes, every man was to blame, so every man would suffer.

Before his assignment to France, von der Meer had fought on the Eastern Front. After the lost battle for Kursk, he went west. In Poland, von der Meer saw the incredible. He met an old comrade from Russia and was offered a tour of Sobibor. Later in Czechoslovakia, he passed through Flossenbürg and entered the camp on his own. He did the same at Mauthausen in Austria, Dachau in Germany, Natzweiler-Struthof in France.

Over his cold teacup, the Major said, "The phrase one hears is 'the final solution.' "

He told Ben about slave labor camps, where Jews were worked to death. They were starved and they were beaten to make sure the labor killed them. Other camps kept alive only those Jews it took to help murder the rest in ten thousands, a cadre to haul carts, sweep ash, and dig pits. The Jews arrived at the camps in droves packed into railroad cattle cars. There were enough in each load to people a village, so with every train another name on the maps of Poland, Russia, Ukraine, France, Italy, Holland, Belgium, the Slavic nations, Germany, was liberated from the Jews. Within minutes of arriving in the camp, the Jews were stripped to the skin, their clothes and possessions vetted in piles for what would be burned and what would be returned to Berlin for reuse. Naked women clutched themselves in shame while the men stood dumb and dangling. Guards herded them to warehouse-size rooms. Their corpses were shoveled out the back by their neighbors, by their children, by their brothers. . . .

Ben's horror was complete in the first minutes. But von der Meer spoke on, about the pits of lime-coated corpses where the ovens were overworked or broken, about the mountains of ownerless luggage and shoes when the transports back to Germany were too slow.

The paratrooper had watched his countrymen and the men of Allied nations do these monstrous things in the camps. At first he held each man responsible for his own morality. He had looked into the soldiers' faces, searched there for the insanity of their work, and could not find it. How could this be? Where was the disfigurement, the twisting? How can such a thing leave no mark on a man more than smoke?

Von der Meer told Ben how he held his tongue. Most regular German infantrymen knew nothing about the real nature of the camps. They lived and fought in pleasant oblivion, but that luxury had been stolen from von der Meer. He had seen the camps and so had begun to question, not the killers, but himself. Perhaps, he thought, there was no longer individual morality in this war, a war to bring forth a new Germany, a new world order. Perhaps morality had been replaced by a national code, perhaps duty and strength had redefined decency. Von der

Meer knew—everyone knew—the Jews had to be relocated, isolated from German culture. The Jews were a curse, they controlled too much money, they were a cabal of liars and leeches. Certainly there was no role in the new Reich for the Jew. Von der Meer had grown into manhood with this belief, he held it still. And when he saw firsthand Hitler's solution, the extermination of a people in millions, and the calmness of the men who did this, von der Meer's shock was short-lived. The soldiers, many of them SS *Totenkopf,* were harsh men but it was a harsh job. Perhaps the Jews must be vermin after all. For the decade leading up to the camps, posters had said this, boycotts followed, the cinema agreed. Good Germans took part in isolating the Jew. Not criminals or paranoids or maniacs, not just Nazis, but respected men and women in every walk, all of German society turned its back. Once the Jews' businesses were taken from them and their possessions deposited with the state, what further purpose did the Hebrew serve? The Jews were rats in the house, and Hitler the Father had sworn to clean them out. To be *judenfrei* was to be fully, finally, German.

Who was there to question this? Few voices were raised for the Jews, hardly even their own. These were quickly ignored or silenced. Some protests came from outside Germany, but proper *Deutschlanders* did not listen to outsiders; this was considered a strength, a patriotism.

It was war that returned von der Meer his senses. Two months earlier, America had invaded Normandy. Von der Meer fought Ben and his GIs in the terrible hedges and sucking swamps and he awoke to fear. What would America think if they discovered the camps? America would not understand what Germany had to do to free itself from shame and the Jew. If America won this war, they would question. There would surely arise in the world a new hatred, for Germans themselves.

"That is why I fight," the Major told Ben. "To keep you away from the camps."

Ben could not look at von der Meer speaking, the German's lips making the words were too horrible. In Ben's chair, the weight of cattle cars crushed him. Bullets exploded his head, gas gagged him. Fire cleansed the chair, he was gone. Ben lay in ashes with his people.

On the desk in front of him rested Phineas's pistol. Ben found only the power to take the gun in hand, and, when von der Meer was done, to ask:

"Why tell me this?"

"Because you're a Jew, and an American. You've hurt Germany. Since I'm letting you go, I had to hurt you somehow. It's only fair."

"Fair?"

"It's a war, Rabbi. In war, we hurt people. Stop sniveling like you didn't know this."

Von der Meer stood behind his desk. The interview was finished.

"Get up," the Major snarled when Ben had not risen.

Ben pushed back the chair. The heft of the pistol felt enough to collapse him.

"Put that gun away and take out your white flag. You'll get shot or they'll bring you back to me."

Ben put the .45 in his belt, under his jacket.

"Rabbi Kahn."

"What?"

"Look well into the faces of your soldiers when you tell them what I have told you today. Look deep into their eyes. And you will see that they won't care. Roosevelt, Churchill, your Generals—they know what we are doing and they've done nothing to stop us. No camps have been bombed, no railroads leading to them have been blown. There has been no outcry in the world newspapers. We have murdered millions of Jews, Rabbi, and no one cares. In any land you live, in any time, you are Jews."

Ben turned. The Major spoke to his back.

"When the camps are discovered, they won't say the rotten Germans killed men, women, and children. They'll say we killed Jews."

Ben stumbled down the stairs and out of the farmhouse. He walked north alone, out of St. Germain. He unfurled the Red Cross flag but did not raise it. The banner dragged in the grass beside his boots.

In the fields approaching the river, litter bearers, medics, and Chaplains Bolick and McGwire continued the search for wounded. Some German gunners pointed out soldiers they'd shot near their positions. The swap of enemy wounded for eight wounded GIs was done.

Ben saw Sam running across the reeds to him.

Ben dropped the white flag. His knees buckled. Sam could not lift him out of the grass. The private called for a litter squad to carry Ben off the meadow. When McGwire and Bolick heard this, they came running, too. Ben told them Phineas would not be released, and nothing else the German Major had said.

Now, piecing himself back together, Ben did not recall what happened next in the field, and not much of the time since. For two weeks Sam was his only conduit, feeding him news with bites of food. Forty-eight hours after the surrender on Sèves Island, the 90th surrounded the village and found the Germans had withdrawn. At St. Lô, the carpet bombing and breakout had gone better than hoped. The T-Os moved forward, taking Périers, then the division was assigned to a week of rest in the rear. Again, the division's CO was relieved in disgrace, for the failure on Sèves Island. Another General was in charge of the 90th, and one more blow was delivered to the men's morale. This morning they were on the way to take another town, Mayenne. Ben was in the back of a truck.

A dough reached a hand to his knee. Ben leaned out to him. This was a good-looking boy, blue-eyed. Stubble roughed his chin. He'd seen some action.

"Chaplain, I was wonderin' maybe you'd say a prayer for us."

If I told him, Ben thought, if I told him five hundred miles from here Jews were dying in mounds? If I spoke, would it crush him, too, would he help me bear this?

"You do it," Ben said.

A bouquet flew in the cab, straight toward McGee's face. The boy dodged, flashed a grin at Joe Amos, then grabbed the flowers off the floorboard. He leaned out his window and tossed the stems back to the crowd one by one.

Two women climbed on the running board beside Joe Amos. One reached out to tug him for a kiss. Joe Amos said, "Thank you."

He grabbed McGee by the belt, to pull the boy back from being hauled out his own window into the arms of the women of Fougères. Joe Amos didn't know why the thirty-truck convoy had stopped, but he guessed it was to keep from running over the townspeople thronging the street.

Everywhere Joe Amos looked, people bobbed and shouted. Young girls wore print dresses, pastels and florals. Some swirled their skirts like gypsy dancers, showing good legs. The older women wore dark colors, even in the heat. Their hair was done up and they wore makeup and heels. Every lady waved or flung kisses. The girls bounced on toes. They beat on the truck panels with flat palms to make noise beyond their calls of *"Amour," "Bienvenue," "Merci!"* While the women held up bottles of wine for the black drivers, old pensioners, dressed for church, drank to each other, often hoisting a glass in the direction of the American column.

A young boy climbed on Lucky's hood. He raised his arms to the crowd to cheers. He brought his face close to the windshield and clapped his lips to the glass, blowing and puffing his cheeks. Joe Amos smiled at the catfish face the boy made, but he pointed off the truck. The boy stood again and fell into the arms of his mates and more girls. Laughing, Joe Amos held out a cigarette. The lad leaped out of the crowd and grabbed it, shouting, "Okay!" Other hands went up. Joe Amos tossed the rest of the pack to the people, flinging each fag to the folks far back in the mob.

Every truck in the column was swarmed like this with revelers hanging off the fenders, running boards, and hoods. Every balcony and doorway along the main street of Fougères was crowded. McGee reached down out his window, accepting daisies, which he threw back to other girls. Joe Amos heard him laughing.

McGee pried himself back into the cab. His black face gleamed with sweat and red glossy lip prints.

"Sarge, can I get out?"

"Go ahead. But when I honk the horn you get your ass back in here pretty quick. We're gonna be movin' any minute. Soon as the MPs clear the road."

McGee opened his door with care to avoid banging the pressing crowd. He stepped into a foam of white uplifted arms. He said, "Alright now," then his voice was drowned.

Joe Amos watched the girls clot on the boy. They squealed to each other. Joe Amos supposed they were saying in French what McGee would never hear from white women in America, how much they liked him. Joe Amos stayed at the wheel, shooing people off the truck, keeping his senses aware should anyone try to climb on the back and lift any of the rations and uniforms he carried behind the 79th Division.

Two weeks ago, Joe Amos had ridden through the breakout blast zone. He'd never forget what the carpet bombing had done there. Who could have known that dirt could burn, that metal would melt like wax, that human bodies smelled sweet when fried? The tanks of 2nd Armored had smashed German resistance for ten miles without slowing down. Suddenly, in one day, the round-trip to supply these forces became twenty miles longer. Every sunrise since had added more road and field between the beaches and the surging edge of the American assault. Since August first, when Patton took over the newly formed Third Army, the Krauts had backpedaled south out of Normandy like they'd been socked in the jaw. Twenty-one divisions under Patton and Courtney Hodges had spread out, heading west into the Breton peninsula, south to the Loire and east toward the Seine. The GIs were gobbling up France. Joe Amos never imagined he'd see so much of the country so fast. If the 90th took Mayenne today, thirty miles east of Fougères, the supply trip would get sixty miles longer, just like that. Already Lucky was rumbling and spitting, complaining about the abuse and lack of rest or maintenance.

Joe Amos looked over at McGee. This crowd patting and hugging him was the first reward the boy had got since Joe Amos met him. McGee had seen little but long hours and a devastated countryside. For his hard work, he'd been called names by the same men he drove day and night to support. Like all the coloreds in France, he bit back an anger, but something else was building in McGee. Seeing the boy holding flowers, filled glasses, and girls, Joe Amos hoped this might relax him a little, bleed off some of his percolating unease.

Joe Amos wondered, too, about Boogie John. Boog would have gotten out almost a week ago. The big man would love this elated crowd, he deserved it. Joe Amos would have to find his old partner, even though after the breakout that wasn't going to be easy. Since the breakout, every driver was either behind the wheel all day or sitting next to the man who was.

One of the bullet holes in the dash snared Joe Amos's attention. He snugged a finger into it. Joe Amos had his rewards. The memory of the Messerschmitt trailing flames. The three stripes on his arm. And Geneviève.

He hadn't seen her in two weeks. Only once had he been through Couvains, but he could not split from his column. He leaned on his horn all the way past the road leading to the big house and drove on.

Joe Amos sat high in the Jimmy, rubbing his chin, thinking about his girl. The Army can't keep pushing like this, he figured. There'll be a pause soon, and he'll go visit her. The Marquis will squeeze him and welcome him. Geneviève will cook. They'll all drink, and the Marquis and McGee will leave the two of them in private.

The truck rocked and Joe Amos shouted, "Hey, come on now, get down!"

The Mayenne River flowed north, splitting the town of Mayenne east and west. Three stone bridges had been built across the river; two of them were blown. The third had eight 500-pound aerial bombs wired to it.

Ben perched on the second floor of an emptied warehouse. He stared east, across the river, into the German-held half of Mayenne. An artillery spotter in the window beside him had just called in a cannon and mortar preparation on the Kraut positions, to begin at 1750 hours. Ben looked down into an alley, where two hundred men of B Company, 357th Infantry, checked weapons, readying to charge over the bridge.

The first big rounds whistled in. Across the water, the town rocked. In the opening minutes of the barrage, a shell struck the ammunition caisson of a Kraut 88 that had been guarding the lone standing bridge. The massive explosion set off a cloud of smoke that blew over the river, obscuring the bridge. The spotter's radio screeched an order to call off the mortars and artillery. B Company was ready to cross under the pall now. The spotter forwarded the cancellation to fire control.

From the alley below Ben's window, the lead platoon lit out for the bridge. They ran straight up the street, into the gray coils of gunpowder stench. Before the first foot was set above the river, machine guns opened up from buildings on the east bank. The Kraut guns fired wildly at the fifty doughs scrambling and ducking behind the lean rails of the bridgework. A lieutenant at the head of the unit did not let his men falter. Ben heard him shouting orders, curses, encouragement, and every GI made it over the bridge behind him. Along the way, under pinging fire, they clipped all the bomb wires. The Germans, waiting to the last moment to blow the bridge, had lost their chance to the lightning charge of the platoon. Other soldiers on the west bank laid machine-gun fire into windows and doors across the river to keep the Krauts' heads down.

Onto the bridge, at the platoon's heels, two Sherman tanks clanked, blasting rounds above the boys' heads into any crevice that might hold defenders. In front of the Shermans crept a pair of engineers, clearing the bridge path of mines. Ben borrowed the artillery man's binoculars and scanned the action.

Halfway across the span, a fireball erupted with a *boom* that shook Ben's building. When the haze cleared, both engineers were down, one missing a leg. On the bridge a soldier dragged the engineers out of the way and the tanks continued, shooting up the town.

The first unit reached the far end of the bridge, and disappeared into the buildings to secure a bridgehead. Behind them, no more troops set out over the bridge. Ben swung the binoculars to find the problem. The next platoon in line had balked. They were cramming themselves into doorjambs and crannies in the alley. No one was leading them across.

Then something happened that Ben had not seen in the 90th. A Major stepped out from his own cover to march up and down the alleyway, excoriating the soldiers for abandoning their buddies on the other side of the river to fight by themselves. The lieutenant who'd led his platoon across the smoky bridge ran back, picking up a rifle from one of the fallen engineers. In the alley he lent his voice to the Major's berating. Prodded by the two officers, the platoon fell in. Behind the lieutenant, under covering fire from both sides of the river, they scampered across the bridge. Every soldier made it.

In two and a half hours, the second half of Mayenne fell to the Tough Ombres. A/T guns and tanks were positioned north and south to guard the flank approaches. The leading edge of 1st Battalion had already chased the Krauts a half mile east out of town. Ben walked over the river with Sam at his shoulder. Snipped detonation cords lay useless in their path. A blood smear rouged the road.

Ben gazed into the green ripples of the river, and into the punched holes in buildings lining the bank where the Krauts had been routed. He marveled. What he had seen was perfect coordination between armor, infantry, and artillery. When a unit of riflemen hesitated, their officers had stepped in and shown leadership. Once they got their heads up, the boys beat the Krauts out of town like dust out of a rug.

Ben asked Sam, "Was that the same 90th?"

Sam picked up a bit of tar gouged by the tanks' treads. He tossed it over the rail into the water. He hesitated before he replied.

"I guess everybody just needs someone good to follow."

Ben nodded. The 90th had a fresh CO now, and was assigned to Patton's Third Army. Under these new Generals, the doughs were streaking over France, racking up victories; that meant fewer casualties, and fewer replacements of men and officers. The bocage and Sèves Island were fading behind them. After two months, the T-Os, the problem division, were becoming a fighting unit.

"I was talking about you, Chaplain. You and me?"

Ben had missed the compliment. Sam rattled his head and spit over the rails.

"Well," Ben said, "I suppose that's true. After all, I've been following you since we met. Schenley."

Sam lowered his head to hide his smile. "Alderdise."

Dusk settled. More than a hundred German prisoners were marched back over the bridge, to be loaded into trucks and taken north to Normandy for processing. Ben sent Sam to scout out a place where he could hold a service that evening. Behind him, in the river, stripped GIs bathed beneath the bridge, jeering at the POWs crossing above them, and ogling the eight massive bombs still strapped to the stone pillars.

Ben strode through the town. He watched the battalion gird itself into Mayenne, hardening its hold with foxholes, sandbags, tanks, mortars, and tramping, confident boys. Many of them greeted Ben with calls of "Hey, Chap!" It seemed to Ben a way of chest thumping, of saying "Hey, look at me, I crossed a bridge and took a town and didn't get shot!" Confidence was taking hold in the T-Os.

Ben reached the eastern outskirts, only a few blocks from the town center and the blackened wreck of a Kraut 88. He looked east, where the rest of the war was to be fought. Phineas was already out there, way ahead of him. So was Thomas, maybe.

Ben's thoughts of his son were interrupted by the winding roars of car engines. Standing in the road, he turned to look back into town. Two vehicles he did not recognize barreled straight at him, headlights off. Belatedly, he realized they were German staff cars, making a break.

Ben held his place in the road. He slid his hand under his jacket and gripped Phineas's .45. He pulled back the slide and lifted the gun two-handed to aim at one speeding windshield.

"Chaplain," someone shouted, "get out of the way!" Tightening on the trigger, Ben considered how the way had grown too large for there to be anyplace left to get out of it.

The gun sight followed the lead car, now tearing right at him. Ben leaned into the pistol, to take the kick.

Before he could squeeze a long shot, an Army jeep screeched around the bend. The jeep slammed its brakes between Ben and the onrushing cars. In the rear of the jeep, a soldier manned a mounted .50 caliber machine gun. Two captains leaped out of the seats, Tommy guns spitting fire. The .50 cal joined them. The lead Kraut car wobbled, the escaping driver dodged too hastily. Two wheels came off the road and the vehicle rolled over, just twenty yards in front of Ben. Slugs ate into the roof of the car, even before it stopped skidding on its side.

The second car charged through the gunsmoke and steam. Ben lowered the pistol and stepped back, knowing this car was dead, too. When it passed him he saw the hundred splinters in the windshield and doors from the weapons that continued to blaze at it. There men slumped inside. He heard the bullets bite metal and glass, could not hear them hitting bone. The car slowed after it raced by. The two GI officers and the soldier on the .50 cal tracked it, never taking their fingers off their triggers, until the car faded off the road and stopped against a pole just outside town, fifty yards away. Amazingly, one Kraut staggered from the car. The dough on the .50 cal plastered him with a long burst, plowing so many rounds into and through the German that the car from which he'd emerged caught fire.

Soldiers milled out of doorways, to look down the street at the burning vehicle and the body. A sergeant shouted to get back to work, it was just a stiff. The GI behind the .50 caliber and the two captains lowered their hot guns and walked side by side like Western sheriffs to the edge of town. Ben fell in beside them. The gas tank of the staff car detonated. Greasy smoke pulsed over the flames. The sound of the car burning was like a heartbeat.

In the thickening night, the four men stood ten yards from the fire. The body was an officer, that much Ben could tell from the collars and sleeves of the uniform. The rest of the man was so bullet-riddled he was mash.

"Padre." One of the captains spoke.

"Yeah."

"I didn't know you fellas carried guns."

Ben realized the .45 still hung in his hand. He kept his eyes on the pulverized corpse laying close to the fire. The skin on the Kraut's spoiled face began to bubble. His blood on the cobbled street shone. The other two bodies were out of sight, fallen over inside the car. Ben tried to smell them through the oil and burning rubber.

"Some do," he answered.

Ben and this captain stayed behind when the GI and the other officer walked off. For a time, neither spoke into the throbbing heat.

Then the captain asked, "Would you have shot him?"

Ben thought back to the frenzied moments when the cars were charging at him. He recalled feeling nothing, not reluctance or anger. Just the heft of the Colt, the balance of the thing. He had a bead on the windshield.

"No."

The captain shouldered his Tommy gun. "Maybe you should holster that, Padre."

The officer turned from the greedy flames, walking back into Mayenne. Ben lingered, letting the heat sting his cheeks. The weight of the gun still tugged in his hand.

The fire had baked the scarlet of the blood into black crust. The body had been busted by slugs in so many places, the Kraut looked almost turned inside-out, more gut than flesh. Ben could tell little about what this man had looked like, his hair had already burned off, his face was boiling and flat.

Ben lifted the pistol, already cocked. He fired once into the middle of the corpse. Nothing in the body moved. Ben was not satisfied. The report fled upward and out, echoing over the gobbling fire. Ben stuck the gun in his waistband. He stayed another minute, glaring into the heat, smelling at last the cooking men.

An hour later he conducted a service for fifty doughs in a parking lot. The soldiers knelt while Ben spoke.

He told the boys of his pride in their actions that day. He described what he'd seen of them, and of the enemy fleeing Mayenne. He foretold swift and great things for the coming battles, and for the 90th Division.

Ben said the *Shema*. After that, he led the Lord's Prayer. Not once did he close his eyes.

D+62

Joe Amos chucked the last jerrican into the sand with a gallon left in it. Lucky's tank was full. He lit a cigarette, too tired to worry about the spilled gas on his hands.

OMAHA at dawn was like a starter's pistol going off. The moment the light rose on ebb tide, landing craft started hitting the sand out of the pea-soup fog. Out in the mist, Joe Amos heard them churn their engines, starting a hundred yards out. He listened to the boats bull through the surf to ram the beach, jumping out of the mist onto the sand where they dropped their gates and spit trucks, tractors, tanks, tank destroyers, ambulances, artillery pieces, jeeps—everything and anything that was green and came on wheels or tracks barged onto the packed sand. Without pause, without orientation or ceremony, every vehicle either headed up the draws to find the fighting or got in line to get a load. Big cargo ships offshore that couldn't hit the beach were off-loaded by cranes onto barges and DUKWs. These came in from the fog, too. While the water was low, supplies were stacked everywhere on the beach, like sandcastles to be washed away by waves of Jimmies rolling past. At high water, everything was taken to chaotic depots in the nearby hedges. Joe Amos turned to look up at the gray shapes of the bluffs. When he faced the water again, another ship had beached, grinding and ungainly, one more pile of supplies took shape, and another pile was whittled and sent to war.

The American supply effort was immense and astonishing, Joe Amos thought, and still it strained the strength of every man involved to keep up with the advances, still it was not enough. None of the French ports had come online in a major way. Cherbourg realized only a trickle through its tangles. On the Breton peninsula, Patton had chased the Germans out of the middle and into the harbors. The Krauts responded by demolishing St. Malo and Nantes, while Brest, St. Nazaire, and Lorient stayed in the hands of defenders holed up in rock-hard citadels. Two months after the invasion, the beaches and Joe Amos's trucks remained the Allies' only lifeline.

He clamped the cigarette in his teeth. He rubbed sand in his mitts to scour away the smell and itch of gas on his skin. Lieutenant Garner walked down the line of Joe Amos's truck platoon holding a clipboard. Joe Amos was always amazed that in the middle of all this anthill action, Garner could find him to give him orders.

Joe Amos reached into the passenger side and took out a pack of Chesterfields. These were bought from Speedy Clapp before sunup, in bulk for the better price of a dollar a pack. Joe Amos was no longer buying cartons but crates from Speedy, sometimes from Thalhimer in Cherbourg. Every day he sold no fewer than twenty packs for two bucks each. His roll of dollars and francs had grown as thick as his wrist. He spun the Chesterfields to the lieutenant.

"You look like shit," Garner said.

McGee rolled from beneath Lucky, where he'd tried to sleep for the two hours they'd not been driving.

The lieutenant tore into the cigarettes. "And he looks worse," he added.

"When do we get a day off?"

Garner puckered behind his Zippo. "I don't know what chicken farm you're from back home, son, but this is a real war. We get a day off when we win. Maybe."

Garner pocketed his lighter. McGee didn't bother speaking to the officer but climbed into the passenger seat and put his head on the dash.

Garner gave Joe Amos his instructions: forty trucks, hauling half rations, half small-arms ammo, south to the 30th. Joe Amos didn't expect a piece of paper from the clipboard. Ten thousand tons of supplies were stacked on the sand; most of it moved a hundred miles inland with a word.

Garner ran a hand over the truck's fender. "Lucky holding up okay?"

"She gets by. Might need some looking after."

Joe Amos took from his pocket his mostly full pack of Lucky Strikes. He clapped them into Garner's hand. "Soon."

Garner stuffed the cigarettes away. "Sure. Assuming you get back."

Up in the cab, McGee's head popped out the window. "Assuming?" he echoed.

"Why?" Joe Amos asked the white officer. "What happened?"

"Early this morning, the Kraut Seventh Army counterattacked. They're heading west for Avranches, trying to close our corridor. If they get to the ocean, they'll lock us up again in Normandy. All the troops south of there'll be cut off from the supply lines. You move fast, and the 30th holds its positions, you shouldn't get stuck down there."

In the cab, McGee moaned into the dash.

Joe Amos asked, "Down where?"

"Last I heard, the 30th was still in Mortain. You'll have to go find out."

"Where's everybody else going?"

Garner patted the blue sheets on his clipboard. "Says here I got forty more going to the 4th near Vire, and the 35th around Landivy. The rest are loading up for Third Army down in Le Mans."

Forty trucks each to Mortain, Landivy, and Vire, to contain a Kraut counterattack? And another three hundred trucks sent to Le Mans? Why shift so much supply so far south of the attack? It didn't make . . .

Joe Amos asked, "Where's Third Army headed?"

"North."

In a snap, Joe Amos figured it out. He had a road map in his head. He drew the lines of assault and saw the gambit.

The Generals were betting the 30th would hold at Mortain. The other divisions would pound at the Kraut's exposed flanks, like hitting a boxer in the ribs to slow him down. In the meantime, Patton was going to rage north out of Le Mans with everything he's got. Patton was going to spank the Krauts on the behind. An end run.

And the Brits were positioned due north of Patton, coming out of Caen.

Holy smokes. They're going to try and surround the whole German Seventh Army!

Garner nodded at Joe Amos.

"Yep. You got it, sport. This is big. The Krauts might pull this off. Or they might have fucked up. We'll see."

The lieutenant spat and pivoted on the sand. Walking past the passenger door, he smacked a palm against the thin metal.

"Cheer up, boy," he called to McGee. "You're getting to serve your country."

By 0600, Joe Amos's column was loaded and on the way to Mortain. The fog kept the road clotted with traffic, headlamps on. Joe Amos drove second in line behind the lead jeep. He fought the urge to lean on the horn, pull the whole convoy into the passing lane, and haul ass the fifty miles to Mortain. The Krauts were coming down there, and from the sound of things, coming hard. This morning, all his tiredness was gone. Yet there was little Joe Amos could do but tap on the wheel while he and his ammo crates crept through the mist, bumper to bumper, double-clutching in and out of third gear all the way to St. Lô.

McGee said nothing. The boy crossed his arms and gazed into the fog. Since the street celebration in Fougères, McGee, quiet by nature, had spoken even less. He drove his shifts alright. But something about the flowers and the elated girls had sparked some lament inside McGee, or snuffed some spark, Joe Amos couldn't tell. Either way, even though he took the money Joe Amos gave him from the cigarettes, and never turned down a free smoke for himself, lately the boy wasn't good company.

Ten miles south of St. Lô, the column left the main road, headed down a narrow backwoods lane southeast to Mortain. The trucks gained speed. Tree branches whizzed close to Joe Amos's elbow. The convoy leaned around curves in the fog. Joe Amos liked this kind of driving, it was dangerous, and war was supposed to be that.

At 0730, the column passed a roadblock at Les Rocheaux, four miles west of Mortain. On all sides of the MPs' sandbag positions, artillery pieces under camo netting stood by stacks of shells. Every cannon tilted east. Joe Amos could only see a few of the big guns through the haze, but he was sure there were plenty more in the fields around the village. The big tubes waited, ready for the cover to lift, for someone to tell them where the enemy was. Joe Amos rolled into the mist under their aim.

The column crept forward. Whatever the MPs told the boys in the lead jeep, it slowed them down. Trees closed in again on the road. All forty trucks moved like blind men, almost tapping the pavement before moving over it.

"Take the wheel," Joe Amos told McGee.

"Where you goin'?"

"Take it."

McGee slid over. Joe Amos opened his door and stepped on the running board. With a swing over the panels, he landed on the ammo crates. He dropped behind the .50 cal and charged the bolt. Up here, out of the cab, the fog was thick as lace against his cheeks. In the truck close behind, Philly boy Baskerville gave him the okay sign.

A slow gray mile slipped past. The road emerged from the trees into fields. The mist had begun to thin, but still the vista was kept short and cottony. Overhead, airplane engines muttered. These weren't fighters but slower planes, spotters looking down through cloud breaks for the German assault. Or maybe they were Kraut planes looking for the Americans.

The column inched ahead. Joe Amos keyed his senses into the emptiness. Nothing but uncut grasses and low stone walls edged the road. Barns, some of them wrecked, studded the pastures. His fingers rubbed the machine-gun grips. Today was a Monday. His mother and sisters would be off to the mill, his brothers-in-law would be up with this early fog driving tractors and mules. Geneviève was a country girl, she'd be up, too, tending to her kitchen and chickens.

The planes faded. The morning hushed except for the gears of forty laboring Jimmies and a jeep. Where was the giant Kraut attack? Where was the 30th Division? A sign read Mortain was three kilometers ahead.

In the mist, what Joe Amos thought was a fence post raised an arm. A young boy stood beside the road. When the convoy rolled past, the boy, in a cap and dark vest over a white-sleeved shirt, dressed like a little man, pointed east. Joe Amos watched the boy disappear behind him. Drivers tossed him chocolate bars, but the boy did not bend to gather them: he kept his hand up, showing the way to the battle.

Joe Amos saw the first tanks before he heard them. They came through the hazy fields, as big as trucks themselves, headed away from

Mortain. The lead jeep stopped. A Sherman halted in the road across the convoy's path, others pulled alongside the column. Riflemen rode on the tanks' decks, high enough to look right into the truck drivers' windows.

McGee braked, the whole convoy halted. Joe Amos swung the .50 caliber into the fog. He took his finger off the trigger when he recognized GIs filtering out of the fields.

Tanks rolled alongside the stalled column, inspecting, heading for the rear. Men tramped out of the mist, stepping over low fences and hopping ditches. The morning jangled with the noises of soldiers streaming west away from Mortain and the grumbles of tanks sizing up Joe Amos's column. Had the 30th broken ranks? Were they retreating?

Soldiers began to stop on the road beside the trucks. One called up to Joe Amos behind his machine gun. "Hey, pal, what you got for us?"

Joe Amos called down, "You the 30th?"

"You got it."

"Where's y'all's depot? We got a load of gas and ammo for you guys."

The soldier was joined by several of his mates. All laughed, shaking dirty faces.

One pointed east into the mist. "She's 'bout two miles thataway."

Another said, "I reckon you're the depot, pal."

Joe Amos climbed out of the gun ring, onto the boxes.

"Catch," he said. He hoisted one crate over the rails and dropped it into a dough's arms. The soldier hefted the box away. Hands went up and Joe Amos filled them, unloading the Jimmy as fast as he could until McGee and a white soldier climbed up to help dump the crates over the side. Joe Amos looked down the length of the convoy. A thousand soldiers had come out of the fog. Every truck in line was tossing its cargo to them a box at a time. A dozen Shermans idled in the lifting mist, waiting for their foot soldiers to load up and resume the retreat.

Working, Joe Amos asked one of the doughs, "What's goin' on in Mortain?"

The boy strapped his rifle to catch a crate. "Krauts got it. Came outa nowhere last night. Don't worry, buddy, we ain't runnin'. Old Hickory's just fallin' back a little. We'll get it back. We still got a battalion up on a hill back there lookin' right down their throats, and they ain't goin' nowhere. Gimme a box."

By 0800, Lucky's load was gone. The convoy's two hundred tons were stripped and shouldered. The soldiers of the 30th marched off like ants from a picnic. Joe Amos's back ached. McGee got behind the wheel.

A captain approached. Joe Amos had nothing to give him.

"Thanks, Sergeant," the officer said.

"No problem, sir."

"You'll probably want to be gettin' your trucks out of here pretty quick."

He turned, lifting a finger to the east.

Joe Amos had kept his head down for a busy half hour. Looking out now, he noted the mist was burning off. Visibility to the east had picked up.

"Hear that?" the captain asked.

A distant squeak disguised the power of the sound. These were tracks, not like the Shermans but something bigger, slower. A howl like a huge farm tractor grumbled under the peal of rolling metal. Joe Amos narrowed his eyes to see into the fields beyond the fences and barns. The fields showed the trails of a thousand men's boots stepping through the dew. The brown outline of a village rose at the crossroads of two hedges. This was Mortain, out of the clouds at last. In front of the town, at the edge of the meadow, just over a mile off, Tiger tanks were headed this way.

Behind the Tigers, a column of smaller German armor rolled west in wedge formations. Joe Amos spotted no fewer than thirty panzers. He'd never seen a real Tiger before, but he guessed he was well within the be-hemoth's gun range.

"We'll be goin' now, Captain. McGee!"

Joe Amos shot the officer a sloppy salute. The man hurried off with the stragglers in his troop. Before jumping off Lucky's bed, Joe Amos took one more look at the advancing Kraut tanks. He saw the long barrel of one tank puff.

Five trucks behind him, a blast rocked Morales's truck, hitting so hard, the Jimmy exploded as it tumbled over. Morales and his assistant were in the truck bed finishing handing out supplies when the shell struck. Joe Amos saw the miracle of them thrown clear. The two sailed out of the fireball, then hit the road, rolled to their feet, and scampered out of the way. Joe Amos was in mid-air off the bed of his own truck when the second explosion hit. The shell missed the convoy, blowing a pillar of dirt and black smoke fifty yards beside the road. Joe Amos

leaped into the passenger door just as McGee flung the gears into reverse.

The jeep in front of the line, with its shorter turning radius, was already burning rubber the other direction. The convoy was bunched too
tightly, no one could turn in the road, no one could back up.

"Go forward!" Joe Amos screamed at McGee. "Turn around!"

The boy shifted gears in a blur and stomped too hard on the gas. The
Jimmy shot forward, McGee hauling hard on the wheel. The truck's
front wheel dropped into the ditch.

"Goddammit!" Joe Amos had to pull back his own hands, instinc-
tively reaching for the wheel and the gearshift. McGee snapped into reverse again, nailing the gas, trying to heave the front axle out of the
ditch. The rear tires spun and smoked, raising a stink and a whine.
Lucky didn't budge.

McGee hit neutral.

"Stuck."

"I know!" Joe Amos hollered in the boy's face. "I fucking know!"

The middle of the convoy was a confusion, two dozen trucks at all
angles struggling to find room to turn in the narrow lane. The Jimmies at
the far end were in reverse, winding fast and already gaining distance.
Fire and smoke from the gutted truck lent the road a battle chaos.

"Come on!"

Joe Amos leaped out of Lucky. McGee followed. The boy ran ahead
to Baskerville's truck and flew onto the bed. Baskerville was leaning on
his horn for the truck blocking him to get straight. No more rounds came
in from the enemy tanks. Joe Amos glanced back. The Krauts were mid-
way through the field, clanking louder by the second. He figured there
must be at least fifty panzers, packed tight and coming right at him.

Joe Amos patted Lucky's fender. "I'm sorry, gal. Really."

He grabbed the two M-1s from beneath the seat. He flagged down a
soldier jogging out of the field, one of the last doughs to flee Mortain. Joe
Amos asked him for a grenade.

He lifted Lucky's hood, pulled the pin, and left the grenade on the
engine block. He sprinted away from his truck, heading for Baskerville,
who idled, waiting and honking for him. The explosion made Lucky
jump, surprised. The two tires in the ditch went flat and Lucky kneeled
down. She was left there, smoking and useless.

The convoy straightened itself. Joe Amos jumped up and held tight
beside McGee while Baskerville sped away. They passed Morales's

burning Jimmy, and the smoldering crater from the wayward tank round. The road ran without curves and the fog was gone. Joe Amos watched behind him for a long mile, until Lucky and Morales's truck were smoke markers behind a bend. The convoy rolled by some of the soldiers from the 30th, still carrying their crates. The GIs waved and hooted, in good spirits.

"I'm sorry," McGee said. The boy's face sagged with failure. Joe Amos nodded to him, not sure what to say. He was worried about Morales, and damned sorry to leave his bullet-scarred truck. But of all the things he might yet lose, his own life or a limb, or McGee, another driver in his unit, his stripes, Geneviève, the one thing he lost—his vehicle—was something he could stand. Boogie was right. Joe Amos was not going to be a hero in this war. He stood in the back of a truck zooming away from the fight, leaving it to the white boys, as always. Lucky was a symbol of what he would not achieve, so in a way it was right that he should lose her. The roll of dollars in his pocket, the beautiful French girl he would see in the next few days even if he had to buy the time off from Garner, his sergeant stripes—these were Joe Amos's real victories.

McGee had panicked, sure. But nothing would be gained from throwing it up to him. Joe Amos would get them another Jimmy with a machine-gun cherry on top.

"No sweat," he told McGee. He held out a hand. McGee smiled and gave him some skin.

Overhead, artillery rounds ripped. The big guns the convoy had passed that morning in the fog were starting to hammer the Kraut advance. Shells flew thick, a whistling flock. Joe Amos had a feeling the dough who'd said the 30th "ain't goin' nowhere" was right. Other convoys will be feeding them, too. But at least now the boys had two hundred more tons of bullets and C-rations for their stay, compliments of his Lucky.

D+66
AUGUST 11

"Don't seem like the same war, does it, Rabbi?"

Sam leaned back in the open jeep, one hand on the wheel, the other offering Ben a canteen. Three days ago someone from the 359th's motor pool tossed Sam the keys to this vehicle. Ben accepted, and he and Sam had been riding since.

Ben took the canteen. He doffed his helmet and dripped water over his face with his mouth open. The August sun baked the fields, the jeep's green metal was hot to the touch. Traffic on the road to Alençon moved slower than the walking GIs. Ben rubbed water into the bristles of his hair, feeling it dribble down his back without cooling him. The air was silted with dust from thousands of boots and exhaust from slow-moving trucks. In the fields, three dozen Sherman tanks paced the convoy. A mile overhead, P-47s circled to protect the strike force from wandering Luftwaffe fighters.

"No," Ben answered, almost a minute after Sam made his comment, "it doesn't."

Everywhere he looked, Ben saw proof that this was a new war. Instead of staring into the matted walls of roots and leaves in the bocage and the dark cloisters of branches in the forest, he looked to distant hills, saw the steeples of the next town. Instead of a hundred bodies and quick-dug holes to lay them out of sight, he moved beside men strong on their feet. They liberated thirty miles a day instead of dying for that number of yards. The aid stations were not so full, the Graves Registration teams not so busy.

Not just the war but the men themselves were transformed. Since Sèves Island, the 90th had hung a few pelts on their shed: Périers, St. Hilaire du Harcouet, Mayenne, Laval. Now they spoiled for a fight with the Krauts. They sang on their marches, they ribbed each other, even the replacements whom they no longer feared as Jonahs and rookies.

Momentum swept the Tough Ombres, a tide raising all spirits. Even Sam sauntered, proud to be assistant to Rabbi Ben Kahn, who had walked into the Kraut's camp. Yesterday, Ben overheard him sharing a smoke with some doughs, telling them he'd run under more Kraut fire behind his chaplain than he ever did as a foot soldier.

The next targets were Alençon and Carrouges. The 90th followed behind the French 2nd Armored leading the spearhead north. The 2nd was supplied with American uniforms, half tracks, guns, and Shermans. The French force was ragtag, made up of regulars who'd fought in the Sahara, plus sailors with no Navy, North African Arabs and Senegalese, and French colonials who'd never set foot in France. The GIs trudging along the road complained about how slowly the 2nd was moving. They joked how the Frogs were handed new American tanks, and were busy practicing driving them in reverse.

Soldiers passed the creeping jeep. The column, made up of the two divisions plus their supply trains, was probably fifteen miles long. Tomorrow, the leading elements would likely take Alençon before most of the Tough Ombres reached the town. GIs saw Ben in his seat and took liberties with him, calling out "Chap" and "Padre." Some cursed, "We're gonna go kick some fucking Jerry ass!" just to be bad boys and get Ben's attention. Many walking by touched him on the shoulder, some that were Jews wanted to shake his hand. Ben could not rest or close his eyes in the heat from the constant contact.

The momentum of the advance did not take hold in him, though he was carried along on its current. He was too troubled to be buoyed by distance gained and easy battles. Every day was too long now for Ben, even if it brought another victory over the Germans, another freed point on the map. Every rising sun did not rise on another thousand Jews somewhere to the east. This new war, the fast-paced skipping over

France, was not fast enough, because it was already too late. In his heart, he'd begun to lose hope for Thomas, Phineas, for his people, and for his own faith.

He suspected he'd been wrong to bargain with God. Perhaps God did not pay as much attention to proud Ben Kahn as he'd thought. If that turned out to be true, then Thomas and Phineas were indeed lost, like the Jews of Europe already were, because then they, too, were subject only to the mercies of Germany, and these were paltry. Ben could have no effect at all.

"So, Rabbi," Sam asked, "what do you think the Frenchies'll do tonight? Throw a dance party?"

Last night, after dark, the French armored column lit campfires throughout their bivouac. Alençon was to be their first combat as a unit in France since 1940. Their lack of camouflage discipline came back to haunt the entire column around midnight when a handful of German nightfighters swooped in for a few harassing runs. A couple thousand guns in the 2nd and 90th opened up, waking Ben and anyone else fortunate enough to catch a snooze. No casualties were reported, but the affair did little to raise the GIs' confidence about their French fighting partners.

Sam kept up his chatter, trying to cajole Ben. He mentioned more spots in Pittsburgh they might both know. He pointed out the neat, square pits beside the road every seventy-five yards, emergency foxholes dug for Kraut truck drivers to escape Allied air raids. For two weeks, Sam had taken to typing a lot of Ben's correspondence, making sure the older man got rest and meals, even intervening with the men always tugging at the chaplain for conversation, favors, requests to be excused from duty, complaints, letters to be mailed. Sam did his best to spare Ben's energies, saving him for the hurt and dead, and for Friday night *Shabat* services among the riflemen. Ben figured Sam had secured the jeep, to ease their movements between the three regiments of the 90th. The boy steered Ben to the company of other officers, men he could try to relax and talk with, while Sam waited nearby on a stump or in the jeep. He monitored Ben's moods, and talked a blue streak when Ben went quiet for too long.

"We got a big surprise comin' for the Krauts, huh, Rabbi? Gonna jump right up behind 'em."

Ben could not tell the boy to shut up. He wanted to fall and stay down, and Sam would not let him.

Sam thumped on the steering wheel.

"If we ever get there, that is. Come on, guys. Geez."

All the way down the shady lane, Joe Amos honked the horn on Garner's jeep.

The Marquis waited in the circular drive with his arms spread wide. He did not drop them even while Joe Amos climbed from behind the wheel.

"Joe Amos! We thought you had forgotten us. But no. Ha-ha, no, you have not, *mon frère!*"

Joe Amos stepped forward. The man shut his embrace like a mouse-trap. Joe Amos took kisses on both cheeks.

"But, where is Lucky, eh? You are not driving the bullet truck today?"

Joe Amos waited until the Marquis let him go. He couldn't have a conversation with a man's face this close after being kissed. He stepped back.

"I had to borrow this."

The truth was the jeep and the afternoon to drive it down here had cost Joe Amos fifty dollars cash. Garner wouldn't take it in cigarettes.

"Lucky kinda ran out of luck."

Joe Amos intended to hold back the exciting story of how he lost his truck in the teeth of the German advance, to tell it in front of Geneviève.

He watched how the Marquis looked over the jeep, inspecting it for gifts. Joe Amos had brought no jerricans or cigarettes, not even McGee this time.

"Where's Geneviève? She in the kitchen?"

The Marquis seemed startled away from his scrutiny of the jeep. He had a sort of Christmas-morning disappointment on his face.

"Ah? Yes, she is in the house somewhere."

Joe Amos left the vehicle. The Marquis came alongside, quick and cheery again, chatting about how much he liked the jeep up close, he'd only seen them flying past on the road. It seemed quite basic and hardy, a car for survival. The Peugeot was running well, he said. The recent hot weather and rains were making it difficult to keep up with the grass, though the grounds looked manicured.

Inside the house, Geneviève hurried down the curved stairwell, still twisting her hair into a bun. Like her father, she pecked Joe Amos on both cheeks. Then she took his hand in hers. The Marquis clapped, playful but impatient.

"We have a visitor, child. Put food on the table."

Joe Amos noticed both daughter and father looked rosy. They'd fleshed out since he'd seen them two and a half weeks ago. Joe Amos figured the Marquis had traded the gasoline well for victuals.

In the kitchen, Joe Amos said, "Wait a minute. I got something for the two of you."

Over the table, he spread a fan of bills, one hundred and seventy dollars and five hundred eighty francs. The francs, set officially at fifty to the dollar, had even more buying power in the black market than the bucks.

The bills on the table were just bits of paper, Joe Amos thought. They hadn't been that hard to collect, it took some wit and enterprise and here they were. But the eyes of the Marquis and Geneviève frozen on the tabletop said that the money was life. Joe Amos had killed a German pilot and fed an army, he'd escaped tanks and washed gummy blood from the bed of his truck. These bills weren't life to him: the girl with her hands to her mouth was. The job ahead, miles to drive, an enemy to beat, his uniform, the future to win, these were life. He would give Geneviève every dollar he came across if it put that look on her face again.

"*Mes cieux!*" Geneviève gasped through her fingers. "This is too wonderful."

The Marquis said nothing. Joe Amos caught his eyes scanning the bills, counting. Geneviève slid an arm around her father's waist.

The Marquis reeled his attention away from the money. With his arm around Geneviève, he smiled and reached for Joe Amos's hand.

"*Merci. Merci.*"

The Marquis's head dipped. With his thumb, he bladed a tear from his cheek.

The Marquis sniffed and released Joe Amos. He stepped away from Geneviève and the cluttered table.

"Go. Leave me here. Take a picnic."

"Marquis," Joe Amos asked, "you alright?"

The man laid a hand over his heart. "*Oui, oui.* Go. I will see you when you return."

The Marquis headed for the back door out of the kitchen, to his vast lawn. In the doorway, he turned.

"Geneviève?"

"Oui?"

"Rendez le garçon heureux."

The Marquis went out to the yard. Joe Amos and Geneviève stood on opposite sides of the money.

"What did he say?"

The girl turned to the cabinets. She went on tiptoes to take plates from the back of a shelf. Joe Amos admired her white ankles, the softness of her reaching arms. She spoke without turning to him. Joe Amos didn't mind.

"He is very grateful. We will go into the *Forêt de Cerisy*. I know a place."

"That'll be nice."

The girl assembled the picnic meal and loaded it into a wicker basket, bread, meat, and vegetables. She narrated, "Do you like cheese?" and "We will drink Cabernet today." Joe Amos glowed. He'd laid out for this French girl and her father more money than he had ever brought home in Danville to his mother. He lit a cigarette and crossed his legs at the table. Conversation stopped while she finished the preparation. Joe Amos fingered the bills. He wished McGee, Garner, someone could be here to see this. Major Clay, that's who he wanted. Major Clay, who'd said he'd never be a hero.

Geneviève was pleased with the open-top jeep. She ran back into the house for a scarf, tied it around her hair, and climbed in. She wore a simple, light frock, and the scarf was white. On the seat beside him, in the sunny afternoon, the girl could not have been more his creamy opposite.

The road led east out of Couvains. For five miles they drove through uncontested hills and fields, where buildings and fences had not been knocked over. France gleamed in emerald and gold, a lush land of cattle and gray boulders. Small churches anchored even the tiniest villages, flower wreaths lay at the foot of crucifixes at country crossroads. The figures of Jesus were carved from old wood and varnished, to hang for mankind every kilometer, never enough. From his truck seat, Joe Amos had seen only the France that had been battlefields. On this summer day in an open car, he breathed the pollen of flowering trees and weeds, and slid past crop rows and elderly women in smocks picking in the green. Geneviève's white scarf fluttered beside him, she smiled and looked like a movie starlet.

When they reached the Bayeux–St. Lô highway, she told him to turn right into the *Forêt*. The road burst with military traffic. Column after column powered past, packed so tightly no one could slow to let him in. Joe Amos waited for an opening. Geneviève commented on the unremitting line of trucks and tractors, saying, "So this is America. *Mon Dieu.*"

After several minutes, a gap appeared. He told Geneviève to hold on and gunned the jeep into the crevice. In the backseat, the picnic basket slid. She checked, nothing had broken.

Joe Amos closed on the deuce-and-a-half in front of him. The Jimmy's bed was full of replacement GIs heading to St. Lô. He could spot them, anyone could who'd been in the war more than a week.

A few of the clean faces crowded over the tailgate, looking down at Joe Amos and Geneviève and their picnic basket. A cigarette was passed around, the boys smoked between finger and thumb. The shared cigarette was a bond for them, a cheap one, Joe Amos thought, just smoke on lips that would be bloodied soon enough. Then they'll know who's their brother. Then they'll learn if they're as tough as they're trying to look.

Geneviève lifted her chin at them waving to her. One soldier wolf whistled. She set her hand over Joe Amos's on the stick shift. Joe Amos wanted to back off the rear of the Jimmy, but the truck behind him was on his bumper. She pulled her hand from his when the first dough shouted at them.

"Hey, boy! Get your hand off her!"

"Hey, lady, what're you doin' with a nigger?"

One soldier tossed the cigarette overboard, bouncing it off the jeep's hood. He unshouldered his carbine.

The GI worked the bolt on his rifle. He lifted the gun, pointing straight at Joe Amos's head. Other doughs pushed the long barrel down. The soldier glared through the shoving hands around him, taking away the rifle but never his eyes. Joe Amos pulled the jeep out of the convoy. He stopped on the shoulder.

Trucks roared past. The gargle of worn mufflers and the stink of tired pistons made the shoulder of the road a hard place to sit. More soldiers hooted when they rolled by. Joe Amos put his eyes into the woods. The trees were skinny chestnuts and oaks, kept stunted by the winds of Normandy. Geneviève said something to him. Joe Amos clamped his teeth so hard, the column next to him made such a racket, that he did not hear her. Geneviève sat back in her seat, waiting.

Joe Amos chewed on his anger, that some cracker would do that in front of his girl, just to spoil his good time, his one day off. That dumbass was never going to shoot him; the boy was just spouting off, pretending he wasn't scared out of his country wits to be rolling off to war. Joe Amos rapped his fist on the steering wheel. How could he explain to Geneviève what she just saw? What did she know about blacks and whites in America? Was he supposed to tell her the man she was with was despised, that he got treated like an animal by some of his own countrymen? What was he to say when she asked why? Because he was brown? It was the truth, but that would make no sense to someone who hadn't grown up with Jim Crow. Joe Amos reckoned he'd just tell her what his mother had told him when he was a boy, that hate and love were like bullets, once they got in your heart it was near impossible to save yourself from them. When it came to heaven and some white folks, it looked like the best you could do was hold on and hope better days were ahead.

A truck horn sounded. Joe Amos sighed, reluctant to look, guessing it was just more soldiers hazing him. He looked instead at Geneviève. She smiled, and just like that she made this a better day. The horn beeped again. He looked over his shoulder to see a stopped Jimmy. Behind this truck, another horizon of vehicles bunched on the highway. The truck's driver was white. He waved Joe Amos back onto the road.

Joe Amos punched the gears and pulled off the shoulder. He lifted a hand to the driver in thanks.

A minute later Geneviève showed him the turnoff for her picnic spot in the *Forêt*. Joe Amos bounced the jeep down a logging road. Every moment the noisy highway was left farther behind; the trees cushioned the engines and summer light. His thoughts of the crackers in the truck and of America faded, too. The girl guided them beside a stream, under a copse of pines where the ground was a ginger patch of soft needles.

Geneviève spread a blanket and set out the picnic. Joe Amos smoked beside the stream. The tumbling water and breeze covered the sounds from the highway.

"Sit," she said.

Geneviève busied herself cutting a tomato, laying slices over bread and cheese.

"They are bastards," she said, after a time.

"They don't mean nothin'."

"Not to me, no." She spoke without looking up from her hands. "But to you, they mean everything. They are your Americans." She handed him the bread. "You must hate them."

Joe Amos shook his head. He reached for her chin to lift it. He did this gently, like holding a dove.

"No, I don't hate 'em. They don't know any better. After a man knows different, then you can ask him to be different. But those boys back there, they're just stupid. So they're actin' stupid."

"And who will teach them? Who will change them, Joe Amos? You? McGee?"

"Yeah. Us."

"How?"

"By being men, just like them."

"No." The girl reached for the wine bottle to open it. Her movements were agitated. "No, *c'est impossible*. You will never be like them. You are better. *Merde*, even your McGee is better."

Joe Amos leaned back at her flash of anger. She saw him retreat, and softened. She set down the bottle to cover his hand with hers. She lifted his palm to her cheek.

"No," he said, softly. "I don't care about being better. Just the same, is all. That'll be good enough."

Geneviève kissed him. Joe Amos let go her hand and tried to set the bread on the blanket without toppling the tomato, to get both his arms around her. She released the unopened bottle, it thudded on the blanket and rolled off to the pine needles. She wrapped him in her arms and pulled him down.

In the first moments, Joe Amos was lost, tangled in the sounds of her breathing, the caress of her palms running over his back. He kept most of his weight on his elbows but laid his hip across hers. She pulled away her lips, baring her neck for his mouth. Joe Amos opened his eyes and gulped at her skin.

Slowly, as if careful not to blind him, Geneviève undid the buttons on her own blouse. Fixing him with a stare, she uncoupled her brassiere. Joe Amos held himself above her, hands flat on the blanket.

He cupped one of her breasts, toying with the brown nipple. Geneviève's back arched, and she did not take her eyes from him. He traced the curve of her waist, down her ribs, feeling good flesh there. He slid his hand under the loose blouse, to the swale of her back. He pulled himself down.

"Geneviève."

"*Oui?*"

"I ought to tell you. I've never . . ."

Her face pinched, then an odd smile surfaced. She made no move to come from beneath him. She laid both hands to his temples.

"Never what? Oh, Joe Amos, *mon cher.* You are not *un vierge?* I do not know how to say in English."

"A what? No. I'm not. I . . ."

He sat up.

"It's just I never did it with a . . ." He gestured at her naked breast.

"Ahhh," she laughed. "With a white girl?"

He nodded.

"Never in England?"

"No."

"Not in . . ."

"No," he laughed with her, "for damn sure not in America."

"But you have."

"Yeah. Sure."

"Tell me, then, am I so different?" Geneviève laid a finger to her sternum, to point out for him the one woman of the world, without color or nation. "Am I?"

Again, he slipped a hand beneath her back. This time he lifted Geneviève to sit upright on the blanket. He kissed her once.

"Yeah, you're different."

He got lucky and hooked her brassiere on the first try, then buttoned her blouse for her.

D+72
AUGUST 17

Ben gave Sam the option of not coming into Le Bourg–St. Léonard.

"You can stay with the jeep."

Sam kicked at a clod of dung in the barn. Outside, Shermans and M10 tank destroyers moved up. The six hundred doughs of 2nd Battalion, 358th, checked weapons and stepped behind the squealing armor. The Krauts had booted the Tough Ombres out of the town for breakfast. Now, for dinner, the 358th was going to take it back.

"It's alright, Sam. Come up later when it calms down."

Ben opened his pack. He withdrew Phineas's pistol. He stuck the gun in his waistband, then headed for the open barn door.

Outside, dusk hung over the end of the day like something freshly skinned, damp and warm. Men and machines flowed by, aimed at the crossroads village two kilometers east. Walking away from the barn, the evening attack sent Ben back to the other war, crawling into the gloom to the German trenches, a pistol on one hip, knife on the other.

"Rabbi, what are you doin'?" Sam caught up and stomped in front of him.

Ben looked at the boy and did not think him weak for being like the rest, not able to hear. Sam was simply lucky.

"What are you doin'?" Sam asked again.

I'm hating, Ben thought. I'm going into the night.

"This ain't . . ." the boy gestured at all the men and arms moving for the attack, "this ain't your profession."

Ben could tell the boy had thought out in advance this thing to tell him, had prepared it with the word "profession."

Before he turned to Le Bourg–St. Léonard, Ben asked, "You going or staying, Schenley?"

"I'm goin', Alderdise. But doggone it, Rabbi, keep your head down, okay?"

Ben answered Sam's concerns by tromping away from the barnyard into the flow of a company of riflemen. He was certain that Sam stayed somewhere close behind; he was equally sure these men around him would fight harder to protect their chaplain.

The Germans needed to hold Le Bourg–St. Léonard. After four days of fighting at Mortain, their offensive had flopped. The Allied corridor out of Normandy would not be closed. On the 11th, the German Seventh Army began a retreat east to the Seine. Nineteen Kraut divisions—100,000 men with their machines and weapons—stumbled backward through a fifty-mile gauntlet of British, Canadian, Polish, French, and American forces, which paddled them every step with artillery fire and flank attacks. The Allies controlled two of the three major east-to-west roads. This meant that the Krauts had only a small gap to rush through in order to reach their own lines, just fifteen miles between Falaise in the north and Argentan to the south, between the jaws of Montgomery and Patton.

Ben strode among the 358th. This was Phineas's bunch. Nothing remained of the hesitance and nerves of the regiment that foundered in the bocage, lost most of its men on Mont Castre, and surrendered a whole company at Sèves Island. These GIs walked to the town grim and tight-lipped, almost all of them dirty and unkempt. This was a good sign, that they had been alive long enough to get that way.

By the time the first tanks reached Le Bourg–St. Léonard, the sun lay below the horizon. The town ran no farther than a quarter mile, nothing but a string of structures and an intersection. The Krauts wanted the intersection to widen the gap for their escape; more importantly, they needed to deny the 90th the unrestricted view overlooking the valley two miles north, where their comrades fled east in a massive rabble.

2nd Battalion halted four hundred yards from the edge of town. In the fading light, Ben made out the shapes of German tanks slithering among the tight walls. An artillery spotter with Ben's company called in firing solutions. Five TDs rumbled into position, their turrets depressed to aim across open ground. The first artillery rounds whipped in and ranges were adjusted. The observer called in "Fire for effect," and the town was lit up. In the glow of phosphorus and high-explosives, the battalion moved. The armor inched forward, pausing to fire. The men leaned into the sonic storm of shells shattering walls, and turrets booming so hard the Shermans and TDs rocked backward on their treads. Machine-gun fire managed to rattle out of windows in the town, but the Krauts were being cuffed hard by the barrage. The light that flickered to show them the GIs advancing was lightning around their heads. On all sides of Ben, the doughs did not go to ground: they took some hits and kept advancing. The first Sherman clawed to the entrance of the village, standing beside the town's sign. The gunner drew a bead on a facade that he took a dislike to and blew it down with two cannon bursts. The artillery onslaught called up from the rear rolled down the street, to batter the structures at the far end of town. The buildings of Le Bourg–St. Léonard went off like giant flashbulbs taking photos of the doughs charging in.

Small-arms fire hailed against the tank that shielded Ben and the boys.

"Rabbi!" From close behind, Sam's voice cut through the din. "Rabbi!"

Ben did not want to turn around. He knew what he would see. Sam and a medic bent over a dropped boy, the medic tearing open bandages with his teeth, jabbing a morphine spike, Sam's hands stoppering some fount of blood. Ben did not want to turn away from Le Bourg–St. Léonard. He walked on.

Then he stopped. He came back to kneel beside the wounded soldier, the medic, and Sam. He prayed out loud for the injured man, and kept one eye into the burning night.

D+74

The obliteration of the German Seventh Army began at first light.

Ben did not need binoculars to see it, though officers standing around him gazed through field glasses, whistling and approving like they were on the rail at a racetrack. Three miles north from Le Bourg–St. Léonard, the valley floor erupted under a thousand cannons.

Enemy columns of all description scurried in plain view. Tanks, infantry, field kitchens, towed artillery, horse-drawn carts, every one tried to retreat in order but could not. The 90th held the high ground to the south and east; their guns had perfect visibility. The T-Os had taken Ste. Eugenie, Menil, and Fougy, and had cut the road at Chambois. Seventh Army was hemmed into a funnel, with only a few miles left open to squeeze out. Montgomery's Canadians held the north, the Tough Ombres stood alone here at the southern edge. Together, they slammed the Krauts hard, shoving them back into the cauldron to escape or be eliminated.

Twenty battalions of artillery had been attached to the 90th. Ben watched black pillars rise in the valley. He listened to the cannonade blazing along the ridgeline and from the rear, the guns pausing only to let the tubes cool. Each shell made its own whistle overhead, shrill eight-inch howitzers, the tenor *whoosh* of 105 mm cannons, and the gallop-like hooves of 155 mm Long Toms. Each round rent its own blast and crater in the valley floor. Phosphorus rounds bloomed hot white chrysanthemums, each piece scalding enough to melt metal. High explosives killed with shock and shrapnel, armor-piercing rounds drilled through the thickest plating and turned the inside of a tank into a volcano. Timed rounds lay unnoticed in the ground, shattering minutes later.

Forward observers from every battalion crowded the ridge, relaying solutions into walkie-talkies. Their trick was to lay fire on the lead elements of enemy columns, blocking the way with wreckage. Vehicles were forced into the blistered fields, where they slowed or bogged, making them even better targets.

In the 359th's CP, someone had installed a large radio. Standing near the tent, Ben heard the speaker blare reports from the six Cub spotter planes circling over the Krauts in the crystal morning. The Germans were stampeding and confused. One pilot made it clear over the radio he was irritated with the delay between when he called in a target and the firing of the mission.

The flyboy shouted: "Stop computin' and start shootin'!"

The officers who heard this laughed.

Ben watched through the morning. The Krauts clawed at the forces that walled them in, but the T-Os and Canadians around Falaise held fast. Vehicles were tossed in the air on plumes of dirt and fire, to cheers from the officers on the ridge. By noon, white flags of surrender began to sprout in the valley. Where they did, the spotters called off the big guns. The Cub pilots radioed, "Ease up, we got a bunch comin' in."

An officer with the 344th Field Artillery walked over to Ben.

"You been here all morning, Padre. How'd you like the show?" The man was so excited, he forgot himself. "It's a goddammed massacre, isn't it?"

Funny, Ben thought. He'd not considered God at all this morning, not damning the Germans or otherwise. Ben felt no offense at His name taken in vain. In fact, he didn't sense God anywhere, doing anything. He reached inward, into the dark, and found it quiet, an empty hall. The argument's over, he thought.

Ben stared out to the valley floor, at the white flags, the several thousand German lives preserved under them.

He looked to the officer.

"A massacre?" Ben asked. "No."

* * *

White Dog spit in his palm. He spread the gob over his temple. A lock of hair had come dislodged from the grease. He checked the other side, shot his cuffs in the sleeves of his white dinner jacket, and walked into the open.

Avenue Marceau was jammed with traffic heading away from the Étoile and the Arc de Triomphe. Great shiny staff cars, Mercedes torpedoes, made their way east out of Paris, bulging with roped-on luggage. Inside the cars, red-faced officers sat behind chauffeurs, often with a mademoiselle beside them, not so stoic, peering anxiously over her shoulder at the crowds. White Dog blew a kiss to one pretty lady disappearing with her General.

Normally, he would never walk alone in daylight down a broad boulevard. In his pocket he carried false papers and his French was passable to fool a German patrol. But why dare the Krauts, the Vichy police, or a gang from the fascist *Parti Populaire* who might spot him in his zazou getup and try to beat him up? In daylight, Paris held little interest for White Dog, he was not a shopper or a tourist. He preferred the city's splendors by night. But this morning, he felt no need for protection. This morning, White Dog wanted to see the uprising for himself.

Strolling, he thought how history is just dominoes. What some people see as a great event is really the result of something that happened elsewhere. Some GI in the path of a German offensive doesn't have the sense to duck and run. This dumbass stands his ground, other dumbasses get inspired and they hold too; the next thing you know, the Krauts were stopped and Paris was about to be torn apart, or liberated, or both.

On top of the colossal failure of the Mortain attack, the Germans had to deal with the fact that, four days ago, the Yanks made a second major invasion landing in France, this one on the southern coast. The end of the Reich's occupation was only days away.

Blood was in the water. And in Paris, no one went madder at the smell than the Communists.

Posters tacked to benches, poles, and glued to walls called for *l'insurrection populaire*. The color of the ink or paint was always red. The Commies ran the FFI, they owned most of the dead heroes. The Gaullists, to prevent a civil war, were forced to follow along. White Dog figured between the two factions the Resistance was maybe fifteen thousand strong in the city. They had less than a few thousand guns against a crack German garrison of sixteen thousand. The revolt was not going to come from the *fifi* fighters alone but from the people in the streets, a Parisian specialty. This was what White Dog walked to see. He considered his sunny walk a fact-finding mission, taking the measure of both history and the changing marketplace.

He ambled from the Arc de Triomphe toward the opulent hotels on Rue Lafayette. Here the departing German officers were shameless, strapping furniture, paintings, even rolled carpets to their limousines. Some had furnishings piled into trucks to follow them over the Rhine. Parisians who for four years pretended the Germans were invisible glared openly now at the soldiers looting their treasures.

The mood in the city heated under a mounting, hot sun. Stores closed early, a sure sign of trouble, and just as well, White Dog thought; he had more goods stashed in one warehouse than any five government shops, and at better prices. He grinned: after a few days of this nonsense, the black market would be booming.

On every block, shadowy men ran between corners and alleys carrying rifles and gasoline bomb bottles with rags stuffed in the neck. Tensions reared like scared horses. He caught sight of a German patrol stopped on Avenue George V to fire a volley into a tricolor that had been draped over a balcony. Minutes later, in the direction of the Prefecture of Police he heard tank fire. Heading along the Boulevard Saint-Michel, he watched a squad of Krauts taunted by a crowd of old folks waving toilet brushes. The soldiers ordered them to disperse, and when the people did not, they leveled their rifles with execution precision and fired. White Dog slapped his back against a wall at this and decided to head south, across the Seine to Montparnasse.

He picked up his pace, intending to disappear into familiar territory. He would wait out the riots in his covey of hideouts. He'd seen enough, and there was nothing he could do except get nabbed or hurt out in the open. Some Communist would brain him if he said he had no intention of helping the uprising, or a Kraut would shoot him for being in the wrong place, which for the next few days was just about everywhere. White Dog intended to go back to Montparnasse and peep out of his alleys while history wracked itself over Paris.

One thing's for sure, he thought. The Germans aren't going to tolerate this for long. The Commies have put out a call to arms. Silly bastards all over Paris are answering them, and getting shot down for waving toilet brushes. The Krauts have nothing to gain by battling in the streets with Frenchmen for a city they can't hold. They're either going to give

Paris up or blow it up. Either way, in the next few days the Allies' hand is going to be forced. Four million French were going to become nieces and nephews of Uncle Sam. So much matériel was going to flow into Paris that White Dog could get stinking rich just picking up the bits that fell off the trucks by accident.

He stopped by a stall on a rare quiet lane. An old *fournisseur* handed White Dog a *pâtisserie* and charged him one hundred francs.

White Dog bit into the pastry. Whipped cream squirted over his lips.

"Are you selling a lot of these, old man?"

The vendor stepped back from his cart. He flipped down wooden slats to close it. Lacking a horse, the man stepped into the traces himself to haul his business away.

"I only had to sell one, *monsieur. Merci beaucoup.*"

White Dog finished the pastry, watching the old man and liking him. Even more, he liked his own plan for Paris. Wherever history stomped its foot, prices rose.

This was definitely the right time and place for him.

D+76

Sam stopped the jeep under a copse of trees. The column of ambulances could go no farther. The road and fields ahead were too cluttered. Ben hopped out to walk. Sam followed.

Medics, litter bearers, and chaplains clambered out of the column of medical vehicles. Men grabbed sacks of supplies and shouldered stretchers. Loaded, they jogged forward. Ben did not hurry. Sam brought a kerchief to his nose and mouth. The boy muttered, "Holy moley."

Men passed them walking beside the ambulances. Sam edged in front of Ben, agitating to speed up, but Ben kept his pace. When they emerged from the trees at the head of the line, they were the last ones, exasperating Sam.

The road was gone, cratered out of existence. The pileup blocking the way told an instant and violent story: a German tank had been destroyed, a second tank tried to shove it off the road and was hit, trucks and carts moved into the fields to go around, they, too, were struck, everything burned, and this escape route grew choked.

Ben entered the forest of ruined machines, a hundred yards of scrambled steel. Sam kept his rag pressed over his face. Ben breathed in the burned metal, like the smelters in Pittsburgh.

Behind the vehicles, the pasture of dead was vast. The cadre of medics had run into it and got no farther than fifty yards before every one of them and the litter bearers had work. Ben lost sight of the handful of other chaplains in their scurrying to save.

He walked, skirting bodies and limbs, and craters with debris flung against the walls. The distinction between what had been human and what was a cow, horse, or machine mingled around his boots. The smells of torn flesh did not stand out from the odors of oil and cordite sown in the ground. Sam had dropped his cloth. His face was white and dashed. Ben turned and waded on.

Only when the rushing medics were just figurines across the field did he stop. He looked south to the high ground where for two days he'd watched the bombardment that did this. He marveled at the accuracy of the big guns, as well as the constant bombers and fighters that harassed the great enemy retreat. On all sides, emerald land and trees gleamed as they did everywhere in Normandy. Many houses and farm buildings were untouched. Everything else—everything German—was smashed. The road was ripped up like tape. A standing horse, still harnessed to a charred cart, watched Ben weave through the remains of Seventh Army.

Ben passed artillery pieces twisted by Allied shells, others that had been spiked and abandoned by the Krauts. Overturned trucks spilled food, ammo, stolen artwork. Every vehicle of every sort, from wheelbarrows to bulldozers, and thousands more stretching west, had been devastated. The loss to the German war effort of this much mechanization would be spectacular.

Strewn everywhere in the ruins, uncountable, were carcasses and corpses. Like the machines in this valley, the German soldiers and their animals had been cut up and scorched. Horses and cattle simply fell to their sides or lay on their backs, legs up like bedposts. The dead men were less composed in their last postures. Soldiers sprawled on tanks, melted into the metal. They lay under trucks that had exploded over their backs. They lay in the open, diced and unrecognizable or stunned and clutching, grimacing or faceless, silent. Nowhere were there foxholes or fortifications that might have given them shelter. The bombs, shells, and rockets never gave them pause to dig. Ben walked on, scanning the demise of this enemy, seeking satisfaction in the absoluteness of it.

The destruction in this valley had been monumental. But it might have been even larger. Five days ago, the prospect among the GIs was for the total surrounding of the Seventh Army, a complete annihilation. Canadian and American troops had fought to within a few miles of each other. Then, for some reason, Patton and Montgomery did not close the ring. Ben and all the officers of the 90th kept waiting for word that 100,000 Germans were in the bag. But for five days, a small escape route remained open, between Argentan and Falaise. Montgomery had only slammed it shut today. Up on the Le Bourg–St. Léonard ridge, talk among the artillery officers was that maybe the Generals had been afraid Canadian and American forces might collide in the heat of battle, perhaps even fighting each other in the confusion, which would have been a catastrophe. Perhaps there were territorial concerns between nations and leaders, even egos. No one knew. But a portion of the Seventh Army had escaped the pocket. Estimates were still unclear; the rumor was that twenty thousand men got out. Even so, that left another eighty thousand killed or captured.

Ben halted his march at the sound of running boots. Before turning, he looked farther into the valley. In the distance, other ambulances moved through the debris field. Medics from another division kneeled in the clusters of hulks. Ben surveyed all of the carnage he could take in. He nodded to himself.

Sam caught up. Ben waited while the boy found his breath.

"Rabbi?"

"I'm fine."

Ben assumed Sam had come to check on him. The look on Sam's face said differently.

"Rabbi, geez. Don't you hear 'em?"

That moment, the moaning of the wounded struck him. The air buzzed with bleating calls.

"You speak German." Sam raised his hands to Ben. "You know what they're saying. How can you just . . . ?"

Ben smelled the stench of the bodies floating on August heat. He noticed the lifted hands.

"Rabbi, open your eyes."

Ben looked around, no longer in a landscape of victory or vengeance. There was horror here, miles and miles of it.

"They're open."

Sam's lifted hands shoveled at Ben. The boy needed an explanation. Ben said, "Multiply this."

"What are you talking about?"

Ben grabbed Sam by the lapel.

"Do it. Multiply every dead man you see by five hundred."

He pivoted the boy in a circle, tugging him hard. He swept his other hand across the terrible landscape.

"Every corpse, every voice, by five hundred. Look, look down that way, there's more. See them? Multiply them, too. Five hundred times. More, six hundred. The dead won't fit in this valley, Sam."

Ben struck his own chest, his heart.

"They won't fit. You understand?"

He let the boy go. Sam backed away, timid and leery. He looked over the field. Ben could tell the boy was trying to do what he was told, to imagine.

"It's not about my son or Phineas anymore," Ben said, gentler, at last giving his son and his friend their rest. "They're gone."

Sam took several moments with his eyes on the dead Army before asking, "Then what's it about?"

Ben told him, to the backdrop of moans and the ten thousand unburied.

Sam did not believe it.

"Millions? That's . . . that's impossible. Rabbi, if that was the case, we'd know about it. It would've been in all the papers. We'd have put a stop to it. There'd be air raids and . . . and . . . I don't know what, but there's no way we'd let that happen."

Ben let Sam fumble with the obliteration of his people. He listened to Sam deny it, rationalize it, and refuse to lower his assessment of mankind to the possibility of it. Hadn't he, too, doubted when von der Meer told him? Sam was right to stumble over the magnitude, to question that the Allies wouldn't have known or acted, right to find mass murder on an international scale unfathomable. Why would regular German folks allow this to happen under their noses? Wouldn't the Jews fight back somehow? Wouldn't America tell the whole world what the Nazis were doing? Murder millions, how can that be kept secret? Sam was sure that Kraut Major had just made this up to hurt Ben before letting him go. But the German Major had been angry and too precise in his descriptions of the lineage from propaganda to pogroms, group executions to the mass-killing camps, the integers of the final solution. Ben believed von der Meer.

Sam shook his head. Ben read that the boy's rejection of him was total.

Sam dug into his pants pocket. He handed over the keys to the jeep.

"Here you go."

"What are you going to do, Sam?"

"I'll hook up with the stretcher bearers. See if the Army'll let me do some good."

"I'll talk to your CO. Get you reassigned."

Ben watched Sam walk away into the field of metal. He didn't say goodbye to this son, didn't say a word to thank or keep him. Slowly, the boy disappeared behind the slaughter that was everywhere.

D+79

At daybreak, White Dog came out of his alleys.

What the hell, he thought.

In his year and a half of hiding in Montparnasse he'd grown fat in the waist and wallet. But years before that he'd become a bomber pilot for adventure. Over the past five days he watched skinny French boys and girls and doddering old gents have the adventure of a lifetime, rioting to free Paris. While he peered out from shadows, they knocked over trees, tore up cobbles, and tossed them in piles, flipped cars, filled sandbags, and planted their flag on top of the mounds in the middle of boulevards. Obstacles were thrown up all over Paris to restrict the Krauts' movements around the city, making them unable to respond to flare-ups. The brave French flung stones at approaching Germans, fired rounds from a handful of weapons, and shouted curses. The only ones who got hurt were the ones who came out from behind cover or were slow to run away. The rest of the time they congratulated themselves and spread rumors.

White Dog put his white linen jacket over his shoulder. He wore his baggy zazou trousers and spats, topped with a gray fedora. He lit a cigarette and strolled out to the barricade built across Avenue du Maine at

Avenue d'Orleans. White Dog said good morning and helped roll a car over.

After breakfast, he killed a soldier.

It was a remarkable piece of luck. He'd thrown a broken cobblestone dug from Avenue du Maine. The block struck a German soldier who was backing away.

A German patrol, just five gray boys on foot, had turned a corner. They froze at first sight of the barricade, this one constructed of iron railings, bed frames, old furniture, a tipped-over public *pissoir,* and five vehicles rolled on their sides. The soldiers edged around the corner and moved slowly into the open to investigate. When the five were close, one of the Communists behind the barricade fired his rifle, an ancient carbine dusted off from an attic. The shot missed. The young Krauts showed no stomach for a street fight, with no reinforcements and no reason to make a stand. They backed off. More men popped from cover to throw bottles and rocks, brandishing ax handles and crowbars. White Dog, hiding behind a snooker table mounted on the barrier, rose, too. He heaved the cobble as far as he could. The square stone hit one of the soldiers flush in the face, between the eyes. White Dog was amazed. The German fell backward. A battle cry rose from the barricade, the avenue, and every window and doorway. Lamps and household items rained from balconies, women tossed them down with curses. The four soldiers grabbed the legs of their downed mate and dragged him around the corner. Standing at attention, the French sang the "Marseillaise," the hymn banned by the Germans for four years. When some bold souls looked where the Krauts had gone, they found the German boy dead with blood run out of his ears. The *fifis* and Commies and women of the barricade cheered White Dog.

Hugo the mobster approached from one of the many shadows of Paris.

"Careful, *Chien Blanc.* You're coming very close."

"To what?" White Dog asked, basking in the man's grin.

"To choosing a side."

Hugo ambled off, leaving White Dog with a pat on the arm. What fucking luck, he thought. Not just smacking that Kraut with a rock, but Hugo saw me do it. I'm definitely in like Flynn now.

A woman tied a white brassard around his biceps, a blue-and-red patch depicting the tricolor. Other men wore the FFI initials on their armbands. White Dog knew the names of none of the Parisians who manned the barricade, and no one asked him his. None of his regular black market crew were on the street; his cadre of petty thieves kept to their blackness. White Dog stood in the sunlight, tossing another little brick to himself should one more patrol round the corner. He thought he might jettison his old network, specialists in nylons, vegetables, smokes, butchered meats, currency exchange, all trivialities of daily life, and start fresh with Hugo and his Voltaire gang. The mob was well organized. White Dog would need to strike big with his gasoline scheme, and he needed professionals around him, men of action, men like these who stood on the barricades for France today, for profit tomorrow.

He lunched at café tables set up behind the obstacle. Around him were other young men in shirtsleeves, some carrying revolvers, a few in military helmets. In the high windows of buildings framing the street, like opera boxes, people waited for something to happen. White Dog enjoyed being a performer on the barricade, the dose of danger and the safety in numbers, an audience in attendance. He figured some of the other young men might be Hugo's gangsters, and for them especially he kept up his appearance of *patriotisme*. A phone rang in an open window. Someone shouted down news from other districts:

—There's fighting in Neuilly!

—There are Boche tanks in the Place de la Concorde!

—The Mayor's office in the fifth *arrondissement* is under attack!

In the early afternoon, the phones went out again. On the street, rumors replaced the news: the Americans were only five miles to the southwest; a fresh Panzer Division had entered the city; the Boche had mined every monument and bridge in Paris; the Resistance had cut the wires to the bombs; the *fifis* were out of ammunition. No one could be certain of anything that was happening in the rest of Paris beyond their own street and barricade. Even the new FFI radio station, broadcast only when the power was on, could do little more than read proclamations, play the "Marseillaise," and report that people should stay away from certain areas. The Palaise du Luxembourg and the Place Saint-Michel should be avoided, as the Boche had a clean field of fire from both strongholds. The Germans were strengthening their forces in the Palais Bourbon, the École Militaire, the Invalides, the Hôtel Majestic, and the Hôtel Meurice.

One fact every Parisian knew: the commandant of the German garrison in Paris, Gen. Dietrich von Choltitz, was also called the Butcher of

Stalingrad. Two years earlier the man had reduced that Russian city to ashes. The Butcher might have the same lack of remorse when it came to Paris.

A stout boy with an FFI armband got into a shoving match with another who wore a red kerchief at his neck. Others separated the two, but their shouts continued. White Dog listened out of boredom.

The FFI boy yelled, "This all your fault! Why couldn't you jerks just play along with the truce?"

The red neckerchief shouted back: "It wasn't our truce. It was de Gaulle's!"

"Who cares? Everything was fine. The Germans were quiet, the Americans were coming, and now there's fighting and people are getting killed all over the city. All because you Commies couldn't sit quiet for three days. It's just like Warsaw. Now the Boche are going to burn Paris!"

"No they're not! The Americans are too close." The red armband pointed at White Dog. "What do you think?"

White Dog's ears picked up. Did these boys suspect something about him?

"You know who I am?"

"No." The Communist waved off White Dog's concern. "No one cares. What do you think?"

The barricade had gone quiet watching this squabble. White Dog drew himself up. Hugo and his boys might still be keeping their eye on him.

"To tell you the truth, I don't know where the Yanks are. But you'd better hope they come quick. He's right," White Dog aimed a finger at the FFI, "you Reds should have left the truce in place. Now you've forced von Choltitz's hand. He has to fight back. If he doesn't, Hitler might get impatient and send in the Luftwaffe. Then Paris is really fucked. And who knows if all the bridges are really mined? Or the Eiffel Tower? It could all happen. It might not. I do know one thing, though."

The two antagonists cocked their heads. The rest waited.

"I'm hungry. And I'm buying dinner for everybody."

White Dog recruited the two bickerers to shake hands and come with him. Folks on the barricade patted him on the back while he walked away. Several blocks off was his Montparnasse warehouse. White Dog opened it, put carts in the hands of the amazed *fifi* and the Communist and loaded them with meats, cheeses, breads, Gauloise cigarettes, wine, liquor, and cider. He emptied half his stores into the carts and into a hand-pulled wagon for himself. He tossed on bars of soap, tins of butter, bolts of cloth, boxes of socks, stockings for the girls on the barricade and the old women in the windows, chocolates, anything he could spare to curry favor and celebrate the Liberation. Loading the carts, White Dog exulted. The two boys with him stood laughing at his wealth and generosity.

"You're *Chien Blanc*," the Communist declared.

"Friend to man," White Dog sang, closing the warehouse door.

At the barricade, he sprayed the goods around, feeling like a Vanderbilt or a summer Santa. His name spread with the socks and nylons, the words *Chien Blanc* left mouths just before the meat and cheeses went in. He took a place at a café table where the people of the barricade and the neighborhood came to shake his hand. White Dog was a curio, a celebrity of the night who'd strolled into full light, to mingle and lend himself to the struggle.

Like fucking Flynn, thought White Dog.

Just before eight o'clock, with the sun resting on the roofs of Avenue d'Orleans, a pair of bicyclists in FFI brassards streamed up to the barricade. Their tires skidded when they braked.

"Leclerc has crossed the Pont d'Austerlitz!"

The people on the barricade were stunned. No one knew first whether to shout with joy or wait for the detonations, for if von Choltitz was going to blow up Paris, he would do it now, with de Gaulle's tanks on the Right Bank.

From a doorway, the mobster Hugo started the celebration. He raised a bottle and bellowed, *"Vive la France!"*

Other voices swelled. Embraces and kisses swept the barricade. White Dog was lifted from his seat. In moments, out of the high windows above the barricade, old women shouted for the revelers in the street to hush. The power had come back on. The FFI radio station was broadcasting.

An excited, electric voice floated in the dusk. Windows, like a chorus of mouths, announced the arrival of the French 2nd Armored across the Seine.

No skeptics remained on the street or in the buildings. Every voice and hand lifted, some skirts, too. The Germans weren't going to destroy Paris! The French army itself was the first liberating force!

The radio voice was not drowned out, the old ones in their windows turned up the volume. The Resistance called for every priest in Paris to ring his church bells. Within moments, the radios were drowned in the peals brimming the dusk, from Notre Dame and Sacré Coeur to the little jingles from the handlebars of the bicyclists pedaling off.

After dark, when the festiveness was drained from the barricade, White Dog slunk away, a little drunk on his own cognac. Kraut artillery boomed from the north. The shells landed west in the 15th *arrondissement*, aimed at the advancing French armored columns.

Tomorrow, he thought, when the fight for the city is over, the Germans will be done here. Paris will become America's problem. The floodgates will open.

White Dog tossed his linen coat over his shoulder and headed into Montparnasse.

Near one of his flats, he passed a girl carrying a lantern with the wick low. She was alone in the alley, dressed fine and made up. In the little yellow light she seemed fantastic, sent to him. He kissed her and patted her rump. Handing her a cigarette, he boasted in English, "I was on the barricades today."

D+80
AUGUST 25

"Gentlemen, good morning. Take a seat."

Major Clay doffed his helmet and waited for the three hundred drivers and maintenance men under the mess tent to settle. From the middle of the crowd, Joe Amos saw the Major's hair glisten, gooped in place. McGee dropped the last of his cigarette and ground it under his boot.

The boy muttered, "What they want from us now?"

The company took seats on the benches and tables. Major Clay pursed his lips watching his coloreds mill too slowly into place. Joe Amos chuckled at the drivers showing their disdain for taking an order, even one as simple as "Sit down." These boys had driven twenty hours a day, sometimes two and three days with no break at all. They'd been on their own except for the guy in the cab with them and the bumpers close in front and behind. They'd seen as many French sunups as sundowns. They'd taken their loads right up to the front lines and hauled back prisoners, wounded, and bodies. Their Jimmies sported bullet holes and spiderweb windshields. Major Clay was their CO, but the moment they shifted into gear, each one of them answered only to the convoy and the road.

Major Clay stepped up on a table. He screwed his helmet back on his slick head.

"Shut up, goddammit!"

The room hushed.

"Gentlemen, I have news. This morning, Paris was liberated."

No one in the tent knew whether or not they should cheer. Major Clay had said shut up. Men fidgeted, nodded, and whispered.

The officer continued. "I heard an interesting report this morning, that General von Choltitz was holed up in the Hôtel Meurice and wouldn't come out. A French soldier went inside and asked him why he was laying back. The good General said he could not surrender without some combat, so the Führer would get told at least that he'd been under attack. The Frogs obligingly tossed three purple smoke grenades through a window, and the Krauts came out pleased as punch. Boys, you gotta love this war."

The drivers and mechanics all laughed with Major Clay. The man had the Southerner's front-porch storytelling gift.

"Anyway," the Major said, hoisting a hand for quiet, "everything was fucked up before. Now it's a whole new ball game of fucked up. Here's the situation."

The war had gotten out of whack, the Major said, at least according to the way the battle planners had figured it would unfold. Allied forces were not supposed to cross the Seine and reach the German border until May of 1945. They were now just days away from this goal. Paris was not supposed to be liberated until mid-September; instead it fell this morning. The unexpected and massive victory in the Argentan-Falaise pocket had apparently convinced the Krauts to fold up their tents in France and head back home, to hightail it across the border and man their Siegfried Line defenses. The upshot of all this was that Ike had told Monty, Patton, and Bradley to chase the Krauts east across the Seine, to try and destroy the enemy's armies in France before they could reach Germany and dig in to their prepared defenses there.

"The Germans were not supposed to cut and run like they have," Major Clay told them. "No one saw this coming. So, right now, instead of supporting twelve divisions approaching the Seine a few months from now, like the pre-invasion plan called for, COM Z is supplying sixteen divisions that are crossing the Seine as we speak. One week from today, those divisions will be another two hundred miles even farther east.

And you boys know, every mile them doughs go toward Germany is another two miles we have to drive, out and back. Our supply lines are being stretched pretty thin, and pretty damn far."

The men groaned. "Amen," someone said.

Clay kept up the bad news.

In addition, he explained, instead of supplying a Third Army that was supposed to be just a supporting force while Monty made the main thrust in the north, Patton's recent successes to the south had convinced Ike to bulk up Third Army to almost twice its planned size. That meant twice its supply needs.

Major Clay waved a hand east.

"And you all know George is not gonna slow down. Every day he gets farther and farther away from the plan, which I think we know by now has been thrown pretty far out the damn window."

All told, there were twenty American divisions operating in the ETO. Each division required five hundred tons a day. Another ten divisions waited in England or back in the States to join the fight.

Major Clay looked over the company. He shook his head.

"If this was all we had to deal with, it'd be tough enough. But today, the deal got worse, because starting today we have got to add in . . ."

Most of the men in the tent said the name along with the Major.

". . . Paris!"

The drivers' mood changed instantly. A bunch whooped, shouting, "Yeah, baby!"

Calling over them, Major Clay made it clear they were missing his point.

"Perhaps, gentlemen. I'm eager to see the place myself. But now that we got Paris to take care of, you can throw in another four thousand tons a day. Every goddam day. And we got to take it to them, along with everything else we haul."

Major Clay let the men react. They whistled their amazement and chattered their excitement. Joe Amos looked across the colored faces in the tent. Every driver picked up his loads and drove his routes, steady as a drumbeat. Every mechanic kept his head under a hood or a chassis. Not one of them knew much more than the job at hand and how tired doing it made him. But ever since he first drove through the water and up onto OMAHA beach two and a half months ago, Joe Amos had tried hard to keep an eye on the big picture, assembling how the war was faring from bits and pieces, from where he went and who he delivered what to. He kept a French map in his head, and did his best to keep track of the infantry's progress over it. But he had no idea things had gotten this big, this fast. Just one month ago was the big breakout from Normandy, that everybody now called Operation COBRA. Thirty days later and look at us, he thought. Already knocking on Germany's door. We're feeding Paris. Hot damn.

His thoughts flashed to Geneviève and the Marquis. He wanted to celebrate with them, take them all the news. Where would he get the time to see them? He'd have to be clever. So far, that hadn't been a problem.

Geneviève and Paris. Joe Amos's heart thumped at the prospect. With Paris open, and another four thousand tons heading to the city, there were bound to be opportunities galore. He'd find one, the right one, then he'd make his move.

"Alright," the Major called the men down, "I'm not done up here. Settle."

The drivers and grease monkeys latched their attention back on Major Clay.

"Boys, in case you didn't already suspect this, you and your trucks are pretty much the only game in town. The French railways west of the Seine have been bombed by us and blown by the Resistance to the point where they're no damn good. Cherbourg is barely bringing in a trickle, and the rest of the major French ports in Brittany are either wrecked or still in the Krauts' hands. Some numbskull in Washington figured he'd rather have more bombers than cargo planes, so air freight ain't taking up much of the slack, either. As of today, eighty percent of the supplies for the entire American force is still arriving over the beaches. All that adds up to one thing: for now, it's you and me and a shitload of Jimmies."

Joe Amos didn't know why, he didn't see it coming, but he let out a yell. No one else in the hundreds around him made a sound, his cheer died fast under the warm canvas. He found himself on his feet, McGee gazing confounded at him.

Someone in the rear of the tent said, "Yeah."

Another picked this up. A murmur sputtered, then caught. Someone clapped. In moments, the entire company applauded Major Clay's words, shouting for themselves and their mission, that they, tired and dirty and surely unappreciated, mattered so much.

Major Clay held up his hands a long time before the thunderous clamor dispelled. The men punched shoulders and slapped palms, they rose from the tables and benches to be on their feet. Joe Amos even got dour McGee to root.

"The job ahead," Major Clay called, almost preacher-like now, buoyed in their spirit, "looks impossible, don't it?"

The men laughed at this.

"Back in the Civil War, General Forrest once said the way to win a battle was to get there the fastest with the mostest. Eighty years later that ain't changed. So pay attention, boys. I'm about to tell you how we're gonna do the impossible."

The Red Ball Express began with the call, "Wind 'em up!"

Joe Amos turned the key and gave the gas a rev. Beat-up mufflers beneath three thousand Jimmies growled north at OMAHA, down in St. Lô, and across the bivouac where Joe Amos let out the clutch. A dozen green columns moved together, roaring like a rapid river. Joe Amos shot McGee a grin and rolled out of the field, bumper to bumper.

Twenty minutes later, on the beach, the company took on its first Red Ball load—sixty trucks of clothing, sixty-five for rations. While the Jimmies waited on the sand for the cranes and COM Z crews to shift the tonnage to their beds, each driver painted a red-ball emblem on his front bumper. This was to let the MPs know who was on the Red Ball and who was not.

Joe Amos bought five more cartons of Lucky Strikes from Speedy Clapp, thinking this was small potatoes. So much matériel was arriving over OMAHA that Speedy had dispensed with even the pretense of a clipboard and paperwork. He just played traffic cop on the sand.

When his company was loaded and in line, Joe Amos climbed behind the wheel. Jumping into the cab, McGee looked excited. Joe Amos was glad to see the boy animated, the first time in weeks. McGee had been a pain in the ass and had not bothered to explain why. Joe Amos was left to guess, and hadn't put much effort into it except to figure McGee Mays was one of those boys who just did not like the Army.

"Sarge," McGee said, "I can drive."

"I got it."

"But I'm gon' get to drive later."

"Sure."

"Major Clay said the Red Ball was gonna be historic. I'd like to drive the first leg, you know, on the first day. You don' mind."

Joe Amos took his hands from the wheel. Let the boy have his history, he thought. The Army's not going to give him much else.

McGee guided the loaded Jimmy off the beach. He drove in the middle of the convoy streaming through the draw. Once on the main road, the column built speed and stretched out. Joe Amos could not see Lieutenant Garner's jeep at the head nor could he spot the tail of the convoy, it was so many miles long.

The trucks headed south, to St. Lô, the start of the Red Ball route. The road from OMAHA passed through Couvains. Joe Amos put his elbow in the window and waited.

The column was loud and seemed endless. Joe Amos cast his thoughts ahead: Hear us coming! Passing through Couvains, to his astonishment, she was there, beside the road. This was fantastic! He heard other trucks honking at her when they passed. Joe Amos stuck his head and shoulders out the window, spreading his arms into the wind. He tossed her a carton of Lucky Strikes, landing them in the ditch. Geneviève recognized him only after he was beyond her, shouting and waving like mad. She threw him a kiss, then scrambled in the ditch for the cigarettes. Trucks behind honked at her, too. He watched until she was out of sight, only seconds. The convoy was moving fast.

"Paris," Joe Amos said. "I'm gonna take her to Paris." McGee said nothing, which was right because no one else was involved. She was his alone.

At St. Lô, the column slowed. The town was in such ruin that the trucks had to detour several times. The engineers had plowed only a narrow path through the rubble. Joe Amos stared at the hills of bricks and timbers shoved to the side, all of it knocked down by American shells and bombs. McGee shook his head at the destruction, even though this was the umpteenth time they'd driven through here. This time, tiptoeing through the St. Lô wreckage, Joe Amos felt different. Now they were part of something huge, the Red Ball, like red blood flowing through here, strength returning to all this.

The column hit its stride outside town, stoking south to Tessy-sur-Vire, then to Mortain. The road ran wide, Joe Amos guessed maybe twenty-five feet, and solid. These were the French roads he'd read about in college, roads that dated back to Napoleon, built on granite. Three

years of bombs and one month of fighting had barely scarred their surface.

The Norman countryside, always green and rolling, scissored by
hedges, glowed its brightest today. Joe Amos had never traveled so fast
in so huge a convoy; the roads before had always been choked with traffic going both directions, from vehicles merging out of side roads,
gnarling at intersections. The Red Ball was designed for speed. It was a
one-way loop, utterly dedicated to military transport. Every few miles,
MPs in jeeps sat beside the road, watching the columns fly past. Their
job was to make sure that nothing slowed the Jimmies. No civilian cars
or farm tractors, no cattle, sheep, or geese, no horse-drawn carts, no
tanks or TDs, nothing that couldn't keep up was allowed on the Red Ball
to hold the flow back. At every major crossing, a tall white sign was
nailed to a post, painted with a big red ball and an arrow to show the
way. McGee pounded the gas pedal, the pitted muffler snarled through
the next town, Mayenne. Over this single-purpose highway on the backs
of the great American fleet rode millions of gallons of POL, mounds of
rations and ammo, whole divisions of troops, forests of phone poles, cable, boots, medicine, everything to fight a war, and nothing was going to
slow it down.

McGee did not give up the wheel, staying in the driver's seat after
the first way station at Marmers one hundred twenty miles southeast
from St. Lô. The men jumped down for a piss and coffee, rations were
handed out but the drivers were obliged to tuck into them back on the
road. As soon as Joe Amos's company left the bivouac, another column
sped in.

The Red Ball route rolled east another sixty miles, through Nogent-
le-Rotrou, then to Chartres, the terminus. This was the first time Joe
Amos had seen Chartres. The twin spires of the great medieval cathedral
became visible from a long way off. It was nice to have those great arms
hailing the convoy from a distance, waving them in.

The ASP at Chartres swarmed with activity that rivaled OMAHA.
Matériel arrived at a fevered pitch. The off-loading was furious and haphazard, supplies got dumped into piles to be sorted out later. The object
was to get the Red Ball Jimmies cleared and moving again. A signpost
showed the distance to Paris, just sixty miles; to Berlin, six hundred and
sixty.

For the return trip to St. Lô, Joe Amos took the wheel. After gassing
up, the return leg of the loop ran through Alençon at the halfway mark,

and another bivouac area. This time Lieutenant Garner didn't let the company slow for coffee or a leak, they poured through and powered all the way to St. Lô and OMAHA.

The entire three-hundred-and-ten-mile round-trip took just under nine hours. The summer sun rested on the black bunkers of the bluffs when Joe Amos lowered himself from the cab. He sat in the sand, resting his back against a hot tire. He lit a smoke and tossed the pack to McGee. Both were too tired to say anything. Joe Amos had not sold one cigarette all day, where was the time?

Garner walked bandy-legged through the lines of steaming Jimmies. A dozen radiators had cooked off and their tired drivers tended to them. Garner toured the four platoons of the company, taking stock. He glanced down at Joe Amos and slowed to accept a smoke, then moved on. Joe Amos closed his eyes to the noises of trucks arriving and departing, and the grinding of landing craft ramming the sand, both never ceasing.

Thirty minutes later, with the day pinching shut, Garner returned to the front of the company, carrying orders. He stopped for another cigarette.

The lieutenant stepped back from Joe Amos's lighter and blew a billow. He looked up from the walls of trucks on all sides, to the evening's first stars. Joe Amos started to get up.

Garner shouted into the dusk, "Wind 'em up!"

D+81

Ben got drunk.

He did it quietly, over the course of the afternoon. The townsfolk of Donnemarie never left an empty bottle at his table or in his hand. At midday, the radio reported de Gaulle's walk in Paris—forty miles to the northwest—from the Arc de Triomphe to Notre Dame. A million Frenchmen hailed him along the way. De Gaulle walked in Donnemarie, too, across the radios playing everywhere in the town. The General's stroll set off a celebration here, for the people's freedom and for the Americans who'd delivered it to them.

Ben took a seat at an outdoor bistro table in the warm blue day. He was alone. Sam had given him up, and Ben had given up the jeep. He walked again with the Tough Ombres, or rode with them in the backs of trucks. He hadn't been in the bistro chair for more than a minute before a bottle was plopped on the table by a local, someone else gave him a glass, a girl kissed him on the cheek, and Ben began to drink.

Townsfolk ran around the streets. Ben could figure no reason for this other than to exercise the simple liberty of running and shouting. Even the old hobblers with canes did their best to move somewhere fast. Ben's own liberty was to sit still and pour himself pink bubbles or scarlet wine or the velvet of cognac, whatever he felt like next. An impromptu parade took place. People lined the avenue. Around a corner came the hubbub of an approach, a pack of screeches and jeers. Down the cobblestones of the main street shuffled three women in nightgowns. They had been shorn of their hair down to patchy stubble. The people of Donnemarie booed them and threw things or shook champagne bottles to spray them. Behind these three were a gaggle of older women, driving them on with sharp fingers and tongues. When the collaborators were past, laughter returned easily in their wake. Their misery was nothing but a bobbing cork on the gaiety.

Through the late afternoon and four bottles, no one joined Ben at his table until a priest sat. The old man wore a long black frock and a collar.

"May I?"

"Please," Ben said.

"*Merci.*"

"I do not have a glass for you, Father."

The priest shrugged. He grabbed the champagne bottle by the neck and took a long plug from it. He set it on the metal table with a *clank;* again, Ben thought, such freedom.

"You are a rabbi?"

"Yes."

"You have sat here for hours. Why you do not join?"

"I'm fine, Father. *Merci.*"

The priest raised a hand and shouted something to a running boy. The lad stopped in his tracks, then disappeared into a doorway. Moments later, he returned with a bottle of Camus VSOP and two glasses. The priest patted the boy's head and sent him off.

"A toast?" The priest poured the glasses. Ben took one, the glass was stemmed and more fragile than the cup he'd been drinking out of. He lifted it to the priest.

"*La libération,*" the priest said.

They clinked the lips of their glasses. Ben had to focus to make sure he met the priest's glass with his own.

They drank. Out of the village square came the first sounds of music, from a trumpet, a drum, and an accordion. The people of Donnemarie perked at the strains and headed that way. The priest kept his seat.

"Rabbi."

"Yes, Father?"

"May I tell you? We have lost Jews. They were taken."

"I know."

"We do not know what has happened to them. We fear. We hope."

Ben said nothing.

The priest poured two more cognacs. They touched glasses in silence.

Setting down his glass, the priest said, "I have tried to pray, *oui*? For them. But I am not certain I have God's ear for this. You understand?"

"Yes."

"Would you come with me? To my church to pray?"

Ben drained his cognac.

He stood with the priest, the first time on his feet in hours. The alcohol hit him in his first strides. The priest took his arm and the two walked through the crowds like comrades. The old man talked of the town, how he was born here. Close into Ben's ear he told a joke, about the man who came to confession for having sex with two beautiful sisters. When the priest did not recognize the man's voice, he asked if he was a member of the parish. The man said no, he was Jewish. The priest asked, "Why are you telling me?" The man replied, "I'm telling everyone." Ben had a laugh, appreciating how the priest made the man in the joke Jewish, he could have been anything else. Ben asked the priest to let him take a pee, which he did against a wall with children running behind him.

The church filled an entire block. The priest, linked again to Ben's arm, walked them past a monument for the town's dead from the first war. Ben patted the obelisk above the granite names, thinking he might have fought beside some of these boys.

The arch above the doorway to the church was sooty, as though there had been a fire. Inside, the church was immaculate and coolly lit. None of the windows were stained glass, but regular panes painted over.

"The windows, they are in a bank vault," the priest said, walking Ben to the altar. "Now we will return them. They are beautiful and very old."

Stone steps led to an altar draped in burgundy, topped with silver challises, candlesticks, and a tall cross. Above, a shining wooden Jesus looked to heaven through a crown of thorns. A polished mahogany rail enclosed the altar. Ben thought of a Greek word he'd learned in seminary, *éntheos*, the feeling of possession by the Divine. The hands that carved this Jesus, that hid the stained-glass windows from the war, they had *éntheos*. The priest kissed a white satin stole and laid it around his shoulders. This priest had *éntheos*, too.

The priest kneeled on the steps before the altar. He did not invite Ben to join him, leaving the rabbi to say his prayers on the other side of the railing as he saw fit. Ben had never kneeled to God. That was not something asked of Jews. He wanted to sit, the alcohol in him made him unsteady. He looked back at the first row of pews but wanted to be close to the priest. Ben walked to the steps and bent to his knees beside the old man's shoulder.

The old priest moved his lips to a whispered prayer. Ben had not prayed in weeks, not since Sèves Island. Here, on his knees in an ancient church, he felt at last that he could pray. He was not burdened anymore, not with Sam, Phineas, or even Thomas, not with hope or the Divine. The words felt liberated in his throat. Kaddish was to be said only with a minyan of at least ten, but he figured six million souls made a minyan, too. The Hebrew words came with ease. He did not think to whisper them beside the priest but sang:

"*Yis'ga'dal v'yis'kadash sh'may ra'bbo, b'olmo dee'vro chir'usay v'yamlich malchu'say, b'chayaychon uv'yomay'chon uv'chayay d'chol bais Yisroel, ba'agolo u'viz'man koriv; v'imru Omein . . .*"

When Ben finished, he discovered he'd closed his eyes anyway. He opened his lids and looked beside him to the priest. A tear wet the old man's cheek.

"Amen," the priest said.

Ben stood from his knees. He staggered and caught the priest's arm. The man brought him off the steps and sat him on a pew. The priest returned to the altar, kissed his stole again, then took it off. He muttered a few parting words, crossed himself, and came to gather Ben. The two walked from the church.

In the street, the sounds of the celebration had not slackened. Music and clapping sounded from the cobblestone square. Ben could tell the voices of women and soldiers.

The priest said, "That was beautiful. *Magnifique*. What was it, Rabbi?"

"Kaddish. The prayer for the dead."

"Ahhh," the priest sighed, and shook his gray head. "You think this? They are dead?"

Ben could tell this priest. The old man might believe, might let go of his hope for the missing Jews of his town. But what could the priest do? He was not a soldier, he could do nothing to stop the war. He would only pray more. And he was right, he did not have God's ear for this. No one did, no matter who Ben told. God had chosen. That was why for Ben the Kaddish was a breeze. When your God does not hear, you can pray without gravity. When your God is so distant, you can shout or whimper, you can hold your silence, or your heart in your hands. You are free because God does not care or interfere. You are free because nothing is wanted from you.

Ben unhitched from the priest's arm.

"So long, Father. I'm not mourning anyone else today."

Ben headed toward the square, leaving the old man behind. He would get drunker, he might dance.

D+84
AUGUST 29

Joe Amos sat up with a jolt.

Horns blared in front and behind. Headlamps flashed in his mirrors. Beside him, McGee flailed his hands.

Joe Amos's eyes scrambled for clues, where was he? He stomped on the brake, shifting by reflex to neutral. The loaded Jimmy shuddered off the paved surface onto the soft shoulder. His rear tires locked and skidded. Other trucks in his company leaned on their horns as they passed. The ride got bumpy, Joe Amos gripped the yanking steering wheel as hard as he could. The Jimmy stopped alone in the loud, upturned darkness. He smelled brakes and rubber. He breathed madly, scared and checking his condition and his truck and cargo.

"Fuck!" He hit the steering wheel. McGee cleared his throat and arranged himself from his panicked curl on the passenger side.

"I'm alright," Joe Amos said, regaining himself. He'd fallen asleep but nothing bad happened. Just a fright and a close call. The boys behind him had seen him weave and fade and they'd hit their horns and lights. Joe Amos had snapped awake in time to avoid the concrete pole that stood too close right now bathed in his headlights.

"You okay?" McGee asked anyway.

"Yeah, yeah." Joe Amos exhaled. That would be a rotten way to die in a war, he thought, smacking a pole. The Army didn't hand out medals for that one.

"Where we at?"

"Last town was Marmers," Joe Amos recalled. They were halfway on the outbound leg to Chartres.

He shifted and accelerated along the shoulder until someone let him merge onto the road. He climbed into fourth gear behind another set of cat's eyes. No harm done. He wasn't the first driver to drift off on the Red Ball.

McGee checked his watch. "Three-ten. You wanna switch?"

"At the depot. I'm alright."

Adrenaline needles held Joe Amos bolt upright behind the wheel. He took a swig of water. When he screwed the canteen top on again, he was sleepy. He set his open hand out the window to scoop cool air onto his face. The fading of summer so quickly in France surprised most of the colored drivers, accustomed to lingering Southern heat this time of year.

McGee slumped on the bench. "Lemme see if I can get back to sleep with this shit in my britches."

Joe Amos rapped the boy on the hip. "Shut up." He thought to ask McGee to stay awake with him, but didn't. He knew McGee would have nothing more to say, one jibe per hour was the boy's limit.

Joe Amos made himself ready to resist more slumber. He said, *"Tout de suite."* After four solid days of driving, this had become the unofficial motto on the Red Ball, the French for "right now."

Joe Amos wasn't embarrassed at having fallen asleep at the wheel. All the drivers were getting fuzzy. They went round and round on the one-way loop, starting at OMAHA or St. Lô, often loaded way past their five-ton limit, then barreled flat out for Chartres, sometimes as much as fifty miles past the ASP. Once every eight hours or so, men and panting Jimmies got sixty minutes in the bivouac area to throw off flats, swill some coffee, maybe heat some hash or stew tins on the exhaust manifold for a warm ration, before they hit the road again. The men got dizzier, and the convoys grew more ragged. Some drivers lit out on their own or in small groups, running their loads as fast as they could without waiting for the rest of their column. It didn't take long before confusion was embedded in every detail. The drivers just drove, hard. MPs waved the trucks on. Civilian traffic didn't dare cut in. The drivers ignored anything that held them back, like speed limits, maintenance, waiting for slowpokes, and sleep.

The number of trucks that drove the Red Ball was growing. On August 25, over three thousand vehicles started on the route. Today, that number was six thousand. Three-quarters of those drivers on the Red Ball were colored.

Every non-essential vehicle in the ETO had been press-ganged into service, from COM Z and MTB motor pools, from anti-aircraft units, artillery battalions, engineer companies, even newly arrived infantry were put on foot and their transports taken from under them. Early this morning, with dawn on the beach, Lieutenant Garner spread the word that four days ago, 4,500 tons moved over the Red Ball to Chartres in supply of the combat units chasing the Krauts out of France. Yesterday, Garner said the route carried 12,000 tons. The target for today was 15,000. Then Garner issued the shout, the real motto of the Red Ball Express: "Wind 'em up!"

Joe Amos focused on the crimson slits of the Jimmy beyond his grille. For three more hours into Chartres, he fought his eyelids, tugging his own five tons through the dark.

At the depot, Joe Amos climbed out of the cab with the Jimmies bunched tight and the sun orange and cold. He was almost asleep on his feet. McGee fetched them coffee from a Nissan hut. Joe Amos roused enough to hear a captain call orders to the gathered drivers, all of them stretching their backs.

"Y'all leave these trucks. We'll take 'em from here."

The officer pointed to the far side of the giant lot, at rows of empty Jimmies.

"Take those ones over there. They got good tires and full tanks. They're ready to go." No one reacted to the order. "Come on, boys! Get on it!"

Joe Amos groaned with two hundred others. The hour the drivers normally got to rest while their trucks were being off-loaded had been taken from them. Their turnaround here in Chartres was cut to ten minutes, long enough to grab a coffee and walk across the tarmac to another truck.

The drivers slid their M-1s from their cabs and shuffled like drunks to the dark Jimmies. There were no assignments, just climb on the first truck you found and wind her up. McGee jogged ahead of Joe Amos, to get them a good one, not so worn. When Joe Amos reached the rows of trucks, he saw McGee already standing on a bumper, fiddling under the hood. The boy lifted the governor housing and removed the butterfly valve that held the top speed of the Jimmy to fifty-two mph. Now the truck would do over seventy on a good road. McGee replaced the housing to make it look like nothing had been tampered with, because messing with the governor was forbidden. Getting rid of that valve had quickly become SOP on the Red Ball, and every crew kept a few wrenches in their pockets. In the dangling dawn, hoods went up, some boys cursed, and the hoods clanged shut.

The trucks were a sorry lot. The mufflers were shot on half of them, they resembled tanks with all their squeaks, moans, and the dirty spitting of exhaust. But they ran hard under the lead feet of the colored drivers out of Chartres.

Joe Amos dozed for a hundred miles, all the way to the bivouac at Alençon. There, breakfast was eaten so fast the engines hadn't stopped pinging before they were running again. In the time it took for Joe Amos to down a plate of eggs with hash, five hundred trucks and tractors rumbled in and out of the field. Another hundred bypassed the bivouac altogether, keeping the hammer down for St. Lô.

Back on the road, he thought about Geneviève. Other than tossing her the carton of cigarettes the other morning, he hadn't laid eyes on her in two and a half weeks. This was the longest they had been apart since they'd met. He kicked himself for the thousandth time for not making love to her in the forest. At least right now he'd have that to think about. Instead he was trapped in his head with the recollection of just her breasts and buttoning her blouse. It was like being stuck in second gear, like having a governor on you. In his imagination he romped all over her. She was willing that day, sure enough, a done deal. But that's what being a hero is all about, he thought. You've got to give shit up to be a hero. Sacrifice. The right thing is not often the easiest, or the funnest, or the thing you wish you had done. Burdens come with being a hero. But damn, she wanted it.

Joe Amos thought about seeing her again. He had no idea when COM Z was going to back off this frenzy and give him leave. Also, the Red Ball wasn't allowing him any time to sell cigarettes. When there was a chance, like meals at the bivouacs or downtime during loading and off-loading, his customers were usually dead asleep, or he was. Every day he and McGee smoked four packs between them. The roll of cash in his pocket was not growing fast enough to top what he'd laid out for the Marquis last time. Before he saw her again, Joe Amos needed to figure another way to make a score.

The rest of the day circled along in sameness, although Joe Amos enjoyed the short periods he spent at OMAHA. He got to look out over the Channel and the beach, watching other men, black and white, pitch war supplies up on the sand. He let his eyes play on the infinities of the water and the American invasion. Then the road, dawn into dark, was spent staring at nothing but the smoke-choking rear end of another Jimmy, plus the same fields, hedges, thickets, towns, and ruins he'd already seen, over and over. McGee made so little conversation, as quiet as the black of a well, that Joe Amos began to fantasize that half the time the truck was driving itself.

By 2100 hours, he was behind the wheel again. The sun was newly set and Joe Amos's convoy ran with headlamps full-on; COM Z had changed the rule to allow trucks to use headlights instead of cat's eyes up to ten miles from the front line. Joe Amos's column was just a twelve-truck squad, all with fuel headed for an ASP at Fontainebleau, fifty miles past Chartres. Each Jimmy was loaded with a thousand gallons of gasoline. Morales rode the lead, Joe Amos drove tucked between him and Baskerville. McGee sucked on a Lucky Strike. A nippy wind blew over Joe Amos's arm in the window.

Etampes, a town halfway to the fuel dump, flew by. The dozen trucks barely slowed, gunning down the skinny main street. Their headlights were the brightest things for miles in every direction. Beyond Etamps, the road lay straight. The column was beyond the Red Ball route, and traffic was light. Morales set a fast pace and the rest, with their governors disabled, swayed and sloshed to keep up.

On a dark passage ten miles shy of Fontainebleau, the convoy slowed. A handheld searchlight in the middle of the road waved them down. Morales stopped at a deuce-and-a-half parked on the shoulder. Joe Amos snugged behind Morales.

"What the hell is this?" Joe Amos asked McGee, expecting no answer. "Stay here."

He climbed down. As the lone sergeant on the column, he walked to the light. Morales and Baskerville flanked him. The beam flashed in their faces.

Morales barked, "Hey, *cabrón*, get that fucking thing out my eyes!"

The light pivoted to the ground. Its blue stain hovered in Joe Amos's vision. He couldn't see much in the dark ahead, but he kept walking. A voice answered Morales: "Watch your mouth, Mac."

Joe Amos and his two drivers stopped. They stood blinking to see who they were talking to, who had halted their convoy in the middle of nowhere in the night. By the light of the headlamps shining from his convoy, Joe Amos made out soldiers, twenty at least. From the sounds of rifles shifting on their backs and what little he could see, he guessed they were all infantry. They had with them one Jimmy.

A soldier stepped forward.

Joe Amos said, "Buddy, y'all got to get out the way. We got a delivery to make."

The soldier put hands to his hips. The gesture said plainly he wasn't getting out of anyone's way.

"Sergeant, we've got orders to commandeer these vehicles."

Joe Amos crossed his arms over his chest. Morales and Baskerville stepped up and did the same.

"You got what?" Joe Amos said. "I don't think so."

The soldier came closer. Joe Amos's eyes cleared enough for him to see captain's bars on the man's collar.

"Sir," Joe Amos said.

All three drivers dropped their crossed arms. The infantry captain pulled one fist from his hip. The other rested on a holster.

"General Patton has instructed me to requisition these vehicles and your cargo, sergeant. That's what we're doing. Now get your boys down off 'em."

Joe Amos couldn't believe he was being hijacked by Third Army.

"Sir, can't you just get the gas after we deliver it to the depot?"

The officer shook his head.

"Get your boys down, Sergeant. We been waitin' awhile."

Joe Amos spat on the road. Then he said, "Baskerville."

Joe Amos did not watch Baskerville spread the word down the line. Morales held his ground while Joe Amos moved closer to the captain for a private talk.

"Sir, you want to tell me what's goin' on?"

The officer slipped his hand off the holster. His doughboys moved toward the Jimmies, jangling the weapons clustered all over them.

"Truth is, we're outa gas. The whole damn Third Army is sitting still.

Meanwhile, the Krauts are bailing out of France fast as they can go and we can't stay after 'em. Patton's having a fit. If we can draw 'em into a fight before they get across the Meuse River, we can keep 'em from manning that Siegfried Line of theirs. But we can't fight without gas. Right now the Siegfried Line is just a bunch of empty pillboxes and defense works. But if the Krauts get in there with any kind of numbers, it'll be like D-Day all over again when we try to crack the German border. If that happens, this war might have a little more left in it."

Joe Amos turned to watch his drivers clamber out of their cabs and grab their own rifles. The soldier with the searchlight played the beam over Joe Amos's boys like a white cordon holding them back. The infantrymen were disciplined, they answered none of the curses coming from the Red Ballers.

"So Patton wants my gas enough to steal it."

"Let's just say George wants it enough to make sure he gets it and not First Army."

The searchlight switched off. The captain turned for his own truck. The engines of the Jimmies revved with new boots on the pedals.

"Captain, can we at least get a ride into Fontainebleau?"

"We're not going there. We're headed to Reims."

Reims? That was almost a hundred miles farther east, past the Marne River. Patton was already halfway from Paris to the German border! Joe Amos wanted to know more. He wanted to go with them.

"Then how we gonna get home?" The voice was McGee's. He sounded provoked.

The officer stepped on the running board of his own Jimmy. He grinned in the headlights.

"You fellas do what we did. Wait for a ride."

The twenty-four Red Ball drivers watched their convoy roll away without them. Some of the infantry struggled with the Jimmies' gears. From the shoulder of the road the colored drivers shouted more abuse, some yelled, "Double-clutch it, man! Double-clutch!"

The night closed in. No moon brightened the drivers' situation. By starlight they took seats in the ditch. It made no sense to walk to Chartres or Fontainebleau, both were too far. And no self-respecting driver was going to pull into a depot on foot.

For half an hour, sparse civilian traffic whizzed by. Joe Amos made no effort to flag down any of the cars. He passed out cigarettes; before turning over their Jimmy, McGee'd had the presence of mind to grab the carton from the glove compartment. Twenty-four scarlet embers glowed along the road, a silent and surly constellation in the dark.

At last, the headlamps of a convoy could be seen. The stranded drivers shouldered their carbines and stood from the ditch. 'Bout time, they muttered. Morales cussed in Spanish. Miles away, Joe Amos could hear how fast they were coming, the stove-in mufflers howled down the distance. Red Ballers. When the column arrived it was twenty trucks of rations and small-arms ammo also headed for Fontainebleau. Joe Amos and the rest waved their arms. The lead Jimmy was well past them before the convoy hit the brakes. Passenger windows rolled down. Negro voices called into the wash of the headlamps: What the hell you guys doin' out here? The stranded drivers jumped on running boards to give explanations. Joe Amos watched until all his boys had hitched rides. McGee went off by himself.

Joe Amos walked down the idling line, twirling a finger in the air to signal the column to get rolling again. He figured he'd jump on one of the last Jimmies. A truck in the middle of the pack pulled out of line, into his path on the shoulder, aiming headlamps right at Joe Amos. A voice bellowed from the driver's window: "Get in, College!"

Boogie was let out of the stockade at the end of July. He missed the big breakout from Normandy. Lieutenant Garner greeted him with three weeks of digging latrines. Boog didn't get behind the wheel of a Jimmy until just before the Red Ball started up. Already, he'd earned back his corporal stripe. He was too good a driver, too natural a leader. The supply crisis needed both, and Boogie John Bailey was given another chance.

Boog's assistant driver sat in the middle, trying to sleep for the ten miles to Fontainebleau while Boogie and Joe Amos guffawed and slapped skin across him. He seemed a quiet boy, like McGee. After offloading at the depot, Boogie asked him to ride back to St. Lô with someone else. The boy gladly headed off.

In privacy, rumbling in the middle of the pack headed west, Boogie told Joe Amos about his month and a half behind bars.

"I found out I can do it," he said. "I think I might be a criminal. That shit didn't bother me. I slept all day, did some push-ups, talked mess with the crackers."

"I could do it," Joe Amos said.

"Naw, you'd go nuts in jail." Boogie popped a paw across the back of Joe Amos's helmet. "You'd be in there all thinking. You got to just turn it off."

Over the past month, since meeting Geneviève, Joe Amos had contemplated the stockade, how he'd get a stretch in there if he were caught selling black market smokes.

"I could do it," he repeated. " 'I mean, hell, Boog. We ain't gonna be havin' careers in the Army or nothin'."

Boogie chuckled. "You got that right. But they sure love their niggers now, don't they? Yes, they do."

Joe Amos offered a cigarette from his last pack. Boogie shrugged it off.

"I quit. Jail and latrines made a new man outa me. Lost me some weight. You a new man, too. You lookin' good, College. You still got that French honey?"

Joe Amos told him about Geneviève, about the money he'd taken to the Marquis, and how the old man had teared up at his gift. He said nothing about the picnic in the forest. He said he loved her.

"You'll meet her, Boog. You'll see."

Boogie made no effort to hide his skepticism. Stung, Joe Amos called him on it.

"You got somethin' to say, Boog?"

By the dashboard light the big man widened his eyes, playing surprise at Joe Amos, his former assistant. "You don' mind, Sarge, I'm gonna wait on it."

The mood of their reunion soured for a minute, until Joe Amos finished his cigarette. Then they laughed again over jail, girls, the war, the road. Boogie made fun of Joe Amos losing his entire fuel convoy to Patton.

"I can't wait to see you explain that one to Garner."

Boogie's column sliced through the night fast and recklessly. Their speeds topped sixty on every straightaway. In every small town, if the road was wide they barely tapped their brakes, and if the way was curvy or clogged with debris they dodged and shifted like race-car drivers. The Red Ball was Boogie's meat, slapdash and headlong; finally the big man's get-the-hell-out-of-my-way attitude was something the Army coveted.

At Alençon the column broke for coffee and a midnight snack of stew and soda biscuits. All the drivers in Joe Amos's squad gathered around. Morales continued his Latin swearing at the bandits who'd stolen their trucks.

"I'll take care of it when we get back to the company area," Joe Amos told them.

"They didn't have to steal nothin', man," Grove said over his coffee. "I'd of driven it to Germany for them if they'd asked. Shit. Don't got to steal a brother's truck."

All the Red Ballers agreed. The theft wasn't as insulting as the fact that they were displaced from their steering wheels. Driving was their job, not some fool foot soldier's. They would have driven to Reims or Berlin or goddam Moscow, all Patton or anyone had to do was say what and where, then try to keep up.

Two hours later the column rolled into St. Lô. Boogie stopped in front of Major Clay's Nissan hut.

"Here you go, College. Time to take your medicine."

Joe Amos dropped from the passenger seat. Boogie jumped from the cab, too.

"Where you goin'?"

"I got to see this for myself. This the second time you come back without your truck. It oughta be good."

Inside, a clerk fetched Lieutenant Garner. The officer arrived puffy-eyed, tucking in his tunic.

"Aw, Christ," he said. "You two, please, stay the hell away from each other."

"Good evening, Lieutenant." Boogie smiled. "If you need to take a crap, sir, I can dig you a fresh hole right smart."

"Soon as things slow down, Boogie, I'll take you up on that. Here."

The officer ignored Joe Amos while he shuffled though papers on a clipboard. He handed a blue sheet to Boogie.

"Gas up and take your squad to Cherbourg. COM Z is relocating their HQ to Paris. Thalhimer'll get you squared away. And be quick. We can't spare the trucks for long."

Boogie snickered, elbowing Joe Amos. "No, sir. You sure can't spare no trucks."

Garner glowered at the two. "What?"

Joe Amos cleared his throat. "Lieutenant, I got bad news."

"And I got forty minutes of sleep. What is it?"

"We were waylaid. Outside Fontainebleau. A captain with Third

Army commandeered my column. Said he was taking it all the way back to Reims."

Garner shook his head. "Reims? He's at Reims already?"

"Boogie's boys gave us a ride back."

Garner rubbed his bald pate. "Were you carryin' gas?"

"Yes, sir."

"This captain, he take all your Jimmies?"

"Yes, sir. Twelve of them."

"Son of a bitch. That's the third time since yesterday Patton's done that."

Garner spoke to his clerk. "Alright. Get 'em twelve more from the motor pool." To Joe Amos he said, deadpan, "Got one shot up, got two blown up, got twelve stolen. I can't wait to see what's next with you."

The lieutenant pivoted to head back into the recesses of the hut, a return to his cot.

"That's it?" Joe Amos called after him.

"That's it. Try to hang on to these for a little while, will you, please?" Garner disappeared into the shadows.

The clerk said, "Wait right here." He left Boogie and Joe Amos alone while he disappeared to dig up the locations of another dozen trucks.

"How 'bout that?" Boogie said. "Looks like they can spare some trucks, after all." He thumped Joe Amos on the back. "Gotta roll, College. I'm gonna get my ass to Paris before Garner figures he liked me better with a shovel. I'll catch up with you."

Joe Amos waited in the hut. There were no chairs. He sat against the wall and fell asleep.

D+85

The woman took his arm. Like a couple they walked along the Rue Bénard.

"Ahh, *Chien Blanc*," she said, "I tell you. No one is as big a bore as a collaborator."

Her hand rested in the crook of his elbow. White Dog covered her fingers with his. He liked this feeling, strolling in the open down a boulevard with a woman on a cool, clear eve. Yesterday, she had gone with him to watch the American 28th Division parade down the Champs Élysées. They'd cheered and thrown confetti, he even waved an American flag at his countrymen, a little heartsick at the sight of them. He joined the ten thousand who walked behind the division until they left the city through Bastille. Along the way, Parisians hung from every streetlamp, they draped from balconies, they cavorted into the marching ranks to kiss or hug the Yanks. White Dog heard later that the division entered combat that very afternoon east of Paris. This lifted his spirits.

"Me, I did not collaborate," she continued. "I did not touch the Boche. Not for a ransom did I touch them."

She grabbed a fist of her hair and tugged, to show White Dog she still had her locks when so many women of Paris did not.

"Yes, *cher*," he said, "your hair is lovely."

"Have you noticed? There are surfacing three types of collaborators after the Liberation."

"And they are?"

"They are all miserable."

"The types?"

"Ah, *oui*. First, the ones who worked with the Boche. Them we will put in prison. Some we will shoot, such as Laval, Pétain, and the rest of the Vichy rodents. Then the ones who spoke in favor of the Occupation, *pfff*, they will never get back any good name in France. The worst are the common ones, who did nothing for the Boche but were friendly, let them in their homes. These talk now for hours about how they were forced to do this or that, they explain, they bore. *Ugh*. They get a slap and are told to shut up. I hate them all."

"You hide it well, *cher*."

The jest popped her distemper. She hugged his arm with a laugh, swaying into him on the cobblestones.

"The ones who fought, the heroes, they say nothing. The ones like you."

White Dog did not object.

She said, "I am so happy."

They walked close like this for another block.

"Here," she said, stopping at a bistro. The door stood open to the street. Smoke and piano sounds drained out the door, the place was jammed.

White Dog said, "Show me."

She led him by the hand into the bar. They had to turn sideways to make their way through the crowd. White Dog would have walked in front to part the bodies in their path but she did a better job elbowing through than he would have. The air inside was pleated with smoke and hot with skin and wool. Beer and liquor were lifted in toasts on every side. White Dog had to dodge flying arms and spilling drink. She kept a tight grip on his hand. Partway through the bar he could not see her at the other end of his arm. Someone banged out a rag on a piano. The ringing of a cash register pierced above the plinking and hubbub. *"Pardon,"* he said many times, jarring men's glasses. He noticed several American uniforms in the throng.

Nearing the far wall, her hand stopped tugging. White Dog heaved himself the last steps past some barrel-chested singers of the "Marseillaise." He arrived beside her and released her hand.

At a table, with his back against the wall, sat an American soldier. Beside him was a woman White Dog knew to be a drug addict. On the tabletop were the remains of many beers and shots. With this much debris of drinking and the company of this woman, White Dog expected the man to look up with red-rimmed eyes. But his eyes were clear and astonishingly white against the darkness of his skin.

"Hey now, Missy," the Negro said, not peering at White Dog at all but looking instead at the woman beside White Dog, "did I forget somethin'?"

She smiled, playing the coquette. "No, *monsieur,* you have remembered everything quite well."

"What you drinking?"

"Cognac."

"How 'bout your pal here?"

"The same, *merci.*" White Dog affected a French accent. No need to let out all secrets too soon.

The Negro circled a finger at the waitress, signaling she should bring a round for all four of them. The addict woman slumped sloppily.

"So," the man said, looking now at White Dog, "you her pimp or something?"

White Dog made himself laugh instead of striking the soldier.

"No, *monsieur,* she is my friend. Welcome to Paris. You like the city?"

"Yeah, man, I like very much. Squeeze in here."

Before White Dog sat, he said sweetly to the addict, in French, "Get lost. I have business. Make an excuse."

The woman fixed wobbly eyes on White Dog. He nodded, agreeing by the gesture to pay her money later.

"*Mon cher,*" she blurted to the Negro, "I do not feel well. I must go."

"You sure, baby?"

She rose, unsteady.

"Alright," the man said. He peeled some bills from his roll for her. She took them and stumbled into the crowd.

White Dog's woman patted his shoulder. "I'll make sure she gets a taxi." She left the two of them at the table.

The black man disapproved. He said to White Dog, "Man, you sure know how to clear a room."

Four drinks arrived. Two glasses were slid in front of White Dog.

"Down the hatch," the Negro said.

"*Santé.*"

When all the glasses were empty and lips wiped, White Dog leaned in to be heard without shouting.

"I am told you drive a truck."

"She tell you that?"

"Yes, of course. You told her, *oui*?"

"That I did. What else did I tell her?"

"That you drive trucks of gasoline. That you would like her to guess what a gallon of gasoline might sell for in Paris?"

The Negro leaned in now, brushing aside empty glasses. Their elbows gathered together on the tabletop. White Dog continued in accented English.

"What did she tell you, *mon ami*?"

"She figured about three dollars a gallon."

"And is this price attractive to you?"

The Negro narrowed his bright eyes.

"Who the hell are you?" The man was burly, he glared with malevolence. "*Mon ami.*"

"I am a buyer. And if I am not mistaken, you are clearly interested in being a seller, or you would not have asked the price. That is why she has brought us together. The price is just as she said. I, of course, must mark it up to make my profit."

"To what?"

"Five dollars a gallon is the street price today. But as I said, I will give you three. So tell me, is that attractive to you?"

"Yeah. It'll do." The Negro leaned in his closest. White Dog smelled many things on him, alcohol, exhaust, perhaps the woman. The driver asked, "How much you want?"

"How much, as they say, have you got?"

"A thousand gallons."

The Negro measured him across the table. White Dog whistled.

The Negro grinned. "You ain't got that kind of money, man. And anyway, why the hell you dressed up like that?"

White Dog broke off the negotiation for a moment to feign indignation. "Like what?"

The Negro swirled a finger at White Dog's linen coat and thin black tie, his tux trousers and slicked, piled hair. "Like Cab Calloway or some shit. What's up?"

"I like the American music." White Dog dug his thumbs under his suspenders for one dramatic snap. "And yes," he said, dropping the

French accent, "I have that kind of money. I'll pay you three thousand bucks for your gas."

The Negro retreated from the tabletop as if shoved. White Dog tried to read his face, full of twitches and bared teeth.

"Man," the Negro said, flabbergasted, "what you doin'?"

"Business, my friend. Business."

White Dog reached out his hand over the empty glasses. "My name is White Dog."

The Negro stared at the pale hand for moments, unsure. "You an American?"

"Apple pie, Brooklyn Dodgers, and Cab Calloway. You bet."

The driver took the hand. White Dog's mitt disappeared into it.

"The hell you doin' in civvies?" the Negro asked.

"I'm a B-17 pilot. Got shot down a year and a half ago over Verdun. The Resistance got to me. They brought me through Paris on the way home."

White Dog held wide his two palms, encompassing the crowd, the women, music, life, and profits all around them. "I decided to stay in Paris instead."

"You're black market."

"Le marché noir. Guilty. Built up a nice little network since I been here. I run the show. I got friends, I got connections, and, brother, I got the money. The Krauts are gone and now I got a big, fat, hungry market. The way I see it, you got the gas. I figure it's a match made in heaven."

White Dog turned on the charm in his smile.

The Negro asked, "Why you go by White Dog?"

"Because I don't need Uncle Sam coming to look for me. Far as the U.S. Army knows, I'm dead. I intend to stay that way a little longer. No reason to get nosy, is there, soldier?"

The big man lifted his chin, considering. "You say three thousand dollars."

"Cash on the barrel."

"Four and I throw in the truck."

White Dog whistled. A thousand dollars for a U.S. Army truck.

"A deuce-and-a-half?"

"With a full tank."

"You can do this?"

"Easier than you think, Cab. Hi-dee-hi-dee-hi-dee-ho."

The Negro issued a snarfing laugh. White Dog saw the man was a little drunk.

"Alright," White Dog said. "You got a deal."

The Negro sucked his teeth. "And you're an American, huh?"

"Red-blooded."

"The Krauts knew about you?"

"Everybody did. Everybody in Paris wanted to sell, buy, or steal something. We all got along fine. I kept my face out of daylight and my ass out of trouble. I was even kind of a hero, you wanna know the truth."

"You a hero now, Cab?"

"I might be yours. Let me ask you this. No offense, but how's the Army treating you?"

"What you mean?"

"What do you think I mean? You want me to say it, I'll say it. You're colored. So how's the Army treating you?"

"Like Sambo."

"There you are."

White Dog leaned back, slapping a hand on the table.

"You think it's gonna get any better because you pass up on a shot at four thousand dollars? Why not get a little something for yourself? Four grand worth, by the way. Can I tell you something else?"

"Sure."

"If it goes alright the first time, I'll give you a five-hundred-dollar kicker for every truckload of gas you get brought to me. You look like a friendly fella. You got friends?"

"I got friends."

"There we go."

White Dog hoisted an arm for more drinks. The waitress saw him right off. Two more cognacs were on the table before the Negro spoke.

"How I know I can trust you? You might be a cop or somethin'."

White Dog stood and turned to the crowd. She was by the bar, waiting. He beckoned her. She forged through the backsides and haze. White Dog motioned her to sit where the addict had been, beside the Negro.

"She's yours. On me. Would a cop do that?"

The man eyed her. She stroked his brown hand on the table.

White Dog asked, "What's your name, soldier?"

The big man mulled the question.

"Boogie."

"Just Boogie?"

"Boogie."

White Dog laughed. A counterfeit name. Perfect, he thought, we're a pair.

He hoisted his cognac in toast. The Negro did not take up his glass but busied himself with the girl.

White Dog said, "I like that." The comment went unmarked. He brought the cognac to his lips to drink alone. He whispered to himself, "Hi-dee-ho."

D+91

For six days, Ben walked sunny fields with fifteen thousand soldiers. They saw no resistance. He ate hot chow and fleshy oranges, and at night watched movies. He smoked a lot and drank some during the day from wine stashes among the officers. He found conversation with a few other chaplains who visited the men in their encampment around the town of St. Masmes, a dozen miles east of Reims where the 90th had run out of gas. Ben conducted prayers in the morning and again at dusk, and a Sabbath service with two candles, a glass of wine, and two loaves of bread, attended by over three hundred Jewish doughs. The Suippe River ran narrow north of town. He pulled Thomas's letter from his pocket, set it inside his boots with Phineas's gun, and stripped in the water. Ben washed his uniform, enduring catcalls from the GIs naked and splashing. Afterward he lay alone in his ODs, looking up, listening to the young men. Ben rested with the Tough Ombres. There was no choice, because each in their fashion had run dry, and could not fight.

This morning, word came down it was time to move east again. The 90th folded its tents at St. Masmes and at noon hit the road on foot. There was little reason for haste, the Germans were gone. They'd had most of a week with no pursuit from Patton's army to cross the Saar River and sweep the dust off their Siegfried Line. Reports had it that the Krauts were also manning the old Maginot bastions left over from the Great War. The doughs enjoyed the enforced break but every officer fumed about it, furious at the failure of COM Z to supply them with fuel to catch the Krauts. Maybe they could have hurled a war-stopping blow, they claimed, before the Jerries could scamper into their homeland and border fortresses. But that wasn't going to happen now, and the war would go on longer.

Marching in the fresh 358th Regiment out of St. Masmes, Ben felt none of the foot soldiers' zeal to return to battle. He bore none of the officers' well-informed anger over the fuel shortage and the disappearance of the enemy. Eagerness and anger, these belonged to men who believed they might make a difference. Ben knew better about himself. He walked east into a day that he could not affect. He could not stop the deaths of today's ten thousand in the death camps of the unconquered east. He could not find his son or Phineas, or even Sam. The men on all sides tramping in this war carried weapons they could fire, minds and hearts that could lead and inspire and do battle. Ben's only arsenal were his belief and the God behind that belief; these he could not feel anymore and so could not use them to change a thing. All Ben could do well was walk with the soldiers, talk with them, say words of prayer for them when they had gathered and over them when they were down. The words were not real, they were blanks, shot out of him as simple noise. What was real for Ben were his memories, of the other war, of his living son, of his living people, and the metal nudge at his waist of Phineas's .45.

Ben accompanied 3rd Battalion along the road, covering fifteen miles by 1800 hours. Even walking, swatting bugs and fingering sweat from his brow, he coasted on the momentum of the troops. He liked this lack of choice, the direction of the march, the cadence of the bootsteps. He was not left alone for a moment; for hours there was a dough in front, behind, and beside him, always some voice prodding, singing, or joking in the ranks. The long walk and the talking were easy. In the bright afternoon among the boys Ben became again a soldier. He took on their youth, and becoming young he was not bloody and old, he was not a failed son and a dismissed husband and a grieving father, he was just one of the boys, a Tough Ombre, everything in front of him, ahead lay the chance to be honorable again. Ben lifted his face to the sun. He closed his eyes and walked blindly for a minute, testing the current of men he was in and to no surprise he walked straight and in rhythm. He opened his eyes and considered the pleasures of the march.

With a few hours left of daylight, the battalion stepped off the road into a field with a view across swells of pastureland falling off to the horizon. A mess convoy caught up with them and the infantrymen ate a hot supper. Ben was asked to say a prayer over the meal and he made up a beauty, a rambling paean to thanks, duty, and victory. He spoke so long, some of the soldiers began to eat before he was finished. Ben prayed with his eyes shut the way he had walked in the column, to see if he would stumble and run out of balance, but he did not, the prayer was a wisp and meaningless, so he could have gone on with it past dark. Finally he laughed in the middle of a sentence and said, "Alright, fellas. Amen."

At dusk, with supper done, a column of empty Jimmies pulled up in the road. The battalion was ordered to entruck and continue east by motor. All the doughs gave a cheer, happy not only to be riding instead of walking but knowing this was a signal that the fuel shortage was over. Now they could get back to the purpose of chasing down the Krauts.

Ben climbed onto the bed of a truck with a squad from K Company. A few remembered him from Mont Castre and called him by the name he'd won there, the Running Rabbi. One dough recalled Ben's shouted message to the Krauts who'd surrounded them on the slope: "Go fuck yourselves. I'm a Jew and come fucking get me." The others on the benches howled and every one of them leaned out to clap Ben on the shoulder, like he was a talisman of luck and will. Ben accepted a cigarette, ducking out of the wind for a light. The sun set and the vast countryside faded into dim-lit ghosts fleeing past.

The doughs around him smoked all their cigarettes and exhausted their chat. The breeze grew cool, clouds knocked out stars. A light drizzle dampened them into wrapping their arms and tugging down helmet brims to try for some sleep. Ben sat straight among the slumping soldiers. In the silence of the gears and road he was alone again. Only cat's-eye light from the Jimmy behind lit the dozing squad. Ben rose from the bench to stand behind the cab and take the chill wind face-on. He followed the red glow of the blackout taillights from the convoy in front, little red eyes looking back at him.

Ben stood this way for an hour, catching what pale glimpses he could of the night land flickering by. An eerie sense cloaked his shoulders. He looked out, watching for something. Approaching midnight, he saw the first rotting fence posts slip by in a field. He tightened his grip on the cab. A string of posts emerged out of the thin beams and slow pace of the convoy. Ben wanted the trucks to speed up, to get out of here. But nothing changed for his wanting it. The posts moved closer to the road and he began to see the barbed wire, rusted but clinging still. From his moving perch, he saw in the fields beyond the wire a black row in the earth where the trucks' lamps did not flow. A trench. A scar. In a moment Ben was angry, couldn't the goddam French have filled that in? Why is it still here? His jaw clamped, he made fists. The road ran across a bridge. Ben knew the river without a sign to tell him, the Meuse. Two miles to the right, off to the south, lay Verdun. Seven hundred thousand men had died in those trenches and wire, in a space smaller than ten square kilometers. Somewhere out there in the murk, Thomas Kahn's B-17 had plunged and struck. Fifteen miles farther south, at St. Mihiel, Ben Kahn had crawled under wire, under moon and clouds and God's eye. Ben had come to the sad center of his life. He felt an urge to leap out of the truck, to hit and roll on his belly and stay there, to crawl again under the wire and into these slits in the earth, because this was the last time and place he was sure God had seen him. Instead, Ben did the only other thing he could. He released the cab and sat in his spot on the damp wooden bench, nestling between two sleeping doughboys. He lowered his helmet like them and closed his eyes, enfolding himself in his arms, feeling cold, bloodless.

D+92

The Red Ballers ran.

The operation was so massive, so impromptu and chaotic, that Joe Amos marveled daily how it could get up on its legs for another day without toppling over. Routinely the drivers ignored the rules set out for them by COM Z. They raced at twice the posted speed, bunched up their convoys, and rode each other's tails. They flipped off MPs who tried to slow them or space them out. They ran beyond the limits of the Red Ball, hauling their convoys hundred of miles off the route whenever Army field units asked them to deliver directly to their division's supply points far forward. The drivers liked this bit of spice, flitting up to the front lines, dropping their cargo, then peeling rubber out of there. They ignored maintenance schedules, pushing their Jimmies past the point of reason until batteries dried up, engines overheated, motors seized without oil, bolts came loose, transmissions snapped, drive shafts fell apart, and bald tires blew. Fully loaded and abandoned Jimmies lined the shoulders of the Express route. Drivers shrugged it off, hitched a ride, and got a new truck, leaving the dilemma for someone else. Round-trips began to last more than forty hours of straight driving, and the Red Ballers, colored and white alike, got fuzzy from exhaustion and sabotaged their own trucks to get a break. Often the front lines moved so fast the drivers never found their destinations, so they hawked their loads to whatever soldiers came with their hands out.

The problems that plagued the Red Ball were not all the makings of the boys behind the wheels. There was always a shortage of MPs along the route, traffic snarled easily, and non–Red Ball vehicles crept in, going the wrong way or slowing everything down. Loading and unloading became tedious affairs, often taking over thirty hours to get a convoy filled or emptied. Weight restrictions were ignored: a single row of 155mm shells put a Jimmy over the five-ton limit, and rare was the quartermaster who could resist tossing on another couple rounds. Trucks were sent to depots for loading before the consignment orders arrived from Signal Corps, so the trucks sat empty and the drivers took to malingering. Or not enough trucks were sent to carry a specific load, so the vehicles that arrived were badly overloaded, increasing the wear and tear on the suspension, tires, road, and the Red Ballers themselves. Highway repairs lagged, creating diversions and detours that slowed some convoys and got others completely lost. Many a worn tire met its end in a pothole. Maintenance crews struggled to keep up, encouraging the drivers to skip the long repair lines at the bivouacs and keep driving, eroding their vehicles even faster.

All in all, Joe Amos found it a simple matter to get lost in the shuffle.

"You ready?" Joe Amos asked.

McGee nodded. A Chesterfield hung pasted on his lips.

Joe Amos lightened his foot on the gas. The Jimmy began to coast and slow. In his mirror, Morales's truck closed in. Morales tapped his horn.

Joe Amos put the Jimmy on the shoulder. He braked and stopped. Morales pulled off behind him. The rest of the column motored into the afternoon.

McGee went into action. He hopped down and yanked up the Jimmie's hood. Joe Amos took his time and ambled around to the warm grille. McGee already had his wrench out. Joe Amos put his hands on his hips and waited for Morales.

The Latino walked up, shaking his head.

"The fuck," he said. "What now?"

"Dunno. McGee, what you got?"

The boy cranked a few more turns with his wrench, then lifted out a white spark plug like a dentist pulling a tooth. He drew on his cigarette without taking it into his hands. He jumped off the bumper, tossing the plug to Joe Amos. The porcelain was cool.

"Busted," McGee said.

Joe Amos turned it once to inspect, then chucked the useless plug into the weeds.

Morales asked, "You guys okay?"

"Yeah," Joe Amos replied, pointing at McGee wiping his hands on a rag, "the boy here's got some plugs somewhere. He keeps shit like that under his pillow. We'll straggle and catch you."

"Best mechanic in the company," Morales agreed. "Alright, 'mano. Hasta luego."

McGee stepped back up on the bumper and leaned over the engine. In seconds Morales powered past and slipped into the column. McGee kept his station under the hood, blowing tobacco smoke over the engine and doing nothing more.

Joe Amos sat on the running board, watching his convoy drive by. He waved and gave thumbs-up to his drivers. He'd waited five days for this moment. It was the first convoy he'd had in that time to carry gasoline. He glanced at the boy under the hood.

"Look like you're doin' somethin'," he called to McGee. The boy tapped shave-and-a-haircut with the wrench over and over until Joe Amos told him to stop.

Five minutes passed until the last of the jerrican-laden column was gone. Another line of trucks roared at their heels, but Joe Amos recognized none of these drivers. Time to go, he thought.

He stood from the running board.

"Do it."

McGee reached in his pants pocket for the good spark plug he'd pulled from the engine before Morales walked up. The busted one he'd thrown to Joe Amos—the one to fool Morales—had come out of the same pocket. The boy torqued the good one back into place, connected the greasy spark-plug wire, and slammed the hood. Joe Amos climbed behind the wheel. He cranked the engine as McGee climbed aboard.

The turnoff to Couvains was a half mile ahead.

"Stay here, okay? I'm only gonna be a few minutes."

McGee crossed his arms. He did not look at Joe Amos.

"Whatever."

Joe Amos glared at his assistant. Now was not a good time for McGee to be taking an attitude.

"What are you so aggravated about?"

"I don't see why we gotta come by here, is all."

"I'm just goin' in for a minute. I'll tell you why when I get back out."

"Go ahead, then."

Joe Amos dropped out of the cab. Before closing the door, he turned back to McGee and softened his tone.

"You scared?"

The boy flicked a glance at Joe Amos. He chewed his lips.

"Go on. The faster we're movin', the better."

Joe Amos moved across the grass heading for the mansion's big front doors. Before he got far from the Jimmy, McGee's voice caught up with him.

"Yeah," McGee called. "A little scared."

Joe Amos let himself inside the big foyer, calling for Geneviève and the Marquis. He stepped through the décor, heavy furniture and plush coverings. Walking through the halls he reached a hand up to brush a low-hanging chandelier. The smells of simmering chicken and vegetables breathed from the warm stove. A corkscrew lay on the chopping block with a cork stuck on it. Joe Amos looked out the window to the rear yard. The Marquis was there on the lawn, shirtless and shoving his mower. Joe Amos made for the door. He pushed and collided with the girl.

Today she wore slacks and a linen blouse. Her hair, knotted in a bun, let loose stray strands over her face. Her flesh was flushed. On seeing Joe Amos, she backed away and ran a sleeve over her cheeks. She smelled of grass cuttings and sweat, green and pink odors that went straight to Joe Amos's gut and groin.

"Hey," he said, backing up, too, surprised.

"Joe Amos." The girl straightened herself, hastily tucking hair behind her ears. "You are here."

"Yeah." He laughed, amused at her efforts to prettify herself. He held out his arms for her to step in for a kiss. She stayed back, then came close for a peck. It's because she's sweaty, he realized.

"I can only stay a few minutes. I'm in a convoy but I hung back to come see you."

"I am cooking," she said, pointing to the kitchen.

He brushed a blade of grass from her shoulder. "And yard work, too," he added.

"*Oui*, very busy."

Joe Amos got the feeling she was in a hustle about something.

By now the Marquis had seen them. He waved Joe Amos to come where he labored behind his mower. Joe Amos reached for Geneviève's hand.

"Come on. I want to talk to you and your father for a minute."

The girl did not put her hand in his. Her head tilted, her forehead crinkled. All her hurry disappeared.

"Joe Amos," she whispered. "No."

He didn't understand why she was laying back. He had a truckload of gasoline parked out front he was going to sell tonight in Paris for a fortune. He was going to be rich and he was going to rescue her and her father and this property. Joe Amos grabbed the girl's hand and towed her across the lawn. She lagged for the first steps then caught up and strode beside him. The Marquis quit his mowing and buttoned on his shirt. He poured a glass of wine from the bottle Geneviève had brought out from their wonderful warm kitchen that Joe Amos would protect and fill with food and delights.

"Joe Amos Biggs!" the Marquis called, holding up the ruby-filled glass. "Again you have come. Have a drink!"

Joe Amos took the glass and emptied it in one gulp. This was a toast to himself. He did not let the girl's hand go.

"Marquis, I can only stay a few minutes."

"Yes, of course. So."

Again, Joe Amos felt a rush in their welcome.

"Well, I wanted to tell you something, and then ask you something."

Geneviève tugged enough to have Joe Amos release her hand. She did not meet his glance.

"Yes?" the Marquis said.

"Okay. Well, here goes . . ."

Joe Amos hesitated. He cleared his throat and did not speak, arranging his words, remembering what he had planned and hoped to say. The Marquis, like his daughter, changed his posture, the energy to usher Joe Amos off the place softened. The Marquis set a kind hand on Joe Amos's shoulder and said like a father, "Whatever it is, say it. Get it over with."

Joe Amos stood confused. Where were the high spirits of his other visits? The embraces, the affection and gratitude, what happened to all that? I'll tell them, he thought. I'll just tell them straight out and the news will be so good everything will snap back to normal.

"Alright. Marquis, Geneviève. Look. I've got a deal going down tonight that's gonna make me a lot of money. I know this guy who knows another guy in Paris. An American who's a bigwig in the black market there. He was some kind of pilot who got shot down and stayed in Paris and now he's getting rich. He's buying gasoline as fast as he can get it, and he's buying trucks. This friend of mine, another driver, he's arranged for me to sell my whole load and the Jimmy for four thousand dollars. I gotta give McGee a thousand, but I keep the rest. And don't worry, it's foolproof. My friend did it and he got away with it easy. The Army's got no way of knowing what happens to any of our trucks. Things are moving too fast for them to keep up. I'm just gonna say it broke down and I left it on the side of the road somewhere. I done it before. So how 'bout that? Three thousand dollars. Wow."

The Marquis had left his gentle hand on Joe Amos's shoulder. Now he dropped it.

"That is a lot of money, my friend."

"Yeah. It is. And I'm gonna give it all to you."

Joe Amos waited for the Marquis to react, to click his heels, grab his daughter, and do a do-si-do, or something. The Marquis spoke to the ground.

"And in return?"

Joe Amos was rocked. He never looked at it in terms of a trade.

"No, man, not like that. That ain't it."

"And in return, Joe Amos?"

Joe Amos heaved a sigh. What was going on? He'd just said he was going to give the Marquis three thousand dollars! Again, confusion swirled and he could figure no other course but to press on and trust that what he would say next would be such good news that all this gloom and reluctance would disappear, and the kisses and wine would flow like he had expected.

"I want to marry Geneviève."

No reaction came from the Marquis or the girl. Joe Amos looked to Geneviève but her eyes were fixed on her father.

"I said I want to marry you."

"Joe Amos," the Marquis spoke. "Look at me."

He pulled his eyes from the girl. She was the reason he would do anything, be anything, a hero, a criminal.

"My friend, my good boy. No."

The Marquis set his arm around Joe Amos's waist to lead him away from Geneviève. Joe Amos held firm.

"No?"

The Marquis waited. Joe Amos repeated, louder, "No?"

"It is not what you think," the Marquis said.

The Marquis gave up trying to pull Joe Amos from the girl. He said to her, "Go in the house."

"No. She stays."

"Joe Amos, you are not the master of this home." To his daughter, he said again, "Go in the house."

Before walking away, the girl shook her head at Joe Amos. The gesture broke his heart. He could not tell if she was repeating her father's refusal of his proposal, or if she was saying to him, Go now. Do not stay and ask questions. Go.

Joe Amos watched her leave. He caught himself leaning after her, sucked in her wake, aching to dash across the lawn.

She entered the kitchen and closed the door. Joe Amos watched the window; she did not look out.

"Alright, man." Joe Amos yanked his arm from the Marquis's grip. "What's up? You don't want my money anymore or you don't want my color? Which is it?"

Joe Amos took steps away, angered now, done with being confused. The Marquis lifted his hands into the breech between them. Joe Amos wanted the betrayal out in the open and he wanted it now.

"What is it, Marquis? You fuckin' owe me this."

"*Oui.* I owe you."

The Marquis dropped his arms.

He said, "Do not think this is easy."

"Get on with it."

The Frenchman drew a breath.

"The Nazis. I told you, they were here for four years. My wife."

"Yeah, you said before, she died of the flu."

"No. There was no flu. My wife is alive."

Joe Amos pulled himself erect at this, suddenly afraid of where the Marquis's explanation might go.

"If she's not dead, where is she?"

"She is there. In the house."

Joe Amos's jaw dropped to speak, but his lips would not part. He leaned onto his toes, wanting to leap at the man and shake him.

"My wife," the Marquis said, "Geneviève." It was the worst word he could have spoken.

Humiliation reared at Joe Amos like flames, stopping him from grabbing the Marquis. He'd been made such a fool. He felt pulverized, without the bones to strike the man.

"You used me." Joe Amos put all the venom he could muster into his voice.

Still, he sounded to himself like a hoodwinked yokel.

The Marquis drew himself up, proud in his posture. Joe Amos marveled, Where does he get the balls?

"No worse than I have been used."

"You *used*? Go to hell."

"That journey has already been made. Tell me, do you think the Germans in their four years in my house asked my permission before they had their way with my young wife? Do you think I stood by and did nothing? I was dragged into this yard and beaten more times than I recall. What can a man tolerate, Joe Amos? What can he stand by and watch, what brokenhearted sob can he swallow? Hmm? Do you think you will stand this, to have been used so badly as you claim? Perhaps, perhaps not. You will learn, I suppose. As have I."

Joe Amos looked back to the house to see if Geneviève was watching. The windows were all empty of her. The mansion seemed small and desperate.

"You son of a bitch," Joe Amos said.

"*Oui.*"

"Your wife's a whore."

The Marquis made no move to avenge this remark.

Instead, he raised his chin and said, unblinking, "I see this makes you feel better, to curse us. Go on, then, if this is what you must do. But understand. My wife that you say is a whore has more courage and honor than you and me and a thousand men. You cannot marry her because she is my wife, yes. But even if she were not, you do not deserve her. You have not suffered like her, like this house. You are just like me, Joe Amos. You are a thief."

"I'm a what?"

The older man held his ground.

"Go ahead, strike me. You think you will be the first? After four years with the Boche in my home, you think I have not had a blow? *Pff*, I will not even feel your hand, Joe Amos Biggs."

Joe Amos reined himself in. He spoke though clamped teeth.

"If I'm a thief, what about her?"

"What did she steal from you? Your heart? I have given it back to you. So. You are made whole. But did you think for one minute what was stolen from us? Did you really think yourself the man to give it all back? With what? Three thousand stolen dollars? An offer of marriage? That is *merde* for what this house has lost."

The Marquis paused but did not look away.

"What else?" Joe Amos asked, to purge everything.

"You have not heard enough?"

"What else?"

"*Bon*. We continue to survive. Geneviève, she does what she has to do even now, with the Americans in France. My young wife, she has the heart of a warrior. She knows what must be done to survive."

"What are you saying to me?"

"I am saying that if you wait long enough, another truck will come up our drive and you will meet another man. And if the two of you wait, you will meet a third."

Joe Amos nodded, heaped with more shame than he ever thought he could bear. What can a man tolerate? This?

The Marquis took up the bottle from the grass. He offered the wine to the glass still in Joe Amos's hand. Joe Amos let him pour.

"One more drink, my friend, then you should go. Take your gasoline, sell it, and keep the money for you and your fine McGee. The money, you deserve."

Joe Amos drank the wine, then let the glass drop to the lawn.

"Did she care for me at all?"

"Of course. You are a good boy."

Joe Amos walked around the long edge of the ancient house. He kept his eyes down and did not look in any windows. The sound of the Marquis's mowing ushered him from the property. McGee and the Jimmy waited out front in the big circular drive.

Joe Amos climbed in the cab. He cranked the motor and pulled away. Along the shady drive, he feared another Jimmy coming up the road. He would stop the driver and warn him, tell the Marquis's whole story, the truth about that house. Had another man told him those things ten minutes ago, he would have fought. The jerricans jittered in the back.

McGee smoked and said nothing. Joe Amos brooded over the wheel, flinging the Jimmy south to St. Lô inside a long column that had let him in. The two did not speak for hours, until the convoy had passed Vire, then Domfront, and approached the first bivouac area at Couptrain. Joe Amos paid no attention to the time. He flew past MPs flagging the column to slow down and the large Red Ball billboards marking the one-way route. Afternoon light frayed to the east, the sun swelled orange the lower it sat on the faraway fields west. Joe Amos finally noticed the day ending, and was glad of it. He listened to the pistons and springs of the truck, the gearbox and slick rubber against the road, and thought how sick and tired this Jimmy was, how overworked. It needed to rest, not to be sold into slavery. And the thousand gallons of gas in the back, they belonged at the front, not in Paris. I've been chumped, Joe Amos thought. The Marquis said he gave me back my heart. He gave it back beaten up to hell.

Joe Amos followed the convoy into the bivouac. Dozens of Nissan huts had been erected for maintenance, sleeping areas, offices, and spare parts in the great pasture where not one blade of grass or weed was left standing. Hundreds of vehicles rolled and a thousand men walked in crisscross patterns, honking horns and yelling everywhere. The frenzied activity on the Red Ball followed them, even here where they came to a halt for a while. Joe Amos guided his Jimmy out of the column, aiming to stay just long enough for a coffee. He intended to get back on the road to catch up with Morales, Grove, Baskerville, and the rest of the boys at Chartres. He wished time was like the road, wished he could drive faster through it and leave her behind months before sunup.

McGee jumped down to stretch. Joe Amos brought him a coffee, too.

McGee asked, "You want me to take her for a while?"

"Sure. Hey, McGee."

"Yeah?"

"Look, I reckon the deal's off."

The boy sipped his coffee.

"What you mean?"

"I mean, we ain't taking the gas to Paris. I changed my mind."

McGee's gaze narrowed. "Somethin' happen back there with the Marquis?"

"None of your business."

"None of my business? I get in the same trouble you get in, but I only get me a thousand dollars out the deal. I didn't say nothin' 'bout that. But I'm gonna say somethin' 'bout this here. This is my business."

"McGee, back off."

"That girl told you she don' want you no more. That's what happened. Now you don' want no money. I ain't stupid, Sarge."

"I said back off."

"No, I think you back off. You change your mind, but what about my mind? I ain't changed. I want this."

"And I said no. Forget it. Get in the truck. I'll drive."

McGee dropped his coffee mug on the dirt.

"No, Sarge. I'll drive. And you stay here."

"McGee, think about this. It's not a good idea."

The boy shook his head and all his hardness fell away.

"What else I got? Really, Sarge, what else? You and I both know I got nothin' after this war. And I ain't got a damn thing to show now. I ain't like you. I ain't shot down no plane, got me some stripes. I didn't get no girl. Come on, man, lemme have this."

"You'll get caught."

"Maybe. Maybe not. But 'til I do I'm gonna have me four thousand dollars in Paris, France."

Joe Amos looked the boy over. McGee knew the risk, and he was willing to take it. Like Joe Amos had been.

"I won't tell nobody, Sarge. I get caught, I'll say I stole the truck out from under you. Go on inside and get another coffee. Here. Get one for me."

McGee bent for the dropped cup. He walked close and handed the mug over. Joe Amos took it. The two shook hands.

"You know the address in Montparnasse?" he asked.

"Yeah. I got it. Rue Stanislas. I got the map in the glove box."

"You know the man's name?"

"White Dog."

"Alright. Good luck."

"I get away with it, I'm gonna bring you a thousand dollars."

"Don't, McGee. Keep it all."

Joe Amos let the boy's hand loose. He took the empty coffee cups inside the tent. He kept his back turned until he heard the rush of the motor and the lunge of gears. He walked outside with the two mugs steaming, to watch McGee pull away. Joe Amos's M-1 lay on the ground. He dumped out McGee's cup.

Another colored driver came beside him, sipping coffee.

"That your rifle?"

"Yep."

"That your rig?"

"It was."

"What's up?"

"Me and my assistant had a little argument. He drove off without me."

"Asshole."

"Not really. I need a ride to Chartres."

"Sorry. We ain't stopping there."

"Where you goin'?"

"Long fucking way, out toward Metz. Right up to the front."

"Who's in Metz? Patton?"

"Patton. We're takin' ammo to the 90th, outside some town called Thionville, on the Moselle."

The Tough Ombres were at the Moselle? Damn. The last time Joe Amos looked, the 90th was just east of Paris. Now they're knocking on the German border.

The driver shrugged. "Like I said, it's a long drive."

Joe Amos laughed into his coffee cup.

"Man, you don't know. I'd walk it."

D+93

Ben took his second bullet of the war. This round nipped his web belt at the waist, spinning him around full circle before he went down. His left hip stung like he'd been cut with a scythe. On the ground he burrowed hard, scared and mad. The gunner knew he was down and plowed the soil left and right but missed Ben, flat in the high grass. Once the zings of bullets swept away elsewhere, Ben rolled over gingerly to pick at his belt buckle, to get it off and take a look at where he'd been hit. I Company had walked right into the Kraut MG's sights, which blasted from a stand of trees a hundred yards ahead outside the village of Mont. The target for the day's march was the town of Fontoy, and this sudden resistance along the way was unexpected; the Kraut MG was the first combat for the whole division in over two weeks, spent resting without an enemy to pursue or gasoline to chase them with. This wasn't much in the way of a fight: some unlucky Kraut unit got left behind to slow the Americans down while the rest of their bunch hotfooted it farther east. Even so, two hundred shocked doughs of I Company went to ground fast. Shouts went up from a handful of wounded. An officer scrambled for the radio, calling for an A/T gun to move up. Sergeants yelled at their squads to get on their feet and circle the trees.

A medic skidded beside Ben and helped him ease off the belt. The lattice was sliced where the bullet struck. The weeds gave some cover for Ben and the medic as the Jerry machine gun busied itself, hacking away at the company spreading out.

The medic muttered, "What kind of sumbitch shoots a chaplain. I mean, that ain't right. He can see plain as day you got a red cross on your dang helmet. I swear."

Ben sucked through his teeth. The medic's annoyance at a chaplain's being shot made his hands brusque exposing the wound.

"It's alright," Ben said to get the boy to ease up tugging at his shirt and pants. "It's . . . ow! It's fine, I been shot before. Just . . . !"

Phineas's pistol tumbled out when the belt went slack. The medic raised an eyebrow.

"Looky here. Maybe that Kraut saw you comin', Padre, and just shot you first."

"Could be. How's it look?"

In answer, the medic stuck a thumb and forefinger into the cardinal depths of the gash, checking for fragments. Ben felt speared. His mouth gaped and his eyes crossed. He blinked into an encroaching blackness, ready to faint.

"Looks clean," the medic said. "Come on, Padre, hang with me now. Attaboy." Ben sensed a hand on his back and a canteen at his mouth. Water ran over his chin before he could remember to part his lips to drink.

"There you go."

With the medic's mitts finally away from the wound, Ben's vision unclouded. He noticed the size of the boy, big as a bull.

"Were you . . . uh . . . ," Ben asked, "were you a boxer or something?"

"No, why you ask?" the medic sprinkled sulfa powder over the channel punched through the fleshy part of his waist. Ben sucked air at the new, smaller stabs of pain. The medic dug into his pack for a gauze wrap and a bandage. The gash bled into Ben's OD underpants.

"Nothing," Ben groaned. "Forget it."

"My dad runs a meat-packing plant in Wyoming. That what you mean?"

"Yeah. Must be."

"You got lucky here, Padre. There ain't much of you where a bullet could miss an organ. But this one did."

"I got one in the fanny a couple weeks ago. Same side."

"Who shoots a chaplain?" the medic grumbled again.

The boy pressed Ben's hand over the bandage patch. He helped Ben sit up while he spun the gauze wrap around Ben's midsection. When he was done, the boy smacked him on the shoulder. Ben flinched.

"Good as new, Padre. We'll get you back to the aid station and have a doc look at that. But you're gonna be okay, maybe a couple stitches. Here." He poured some sulfa tablets on Ben's palm.

"Thanks . . . what's your name?"

"Bubba."

Ben snorted. "I could have guessed. Stay low, Bubba."

"See you later, Padre. Do you need a stretcher or can you get back on your own steam?"

"I got a little steam left."

The medic scampered away. The morning stayed splintered by potshots from I Company still trying to ferret out the Kraut machine gun hidden and flailing at the doughs from the trees. Ben hunched under the grass to tuck in his shirt over the wrapping and pull up his trousers. He finished with difficulty, then shoved Phineas's .45 back into his waistband. That smarted.

I Company kept the Kraut MG busy. Ben struggled to his feet and hobbled, bent over, as fast as he could to the rear. Once he covered fifty yards, he straightened. The pain in his side was bad but he gritted his teeth and found he could walk with a limp.

Ben moved past more soldiers easing forward to join the hunt. The company needed to clear the woods so they could take Mont and stay on course for Fontoy. A few doughs who saw Ben called out sympathy and curses, "We'll get the sumbitch did that, Chap, don't you worry. Damn Krauts." Ben waved a bloody hand.

An A/T gun crew hauled their 57 mm cannon into the clearing, then swung it to face the woods. Ben sat on a stump to watch them load and fire five rounds at flat trajectories into the trees. Trunks and branches blew sky high. The doughs of I Company ducked flying shavings. When the smoke cleared and the last bark and chips fluttered to earth, the woods were gouged and hazy. A squad stepped into the brush, guns ready. Ben turned away. More men moved up, running now.

Ben limped to the rear, his first strides backward since stumbling down Mont Castre two months ago. Every trod yard, every trucked mile since then had been east, running down the Germans, chasing what he thought God wanted from him, holding himself out in the argument.

Now he was in retreat. He considered whether he might keep retreating, catch a ride back to the rear, take his stitches and head west until he was home and done. Nothing was left for him in France. He'd come back to this war thinking he could make some difference, sway God in Thomas's fate, win over soldiers to fight for his reasons. He'd thought he might wipe off the blood from his hands onto the new battlefield, wash his hands in old rivers. He'd found that the blood clung, and beyond that he'd mattered not at all, only enough for God to turn from him. Who shoots a chaplain? Ben knew the answer now. No one. This was God's last statement to him, that Ben Kahn was no chaplain. No rabbi.

An ambulance driver spotted him making his way to the rear. The private jogged to help him.

"Who shoots a chaplain?" the boy asked, taking Ben's arm. Ben shook his head and said nothing.

He asked to sit up front with the driver, not on a litter in the rear. The boy was glad to say yes. Escorting Ben over the last of the field, he carried on a one-sided chat, about his home and folks and why he was a driver and not a fighter. He was a Mormon from Provo. Ben let him prattle, then stood aside while the boy and a medic settled two stretchers into the rear of the ambulance. Each of these wounded doughs had been hit in the leg by the MG before the A/T gun smashed the woods around it. Ben spoke to the two boys briefly. Both reached from their litters to point at the red blemish at Ben's waist where his bandage was soaking through. Ben grimaced when the boys asked, "Does that hurt?" "Sure does," he told them.

The driver took the wheel, gabbing again. The ambulance rolled in a convoy of a dozen vehicles, a mix of Red Cross trucks and emptied Jimmies with an infantry squad in the back. These doughs were headed to the ASP at Mairy to pick up supplies. The road was a one-lane, narrow, bouncy path, barely paved. Ben bit his lip and put a hand over the rip in his side to press it shut.

Mairy lay two miles away, and the ride was quick. The boy was a terrible driver, dodging potholes, making the stretchers in the rear bang the sides of the ambulance. He scraped the panels of the vehicle against branches grown wild along the road. In five minutes the village appeared at a crossroads. It had its own church and a welcoming wooden icon of Jesus posted outside the town limits. The column stopped beside a circle of crates, an ASP in a field where the carved Jesus gazed over the heads of the soldiers jumping out of trucks. Ben eased from the cab. The Mormon driver bustled to the back of the ambulance. The wounded were to be transferred to another set of vehicles shuttling two more miles to the rear, to the 90th's CP at Landres. That will be four miles away from the fighting, Ben thought. That's a start.

Ben's side pulsed. He looked into his palm; blood tacked his fingers.

Another convoy arrived on the road at the edge of the field, this one coming from the west. Quartermasters waved clipboards to greet them, showing the newly arrived Jimmies where to park. The trucks all bore the Red Ball emblem on their bumpers. They halted in a tight echelon, with parade precision. Every driver who stepped from the dusty cabs was a colored boy.

Ben forged ahead, figuring he'd catch a ride with one of these Red Ballers back to the CP. He looked at the thirty Negroes gathering on the grass. Some of their trucks steamed under the hoods. But even from a distance he could tell the dark boys had a swagger to them. They shared cigarettes and slapped hands. Not a one of them made a move to off-load their beds filled with ammo. Some stretched, others loitered in the shade of their Jimmies. None of the white soldiers spoke to them. Ben headed their way.

Halfway to the line of trucks, he noticed several GIs and drivers standing in place or sitting up on the grass. Ben halted, lifting his senses to the morning. He followed the looks of the stilled soldiers. He turned to the village and the road behind him.

Squeals were the first thing he heard. The stretcher crews took off running with the wounded between them. In seconds, every dough in the field with a crate in his hand dropped it and dashed. The Negro soldiers sprinted for their trucks. Like the wooden Jesus across the field, Ben stared.

The thrum of motors clawed beneath the squeaks of rolling tracks. Three hundred yards away, where the lane emerged out of its summer cloak of brush and trees, a Mark IV panzer powered into the open. The tank did not stop, clearing the way for two more panzers to roll into the field. A hundred grenadiers jogged behind the tanks.

The lead machine's turret whined and rotated, a robotic, ugly gesture. The long cannon pointed at the mound of supplies. Ben clapped one hand over the hole in his side and the other on Phineas's pistol, and ran.

The great cannon cut loose from seventy yards, point-blank range, so that the blast from the Kraut tank and the eruption in the supply dump happened at the same instant. With a black-and-orange fireball and a piercing yowl, a corner of the dump was hurled into the air. Busted wood slats and C-ration tins snowed over the field and running doughs.

Joe Amos was pissed off, scared, too. He stood rooted. What the hell was going on, where'd all these Germans come from out of nowhere? Damn, this was the front line alright! It's what he said he always wanted, but suddenly he wasn't so sure. The shit had hit the fan and he didn't know what to do, where to run. It seemed like a hundred soldiers black and white were in the same quandary, either frozen and gaping at the charging enemy or just darting around. A second tank fired into another portion of the dump, blowing it to bits. Joe Amos jerked at this detonation. By instinct he growled; someone had to haul those crates all the way out here from the beaches and now these Krauts were shooting them up.

The three tanks fanned into the field. In seconds the dump took two more shells. In moments more every truck and ambulance parked beside the dump was in ruins. German soldiers galloped through the smoke from the fires set in the vehicles and the crates of uniforms and food. They headed across the field, for the convoy.

Joe Amos looked for Hull and Franklin, the two drivers he'd ridden out here with over the past day and a half. He didn't see them, he didn't even know where he was exactly, didn't know the name of that village on the far side of the smoky field. White infantry and quartermaster crews flung themselves into foxholes, dug either by them or by Germans in their four years here. Colored drivers dove for their truck cabs to grab their M-1s, then scattered for cover. This struck Joe Amos as the best thing to do, but he was too far from Hull's truck to fetch his rifle. Already shots rang from both edges of the field. The fight was on.

He whirled for the column parked on the road and ran flat out thirty yards. In one bound he was on the tailgate of a truck, with another jump he stood on top of the ammo crates. He hurtled across them and dropped inside the ring of the .50 caliber machine gun. Flinging the ammo belt out flat on the boxes to help it flow smoothly, he charged the chamber and swung the barrel at the onrushing Krauts.

"Alright, boy," he muttered, taking aim, "let's do somethin' right."

Joe Amos squeezed the trigger and spit a gale of bullets right through the swirling smoke, aiming blind at the advancing Krauts but sure in their direction. The ammo belt jiggled across the crates, empty brass casings tinkled around his boots. The fat gun shook but Joe Amos threw every muscle into keeping it steady on the Krauts. Through a gap in the smoke he saw them dive to their gray bellies in the field. He let off the trigger.

"Whoo!" he shouted into the battle. "Whoo-ee!"

In the moments he'd bought, two teams of doughs had worked their way forward with bazookas. Where the hell did those boys get bazookas? he wondered, then figured they must have grabbed them out of the supply dump before the Krauts blew it up.

All four men ran ahead and Joe Amos swung the gun again, shooting the daylights out of anything that moved in front of them while the GIs dropped to their knees. The teams took aim at the lead panzer, which growled past the burning supply dump in the center of the field. Joe Amos wasted ammo on the tank, hoping to draw its attention away from the bazooka teams. He succeeded, and whooped again.

The Mark IV spotted him. Like a slow death's finger, the turret turned for him standing on top of his Jimmy. Joe Amos blasted the last of the ammo belt right into the face of the tank until he stared straight into the black eye of the cannon. Then he sprang over the side of the truck.

The ground hit him hard. He didn't try to stand and run but rolled like a barrel as fast as he could away from the Jimmy. The explosion blew over him, rolling him faster. He stopped and looked dizzily into the black heat of an inferno where the Jimmy had been. Nothing but the chassis and flaming wheels were left. He covered his head from the falling pieces of truck and cargo. The Jimmy's hood landed with a clang five feet from him.

Joe Amos scrambled to his feet and peered through the blaze at the panzer. Its cannon was pivoting to take out another truck just when the first bazooka round struck. A flash bloomed on the panzer's temple and the turret stopped its whine. The second shell pounded on the same spot and that did it, the turret popped like a cork out of its ring and settled cockeyed. Hatches flung open and the tank crew bailed out. Oily billows coiled from the wounded panzer. Hollers went up everywhere in the field from the doughs and drivers.

He ran along the line of Jimmies, but the other .50 cal already had a colored boy behind it, working it hard. Joe Amos needed a gun. He skipped between bumpers and scooted back into the field's edge, scanning for a weapon and cover to shoot from. Behind him, from the charring truck, crates of ammo began to cook off. Zings and snaps of un-aimed rounds made Joe Amos dive into the nearest hole dug beside the road.

He gaped at the skirmish fought across the broad pasture. Smoke rising from the ruined tank and blazing depot obscured the fighting. Haze from the smoldering Jimmy hugged the ground. A carved Jesus high on a cross looked over the smoky combat, impassive, head down. Joe Amos figured Christ had seen plenty in His time.

There was nothing for Joe Amos to do in the battle without a rifle. From the foxhole he watched the two remaining tanks career over the field, making themselves harder targets for the doughs with the bazookas. Both tanks kept shooting on the run at the Jimmies, hitting two more trucks and missing three. More ammo flared and fired crazy rounds in every direction. The bazooka teams kept trying to creep close but the tanks sped away or the doughs were chased back to cover by Kraut infantry.

The fighting was simple to follow, even with the smoke thickening from burning vehicles and black exhaust from the tanks. The Krauts moved in from the north, the GIs and drivers defended the south and the convoy, while tanks dodged in the middle, working to get clear shots at the Jimmies and to finish off the supply dump. No more than two hundred yards now separated the forces: in some places, only a hundred lay between them.

Joe Amos's legs stayed tensed, waiting for a reason to fly out of this hole. It was a clashing, flaming time, with the colored driver and the machine gun blaring from the Jimmy on the road, the carping of small arms on all sides, the screech of armored treads everywhere. The two remaining tanks roared at the trucks and hit another three, adding more blaze and smoke to the battlefield. The Krauts tried to move up, the doughs and drivers tried to nail them down under a flail of bullets. The haze leaked thin glimpses of the enemy, hardly enough to take aim. Joe Amos coughed and cursed without a gun.

Glaring into the smoke, he caught sight of a soldier staggering forward, still amazingly on his feet in the heart of the fighting. The guy had been hit, he struggled with a limp. A pistol hung in his hand.

A dough ran across the field, into the smoke to help this straggler. Joe Amos spotted the red cross on the hobbling soldier's helmet, he was a medic. No. The running dough called to him, "Padre!" He was a chaplain.

The soldier made it most of the way before he got hit. The GI threw out his arms and landed like a duck on water, skidding and collapsing, facedown. The chaplain stumbled to the dough and kneeled. He rolled the soldier over, and didn't seem to notice he was in a crossfire with tanks rumbling at his backside. For a moment the chaplain laid his face close to the downed soldier, then tried to stand. He reeled and sank back to his knees. Joe Amos could tell he was finished.

Ben looked at the dead soldier.

No name, no religion, he knew nothing about the boy except that he'd taken a bullet through the throat coming to a chaplain's rescue.

From his knees he looked from the soldier's face into the twirls of smoke. Breathing was hard; the hole in his side knifed him and said he was going nowhere. Behind him came German boots and rattles, shouts closing in on the raging dump. Around his head, rounds sizzled.

"I'm sorry," he told the body. This boy surely hadn't considered dying here, in a raid on a supply dump outside some out-of-the-way village. He'd just wanted to be brave, get the hurt padre off the field. Trusting he was doing a good thing had killed him. Ben had killed him. Ben asked himself for remorse and couldn't find it. Instead, he'd given the boy the only thing he had, a quick and empty Lord's Prayer, guessing he was likely a Christian. Ben couldn't feel any pride for the courage of this soldier, or gratitude at the sacrifice. All he felt was the waste.

This moment had been coming. He'd held it at bay as long as he could with denial, lies, and hope, patching the cracks with faith, but finally he felt death rising in him. Father, mother, brother, enemies, pals, son, Phineas, and now he was cracked open, at last his own spilled out. He coughed again and seized at the pain. He took in his surroundings. The circumstances of his death were going to be the same as this squandered soldier's.

No, they weren't.

Ben glared at the earth, at his folded knees on it, and remembered that God had turned His back. God asked nothing from Ben any longer, and though Ben did not want this freedom, he had it. God was not deciding Ben's life or death on this battlefield. Ben chose for himself.

He pushed his foot into the ground. The pain in his side tried to trip him but he drove the boot harder into the grass. The pain reared but could not stop him. Ben rose above the dead boy.

He took a step. He couldn't make it to the doughs defending the field. They were too far, there was too much lead in the air, the Germans were close behind him. Ben chuckled in a dry mouth.

He walked anyway.

A voice screamed from the rear.

"Halt! Halten Sie! Aus den Grund!"

Ben pivoted. He found all the strength he needed.

He hoisted the .45 and fired. The first round hit the grenadier high in the chest at twenty yards, knocking him backward like a pratfall. The second and third rounds winged two more soldiers who had their rifles poised. Ben put one down with a bullet to the leg, the other twisted with a round in his shoulder. Ben dropped him with two more shots. The German with the hole in his leg raised his hands. Ben aimed between the palms and put a bullet in the man's torso.

He turned for the convoy. There, standing five feet off, with smoke and flickering fires as a backdrop, stood one of the colored drivers.

"Damn," the boy said.

The chaplain lowered his pistol and turned away from the three dead Krauts. He looked ready to buckle again. His left side was soaked with blood. Joe Amos hurried to the chaplain and propped him up, then leaped to the GI's body to fetch the spilled rifle.

"Sorry, man," Joe Amos said to the corpse. Moving fast, he hoped this boy had at least heard whatever blessing the padre had given him dying. Joe Amos shouldered the M-1 and grabbed the chaplain by his gun arm.

"Come on," he said, already hauling the chaplain over the grass. The man stifled a cry. His feet barely kept up. Joe Amos took the chaplain's arm over his shoulders and ran, almost lifting him over the ground. The sounds of their boots and the wounded groans from the chaplain did not hide the hiss of bullets. Joe Amos blurted with every stride, "Come on, come on, come on . . ."

The run was forty yards to the road. Joe Amos glanced up from their feet to see the colored driver on top of the Jimmy still raking his machine gun behind them, keeping the Krauts' heads down. Smoke from the blazing dump scraped in Joe Amos's chest but he ran into it, gulping. The chaplain grunted with every step. Joe Amos answered him, "Come on . . ."

Ten yards from the foxhole, the tanks hit another Jimmy. The roar was immense, this truck had been carrying artillery shells. Joe Amos flinched sideways at the explosion. The chaplain slipped from his grip. The man stumbled and the blast toppled him. Joe Amos dove, flames mushrooming over their heads. The concussion flipped the Jimmy into the air. The two trucks in line snugged front and rear were jacked off the road to crunch on their sides. Only three of the dozen trucks remained. The colored boy and his machine gun had vanished.

Joe Amos scrabbled on his belly to the chaplain. The man waved him off.

"Go," the chaplain rasped.

"Can you make it?"

"Go!"

Joe Amos skittered for the foxhole. The chaplain bared his teeth and crawled. Joe Amos helped him slide into the hole. The chaplain folded to the dirt bottom. He had not let loose his pistol.

Joe Amos squatted next to him.

"You gonna be alright?"

The chaplain nodded. One hand went into his lap with the Colt, the other pressed over his bloody side.

"What were you doin' out there?"

There wasn't much to the man. He was scrawny, with a few days' growth of gray beard. There wasn't much to his answer, either.

"Walking."

"I guess. Man, look at you. How bad is it?"

"I'll live."

"You weren't gonna do much livin' out there."

The chaplain returned the nod, an acknowledgment of the rescue. The red splotch on his tunic was spreading.

Joe Amos saw the Ten Commandments insignia at the chaplain's collar.

"You're a rabbi."

"Yes."

"Man. Who shoots a rabbi?"

The chaplain snorted and shook his head. "Everyone."

"Well, you damn sure shot back. I didn't know you guys could handle a gun like that."

The man's eyes brimmed with tears. He dropped his head to his chest, obscuring his face below the rim of his helmet. That hole in his side must be hurting him a lot, Joe Amos thought. Probably he's scared, too.

"I know you from somewhere?"

The rabbi shrugged and did not look up.

Joe Amos slid the rifle off his shoulder. "Don't you worry about a thing, Chap. You're with Joe Amos Biggs. Ain't nothin' gonna happen to you."

Joe Amos rose to lean over the lip of the trench. He set his cheek to the rifle stock, aware that this was a dead man's gun, feeling that it might for that reason be better, maybe vengeful on the Germans. He found a target, a grenadier sneaking up through the smoke. The depot was in full blaze. Nine wrecked Jimmies crackled and fumed. Joe Amos lost the Kraut for a moment in the haze but got him back on the end of the rifle. He closed one eye and walked the Kraut over the sight. He squeezed the trigger. The rifle bucked. The gray soldier kept moving up. Joe Amos made no adjustment in his aim but fired again twice, then the Kraut went down.

"Yeah!" he shouted. "You see that, Padre? Got him."

The chaplain's head was down, not watching.

Joe Amos lined up another target. He fired and missed, but this didn't matter. What counted was the gun in his hands, the colored boys all around mixing it up, and the white boys fighting, too, everyone together.

"You ain't lookin', Chap." Joe Amos spoke without taking his cheek from the stock, scanning for someone to shoot. "But this is what I been talkin' about since I got here. Say a colored man can't fight. The hell with that. Look here, man. Come on, get your head up, look around. What do you call this? Can't fight, my ass." Joe Amos glanced down to the chaplain, thinking perhaps the vulgarity would rouse him. The chaplain stayed curled and quiet.

Kraut infantry had gathered again behind one of the panzers. Joe Amos eased the barrel and waited. The tank powered closer, inexorable and dangerous. The machine gun in its face spewed bullets at a lightning rate. Joe Amos wasted a shot down the length of the machine, then another. He was firing not so much to hit someone as he was making the bullets fly, for the driver with his .50 cal who'd looked out for him in the field, and for that dead white boy whose gun this was. Joe Amos squeezed off two more rounds, for both of them.

He lifted his eyes from the barrel to the battlefield. Both tanks pressed slowly forward through the smoke, with plenty of infantry hunkered behind. Off to his right, another bazooka team snuck into the field. At their backs, their squad fired volley after volley to try and get them in close.

On his left, the drivers did the same, plopped on the ground, ducking in holes or behind smoldering pieces of their blasted trucks. Every one of them held a barking rifle.

Joe Amos lifted the M-1 and let fly at one of the tanks, careless but carried away on the din. He tugged the trigger again. One more bullet grazed the side of a panzer, then the M-1 cartridge was empty and ejected.

"Out," he said.

The chaplain looked up. There was nothing like fear on the man's face. There was nothing at all, Joe Amos thought. Whatever tears or pain had been there were gone. This was a blank man. Joe Amos had seen this look on dead faces, after the spirit had flown.

The chaplain struggled to his feet. Joe Amos thought he might say something, but the chaplain did not speak or meet his eyes. He gained his balance and lifted the .45 to pop out the clip. The man palmed the gun like he knew his way around it. He had four rounds left. He slapped the clip back into the butt and turned to face the battle.

In the field, the tanks and grenadiers had advanced inside a hundred yards. The smoke from the dump pulsed behind them. The panzers' turrets took the measure of the last three Jimmies.

"Alright," Joe Amos said to the silent chaplain. He laid down the rifle. "Okay, then. Be right back."

He jumped out of the foxhole and hit the grass running for the nearest Jimmy. Pumping his arms, he glanced over his shoulder at the tanks, racing a turning turret, hoping the bazooka boys would keep it off him for fifteen more seconds. There was no cover, the Jimmies had been blown catawampus all over the road and Joe Amos had to dodge bits and clumps of them, running so close to flames he felt his uniform singe. Small-arms fire pinged off the wreckage until he reached a loaded Jimmy and scrambled on top. He was lucky and found what he was looking for fast. He lifted the box of .30–06 ammo and tossed it over the rail to the ground, hoping it would break open. It didn't. He jumped down after it. There was no time to try and crack the crate and grab just a handful of cartridges, and he'd brought no tool to do that. He hefted the box to his shoulder. On an impulse, he jerked open the driver's-side door and looked under the seat. He felt his luck running strong with him, there was another M-1. He grabbed it, figuring maybe that chaplain could handle a rifle, the way he worked that Colt.

Joe Amos ran back to the foxhole by the same flaming, serpentine course. More bullets searched him out but he stayed behind the wrecks as much as possible, moving slower with his load through the smoke and heat. Five yards from the hole, he threw the ammo box like a shot put, hoping again it would crack open. It held firm. Joe Amos clambered into the safety of the hole and unshouldered the rifle, winded. Before he could catch his breath, the chaplain had smashed the crate twice with the butt of the rifle Joe Amos had left behind. A plank on the top gave way. The chaplain yanked out cartridges. He tossed one to Joe Amos just as the Kraut tank blew away the Jimmy where Joe Amos had fetched the crate two minutes earlier. Both of them cringed into the hole, away from spinning debris.

The tank had come to a standstill to take aim at the last two Jimmies, confident it was being protected by the grenadiers at its rear and flanks. Covering fire coming from the Red Ballers and the quartermasters was intense. The bazooka team took advantage to creep close. With one shot they scored a powerful blast on the tank's treads. The behemoth shuddered and screamed as the tracks running over its right bogey wheels broke loose and spilled on the grass like a great busted watchband. The tank was hobbled. Now the bazooka team drew careful aim on the side of the stilled turret. Hatches on the tank were opening when the next shell hit. The blast enveloped the Mark IV. When the fire swirled away and the echoes had died, no one came out of the lifted hatches.

The chaplain had laid his pistol on the edge of the foxhole. He loaded the M-1. Joe Amos shoved a fresh cartridge into his. The two lifted their rifles in tandem, shoulder to shoulder.

Joe Amos fired. He had hundreds of bullets in the crate, why not let them fly? He shot at the grenadiers scattering away from their killed panzer. He found the soldiers hard to hit at a hundred yards, running or diving to their stomachs. But he exulted with the rifle. He muttered "Bang" and "You want some?" with every few rounds. He liked it when the spent cartridges kicked themselves out of the rifle, collecting on the ground in front of the foxhole. They were like medallions, proof. Beside him, the chaplain fired more slowly, calm on the trigger. He had the strap wrapped around his extended left arm. He used one clip in the time Joe Amos went through four. Before reloading, Joe Amos paused and watched the chaplain fire. Sure enough, a grenadier went down.

Joe Amos loaded and returned to his own rifle. The Germans were down to a single tank but this one was a bastard. It roared fast back and forth across the field, never setting itself up for a bazooka shell. It pivoted fast on its tracks, and whenever it faced the GIs or the colored drivers it let loose with a cannon blast or a burst of machine gun. All the defenders cringed when the tank faced them; the Kraut grenadiers used that gap to move up. They were hard to hit, still shrouded in smoke. They fired and moved with precision, ducking behind the tank, then flashing out to charge and take more ground.

The quartermasters and drivers fought back with everything they had, but it wasn't enough. The enemy was well drilled and coordinated. The battle was ten minutes old and already the Krauts had advanced over half the width of the field. At this rate they'd be in grenade range in another five. Joe Amos had no grenades, and he didn't think any of the drivers or QM boys did, either.

He started getting nervous. Bullets whizzed close to where he set his left elbow in the dirt, the rifle kicking at his cheek and shoulder. The chaplain beside him never changed his tempo. The man said nothing.

"You know," Joe Amos spoke to him, "I almost made a big mistake the other day. I might've missed this."

The chaplain fired. His clip was done. He reached behind him for another, not hurrying. He surprised Joe Amos when he uttered, "Maybe that wasn't a mistake, then."

Joe Amos fired off two quick rounds while he had the chaplain's attention. He kept talking.

"Naw, it was a mistake. I almost did something really bad. I got involved with a French girl. I was gonna sell my whole load of gas on the black market just to kiss up to her father."

The chaplain loaded and took his position. Again he selected targets slowly. Joe Amos kept talking, focusing away from his weapon. He figured the chaplain was doing more good anyway with fewer shots.

"Buddy of mine found some guy in Paris who was gonna buy the gas and the truck for four thousand dollars. I mean, that's a lot of jack. I was gonna do it, too. But it didn't work out. The girl, I mean. She didn't work out. So I didn't go through with it. My assistant did. McGee. McGee Mays. His real name is Adolph. That's somethin'. I reckon he's in

Paris right now having a high time. Probably ain't comin back, either. He didn't seem like he cared much for the Army."

Joe Amos fired again at the approaching Krauts. The chaplain fired, too. Joe Amos guessed the grenadier who went down took the chaplain's round.

"Weird thing is," he spoke into the rifle stock, "the black market fella in Paris who was gonna buy me out, my buddy said he was an American. Some B-17 pilot shot down in '43 over Verdun."

Joe Amos quit shooting and laid down his rifle. To his astonishment, he wasn't frightened, nowhere near like he ought to be. Not next to this chaplain. The white man had an aura, something hard like fired steel. He was quiet, and he seemed a good man, the way he'd knelt with that soldier who'd got shot coming to save him. He wasn't blank, Joe Amos thought, he was filled with will and spirit but grim like one of the prophets. He was wounded bad and still had strength to fight, the kind of peace and power that comes from belief. Next to him, touching shoulders and feeling the snap of the man's rifle through his body and into Joe Amos's own, Joe Amos believed, too. There was indeed a God, there had to be, especially at times and places like this. God was here, and all this was in His hands. Out there in the smoke, wasn't that Jesus on that cross? Joe Amos only had to have faith, and he had to be brave in that faith. Everything else would work itself out. God was on the chaplain's side, sure enough, and Joe Amos was at his side. Geneviève, the Marquis, Boogie, McGee, the Messerschmitt, Garner, Speedy, Himey— every one of them had brought Joe Amos here like road signs.

The chaplain had stopped firing. He was staring at Joe Amos.

He asked, "What did you say?"

Joe Amos looked away, to the two remaining Jimmies.

"I bet one of those trucks has got grenades."

"Wait," the chaplain said.

Joe Amos set his palms on the lip of the trench. He bent his knees to spring.

"Don't worry, Chap. I'm a hero today."

The driver took a bullet the moment he was out of the foxhole.

The round struck him high in the back. He staggered, waving his arms like a man out of balance. Something strong ran in him and he kept his feet, even took a step. Then another bullet thudded low in his back and knocked whatever it was out of him. He swayed backward.

Joe Amos Biggs fell hard. Ben collapsed beneath him to the bottom of the foxhole. The boy lay faceup in his lap.

Quickly Ben undid the boy's chin strap and tugged off his helmet to clear his face. Joe Amos Biggs's eyes were flung wildly open, whites showed all around his dark pupils. Ben felt the boy's heartbeat as wild as his eyes, thumping.

The boy panted. Sweat broke on his brow. Ben wiped it with a palm. He ran his hand over the boy's short, brushy hair.

"Damn," Joe Amos growled. "Man, what'd I do?"

The boy swallowed. No blood foamed on his lips. The bullets had missed his lungs but hadn't come out the front. They stayed cozied inside him, making sure whatever damage they'd done stayed lodged open.

He began to shiver. This was bad, a sign of severe blood loss. Ben rolled him over enough to see the two rips in the boy's jacket. The first bullet had drilled all shoulder, just meat and broken bones. The second round had hit low, close to the spine. Ben probed the puncture, the boy made a guttural mewl. The wound did not gush blood but dribbled a steady pulse. Ben guessed this second bullet had cut a renal artery. Even if the hole was bandaged and stoppered by a medic, the boy would bleed out internally in a minute, more or less.

"Joe Amos."

The boy closed his eyes. Ben stroked his cheek to bring his eyes open again. When he looked up his drifting gaze fixed on Ben.

"I'm thinking. . . . I'm thinking maybe you go get the grenades. I'm not gonna make this run."

"You sit this one out."

"But hey, I got you off that field, didn't I?"

"Yes. You did."

"Fought, too."

Ben nodded.

Joe Amos gathered some strength.

"Tell Major Clay."

"I will."

"Tell . . . tell my mama. Danville."

"Joe Amos."

The boy went silent, mustering his last reserves. He shut his eyes and shook his head in a small tremor. Joe Amos felt some new pain. Ben couldn't tell if it was in his waning body or his spirit.

The boy opened his eyes and his mouth. Tears glistened in his eyes, blood on his tongue.

"Geneviève," he muttered. "You tell Geneviève."

Ben did not know who Geneviève was, and he did not figure he would find out. He nodded.

"Joe Amos, listen to me."

"Okay, Chap. Okay."

The driver lifted a hand to cover Ben's on his chest. "Chap, say something." The shivering grew worse. The hammering of his heart pounded in Ben's lap.

He wanted Ben to pray for him.

"Jesus," he said, as though telling Ben where to start.

Ben spoke quickly. "Joe Amos. The man you were going to sell your gas to. The American pilot in Paris. What was his name?"

"What? I . . . I . . . white something. White Dog."

"Where is he in Paris? Did your friend say? Where were you going to take the gas?"

The boy's mouth worked but he did not speak. Ben saw him baffled on the footbridge between life and death, between asking for comfort in his passage and giving over his last seconds to one more chore, for this chaplain, and not knowing why. Ben willed the boy to live those few seconds for him. *Save me one more time, Joe Amos Biggs. I know my duty to you as a rabbi and I cast it aside, for this. For my life. For my own boy.*

Ben shook the dying driver.

"Where is White Dog in Paris?"

The boy coughed. His back arched. His face skewed. Ben could not wait for the pain to pass. He rammed his words into the boy's agony.

"Where is he? Joe Amos?"

The driver stayed rigid for terrible moments, then released into Ben's lap. His jaw and spine slacked. The engine of his heart eased. His black eyes stayed on Ben.

"Joe Amos. Please. Tell me. I think it's my son."

The boy made no reaction. Ben feared he had slipped too far.

Then Joe Amos Biggs smiled. Ben saw, in that moment the boy had become sure of something, a truth, a guarantee. His hand relaxed over Ben's, to let him go, and to be on his own way.

He whispered, "Montparnasse." With one more heave, he added, "Rue . . . Stanislas."

These were the boy's last words, an address. He did not die for several minutes. Ben cradled him in his lap at the bottom of the foxhole, he laid his hands to the boy's chest, to ride the rise and fall of his idling breaths. Ben did not pray for Joe Amos. Again, he gave only what he had, and he knew God was no longer among his presents. Ben told him when a company of infantry from the 90th and three Shermans arrived to rescue the remaining doughs and his fellow Red Ballers. When this was said, the boy died.

Later, when the Tough Ombres walked the battle area, they found Ben in the hole, beneath the body. Joe Amos Biggs was lifted away and laid in the back of a Jimmy. Ben struggled to his feet, very bloody.

D+100
SEPTEMBER 14

Ben woke before sunup.

His fifteen stitches itched but did not ache. His bandage did not seep. By the light of a lantern at the end of the ward he put on the fresh uniform that had been brought for him and laid across a chair at the foot of his bed. The fit was fine; the nurse who'd fetched it for him had said her husband was exactly his size. She had transferred all his rank and chaplain's insignia to the new outfit. He did not remove any of the markings, they would have use yet. He pulled Phineas's Colt from the bedside table and checked the clip for the four rounds. They were there. He stuffed the pistol into his waistband. From a medical cart he gathered a clean bandage, tape, and a roll of gauze and dropped them in his new pack. He slipped on crisp socks but carried his boots, which had been cleaned. His Red Cross helmet remained the same filthy thing he'd worn into the hospital.

He tiptoed out of his ward, avoiding the night nurse. When he was in another hallway, he put on the boots and walked for the front door. Anyone noticing him saw a chaplain leaving the hospital and had no reason to stop him.

Ben flagged a ride. Traffic ran thick in Fontainebleau even in the early morning. The city on the Seine was a major crossroads and a depot for Third Army. It held several headquarters and was on the return route of the Red Ball Express. Bonaparte's last palace was here, too. When Napoleon departed Fontainebleau in 1814 he went into exile.

Ben rode east to the sprawling depot near the river. He thanked the driver, who was headed for breakfast and a cot, then walked to the motor pool. Before he'd gone fifty feet into the depot he found himself pressing against walls of crates and sliding sideways along lines of parked vehicles to avoid the crush of activity. Trucks roared in and out of the depot in immense echelons. The pace of exchange was feverish. Empty was traded for full, loads were lifted and shifted by hand or crane, engines and shouts rang as loud and urgent as a battleground. After a week in a hospital bed, Ben's strength still wavered. Several times men, white and colored both, yelled at him to look out, he had wandered straight into their paths. Ben winced at truck horns and at the clout of loads dropped, unable to separate the clash of battlefields from this depot.

With dawn rising, needing a chair and water, he found a motor-pool garage. A sergeant behind a desk directed Ben elsewhere. Ben walked off, but the sergeant came to haul him back. The man gave up his seat, set out a canteen, and told Ben to wait right there. Ten minutes later, with dawn filtering through grimy windows, the sergeant rolled a newly painted jeep in front of his desk, headlamps on. He honked the horn, happy with his good deed for a chaplain. Ben jerked, he'd been dozing and almost dove from the chair. The sergeant said, "You okay?" Ben calmed himself, it was just a jeep. He asked to keep the canteen and was given it. He tossed in his pack and drove off for Paris.

Ben had never been in Paris. But once he found Montparnasse, Rue Stanislas was not difficult to find. It was a two-block stretch linking two major avenues, just three hundred yards from the Luxembourg Gardens. A series of Parisians directed him ever closer with hand signs or passing English. The street was a narrow canyon of high, ornate facades with storefronts and garage doors at the bottoms and balconied flats farther up. When he arrived the mid-morning sun had just climbed the tops of the buildings and cast sharp shadows down the cobblestones.

Ben parked in a shadow, the only vehicle on the cobbles. On the sidewalks, old women lugged fresh loaves and mesh bags of victuals. They wore kerchiefs and coats. Ben looked at their fat ankles. He finished the last of the canteen. The ride in the open and stiff-riding jeep had exhausted him.

He waited, gazing the length of Rue Stanislas. He unbuttoned his tunic, pulled up his OD undershirt, and glanced at his midriff. The wrapping was clean, the ride from Fontainebleau had not ripped his stitches. He tucked himself neat again.

Ben was reluctant to get out of the jeep. This street held secrets he did not want to know. If he had a bullhorn he would stay put and call out for Thomas. This is your father. I've come for you. Come out, come out. . . . The boy would step from a shadow of Rue Stanislas into the light, climb into the empty seat, and they would drive away. Ben would need to know nothing of what Thomas had done, why he was here, why he was White Dog and not Thomas Kahn. They could unravel it later, when they were safe, when Ben was strong and they were together.

Ben tasted hope. He knew the best he could expect was that he would take Thomas back to a court-martial and prison as a deserter. No matter. The boy was young yet, he had hurt no one. He was in the black market. Ben had done far worse in his youth in the name of duty than what Thomas might have done for money. There was time to heal Thomas, too. Ben forgave his son for being alive the way he'd had to forgive him for being dead. Ben tapped the letter in his breast pocket, the nurse had been careful to put it there.

An elder gentleman in a bowler hat approached. Ben raised a hand in greeting. The man smiled in return.

"*Pardonnez-moi.*"

"*Oui?*"

"I'm sorry, I don't speak French. But do you know a man who calls himself White Dog?"

The man cocked his head.

"*Chien Blanc?*"

"Yes. *Oui.*"

The man waggled a wrinkled finger.

"*Non,*" the old man said, "*non.*" He walked off, shaking his head.

Ben stood beside the jeep. He asked two younger women walking together. They spoke English and greeted him. One welcomed him to Paris and kissed him on a cheek before he could ask about *Chien Blanc.*

They looked at each other and said they did not know him. An older woman followed. She lifted her cane to make her point. *"Non!"*

Ben waited and selected a middle-aged man in dirty coveralls. He had a bulbous belly. This told Ben he had eaten during the Occupation. He might know White Dog the black marketeer.

"Chien Blanc?" The man stopped and scratched his chin. He wore two rings on that hand. "Why do you want him?"

"I want to sell him this jeep."

"But you are a rabbi, yes? You do not do this."

"This is a disguise. I have been shot. Look."

Ben opened a few buttons to show his gauze wrap. He lifted the hem of his coat to display the butt of the .45.

"I know *Chien Blanc*," Ben insisted. "He said to meet him here on Rue Stanislas but I do not know which building."

The man nodded, impressed. "A rabbi. That is clever."

"No one suspects."

"Give me something," the man said.

"I have nothing."

"The gun."

"No."

"The pack."

"Take it."

The man hefted the bag and peered inside. He dumped the gauze and bandage on the floorboard.

"Keep those, Rabbi. Number three ten, if he is there."

"Merci."

"Monsieur, I would not take the pistol."

"Why not?"

"Chien Blanc, he has been good to the people of Montparnasse. He has kept many from starving. Yes? He was on the barricades. Many think him a hero. But I know him, too."

The man used the bejeweled hand to pull back the hair above an ear. He tilted his head to show Ben a new scar.

"He gave me this."

"What are you saying?"

"I am saying if you find you need that pistol, you will also find it is not enough."

The man shouldered the backpack.

"Please do not tell *Chien Blanc* you spoke with me."

"I won't."

"I hope you sell for a good price. *Bonne chance*, Rabbi."

White Dog shot his cuffs and straightened his tie. He laid out a hand and watched the green dollars pile up. He always made Hugo pay him in American money. One, two, three thousand bucks, all in hundreds. He held up his other hand for Hugo to stop while he folded these bills and slipped them into his coat. Then he put the hand out again for Hugo to fill it with three thousand more.

He stowed this wad in his baggy pants and withdrew the key to the deuce-and-a-half. White Dog made the biggest profit here, selling the trucks to the Voltaire gang for two thousand when he only paid one for them. He jangled the key over his head for Hugo like a doggie treat, making the mobster reach up for it. Hugo took the key with no expression. Both men turned to the alley to watch the last of the jerricans handed down from the Jimmy's bed. A line of twenty cars hunkered on the shaded cobbles. Each driver took ten containers and covered them with blankets in their trunks and backseats. Two big guards in leather jackets blocked the entrances to the alley.

"Let's go inside," White Dog said, laying a hand to Hugo's back. "Talk a little more business."

Hugo followed White Dog to the back door of the garage. Four other gangsters who had been unloading the Jimmy clapped their hands, finished with the labor, and fell behind them. The column of cars and the truck pulled out of the alley like a funeral. The two behemoth guards got in cars. Before White Dog entered the garage door, the alley was empty. All that remained were the two rolls in his pockets and the five ugly men he held the door open for.

Inside, White Dog moved carefully not to brush anything on his white coat. Everything was dusty, the walls held tools unused for years. The ceiling rose high, slung with chains like a dungeon. Hugo and his henchmen took up a semicircle. One of them sat on the fender of a forgotten Citroën, careless about getting his pants dirty.

"*Bon*," said White Dog, rubbing his palms. He switched to English, for him and Hugo alone. "Okay, we've made a lot of money in the last three weeks. Right?"

Hugo took in the surroundings. His jowls tightened, showing how little he liked coming into the garage. Hugo was not the night creature White Dog had become, he did not have the same tolerance for grit and dark. Hugo was about power and its many bright rewards. White Dog was driven only by greed, and that was why he considered himself the stronger man.

"Yes," the mobster answered. He raised his eyes from the oil-stained concrete.

"I've lost track. What, a dozen truckloads so far?"

"Perhaps. Quite a few, *Chien Blanc.*"

White Dog grinned. He had bad news.

"This first part has been easy, getting up and running. I'm hooked in with a couple of GIs I can rely on. No problems there. But, here's the kick in the pants. They're telling me it's getting tougher on them to come up with whole truckloads of gas. COM Z is starting to crack down. So much gas is disappearing into Paris that even fucking Patton is stealing it. So."

Hugo waited. "So?"

"So, it's getting more risky for them." White Dog folded fingertips into his own chest. "So, it's getting more expensive for me. Hey, this was bound to happen. Now I got to raise my prices. You gotta see that, right?"

Hugo rubbed his forehead. "How much?"

"Four-fifty a gallon. Hugo, just hand it off downstream. Sell it for five-fifty. What's the big deal?"

"I will have to speak with Voltaire about this."

"Okay, you square it with him. Tell you what. I'll hold the line on the trucks. Still an even two grand, no price jack there. That's all I can do."

Hugo turned to his four men. In French he told them, *"Chien Blanc* wants to raise his prices." The four shifted and cursed. One of them spat and the dab slapped the concrete.

Hugo faced White Dog.

The goon resting on the Citroën leaped to his feet. All four of Hugo's men flashed hands under their jackets. They drew a firing squad of pistols. Hugo, more slowly, pulled a revolver from his hip. Stunned at the weapons, White Dog backed into a workbench, knocking it over. Wrenches spilled on the floor in a tinny clamor. White Dog focused and noted the five guns were not pointed at him but past his head, behind him.

Someone else was in the room. White Dog grew furious as he turned.

A soldier stood there, a medic with a Red Cross emblem on his helmet. He was too old to be a medic. He looked familiar, which was impossible.

White Dog checked the back of his white coat. The bench he'd bumped had imprinted a stripe of grease across the vent.

"*Monsieur*," Hugo said, dead calm, "you are in the wrong place. I suggest you go out the way you came in, right now."

The medic held his ground. One gun cocked.

Not a medic. A chaplain. A rabbi.

No fucking way, thought White Dog.

"I'm looking for White Dog," the rabbi said.

Hugo answered. "What is your business with him?"

"I will discuss that with him."

"Who are you, *monsieur?*"

"Ben Kahn."

White Dog coughed a laugh, shocked. "You're his old man."

Without moving his revolver from the rabbi, Hugo turned to White Dog. In French he asked, "You know this man?"

"Yeah," White Dog answered in English, to include Ben Kahn. "Yeah, I do. That's *Acier*'s father."

The rabbi reacted to this. He stepped closer in the room, pulled into the guns aimed at him.

"You're White Dog?"

"One and only."

"You know my son?"

"I knew him."

The man stopped advancing. He tightened his lips, his hands worked.

"Knew him?"

"Yeah. I was his co-pilot. After we got shot down the Resistance brought us to Paris. Tommy got the big idea to stay. So we set up our little operation, which by the way you're interrupting. So if you don't mind . . ."

"Where is he?"

"Gone."

"Gone where?"

"Honest to Pete, this is not a good time."

Hugo lowered his gun. The four behind him followed suit.

"Tell him," Hugo told White Dog.

"Aw, geez, Hugo." White Dog flapped his hands against his sides.

"Tell the man what happened to his son."

White Dog was exasperated. This was old news. This rabbi had popped up out of nowhere. White Dog was amazed that he'd found this garage. Now, because one old guy couldn't let go, a very simple and profitable afternoon was going to turn complicated and sour.

"Tommy got picked up. By the Gestapo."

The rabbi seized as if gut-struck. One hand went to his side like he was holding something in.

"When?"

"You want to know exactly? I'll tell you exactly. June 12. Nobody's seen him since. Okay, Rabbi? That what you needed to know?"

Hugo asked, "He is a rabbi?"

Acier's father's gaze stayed on the floor. His breathing filled the room. He did not speak.

Hugo spun on White Dog.

In French, he growled, *"Acier* was a Jew?"

"Sure. Sure, he never mentioned it?"

"He did not. But you knew this?"

"Yeah. I knew. What's the big deal?"

"Then he is dead."

"I don't know, Hugo. I guess he's in a camp somewhere."

"Yes. A camp somewhere."

Hugo shook his head.

"Tell the rabbi what you did. Or I will."

"What? What did I do?"

"Chien Blanc, do not think you are the only one who ever spoke to the Germans. Voltaire was not without friends in the Occupation. Now tell the rabbi, or our dealings are at an end."

"You're shitting me. Over this? Come on, Hugo, we're making money hand over fist—"

"Do you think I am telling a joke?"

"Fine. Whatever."

White Dog smoothed the slicked hair on his temples. He shot his cuffs again and switched back to English.

"Look, Rabbi. It was business. Okay? I might have put a bug in the Gestapo's ear. That's all. But they had plenty of reason to pick him up anyway, Jew or not. You know? The black market is illegal, and *Acier* was a big fish. I mean, it's a dog-eat-dog world out there. We all do what we got to do. Tommy did it to others. I did it to him. No big surprise."

White Dog turned toward Hugo. "Happy? Can we finish our discussion in private now?"

"You killed my son."

White Dog sighed. Was this not going to end, he wondered? Hugo glared. White Dog turned back to the rabbi.

"You got me all wrong, Pop."

"Don't call me Pop." The man winced. He reached under his jacket to press a hand to his side. This time when he pulled it away, he looked into it.

"S'matter?" White Dog asked. "You got no stomach for business?"

He intended this as a pun. It landed flat, so he kept talking.

"That's all it ever was. Business. Everybody did it. Get real, Rabbi."

The rabbi staggered. He set a hand to a tabletop to steady himself. When he pulled the hand up, the table bore a crimson smear.

The rabbi had been shot. Who shoots a rabbi? This was one determined old buzzard.

"So, Pop. What are we gonna do? I can't stand here all day chattin' about old times. You don't look like you want to, either."

The rabbi did not correct White Dog this time for calling him Pop. White Dog figured *Acier*'s father was just about finished, bleeding and with five armed mobsters staring at him. Still, he must be some guy, this Rabbi Kahn, to come all this way. Tommy had described him like that— tough, a hard nut, he'd said.

Ben Kahn reached again under his olive jacket. He hoisted a big pistol, a Colt .45, out of his waistband.

The man was trying to scare him, humiliate him in front of his associates. But the old guy held the gun hard, harsh, like he meant it.

"What are you gonna do, shoot me?"

"Yes."

White Dog pivoted for Hugo. The mobster had not lifted his own pistol.

"I think," said Hugo, "our business is concluded, *Chien Blanc*."

The first wash of panic sprayed in White Dog's stomach. What was going on?

Hugo put away his revolver. His henchmen did the same. Hugo flicked a finger at the biggest, the one who had sat on the car. The man came close. White Dog, breathing hard, smelled his cologne. He rifled

White Dog's jacket for the three thousand dollar wad. When he had it, he snapped his fingers and flattened the palm. From his trousers White Dog dug up the other roll. The thug gave the money to Hugo.

The mobster pocketed the cash. He sidled next to White Dog and whispered in his ear.

"*Mamzer.* That is Yiddish, *Chien Blanc.* It means 'bastard.' "

Without another word or glance, Hugo and his men left the garage. White Dog stared into the black socket of the Colt until he heard the door slam.

He began to shake.

The search for Ben's son ended here.

The letter in his breast pocket, which like another heart had beat and bothered him, had carried him, went silent. Ben set his hand over the pocket. The paper inside seemed old, an artifact. The last of its kind.

An end had been put to everything.

Almost everything.

The young man on the other end of the Colt began to quiver. Ben wondered what this coward White Dog saw that convinced him he was about to die. It wasn't just the pistol pointed at him. Looking over the gun Ben felt exactly, to the breath, the way he'd felt in the Great War, cutting throats, cracking heads, crawling by dark to do those dark acts. A week ago, at Mairy, at the battle of the burning depot, he'd wept to kill while the colored boy had celebrated. Both arrived at their destinies in that foxhole. In front of White Dog stood an abandoned man.

Ben fixed the pistol between White Dog's eyes.

The boy stammered, "You can't do that!"

Ben's voice was cool.

"Yes I can."

"No, no, no, you're a rabbi. You're . . . you're a man of God."

Ben answered down the barrel.

"Not anymore."

He did not ask what his son was like, what kind of man was he?

The first round Ben fired into White Dog would not bring Thomas back. The second bullet would not return the betrayed millions. The third would not lead God back to him. The fourth missed and went into the wall after White Dog was down and dead.

But Moses said to Elohim, "Who am I that I should go to Pharaoh and bring the sons of Israel out of Egypt?"

Exodus 11

December 24, 1944

Ben did not intend to arrive on Christmas Eve. The drive south from Pittsburgh took four days instead of two. He meant to come and go on Friday. Now it was Sunday. The roads through the Appalachians were stripes of snow, the mountains blotted white. With all the young men gone to the Pacific or Europe, clearing the highways took a long time. In his old Ford, Ben crept behind tractors and their skimming blades, his windshield wipers smearing snow. He slept in roadside motels in socked-in hollers. Beyond ordering food, fuel, or a room, he'd spoken to no one. The snow thinned when he lowered out of the Blue Ridge into Virginia. No snow clung on the brown banks of the Dan River.

He knew her address. He'd written her the letter she must have gotten in the autumn. Crossing the river into Danville, Ben stopped for gas. On the western outskirts, smokestacks from the textile mill jutted, probably visible from anywhere in the town. At the lunch counter inside the gas station, he ordered a slice of pie. A sign above the counter read Whites Only. Ben took the pie plate outside and ate watching an old fellow pump the gas. He got instructions to Gypsum Road from the man, who also checked his oil and recommended another quart for the aging car. Ben left the plate and fork outside.

The directions to the farm carried Ben to the sparse eastern part of town, on the other side of Pumpkin Creek and the rail tracks. His tires thumped over the rails. The sound was notice of a boundary crossed. His foot left the accelerator. He coasted, unsure. For weeks since he'd been back he'd practiced what to say, but for the four days' driving he'd done other thinking and now he was unsure. The Ford slowed almost to a stop. A pickup truck closed behind him and tapped the horn. Ben stepped on the gas.

The day had been sunny in Danville while Ben drove down out of the mountain clouds. Now the last light over the river beamed blue and icy. Ben found the house set back behind bare acres, the soil plowed and cold. He turned past a battered tin mailbox. The Ford's tires ground gravel. A small white dog barked and ran halfway to see him, then stopped in the yard. A chicken stuttered around the corner of the house. Taped in the picture window was a cloth banner, a gold star on a white rectangle surrounded by a red border. The flag said a member of this family had died in service. Before Ben could shut the engine, she was on the front stoop in a shawl.

Ben got out of the car. He did not wave while he approached. She waited on her steps, her shawl pulled tight. She wore a colorful dress, to go out somewhere, and boots with fur tufted at the ankles. Both their breaths made mists in the chill.

"Mister, how are you?" She spoke first. Ben was not in uniform, he never would be again. She lifted a hand from under the shawl. She was a small woman but not frail. Ben walked without speaking but she did not lower her hand, her greeting did not fade. When close enough, Ben saw the calluses on her palm.

"Mrs. Biggs."

Her hand lowered. It rested over her breast, like a woman preparing herself.

"Yes, sir?"

Her hair was gray, worn long and straight, pulled tight behind her head. She was darker skinned than her son, the color of her winter land.

"I'm Ben Kahn."

Stock-still, she said, "You're the chaplain wrote me the letter."

"Yes, ma'am."

"You were with my boy."

"Yes, ma'am. I was with Joe Amos."

Her breathing clutched. The hand on her breast flattened against the shawl.

"What you doin' here, Chaplain?"

"I'm not a chaplain anymore, Mrs. Biggs. Just Ben Kahn."

The boy's mother eyed him, frosty as the air.

"Well, Mr. Kahn, would you like to come in out the cold?"

"Yes. Thank you."

She turned and went into her house, not holding the storm door open for him. When he followed inside, the warmth of a woodstove stroked him. The house was tidy, doilies on every table, comforters folded over the sofa and chairs. A knit oval rug centered the room. Mrs. Biggs went into her kitchen. Ben walked to a wall tiled with dozens of photos, of children all ages, mostly girls. In the center, black crepe curtained one frame, a picture of a young man in a green uniform and cloth cap. Ben had looked into this same face; war and even the minutes bleeding to death had not stolen its contours from his memory. Ben could not think how to tell the boy's mother this, how her son looked fighting, how he looked dying; at the end, the same odd smile that was on his young face was there when this photo was taken just after basic training. Each time, Ben knew, the boy had seen something hopeful ahead. On the right side of this picture hung a Silver Star medal, framed in gold. The decoration was a five-pointed star cast in gilt bronze. In its heart lay a smaller silver star. The medal dangled from a ribbon of blue-and-white stripes, with one broad red stripe down the center. Ben was glad to see the decoration. From his hospital bed he'd written the CO of Joe Amos's trucking company, a Major Clay. Opposite the star, on the left side of Joe Amos's mourning frame, hung an illustration of Jesus capped with a golden halo, hands clasped.

"Have a seat, Mr. Kahn," Mrs. Biggs said.

Ben chose the sofa, with the service flag taped to the window behind his head.

She entered the room holding two glasses, iced tea on a December day. Ben thanked her while she sat in a facing rocker. He drank first, his mouth puckered at the amount of sugar. She sipped and licked her lips dry.

"Where did you come in from, Mr. Kahn?"

"Pittsburgh."

"That's a long way to drive to see an old colored woman. May I ask your business?"

Ben set the glass on a doily. The ice numbed his hand. He looked at the stove beaming heat and thought of the son who before the war had chopped wood for it.

"I came to tell you how brave your son was."

On the table between them sat a worn Bible. The woman rocked forward to set her tea down and pick up the book. Inside the cover was folded Ben's blue letter. She unfurled it and held it out to him.

"You already told me that, Mr. Kahn. In this."

He did not take the letter. She looked at it for moments, then folded it back inside the Bible.

She took up the tea again and rocked. She did not drink. The ice in the glass moved.

"He was not supposed to get killed, Mr. Kahn. He was a truck driver. That's what they told my boy he was gonna be. How did a truck driver get himself killed?"

Ben told her what he could not write in the letter, what the military censors would not have allowed. He told her the place, Mairy, a tiny village in France that mattered only because supplies had been stacked there. The Germans attacked the depot to disrupt the American supply lines, to slow their advance. Ben had been wounded. Joe Amos ran into a crossfire to lug him off the field. The boy found a foxhole and a rifle and fought until he was out of ammunition. He ran through bullets and flames to a truck, seconds before it was blown to pieces by a German tank. He returned with ammo and another rifle. There were colored drivers and white soldiers all fighting together. When the Germans came too close, the boy leaped again out of the hole to fetch grenades from another truck. He was hit, twice. Bad.

"Mrs. Biggs, your son saved my life. He helped hold off a German attack. Before he died, he asked me to tell you this."

The rocker quit. The woman's furry boots rested flat on the rug.

"Mr. Kahn, thank you. I appreciate that. It rests my soul to know."

"Yes, ma'am."

"He also asked me to tell a Geneviève. Do you know who that might be? Was she his girlfriend or something?"

Mrs. Biggs shook her head, considering the name.

"No, I don't. But my son was a handsome man."

"Yes, ma'am."

"He must have had him a French gal. Don't surprise me none."

"No, ma'am."

"Well, whoever she is . . ." Mrs. Biggs trailed off, seeming to think of another woman who grieved for her son. She rocked again. "I reckon she'll find out when he don't come back."

Ben nodded to the mother as he had to Joe Amos, solely from the habit of listening.

Mrs. Biggs rocked more. Then, like her son had, she shook her head in a small way, to signal some pain had been dealt with, and some decision had been taken.

"Mr. Kahn," she asked, "you could have written me all this in another letter. From Pittsburgh."

She set her sweet tea on the doily beside his. In the wood-warmed room, the two glasses sweat. She asked:

"Why aren't you a chaplain anymore?"

Ben had not driven four days to Virginia to tell her in person that Joe Amos Biggs had died a hero. The medal already told her that. For two weeks he'd stared at the sea from the ship that sailed him home over the cold Atlantic, then at the ceiling of his small bedroom in a sparking steel city, deciding to come to tell her, and only her, something else.

"At the end, your son asked me to pray for him, Mrs. Biggs. I did not."

She tightened the shawl at her shoulders. Her hand fluttered, seeking a place. She touched fingertips to her cheek.

"Before he was hit, he told me about someone in Paris, a man in the black market."

"Was my Joe Amos . . . ?"

"No, ma'am, no, he wasn't. But this man he told me about, I believed it might have been my own son."

She pressed fingertips to her lips.

"Your son was dying. And instead of comforting him I asked him questions. About Paris, about the man I hoped was my Thomas. Where I could find him."

"While he was dying."

"Yes."

Mrs. Biggs paused, glaring.

"Well, Mr. Kahn. Did my son tell you?"

"Yes, he did. And then he died in my arms. After I had traded his comfort for mine. That is what I came to tell you."

The woman nodded, a slow and grim motion.

"Did you find your boy in Paris?"

"I found what happened to him. The man Joe Amos sent me to was my son's partner in the black market. They were both deserters. They were monsters. Both had blood on their hands. This man turned Thomas over to the Gestapo on the day I arrived in France. Thomas is dead."

"How can you be sure?"

Ben did not tell Mrs. Biggs why he was certain, the camps, the Jews. He lowered his hands to his lap and gazed into them, struggling.

She waited, then asked, "What'd you do when you found this man?"

He looked up from his hands.

"I killed him."

She tilted her head at him, as if to see him in some different kind of light. She said nothing.

He explained how he had walked out of the garage and told an MP what he had done. He'd been arrested. Quickly, the Army and the Chaplain Corps agreed it served no purpose to prosecute Rabbi Ben Kahn. The war was ongoing; nothing good could come from making it public that two American flyers had started a black-market ring, robbing the invasion of gasoline. Or that their chaplains were carrying firearms. Ben was told to resign from the military, given an unexplained Honorable Discharge, set loose, and sent home. Thomas was filed as a POW. White Dog, whose name was Lt. Gerome Semmes, was listed as Killed in Action.

Mrs. Biggs stood from the rocker. She collected the two damp glasses. From the kitchen, she asked, "Did you stay with my boy till he passed?"

Ben called to her, she was out of sight at the sink.

"Yes."

She stepped into the living room. She opened the woodstove door and tossed in another log. The swell of heat cuffed Ben on the sofa.

"Did you ever pray for him afterward?"

"No."

"For your own boy?"

"No."

With a creak she closed the iron door.

"What did you come here for, Mr. Kahn? Forgiveness?"

"No, ma'am."

"Good. Then why are you here?"

"Confession."

Mrs. Biggs looked down her nose at him.

"Alright, then. You come with me."

*   *   *

When they left the farmhouse, the sun was down enough to loosen starlight. Ben's Ford was left in the drive. They walked, bundled against the cold.

Mrs. Biggs greeted several colored people on the street. A gathering was taking place. Everyone was decorative. Mrs. Biggs walked in a bright scarf and a knee-length coat, her hands tucked into a fur muffler. Ben stayed at her side, bland, huddled in his great coat. She did not introduce him nor look at him next to her.

The Baptist church stood a half mile from her home, a white clapboard rectangle smoking from twin chimneys. The front doors were flung wide and light spilled to the sidewalk and dead grass. Folks made their way inside after hugs and handshakes. Ben faded behind Mrs. Biggs when she entered the crowd at the church entrance. After a minute she fixed him with a look and held out her hand. He stepped forward.

A thin young man in spectacles bowed when Ben approached. His suit was jet around a starched shirt and string tie. When he spoke, his voice seemed to come out of the church's bell tower, it rang so deeply.

"An honor to have you in my church. I'm Reverend Willis."

"Reverend."

Ben took the man's offered hand. Reverend Willis covered Ben's grip with both warm palms.

"Mrs. Biggs here showed me your letter when it came. A sad affair, sir, but we thank you for your beautiful words. Joe Amos was a light in our community."

Ben could say none of the words that came to him in the grip of this pastor. *I am an outcast. Let that hand free, you do not know what it has done.*

Mrs. Biggs tugged Ben away. The reverend bowed again.

She sat in a middle pew. Ben followed. Four women and their men came behind and leaned over the wooden back to kiss her cheeks. They called her *Mama.* Ben exchanged nods and handshakes, each time feeling wrong and out of place, not because of his singular color in this church but his lack of goodness. These people were black but Ben felt darker than any skin could paint him, he was the one place where God did not look among these rows of worshippers on Christmas Eve, the blind spot in His eye. The hard benches filled, the doors closed behind them. Ben wanted to go, now, before the service began. He felt the collapse of his will, hemmed in on the long bench, and marked this in his caving heart as more evidence of his unrighteousness.

On the altar, candles jiggled beside a limp American flag. The building's interior was spare. The church had likely been built by these folks or their ancestors, sentenced and sequestered out here to the fields on the rim of town but within sight of the smokestacks. Ben glanced at the congregation, at pastel hats and square suited shoulders. He sensed their pride. These folks were called to worship and they came. Their sons were called to war and they sent them. Their rewards in America were ramshackle, but they labored at the mill, they tilled their soil, and hung their gold star banners in their windows when their sons fell. They were not free in America, but neither were they freed from God. Next to Mrs. Biggs, Ben felt cheated.

Reverend Willis ascended the altar. Behind him a chorus in white gowns arranged their ranks. The reverend set his hands on the lectern. He searched the crowd for Ben.

"Before we begin our Christmas Eve service, we have in our presence tonight a special guest."

Mrs. Biggs and Ben faced each other. She whispered, "Pay attention."

The reverend continued.

"As you all know, the fighting in Europe recently got worse. Eight days ago the Germans attacked our forces through the Ardennes in Belgium. It looks like it's going to be a tough Christmas for some of our troops, but I'm confident the boys will hold 'em."

The young reverend bounced a resolved fist on the lectern.

"Now, everyone here knows young Joe Amos Biggs from our congregation was killed in the fighting in France back in September. Joe Amos was awarded the Silver Star for his gallantry in combat. At his side for his last moments was Chaplain Ben Kahn, who's with us tonight as a guest of Mrs. Belinda Biggs. Chaplain Kahn has recently returned from the battleground of Europe. If he doesn't mind, I'd like to ask the kind chaplain to offer our opening prayer. Chaplain?"

Mrs. Biggs had not pulled her eyes from him. Ben did not move. Now two hundred sets of eyes were on him.

"Stand up. God wants you to speak."

"No, He doesn't."

"Then I do. You get up and pray for my boy. You do it in front of his people."

The four women in the row behind reached to touch Ben. One of the men shook the kerchief from his pocket and handed it to one woman who had begun to weep.

"And when you're done," Mrs. Biggs told Ben Kahn, "I'm going to stand and every one of us here is going to pray for your boy."

She laid her hand over Ben's. "And for your people. Now up you go, Rabbi."

The pew squealed when he rose. Mrs. Biggs did not let go his hand.

He opened his mouth to speak, not knowing what to say. He took in the large room, and saw every face down-turned, all hands clasped.

Ben closed his eyes.

GLOSSARY

ASP—advance supply point, often no more than impromptu depots for units on the move

A/T—anti-tank, typically a 57 mm towed cannon

BAR—Browning automatic rifle (M1918), a heavy weapon that uses the same ammunition as the M-1 and can fire 450 shots per minute

CO—commanding officer

COE—cab over engine; 2½-ton cargo truck, like the Jimmy, with slightly more cargo space because the engine was placed below the cab

COM Z—Communication Zone; the command in charge of communication lines and logistics in all liberated territory

CP—command post

DUKW—an amphibious version of the 2½-ton truck, used to ferry supplies to the beach from anchored ships

ETO—European Theater of Operations

FFI—Forces Français de l'Intérieur; the French Forces of the Interior, the underground resistance during the German occupation of France from 1940 to 1945

FUBAR—military jargon for "fucked up beyond all recognition"

G-1—staff personnel and administrative officer

G-2—staff intelligence officer

HQ—headquarters

KIA—killed in action

LCM—landing craft, mechanized; designed to deliver a single 30-ton tank or 100 troops onto a beach

LCT—landing craft, tank; designed to deliver four Sherman tanks onto a beach

LD—line of departure

LP—listening post

LST—landing ship, tank; a specially designed ship that could handle both open seas and shallow draft beaches, for deployment of troops, vehicles, and supplies

MG—machine gun

MLR—main line of resistance

MOS—military occupation specialty

MP—military police

MTB—Motor Transport Brigade—the branch of the Army's Transportation Corps which had authority over many trucking companies in the ETO and inevitably organized and ran the Red Ball Express highway

OD—olive drab; often used to refer to a soldier's underwear

OP—observation post

POL—petroleum, oil, lubricants

QM—Quartermaster; in 1944, the branch of the U.S. Army responsible for supplies

repple depple—GI slang for replacement depot

SNAFU—military jargon for "situation normal, all fucked up"

SOP—standard operating procedure

TD—tank destroyer

ANNOTATIONS

1) Page 16: The Chaplain School at Harvard
In August 1942, Fort Benjamin Harrison in Lawrence, IN, was replaced by Harvard University in Cambridge, MA, as the site for the U.S. Army's Chaplain School.

Each two-month session at the school consisted of eighty applicants. These men were billeted by diversity: each four-chaplain suite was to include one Catholic, one non-liturgical Protestant, one liturgical Protestant, and one Jew. The ability to work with clergymen of other denominations was highly prized.

The main subjects studied were: Practical Duties (instruction in military life); Graves Registration; Discipline, Courtesies and Customs (military custom); Army Morale; Administration; Rules of Land Warfare; Recreation, Education and Music; Military Sanitation; Map Reading; and Chemical Warfare.

2) Page 16: Rabbis in the Chaplain Corps
To ensure a fair and broad distribution of five thousand chaplaincy positions, the military used a quota system based on the 1936 census of America. Forty faith groups were identified and granted chaplaincy positions based on their general population numbers. The largest group represented was the Roman Catholics, which received just over 30 percent of the Army's chaplaincy positions. Following were three Protestant denominations. The fifth-largest group was Judaism, which was allocated just over 4 percent of the chaplaincy positions. This resulted in over two hundred spots for rabbis in the Army and another hundred rabbis in the Navy.

Out of the 311 rabbis who served in the war, 2 were killed in action, 2 were wounded, and 46 were cited for bravery.

By 1943, half the rabbis in America had volunteered to serve in the chaplaincy.

3) Page 20: Red Cross blood

"[By 1942], the Red Cross had literally drawn a line over blood. Later, there was a compromise in which the Red Cross agreed to accept blood from blacks but to label and separate it from that of whites. Red Cross chairman Normal H. Davis agreed that the distinction had no scientific validity but declared, 'The question really is whether or not the views of the majority of those for whom the blood is being produced . . . are to prevail or whether the views of the minority who wish to donate their blood should prevail.' The notion that a seriously wounded battlefield casualty would rather delay his chances of survival until pints with the white label were available is hard to believe. But this separation by race continued in the Red Cross until 1963." (Gerald Astor, *The Right to Fight: A History of African Americans in the Military*, Da Capo Press, 1998, page 164).

4) Pages 33–34: The sinking of the *Susan B. Anthony*

The 1st and 3rd Battalions of the 359th Infantry crossed the Channel in LSTs on June 6 as part of the D-Day invasion, landing at UTAH beach. The following day, 2nd Battalion followed on the *Susan B. Anthony*, an 8,100-ton Navy transport. This ship struck a mine at 0730 and began to sink by the stern. All three thousand troops got off the *Susan B. Anthony*, but the travails of the 90th Division—troubles that would dog them for the first two months of their combat in France—began when half of G Company, approximately one hundred and seventy-five men, boarded the wrong British gunboat that had come to their aid, and returned to England. G Company was not restored to full strength for at least two more weeks. Additionally, many of the men who did reach UTAH beach did so without their weapons, abandoned in their escape from the sinking ship.

5) Page 40: The 90th's first combat CO

This section refers to Brig. Gen. Jay W. McKelvie, who led the 90th to England in April 1944. Prior to being given command of the 90th, McKelvie was the division's artilleryman. Just before embarking for England, the division's CO was reassigned to a corps, and McKelvie was elevated to a job he was not properly trained for. On June 12, as a result of the 90th's foundering in its opening attacks in Normandy, McKelvie was replaced as the division's CO.

In one history of the Tough Ombres, McKelvie was described as follows: "Should never have been given command of a division. In Normandy, critically weak in all aspects of leadership, command, and tactics. Could not communicate with subordinates, enlisted or commissioned. Relieved on 12 June, after 5 days of combat command." (John Colby, *War from the Ground Up: The Ninetieth Division in WWII*, Nortex Press, 1991, pages 148–149).

6) Page 41: The 90th as a "problem" division

In General Omar Bradley's autobiography, *A Soldier's Story*, he made the following comments:

"For the first few days in combat most new divisions suffer a disorder resulting from acute mental shock. Until troops can acclimate themselves to the agony of the wounded and the finality of death, they herd by instinct in fear and confusion. They cannot be driven into attack but must be led, and sometimes even coaxed, by their commanders. Within a few days this shock ordinarily wears off, the division overcomes its baptismal panic, and troops respond normally to assured and intelligent command. Where possible we made an effort to relieve the severity of that shock by conditioning each new unit in a 'quiet' sector before committing it to attack. But when the 90th came ashore on the heels of the 4th Division across Utah Beach, there were no 'quiet' sectors. We had no choice but to fling it into an attack that would have tested the mettle of veterans. But this sudden immersion was not confined to the 90th alone. Other equally green divisions entered the line under even more appalling conditions and most of them weathered the ordeal with distinction. Almost from the moment of its starting attack, however, the 90th became a 'problem' division. So exasperating was its performance that at one point the First Army staff gave up and recommended that we break it up for replacements. Instead, we stayed with the division and in the end the 90th became one of the most outstanding in the European Theater. In the metamorphosis, it demonstrated how swiftly a strong commander can transfuse his own strength into a command. But even more than that it proved what we had long contended: That man-for-man one division is just as good as another— they vary only in the skill and leadership of their commanders." (Omar N. Bradley, *A Soldier's Story*, The Modern Library, 1999, pages 296–297).

7) Page 53: Another CO for the 90th Division

On June 13, 1944, the 90th got its second commanding officer since arriving in France, Maj. Gen. Eugene M. Landrum, who had been deputy CO of VII Corps. After replacing McKelvie, Landrum was advised by General Bradley to "clean house." Also on June 13, the 357th Infantry Regiment got a new CO, Col. John W. Sheehy. Two days later, Sheehy was killed, and replaced by Lt. Col. Charles Schwab, who was replaced on June 17 by Col. George Barth. On June 16, the 358th also got a new CO, Col. Richard Partridge. Several battalion and company commanding officers were also replaced in the first days of Landrum's command of the T-Os.

8) Page 114: The destruction of the Mulberry artificial harbor

The storm of June 19–22 was not a particularly severe one. Winds did not exceed 36 mph. Nevertheless, the artificial harbor moored off OMAHA beach, called Mulberry A, fell apart at the moorings and was battered by free-floating ships.

A second harbor, Mulberry B, sat off the British invasion beach at Arromanches. It survived the storm, though not without taking severe damage, leaving many craft driven ashore. Until the end of August, 9,000 tons a day were off-loaded at Mulberry B.

During the last week of June following the storm, even without its artificial harbor, OMAHA averaged 13,500 tons a day, far exceeding planners' expectations. The decision was made not to repair Mulberry A, principally because of the success of the delivery of American supplies over the open beaches.

9) Page 177: The death of a platoon CO
Each week during the seven weeks of the 90th's combat in the hedges and hills of Normandy, the division lost 48 percent of its infantry platoon leaders. The average tenure of an infantry lieutenant was 2½ weeks.

10) Page 196: The relieving of the 359th's CO
Colonel Clarke Fales, a West Pointer, had commanded the 359th Regiment since 1942. His relief by General Landrum came as a shock to many in the unit, as Fales was a beloved and respected CO. 90th Division histories speculate that Fales's only weakness as a leader was that he was too forgiving of his subordinates. When the regiment bogged down in the bocage and on Mont Castre, Landrum, himself a failing commander, may have let Fales go to shift some of the blame for the poor progress away from himself.

11) Page 199: The gasoline gangs of Paris
Once Paris was liberated, the demand for gasoline became astronomical. Every business that relied on transportation was an overnight success with it, and a pauper without.

Millions of gallons of U.S. Army gasoline disappeared into Paris at the hands of AWOL soldiers who came to the City of Light and stayed behind when their units moved east. These soldiers either joined forces with the existing underworld mobs of Paris—such as the Voltaire gang—or made up their own gangs. The gasoline gangs were centered in the Montmartre and Montparnasse sections.

Gasoline was acquired illegally in many ways. The most common were petty theft, where gang members simply cruised Paris and stole jerricans from unattended vehicles, and the most brazen and simple method of driving up to a POL dump with 200 empty jerricans and saying, "Fill 'em up." Because of the speed of the advance against the crumbling German resistance in France, gas dumps got into the habit of servicing every and all GI trucks, without question. There was no time to ascertain if a soldier was telling the truth, and no proper system of acquisitioning had been set up. The practice was ripe for abuse.

Life in Paris was expensive during the first days of liberation. AWOLs quickly ran out of cash. At the prostitution houses of Montmartre and Montparnasse and on the café grapevine, they were recruited into the gasoline gangs with tales of easy money in the black market.

The gangs could grow as large as sixty men. They were often highly organized, sometimes along the lines of military units, with reveille, special orders, promotions, passes to town, and duty rosters. In each gang, there was always one man who was the "brains." The Vincennes gang was run by an AWOL medic, who dressed as an MP lieutenant and rounded up AWOLs in Montmarte bars. He told them they faced death by hanging for desertion. But if they did him a favor, he would relent. The favor turned out to be driving his trucks and joining his outfit.

The AWOLs made money so fast, their success was what inevitably tripped many of them. CID (Criminal Investigation Division) agents assigned to break up the gas gangs spotted many of them when the GIs tried to send home thousands of dollars in War Bonds or postal orders. The soldiers flashed wads around in cafés or were caught driving expensive cars. Many were nabbed by chance or in AWOL roundups. Other times, the French themselves put the finger on the Americans, such as women jilted by their GI lovers, spurned Frenchmen who lost their girlfriends to the lavish-spending Americans, and otherwise patriotic Parisians who disliked the Yanks exploiting the pain of their city.

12) Page 260: The invention of the steel tusks for the Sherman tanks
For six weeks, the Norman hedgerows had frustrated American efforts to get tanks involved in the fighting. With the breakout—Operation COBRA—looming closer, Eisenhower and his Generals knew that for COBRA to be a success it would be essential that armor forces break loose and not get mired in the bocage.

Several days before COBRA, General Bradley received a phone call to meet Lt. Gen. Leonard Gerow, CO of V Corps, at 2nd Division HQ. "We've got something that will knock your eyes out," Gerow said.

General Bradley wrote:

"The invention came on the eve of its greatest need, for the hedgerows that had frustrated our tanks in Normandy extended into the path of our [COBRA] blitz. . . .

"I found Gerow with several of his staff clustered about a light tank to which a crossbar had been welded. Four tusklike prongs protruded from it. The tank backed off and ran head-on toward a hedgerow at ten miles an hour. Its tusks bored into the wall, pinned down the belly, and the tank broke through under a canopy of dirt. A Sherman similarly equipped duplicated the performance. It, too, crashed into the wall, but instead of bellying skyward, it pushed on through. So absurdly simple that it had baffled an army for more than five weeks, the tusklike device had been fashioned by Curtis G. Culin, Jr., a 29-year-old sergeant from New York City. . . .

"[Lt. Col. John] Medaris [ordnance officer of First Army] sped back to the CP where he ordered every ordnance unit in the army on round-the-clock production of those anti-hedgerow devices. Scrap metal for the tank tusks came from Rommel's underwater obstacles on the beaches. . . . Within a week, three out of every five tanks in the breakout had been equipped with the device. For his invention Culin was awarded the Legion of Merit by corps. Four months later he went home to New York after having left a leg in Huertgen Forest." (Bradley, page 342).

13) Page 267: The surrender on Sèves Island
On July 23, 1944, *Feldwebel* (Sergeant) Alexander Uhlig of the 16th Company of the 6th *Fallschirmjäger* (Parachute) Regiment, led fifty men in a charge across open ground straight at the CP of 1st Battalion, 358th, on Sèves Island. His unit's charge was to avoid being killed by American artillery creeping up behind him. Uhlig's unit was accompanied by two panzers from 2 SS *Das Reich* (Division).

The resultant surrender consisted of eleven officers and two hundred and fifty-four men. The eleven officers were taken to the German CP in the loft of a large farmhouse. There, they were presented to the German CO, Major von der Heydte, who in turn introduced them to their captor, Sergeant Uhlig. Everyone present took tea together.

Three days afterward, Sergeant Uhlig—who had been awarded the Knight's Cross by von der Heydte—was captured by elements of the 357th, while in command of a delaying force. Years later, he hosted a reunion of German paratroopers and T-Os at Sèves Island.

14) Page 271: Chaplains collecting wounded and dead at Sèves Island
Three American chaplains defied strafing aircraft and small-arms fire from both sides to seek out wounded and bodies during the conflict on Sèves Island. Armed only with Red Cross flags, they walked into the open; the Germans were sufficiently impressed with the chaplains' courage to stop firing. The Americans did also, except for the artillery to the rear. The chaplains were: Father Joseph J. Esser, Catholic, Cleveland, Minnesota; Chaplain Edgar H. Stohler, Spavinaw, Oklahoma, Salvation Army; and, Pastor James M. Hamilton, Fort Worth, Texas, Disciples of Christ.

A German captain came forward to greet the chaplains, who were directing stretcher teams to the wounded they had found. The officer and the chaplains spoke with the help of a German-speaking American soldier. The captain decided to inform his CO, Major von der Heydte, of what was happening. Von der Heydte recommended a cease-fire and a trade of wounded prisoners.

The casualty numbers in the 358th for the day of July 23, 1944, on Sèves Island were one officer and sixty-eight men killed, five officers and ninety-nine men wounded, plus the mass surrender mentioned above.

Three weeks earlier, Major von der Heydte had also acted compassionately toward an American unit following battle. On July 4, the 6th *Fallschirmjäger*'s troops had stopped an attack of the 83rd Infantry, causing nearly fourteen hundred American casualties in an assault south of Carentan, toward Périers. Von der Heydte sent captured American medics back to Maj. Gen. Robert C. Macon, the division commander, with a note remarking that he thought Macon probably needed them. Von der Heydte also asked that, if the tables were ever turned, he hoped General Macon would "return the favor."

15) Page 283: Release of the news that Patton was fighting in France
Again, General Bradley:

"For the first two weeks after commitment on the heels of the Breakout, Third Army had been cloaked under a censorship stop. By hiding the identity and strength of that flanking force, we sought to mislead the enemy of our intentions. For had Hitler known it was Patton's tanks which swarmed around von Kluge's flank, he might have called off his attack at Mortain. I knew how impatiently Patton would chafe under the anonymity forced upon him by this censorship stop and for that reason was eager to lift it just as soon as we could. George was stimulated by headlines, the blacker the headlines the more recklessly he fought.

"On August 12, I suggested to Ike that the stop on Patton be removed. . . . 'Not yet,' he said, 'after all the troubles I've had with George, I have only a few gray hairs left on this poor old head of mine. Let George work a while longer for his headlines.' Several days later [August 15] Ike relented and Third Army flashed into the news in the United States. George had begun to fight his way out of the Sicilian doghouse." (Bradley, page 393).

16) Page 294: Another new CO for the 90th
On July 28, 1944, the 90th Division's CO, Major General Landrum, was replaced by Brig. Gen. Raymond McClain, the division's third CO in less than two months of fighting. According to Bradley, Landrum had not yet got the 90th Division in "fighting trim. He had cleaned house but not enough." After the debacle on Sèves Island, the decision was made to replace Landrum, who was described in a 90th Division history as "short, fat, uninspiring; could not lift up or motivate troops. Commanded . . . from an armchair in a cellar. No faith or confidence . . . gloomy and pessimistic."

McClain was the second choice for the 90th, after the untimely death of Brig. Gen. Theodore Roosevelt, one of the heroes of UTAH beach and the oldest man there at 57. Roosevelt passed in his sleep from a heart attack on the eve of being named CO of the 90th. Bradley gave the division to McClain, a distinguished Oklahoma City banker and long-serving National Guardsman. His background was as an artilleryman, and he had served in Africa. Under McClain, the 90th would achieve some of the greatest successes of any combat division in the ETO.

17) Page 304: The defense of Mortain
The powerful German counterattack toward Avranches, which began on August 7, 1944, was designed to drive a wedge between Allied forces in Normandy and force them back to the Channel. Elements of four panzer divisions faced off against a single American infantry division near the town of Mortain. By holding their ground, the 30th enabled the inevitable encirclement of the German forces farther to the east, the Argentan-Falaise pocket. This cost the Germans an army and won France for the Allies. For their dogged defense, the 30th became known as "the Rock of Mortain."

18) Pages 324, 331: The destruction inside the Argentan-Falaise pocket
General Dwight Eisenhower described the scene in chilling language:

"The battle at Falaise was unquestionably one of the greatest 'killing grounds' of any of the war areas. Roads, highways and fields were so choked with destroyed equipment and with dead men and animals that passage through the area was extremely difficult. Forty-eight hours after the closing of the gap I was conducted through it on foot, to encounter scenes that could be described only by Dante. It was literally possible to walk for hundreds of yards at a time, stepping on nothing but dead and decaying flesh." (Dwight D. Eisenhower, *Crusade in Europe*, Doubleday, 1948, page 279).

19) Page 331: The failure to close the Argentan-Falaise gap

On August 12, General Patton telephoned General Bradley to inform him that Patton had troops in Argentan, on the southern shoulder of the gap. "Let me go on to Falaise," Patton urged, "and we'll drive the British back into the sea for another Dunkirk."

Nothing doing, Bradley told Patton. Bradley was afraid of colliding with Montgomery's forces. In the speed and flash of combat, had the two forces not recognized each other on the battlefield the results might have been catastrophic. Patton was ordered not to go beyond Argentan. Patton had already ordered armored elements of his XV Corps to push into the gap. The tanks were recalled immediately.

While the Americans waited for Montgomery to close the gap at Argentan, the Germans reinforced the opening. In the first two days, leading units of panzers and SS troops had already slipped through to the Seine. However, rather than push harder to shut the door, Montgomery chose to attack the fleeing Germans farther to the west, which resulted in squeezing the Germans even faster toward the gap, like a tube of toothpaste. The British tactics mystified Bradley, dismayed Eisenhower, and enraged Patton.

Bradley prevented Patton from spinning a skirmish line across the gap because he doubted Patton could hold it. Nineteen German divisions were heading pell-mell for the opening. Patton had only four divisions in the area, and with them he was already barring three escape routes, at Alençon, Sees, and Argentan. Had Patton stretched his line to Falaise as well, he would have extended his roadblocks to forty miles. Patton's troops would likely have gotten trampled in the stampede. Bradley forbade it.

For two days, Bradley waited for Montgomery to close the gap. In the interim, more Germans slipped through. On August 14, when Montgomery neither asked for help nor moved his forces into the gap, Bradley allowed Patton to send two divisions racing to the Seine to intercept the escaped Germans at their crossing points.

On that day, just after those two divisions had embarked to the northeast, Montgomery contacted Bradley to recommend that their two armies meet at Chambois, fifteen miles south of Falaise. Bradley was flabbergasted; had he hesitated and not allowed Patton to send two divisions to the Seine—seventy-five miles east of Chambois—he might have succeeded with Montgomery in closing the gap immediately. But the die was cast.

The move of the two divisions to the northeast accelerated the Americans' bridgehead on the Seine. It also postponed the closing of the gap, which would have resulted in more POWs taken. Later, Bradley remarked that this was the first and only time during the war that he went to bed worrying about a decision already made. He was never sure if he'd made the right call.

Montgomery closed the trap on August 19. At Chambois, his 10th Polish Dragoons, spearheading for the Canadian force moving south out of Falaise, met with advance units of the 90th Division.

On August 18, Field Marshal Guenther von Kluge was relieved of command of the Normandy theater as a result of the Seventh Army's fiasco. Field Marshal Walter Model took control. The next day, on the road to Metz, von Kluge committed suicide by taking potassium cyanide.

Estimates of the damage to the surrounded German Seventh Army are that over 70,000 men were captured or killed in the pocket, along with an immense loss of vehicles and matériel. Some historians project that as many as 100,000 troops escaped. The battle for France was, in effect, over. However, those German soldiers who escaped the pocket would resurface, at the Siegfried Line, and in December at the Battle of the Bulge.

20) Pages 336–337: General von Choltitz and the surrender of Paris

By August 19, 1944, street fighting in Paris had begun to get out of hand when independent bands of FFI fired on German patrols. Afraid that von Choltitz would retaliate, the Resistance leadership sent an envoy to Raoul Nordling, Swedish consul in Paris for eighteen years, asking him to act as intermediary with the occupying force. Nordling went to see the German commander at his offices in the Hôtel Meurice.

The consul found the German General in a depressed state, bemoaning his fate to have again be left in the rear with the duty of destroying a city. "Now I shall be remembered as the man who destroyed Paris." Nordling begged him not to do it until he could consult with the Resistance to negotiate a truce. Von Choltitz offered these terms: either the attacks on his garrison would stop or he would effectively destroy Paris.

The Resistance accepted the truce, but the quiet lasted no more than a day. Poor communications hampered the spread of the truce. Communist newspapers exhorted the Parisian public to reject the truce and take to the barricades! Also, both the Gaullist and Communist factions within the FFI acted independently to grab as many symbolic buildings as they could during the lull. On August 21, the National Council of the Resistance met and rescinded the truce, with the Communist position prevailing. The Gaullist members followed to avoid the peril of a civil war.

Von Choltitz retaliated by shutting off the city's food. But by this point neither he nor the FFI could restrain their forces in the streets. He told Nordling there was no alternative but to execute his orders, for he would never surrender "to an irregular army."

Nordling recognized that von Choltitz might instead surrender to an Allied army. He received from the General permission to lead a mission through the American lines to bid the Yanks to enter the city and allow von Choltitz to surrender Paris with honor. The General agreed and sent an officer with Nordling for safe conduct.

On August 22, Nordling and a delegation departed Paris in a small Citroën. By the next morning, they had reached Patton's CP southwest of Chartres. The delegation was loaded by Patton into a flight of Piper Cubs and ferried to where General Bradley waited on the airstrip near St. Saveur Lendelin. After clearing Nordling's story, Bradley ordered the French 2nd Armored to start immediately for Paris, paired with an advance of the American 4th Infantry. Bradley then buckled into a Cub himself and flew off to Granville to clear these orders with Eisenhower.

In the meantime, von Choltitz had received a telegram from Adolf Hitler, instructing him that "Paris must not fall into the hands of the enemy except as a field of ruins." The German General had already made his preparations in advance of receiving this message: he had placed three tons of explosives in Notre Dame cathedral, two tons in the Invalides, and one in the Palais Bourbon. He was prepared to level the Arc de Triomphe, the Opéra, and the Madeleine with artillery fire, and had drawn plans to dynamite the Eiffel Tower and use it as a wire entanglement to snarl the Seine. He found it impossible to wreck the more than seventy bridges of Paris, but he determined to do his best. With these plans and Hitler's telegram in hand, von Choltitz awaited the arrival of a "regular" army.

The French tank commander Jacques Leclerc (*nomme de guerre* for Phillipe de Hauteclocque) was ordered to commence for Paris immediately on August 22, but did not get his division under way until the 23rd. For the next twenty-four hours, Leclerc's tanks dallied through a phalanx of exuberant French folk along his path, slowing the advance with celebration. General Bradley wrote, "Although I could not censure them for responding to this hospitality of their countrymen, neither could I wait for them to dance their way to Paris. If von Choltitz was to deliver the city, we had a compact to fulfill." (Bradley, page 392).

Bradley ordered the 4th Division to liberate Paris at once. Hearing this news, Leclerc's men dropped their napkins and mounted their tanks *tout de suite*. By 10 P.M. on August 24, a squad of tanks and a company of infantry from the French 2nd Armored arrived at the Hôtel de Ville in Paris.

The following morning, von Choltitz walked out of the Hôtel Meurice through the billows of three purple smoke grenades heaved into the lobby. He was driven to the Gare Montparnasse, where he formally surrendered the City of Light to the French.

21) Page 344: Naming the Red Ball Express
The Red Ball was an impromptu affair, springing up almost overnight as need dictated. COM Z chose the name for its new delivery service from railway lingo; in the 1940s, Red Ball Express meant "through freights," the fastest form of delivery.

22) Page 351: English translation of the Kaddish, the Hebrew prayer of mourning

"Glorified and sanctified be God's great name throughout the world which He has created according to His will. May He establish His kingdom in your lifetime and during your days, and within the life of the entire House of Israel, speedily and soon; and say, Amen.

"May His great name be blessed forever and to all eternity.

"Blessed and praised, glorified and exalted, extolled and honored, adored and lauded be the name of the Holy One, blessed be He, beyond all the blessings and hymns, praises and consolations that are ever spoken in the world; and say, Amen.

"May there be abundant peace from heaven, and life, for us and for all Israel; and say, Amen.

"He who creates peace in His celestial heights, may He create peace for us and for all Israel; and say, Amen."

(It is worth noting that nowhere in the Kaddish is death mentioned. The theme of the Kaddish is the greatness of God. There is also an appeal for peace, between nations, individuals, and for peace of mind.)

23) Page 362: The relocation of COM Z headquarters to Paris

Eisenhower's chief logistician was Lt. Gen. John C. H. Lee, the commanding officer of COM Z. General Lee's decision to move his gargantuan headquarters from Valognes to Paris came at a particularly bad time, in the middle of the fuel crisis that was interrupting the pursuit of the Germans east to their border.

Months before the liberation of Paris, Ike had ordered that the city was banned to HQ commands. The city's boulevards and hotels were reserved for troops on furlough.

The ban apparently did not reach General Lee, who on August 30 abandoned his immense cantonment at Cherbourg for the comforts of Paris, two hundred miles away. Regardless of how carefully Lee may have orchestrated his move, the shuffle could not have helped but confound COM Z's operations at a time when its full resources should have been dedicated to moving fuel and supplies to the front line. Instead, COM Z itself occupied hundreds of trucks and cargo planes, consuming thousands of gallons of gasoline.

General Lee's indiscretion came at a critical time. His move combined with the immense losses of fuel to the black market in Paris, as well as along the roads through liberated towns, to worsen the fuel shortage and curtail pursuit of the enemy to the German border.

24) A history of the 90th Division in World War II

Despite its rough first steps in Normandy, the 90th went on to become one of the most decorated infantry units in the European Theater, what George Patton called "one of the greatest divisions that ever fought." Here is a record of their medals and casualties:

AWARDS AND DECORATIONS

Medal of Honor	Distinguished Service Cross	Legion of Merit	Distinguished Flying Cross	Silver Star	Soldier's Medal	Bronze Star Heroic	Bronze Star Merit	Air Medal
4	78	6	4	1,311	40	3,526	1,531	115

CASUALTIES
6 June 1944 – 9 May 1945

	KIA		DOW		DOI		SWA		SIA		LWA		LIA		MIA		TOTAL	
1944	O	EM	O	EM	O	EM	O	EM	O	EM	O	EM	O	EM	O	EM	O	EM
June	34	351	1	22	0	0	59	1,033	4	29	45	730	1	76	6	74	150	2,315
July	68	909	12	146	1	5	54	1,076	0	14	147	2,222	10	187	18	629	310	5,188
Aug.	25	251	7	84	0	1	22	385	2	21	17	360	0	95	20	406	93	1,603
Sept.	9	147	2	44	0	1	27	397	0	10	16	272	3	93	1	69	58	1,033
Oct.	5	80	2	18	0	0	10	162	0	6	4	178	0	40	1	60	22	544
Nov.	22	287	1	36	6	2	22	346	0	4	43	874	8	171	12	289	108	2,004
Dec.	9	194	1	35	0	0	15	207	0	5	37	665	8	150	16	424	86	1,680
1945																		
Jan.	12	258	2	49	0	0	18	415	11	676	43	693	13	242	7	248	106	2,581
Feb.	16	245	1	28	0	1	13	296	0	65	22	629	1	186	7	188	60	1,638
Mar.	9	236	1	25	0	0	14	145	1	4	17	330	1	57	3	131	46	928
April	7	121	1	12	0	0	9	14	0	4	13	316	2	212	1	40	33	719
May	0	45	0	1	0	1	0	25	0	0	5	60	0	11	1	14	6	157
Total	216	3,124	31	500	7	11	263	4,501	18	838	409	7,329	47	1,520	93	2,572	1,078	20,390

KIA .... Killed in Action
DOW .... Died of Wounds
DOI .... Died of Injuries
SWA .... Seriously Wounded in Action
O .... Officers

EM .... Enlisted Men
SIA .... Seriously Injured in Action
LWA .... Lightly Wounded in Action
LIA .... Lightly Injured in Action
MIA .... Missing in Action

Assuming the 90th Division's initial strength to be 14,000, the total casualties of 21,371 represents a casualty rate of 153 percent.

Source: John Colby, *War from the Ground Up: The Ninetieth Division in WW II*, Nortex Press, 1991, page 518.

24) A note on infantry casualties

General Bradley observed the following about overall casualties:

"Previous combat had taught us that casualties are lumped primarily in the rifle platoons. For here are concentrated the handful of troops who must advance under enemy fire. It is upon them that the burden of war falls with greater risk and with less likelihood of survival than in any other of the combat arms. An infantry division of WWII consisted of 81 rifle platoons, each with a combat strength of approximately 40 men. Altogether those 81 assault units comprised but 3,240 men in a division of 14,000. In an army of 350,000, fewer than one out of seven soldiers stood in the front line. That does not mean, of course, that none of the other seven fought. Many of them did, but as machine gunners, artillery-men, engineers and tankers. And in Theater, the proportion [was] . . . one man with a rifle for each 15 men behind him.

"Prior to invasion we had estimated that the infantry would incur 70 percent of the losses of combat forces. By August we had boosted that figure to 83 percent on the basis of our experience in the Normandy hedgerows." (Bradley, page 445).

Some rifle platoons lost over 200 percent during the war in Europe; because of the replacement system used by the U.S. Army, more than 80 men may have passed through a platoon's ranks during the eleven months of ground combat.

25) Casualties among the Chaplain Corps
Out of 5,200 total chaplains who served in the U.S. Army or Navy during World War II, 100 were killed in action, 275 were wounded, and 42 were detained as prisoners of war.

Late in the war, the Army Chaplain Corps stated that it had suffered a greater percentage of casualties than any other branch of service except the in-fantry and the Air Corps.

26) Casualties among the Red Ball Express drivers
Because such an immense number and diversity of quartermaster and trans-portation companies drove over the one-way Red Ball Express route, no casualty numbers are available. Certainly thousands of drivers, black and white, put their lives on the line in the ETO, and many suffered wounds or lost their lives in the line of duty. Suffice it to say that delivering supplies to any front line in any war has been, and remains, a highly dangerous duty.

27) The end of the Red Ball
The Red Ball became the "tail" of a U.S. Army that was the most highly mecha-nized and mobile force in military history. The Red Ball Express ran for eighty-one days, from August 25 to November 16, 1944, ending finally when resistance stiffened at the German border and the Allied advance slowed.

In those three months, the Red Ball took its place in the mythology of World War II, becoming one of the great wartime achievements of the American "can-do" mind-set. More than six thousand trucks and trailers and twenty-three thou-sand men moved 412,193 tons of supplies to the advancing American armies all the way to the German and Belgian frontiers.

28) All-black units and the integration of the U.S. Army
In addition to driving trucks, African American soldiers in service units manned en-

gineer units that kept open the supply routes and ordnance companies that maintained vehicles and depots, and they represented three-quarters of the stevedores in port battalions unloading ships bringing supplies from England and the United States.

Blacks were not strictly limited to service units. Some were allowed to serve in a few segregated combat units. The largest of these were the 92nd Infantry Division, which fought in Italy, and the 9th Infantry Division in the Pacific. The most well-known of the black combat units was the 332nd Fighter Group, the "Tuskegee Airmen," made up of the 9th, 100th, 301st, and 302nd Fighter Squadrons. Blacks also saw combat in segregated artillery battalions. In addition, blacks fought in three segregated armored units, including the 84th, the 827th, and the 761st Tank Battalions. In particular, the 761st distinguished itself during 183 days of combat in the ETO.

Another unit, the 555th Parachute Infantry Battalion, known as the "Triple Nickels," was assigned in early 1945 to the Pacific Northwest as smoke jumpers instead of being allowed to fight in Europe. The 555th jumped into forest fires set by Japanese incendiary devices, which had been attached to balloons, then floated across the Pacific on the jet stream. The battalion made more than 1,200 individual jumps during the last summer of the war, covering all the northwestern states, including Montana.

Near the end of the war, a few thousand blacks were integrated into regular combat units. Due to the losses at the Battle of the Bulge and the immense casualty count among inexperienced infantrymen, Eisenhower rushed another 30,000 white troops to Europe. Fresh out of training, these boys were rashly applied and quickly swelled the casualty count. The shortage of riflemen worsened. Eisenhower tried another gambit: amnesty for men in the stockade. If the prisoners would pick up a rifle and fight, he promised their slates would be wiped clean. The response was underwhelming, as most of the men to whom this deal was offered were in the stockade in the first place for their reluctance to fight. Eisenhower tried one more time to dredge up reinforcements for his starving infantry. He looked to the black service units, offering them the chance to fight alongside their white comrades for the remainder of the war. The blacks were to be integrated into infantry divisions only by platoon, never by individual, thus preserving at least a modicum of segregation. Twenty-five hundred blacks volunteered immediately, and by February the total reached 4,562. Because of the prohibition on blacks being in charge of white soldiers, only privates and privates first class were accepted. Many black soldiers took a reduction in rank to be included. The platoons were distributed through the Sixth and Twelfth Army Groups. None of the black volunteers went to Third Army, due to George Patton's dislike of black soldiers.

The exploits and fighting prowess of these units (in particular the Tuskegee pilots, the tankers of the 761st, the Triple Nickel parachutists, and the drivers of the Red Ball) combined to change the entrenched notion that a black man was not fit to fight in the U.S. Army. With the Cold War heating up in 1948, President Truman, on July 26, issued an executive order: "It is hereby declared to be the policy of the President that there shall be equality of treatment and opportunity for all persons in the armed services without regard to race, color, religion or national origin. This policy shall be put into effect as rapidly as possible, having due regard to the time required to effectuate any necessary changes without impairing efficiency or morale."

In memoriam,

Isidore John Previtera

(1924–2004)

ABOUT THE AUTHOR

DAVID L. ROBBINS is the author of *Scorched Earth, The End of War, War of the Rats, Souls to Keep,* and *Last Citadel.* He divides his time among Richmond, Boston, and his sailboat, where he is at work on his next historical thriller.